FIELDWORK IN
MESOPOTAMIA
— BOOK I —

HERE BE JINN

DENNIS TSARSON

ISBN (Paperback): 978-1-7384289-0-8
ISBN (Hardcover): 978-1-7384289-1-5
ISBN (Ebook): 978-1-7384289-2-2

Cover Design by Miblart
Map Design by Rowanvale Books

Published by Dennis Tsarson

MAP OF IRAQ

The River Tigris
Erbil
SYRIA
Baiji
The River Euphrates
Taji
Baqubah
IRAN
Baghdad
Algaara
Ctesiphon
Karbala
Hillah
Babylon
Arabian Desert
Basra
PERSIAN GULF
SAUDI ARABIA
N
W
E
S

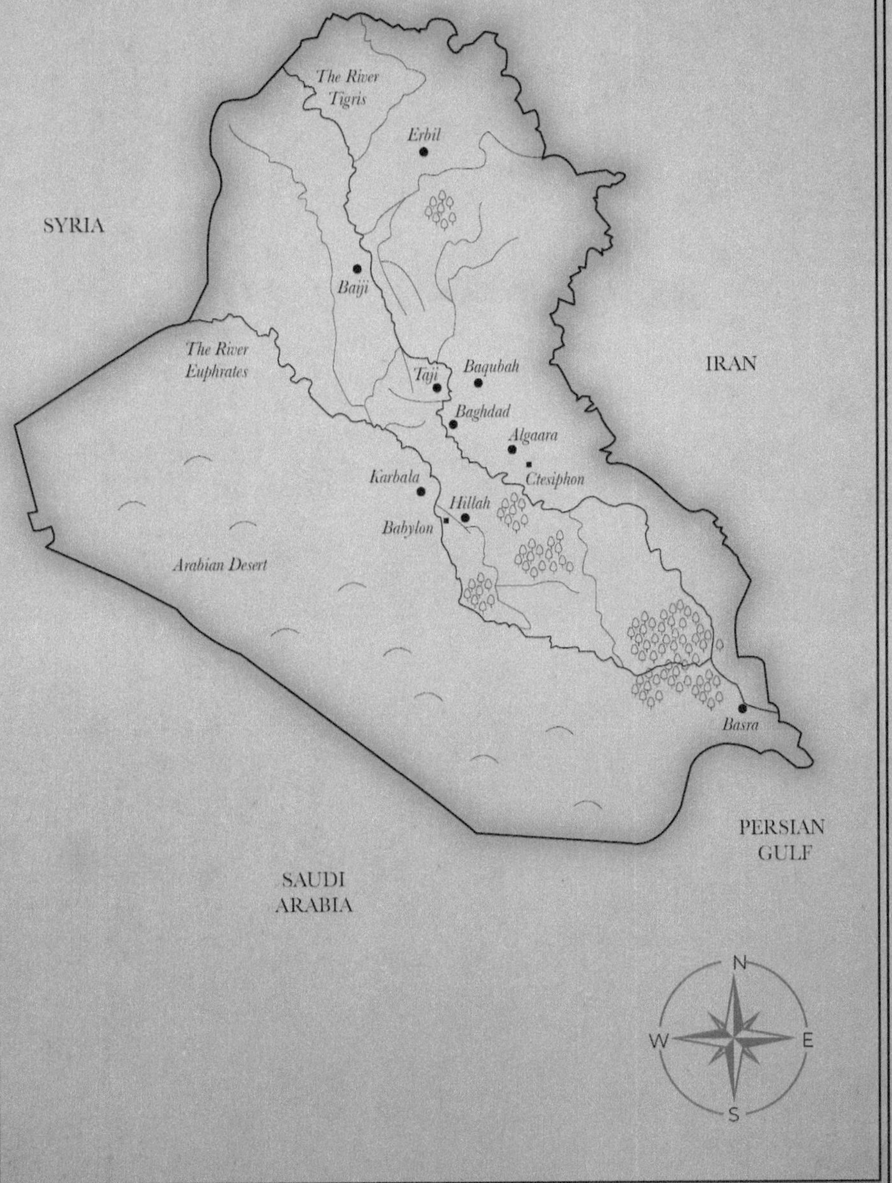

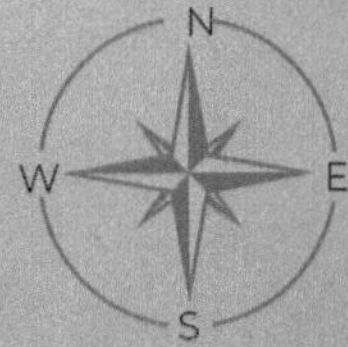

CHAPTER ONE

The Norman warrior stepped forward, proudly and confidently brandishing his sword. He held a leather-clad wooden shield in his other hand bearing the insignia of his duchy: an image of a golden cross along with four green circles, one beside each of the symbol's crossbeams. With a menacing yet theatrical groan, he fixed his eyes on his adversary, a tall Anglo-Saxon swordsman. The Saxon prepared himself; his foothold solid, his weapons ready, his hazel eyes monitoring his adversary. While the sun's rays polished the metal of the warriors' chain mail and helmets, the Norman moved, advancing towards his opponent, cautious and ready to respond to any attack. Silence took reign on the battlefield; even the wind chose not to howl, as though it wished to stand aside and motionlessly observe the duel.

Then, with another feral groan, the Norman began his attack. He lunged; his opponent parried, and the two swords screeched in greeting as they clashed. The Anglo-Saxon pushed, throwing back his enemy's weapon. He attempted to deliver a blow in return, but his blade only thudded against the Norman's shield. Wasting no time, the Norman struck again, now aiming for his adversary's left side, yet just as timely, the Saxon covered it with his own shield. The Norman took a step back, having quickly evaluated the motif adorning his opponent's shield, an attention-grabbing swirl of red and black. The Saxon released a groan of his own and lunged at him.

Many times did their blades clash and many times did sword meet shield. At times, shield too struck against shield, and one of the warriors would stagger back. It happened again, making the Saxon retreat whilst still fending off his opponent's strikes. It was becoming clear that the Norman had the advantage. He intensified his attacks, making each parry a strength-draining endeavour for his enemy.

One more blow kicked the sword out of the Saxon's hand. The weapon fell on the grass as its former wielder staggered. In order to avoid falling himself, he cast the shield aside and drew his left heel back. He did not collapse, but he had lost the battle. He had to watch as the enemy's blade lunged straight at him...

Yet, instead of getting stabbed, he merely got poked. After all, one would probably have struggled to cut butter with the swords they were using, so blunt they were. Then came a round of applause from the witnesses that had assembled around the scene of combat. None of these spectators were knights or pikemen; the majority were dressed as civilians. Moreover, the Norman had never set foot in Normandy and was not completely sure what the duchy's capital was. As for the Anglo-Saxon, had some bard narrated *Beowulf* in the epic's archaic language, he would not have understood a single word of it. He was a re-enactor. All of them were, at a living history event.

"Let's get you back on your feet, Elliott," the Norman said as he extended his hand to the Anglo-Saxon.

"Yeah, thanks."

Elliott grabbed hold. Their audience applauded again as the duo gave bows. Norman—as was indeed the first name of the other cosplayer—chose to overperform by also giving a curtsy.

"Don't get carried away; I don't think warriors used to curtsy," Elliott whispered to him.

"So what's your point?" Norm smirked.

Elliott shook his head lightly. Norm was quite an eccentric. After all, by his own admission, his first name was the only reason he always chose to play Normans at these historical re-enactments.

Worn out by the duel, Elliott trudged to his discarded sword and shield. He picked them up and felt the weight of a gauntleted palm on his shoulder.

"Hey, do you want to grab some lunch?" Norm asked.

"Sounds good to me."

"Let's just put these into the armoury and find Hollie first."

Hollie was Norm's girlfriend and, as far as Elliott knew, the one who'd brought the big guy into the world of historical re-enactment.

They walked up to the armoury, a tent for storing various weapons: swords and shields, lances and battle-axes—all harmless replicas, of course. This session of historical combat was officially over.

They went westwards. They passed the workstation of a smith who was hammering an insignia into a newly-minted coin. In another shop, a potter seated behind an ancient yet complicated mechanism was giving form to a mass of clay on a rotating circle. Yet neither master did so for a fee; educating the spectators was their aim.

The duo approached another stall, one where several peasants had just finished giving a demonstration of basket-weaving. One of them, a young brunette woman in a blue and white dress, simple yet elegant, put the basket on the table upon noticing them. After a quick word with her colleagues, she headed over.

"Hey, guys!"

"Hey, Hollie," Norm said. "Elliott is going to lunch with us too."

"Cool," she said. "So who won?"

"Norm did," Elliott said. "Is there any surprise? He always seems to win when we're pitted against each other."

Elliott had joined the re-enactment society a year before and throughout the passing seasons he'd met up with fellow enthusiasts to hone his skills in swordsmanship. Yet he was still a rookie compared to Norm, a veteran of dozens of reimagined medieval battles and campaigns.

"Well, I do have more experience in combat re-enactment. But frankly, Elliott here put on quite a good fight. There were quite a few occasions when I thought he would knock the sword out of my hand."

"Well, there's always next time," Hollie said encouragingly.

"You mean next year," Elliott corrected. After all, this was the last day of the re-enactment fair.

They wandered into an area where the tables around them were made not out of oak but of plastic, and kiosks replaced open stalls: the food court. The guys split from Hollie for a few minutes in search of the right food merchants, promising to rendezvous at the first vacant table any of them found.

"So, what was I about to say earlier?" Norm said, heading for the tables after he and his sparring partner had got their orders.

"This time, you put too much energy into the first part of the duel, so you got worn out quickly. Hey, there's Hollie."

She was waving at them from behind a table with her order of ploughman's lunch. The guys put down their trays with their preferred choices of morsels: burgers, fries, and sodas.

"Seems like Hollie is the only one of us who chose a more or less authentic medieval meal for lunch," Elliott commented.

"Well, I suggested we have pizza, but you said no. So much for trying something authentic," Norm said.

"I doubt pizza was around during the Middle Ages," Hollie remarked.

"Pizza? Seriously?" Elliott was also sceptical.

"Well, the Romans used to do it like this: they took bread, topped it with cheese and vegetables. No tomato sauce, obviously. Then it was put into an oven to bake. Does this sound like pizza to you?"

"I guess it counts," Elliott reluctantly admitted as he bit into his burger.

"But anyways, back to the topic of sword fighting. Try controlling how much strength you pour into your attack. But if suddenly you really do wear yourself out, then motivate yourself; if there are no stakes, pretend there are. That should make you fight fiercer. I don't know... Imagine you are fighting for the love of a fair maiden." Norm grinned.

"I hope that's what's been motivating you all this time." Hollie threw a mischievous look at her boyfriend.

"Right, babe."

It just had to be one of these boyfriend-girlfriend moments.

A bit later Elliott, still clad in his Anglo-Saxon attire, was again navigating through a multitude of thematically dressed people. There were blacksmiths and merchants, serfs and courtiers. Nearby, a minstrel was performing on a psaltery. Perhaps the idyllic-sounding tune was not really centuries old, yet it fitted the atmosphere. A stalwart falcon watched him from where it sat on its owner's thickly gloved hand.

Elliott stopped in his tracks, giving one more look-over to this part of the re-enactment fair, this unusual world that had temporarily sprung up in rural East Anglia. It would be gone the following day like a broken spell. It might have been a mere game, a land of make-believe, but he had managed to immerse himself in it for the last three days. It offered escape, at least for a few days. Escape from the noose of a job he had grown to despise; escape from the chains of the daily routines he had become sick of.

Yet Bristol would welcome him back tomorrow. He gave a deep sigh and walked back towards the campsite.

***

It was another Friday afternoon at the call centre. Every moment witnessed the ringing of countless phones. Voices merged into a cacophony as employees, some on the edge and with the wide eyes of insomniacs, scurried to make a sale.

Almost a full work week had passed since Elliott returned from his holiday, but the re-enactment fair felt almost as distant as the family barbecue at Grandpa Joey's place around two decades before. Elliott had spent most of the week on the line: talking to new or existing customers and waiting in between calls. He had made only a few sales, which meant practically no commission. On the bright side, the weekend was about to begin.

Elliott kept thinking about bad life choices on his way back home. Every day, he was stuck in the "same old, same old" that had filled him to the brim. Yet it seemed there was no way out of these bonds. What were the options? Exchanging his current job for a different low-paid one? That would just be a case of replacing steel shackles with iron ones: different imagery, similar experience. Learn a technical skill? He had considered it on several occasions, but always ended up concluding that he lacked the personality type to succeed in engineering or medicine. It might have been an error of judgement, but it had already implanted itself deep in his mind and was there to stay.

What other options were there? Move to an uninhabited island? A bit too extreme, especially if one's survival skills were not top notch. Plus, too much planning...

A vibration in his pocket snapped him out of these thoughts. He had returned home barely a minute before. He pulled out his phone. The floating screen of the device displayed one word: **DAD**.

Oh, just what the doctor ordered, Elliott thought.

Still, he clicked to accept the call. "Hello."

"Hey lad." The voice on the other line did not sound enthusiastic. Frankly, Elliott couldn't remember the last time it truly had.

"Oh, hey, Dad," Elliott answered. This would have been a good moment to yawn, but he suppressed the urge. "What's up?"

"Ah, just thought of calling to find out how things are. I'm not interrupting you, am I?"

"Oh, no, no."

"So how's life?"

"Fine." This was promising to be a bland conversation.

"Any big changes happened recently?"

"No."

"What about small ones?"

"Same answer."

"Staying healthy and fit?"

"Yeah, of course. Health and wellness are the most important things in life."

"Attaboy!"

"What about you, Dad?"

"I'm fine, mate. Can't really complain. Planning to hit the gym tomorrow; haven't been to one for a long time."

"Cool."

This awkward exchange was followed by an equally uncomfortable pause.

"Well, it's good to know that everything's going fine. So I guess...until next time?" Dad said.

"Guess so."

"Bye, mate."

"Bye, Dad."

A series of beeps indicated that the caller had hung up. Elliott put the phone back into his pocket.

His mind ventured back in time to one evening in autumn many years ago. Mom and Dad were having a quarrel. This had become a common occurrence by that time. Elliot had never learnt the true reason why, due to different parties telling completely contradictory stories. There was shouting, at high volumes...lots of it. Quite a few things got thrown around, and by the end, a couple of plates, a vase, and a TV remote were not the only things left broken and scattered across the floor. His parents' marriage fell apart. Dad had walked out, never to come back. And it was impossible for a confused eight-year-old boy not to get swept away by the raging waves of this ordeal.

Since then, he'd grown distant from his father. At some point, that distance grew to the width of a chasm. On a philosophic level, Elliott could admit this end result was partially the fault of everybody involved: Dad, Mom and, yes, him. But that was the situation, the end result. It was born in conflict and lived on because nobody had the courage to seek proper closure.

Occasional phone calls between him and Dad could be considered a tradition. But like many traditions, they tended to be empty and useless. Sometimes, Elliott wondered why this tradition even needed to persist.

***

He had a choice to make as he sat behind his laptop that evening. He had subscribed to an online streaming service, one of the many that had been popping up over the last few years. Row upon row of titles and thumbnail images appeared on the screen as he scrolled the mouse down. Fiction and documentaries, any genre and any theme—the choices seemed endless. After some time, an entry appeared in view, immediately grabbing his attention. Its thumbnail was an image of a stone bas-relief depicting one group of figures bowing to another. The title below read: *Mysteries of the Ancient Gods.* This promised to be a good watch. Elliott sat back in his chair.

The documentary opened with shots of observatories standing amidst different landscapes: urban, mountainous, desert.

"Many telescopes and radars across the world vigilantly look beyond the sky's end, into the void of space, searching for signs of extraterrestrial life. Each year, thousands of people come forth with accounts of alien sightings." The narrator read out the introduction in his deep tone.

Everything quickly moved to a studio setting where the audience were introduced to the documentary's host, Dr Leonard Mergham. Tall, lanky, grey-haired, and bespectacled—

the stereotype of a university lecturer. Chances were that he had been one at some point.

"Scientists often look for traces of extraterrestrial activity among celestial bodies and space debris," Mergham began. "But one major source tends to get overlooked: our own distant past. Evidence points to the fact that our ancestors had extensive contact with extraterrestrial civilisations."

The narration continued, accompanied by different scenes, some shot on camera and some computer-generated: felucca boats on the Nile and reed longhouses on the banks of the Euphrates, the Sphinx and the Wall of Babylon, statues of pharaohs and bas-reliefs depicting Assyrian kings.

"Thousands of years ago, human civilisation arose in Egypt and Mesopotamia. But how is it possible that people who had never seen the need to build anything more complex than a single-storey mud-brick hut suddenly began erecting grand monuments? And people who had relied solely on river flood seasons to grow their crops miraculously engineered complex irrigation systems?"

A montage of various works of ancient art made its entry: pottery paintings, wall murals, sculptures, friezes. Each depicted deities worshipped by different cultures: Egyptian and Sumerian, Greek and Roman, Indian and Chinese, Mayan and Incan.

"Myths from different corners of Earth tell stories about gods descending from the heavens to benefit humanity. They brought people fire and introduced them to new work tools. They taught them agriculture, writing, and medicine. But it's very probable that these 'gods', whilst certainly more advanced than us, were merely different rather than divine."

The documentary followed Mergham as he pointed out what he saw as evidence of extraterrestrial contact. He saw it at the Pyramids of Giza and in the colonnaded halls of the temples that stood by the Nile, in papyri and cuneiform tablets, in Egyptian cosmology and Babylonian astronomy. He talked about how some Egyptian wall murals depicted space shuttles, and somehow found references to exoplanets in Sumerian sources.

Later on in the documentary, Mergham was back at the studio.

"But this story has a twist." The camera followed him to a new part of the studio, building up tension. "Studying the pantheons of different ancient cultures gives enough reason to conclude that humans had contact with not just one but several different extraterrestrial civilisations. Let's look at our case studies."

The screen behind him lit up and split into two sections. On the left, against a yellow-brown papyrus-inspired background, a parade of beings manifested. They had the bodies of humans, but their heads were those of different creatures of land, river, and air: a falcon and an ibis, a jackal and a cat, a crocodile and a hippo, among others.

"Exhibit A. Some of the gods worshipped in Ancient Egypt." Mergham extended his hand towards it.

Almost immediately, more figures appeared to his right. Each was caught in the middle of some act. One was warring; another receiving dignitaries; a third stood, looking forth, hands extended, offering a blessing.

"Exhibit B. The gods of the peoples of Mesopotamia: Sumerians, Assyrians, and Babylonians.

"It is clear that these two pantheons were not inspired by the same group of beings!" Mergham declared, looking at the images as if mesmerised. "Let's start with the Mesopotamian...gods. These beings—while clearly regal and exalted—are practically indistinguishable from humans in terms of physical appearance. Their dress code is similar to that of the ancient Mesopotamians. One could easily mistake them for ancient kings and queens, priests and priestesses, the aristocratic class.

"The gods of Egypt, on the other hand, are completely different. There is a strong otherworldly feel about them," he proceeded with his thesis. "And yes, the first thing that catches the eye is their zoomorphic heads. Yet I do not believe that we are dealing with beings that displayed humanoid and bestial hybrid traits. Moreover, these heads actually give us a glimpse into the culture of these extraterrestrials.

"Intriguing, right?" Mergham threw a quick look at his distant audience before turning back to the addictive slides. "However, in order to understand this curiosity better, let's look at some traditions that can be found among some of the cultures on Earth."

The two screens metamorphosed into a new image, that of sand, tents, and camels. There were a couple of people shrouded in navy-blue robes. Cotton turbans wrapped around their heads protected them from the heat whilst veils of the same blue hue concealed their faces.

"The Tuaregs are a nomadic ethnic group that live in the Sahara Desert. According to their traditions, a man ought not to appear in public without covering his face with a traditional shroud called a *tagelmust.*"

A new photo replaced the one of the desert nomads. The roofs of mud huts, conical in shape, could be recognised in the background. But the central spot was dominated by people who seemed to be frozen in motion. Whilst the pink and teal colours of their skirts and tunics might have created a mood of brightness, the long wooden masks they wore, too vague to resemble human faces, gave the photo an eerie feel. Elliott got the impression that no eyes looked back at him through the empty sockets of these false faces.

"The Dogon people of Mali wear these ritual masks whilst performing ceremonies called *dama.* A dama is a mystical dance in honour of the ancestors, during which the Dogon try to reach out to the spirit world in order to get blessings from its denizens."

The next photo to appear was significantly older, in black and white. It showed the façade of a wooden house, its roof rising into a triangle above the entrance. Beside the house stood a giant pole adorned with carvings, culminating in a bird beak at the top.

"The indigenous tribes of the Pacific Northwest believed that every clan had a spirit animal. This is why totem poles were an integral part of their village architecture."

The depiction of the Egyptian pantheon returned to replace the old photo.

"But let's get back to the gods of Ancient Egypt. It's logical to propose that these heads are actually elaborate helmets with stylised masks. For instance, Ra's represents a falcon; Anubis' is that of a jackal. I firmly believe that wearing masks is part of the social etiquette on their home world, possibly a vestige of shamanism and totemism from their civilisation's own past. It's rather fascinating, don't you think? Two worlds can be many lightyears away from each other, but find similarities in the form of certain traditions."

Mergham spent the last minutes of the film narrating from his chair.

"Before I bid you farewell, I would like to talk a bit about my upcoming project. Throughout the years, I have carried out archaeological fieldwork across the world, from Egypt to Peru. But there is still one cradle of civilisation where I have never personally excavated: Iraq, the land that was known as Mesopotamia in ancient times. But this will change early next year when I will be leading archaeological excavations in Iraqi Kurdistan."

Now the screen was displaying a photo that had become yellow with time; a photo of archaeologists working in trenches amidst a barren land.

"Here's a bit of context. In the beginning of the twentieth century, in the drylands to the east of Erbil, a group of German geographers affiliated with the Berlin-Baghdad Railway construction project discovered the ruins of an outpost dating back to the times of the Assyrian Empire. Archaeological excavations subsequently took place at the site; unfortunately, they abruptly ended due to the start of the First World War. However, excavations of the ruins of the outpost's temple revealed quite a few bizarre details. Firstly, every temple in Mesopotamia was dedicated to a particular god, but in this case, they found no hints as to which deity was worshipped at this temple. Even stranger was the rectangular platform in front of it, made out of megalithic blocks that were perfectly fitted together. Nothing similar has been found at any other Mesopotamian archaeological site."

A photo of the platform taken from higher ground appeared on the screen as well.

"I theorise that the platform itself predates the Assyrian outpost and was used as a launch pad for the spacecraft of the extraterrestrials worshipped as gods in ancient Mesopotamia. My team will be the first in over a century to carry out excavations of this site. And I am certain that uncovering the secrets buried in that remote part of the world will help us shed new light on our ancient history and the events humanity forgot many centuries ago. You can find more information about this project on my website."

Strangely, Elliott could not resist the urge to visit Mergham's website. The introduction page described Mergham as a researcher of ancient civilisations and a best-selling author. His books *The Search for Olympus: Aliens and Antiquity* and *The Vessels of Heaven* were splashed across the screen, just the tip of the iceberg of Mergham's bibliography. Elliott headed straight to his blog and found the most recent post about his upcoming project.

Are you interested in an opportunity of a lifetime?

We believe in engaging our online community. That's why we still have places for two volunteers to join this expedition. We will provide you with the necessary training, meals, and accommodation during the dig. We will also handle the procurement of an Iraqi visa on your behalf.

He read on, finding out more relevant information. The expedition was set to take place the following February. A short Q&A was incorporated into the same blog post.

Isn't it dangerous to carry out fieldwork in Iraq?

Whilst Iraq has been plagued by political and sectarian strife for the last two decades, Iraqi Kurdistan has largely remained untouched by conflict and is generally considered safe. A number of travel agencies feel confident enough to operate group tours in this part of the country. The archaeological site itself is located in a remote area of the province which has no recorded instances of insurgent activity.

Elliott slowly rubbed his chin, pondering. He really wanted change. Heck, just earlier that day he had been dreaming of an isolated island he could escape to. Though this was not an island, it was just as remote. And there, in a setting so unlike the one he was used to, he might perhaps become free from all the blandness and nausea of his usual routines. He saw a mental image of himself, clad in a leather jacket and a fedora, slowly and carefully picking up a golden statuette from its pedestal. Yes, this image was not grounded in reality in the least, but maybe it was a sign. Perhaps there, on the edge of the known world, he would finally be able to find something important and life-changing. Perhaps, he would even find himself.

The deadline for submitting applications was the end of September.

"Still the middle of August," Elliott hummed to himself, smiling.

There was still enough time to apply. He would start writing the covering letter the next day.

***

It was a chilly Saturday in early November when the postman slid an envelope through his letter box.

Dear Mr Gildart,

We are delighted to invite you to take part in the upcoming expedition as an Archaeological Trainee.

A document package providing further information about the project and outlining the next steps to be taken can be found attached to this letter. Please carefully read through it...

Chapter Two

"Whoever is in charge here should really turn the air-conditioning on," Jake mumbled.

Neil glanced across at him. "It is on; it's just not enough."

Sweat was dripping down his forehead. He wiped it off with a handkerchief which he then put back into his pocket: he was certain he'd need it on many more occasions before the evening brought forth the desired cool air.

"Better get used to the scorching heat," Neil remarked. "This is Baghdad, not New York."

They made their way through the airport's long, wide corridors. Men and women, in Western-style suits and traditional garb, kept overtaking them as though they all were taking part in a race towards the baggage reclaim area. Random members of staff appeared on occasion. Whilst one was giving some particular spot a round of mopping, another stood invigilating order at the other end of the hall. Men in military attire kept popping up as well. Strategically placed around the airport, a major gate into the country, they served as a reminder of the turbulence of nation's present. One could read a lot of messages in the rifles they firmly held in their hands.

Passport checks happened without problems. The duo picked up their luggage and proceeded towards the arrivals hall. Once they walked through the automated doors, the sounds they had kept contained overwhelmed Neil. The hall was filled with a multitude of people chattering with each other and squealing in joy upon seeing loved ones come through the gates.

"He said he would be standing beside the coffee shop," Neil explained as they went on, followed by the grinding sound of the wheels of their luggage bags.

And, indeed, their arrival was expected. Surrounded by the smell of pastries and coffee, a man stood in the designated place, holding a sign with a name typed on it in block capitals: **NEIL FEAVER**.

His gaze fixed on the duo the moment he glimpsed them among the other travellers. Although they had never met in person, the man clearly knew exactly who he was looking for. Neil was of medium height, with green eyes and short, chestnut-brown hair. It was impossible to mistake him for Jake, whose tall stature made him rise over his boss by a few inches, and whose raven hair was long enough to almost rest on his shoulders.

"Hi there, I believe you're expecting me." Neil smiled and offered a hand. "I'm Neil Feaver."

"Nice to meet you," the man said, shaking his hand. "I recognised you from one of your documentary films. My name is Massoud Mihla."

Neil had heard the name before. Mihla, too, was a journalist, a reporter for one of the country's news channels.

"And this is Jake Parvis, my cameraman."

Jake made a step forward and shook the Iraqi's hand.

"Welcome to Iraq, gentlemen. Throughout your stint here, I will be what you Americans call a 'fixer'," Massoud explained, primarily to Jake, since Neil was already aware of it.

"I'm not sure it's just an American word. I could have sworn Canadians use it too," Jake said with a smile. "And the Brits."

Neil was ready to roll his eyes; the cameraman just had to find an excuse to show off, one way or another—in this case, with his linguistic expertise.

"Oh, and the Aussies too," Jake added, making Massoud chuckle.

"Have you been to Iraq before, gentlemen?" the fixer asked as they made their way towards the exit.

"I haven't," Jake said.

"I have, years ago, but it was a short stint," Neil answered.

"Anyway, I have seen your documentary about Yemen," Massoud said as he led them towards the parking area. "So you've chosen Iraq as your next stop?" Though Massoud was joking, Neil was able to recognise a tint of sadness in his voice.

The Iraqi was referring to Neil's cycle of documentaries. Titled *Turmoil: In the World's Most Dangerous Places*, the series followed Neil as he explored various aspects of life in different conflict zones. This was supposed to be the fifth project in the series.

"Yes," Neil replied. "Like a firefly, I always hover towards a blaze."

They soon reached the airport's parking area.

"And here's our driver," Massoud said, referring to the man obediently standing by the parking lot's gate like a sentinel.

Neil opened his mouth to ask a question, but Massoud responded as though he had read his mind.

"He'll be with us only for today. The driver and vehicle you requested will join you later on since you have stated that you have no need of them during the first few days."

That was true; they would spend the first part of the project embedded with coalition forces.

Once the car doors closed, Neil felt another heatwave come down on him. Judging by Jake's cursing, his cameraman got subjected to it as well. Neil withdrew the handkerchief to wipe the newest coat of sweat off his face. He shot it a quick look when he was done: for a piece of fabric, it promised to be an invaluable possession around these parts. Neil could not wait for this stage of the journey to end so he could finally get a chance to refresh himself in his hotel room, shielded from the sun and heat.

"When the plane was landing, I managed to get a glimpse of the rural area outside the city," Jake was telling Massoud. "I was surprised how lush it is. It was all green as far as the eye could see."

Massoud let out a chuckle in response. "Foreigners often have an impression that the landscape of the whole Middle East is one vast desert," he explained. "In reality, a big part of Iraq lies in the valleys of two rivers, the Tigris and Euphrates. This is why, in ancient times, people used to call this land Mesopotamia: 'the land in between the rivers'. The soil here is one of the most fertile in the world. This is why, throughout history, many of the world's most populous cities sprung up across this country."

They reached the city proper, where high-rise buildings dwarfed any structure they'd passed in the suburbs. Baghdad was a metropolis full of life. The visitors could hear the jabber of the pedestrians as they scurried around on their routines. These mingled with the beeping of thousands of vehicles congesting the roads. It mostly felt like any major city on any continent, yet the military checkpoints that they passed at regular intervals served as a reminder of the constant terror threats that hung over the city like a dagger.

Their accommodation, the Jahwar Al-Tigris Hotel, appeared in view. A tall, grey building, it silently stood watching the eternal flow of the river Tigris beside it.

Neil and Jake bid the fixer and the driver farewell before going inside. They had to wait for some time as their rooms were not ready. And, whilst the hotel's lobby provided shelter from the heat outside, it was not the place Neil wanted to chill at that moment, as cooling and tidy as it was.

Having taken a chair next to the reporter, Jake put his backpack on the floor, unzipped it, and withdrew what Neil assumed was a journal. The cameraman leaned back into his chair, revealing a front cover with cartoonish artwork.

"Is that a comic book?" Neil asked.

"Close, but not exactly. It's a graphic novel." Jake flipped another page. "Though there was a limited comic book series about the same character."

"What is this one about?" Neil asked, rather sarcastically.

"It's called *The Urban Ronin*. It tells the story of a martial arts instructor who, having donned a ninja outfit, fights crime as a masked vigilante."

That was a predictable answer.

"Jake, you're like, what—thirty-two years old?"

"For your information, many if not most comic book readers are actually middle-aged."

"Hmm." Neil felt his philosophical side begin to take over. "You know what? This is actually an intriguing topic. What lures people to all of these superhero-centric comic book stories? There already seems to be a hero for every theme, for every type of power. Practically every storyline has been tapped into and overused. So what keeps driving people to these stories?"

"Maybe it's the lack of justice in real life?" Jake said, closing the graphic novel. "Think about it. Everything is fair in comic books. Everyone gets what is due to them. So when you see authorities and society fail so miserably in real life, why wouldn't you root for a superhero that always gets the job done, no matter how ludicrous their gimmick is?" The cameraman's grey eyes beamed with enthusiasm.

"I've never really thought about it from that angle," Neil said. "After all, I'm thirty-eight; perhaps I'm slightly too old to understand this philosophy." He resorted to dry humour.

"Hey, if you want, I'll lend it to you so you could read it for yourself." Jake held the book out to him. "Only make sure you don't spill coffee on it. It's one of my all-time favourites."

"No thanks, I'll do without."

He had to admit it: Jake, despite his laid-back nature, had the ability to turn the tables on a sarcastic remark.

Hector wasn't like this, Neil thought, remembering his previous colleague and cameraman. Melancholia pinched him as he thought about the reporting he and Hector had done in environments heated up by the firing of bullets, the places where the sound of exploding shells was as natural as the singing of birds. He wished he could do another documentary with his rowdy yet punctual former cameraman. Alas, there was no way Hector would ever film another video...

Neil sighed in regret.

***

To Neil's joy, the hotel had a lounge. It was his first destination after he had freshened himself up in his hotel room. The lounge was not particularly posh, but its Art Deco atmosphere, despite its amateurism, manifested almost immediately. It was a domain where the colour maroon reigned. Everything looked like it had been soaked in it: the lights, the simple wall paint, the leather chairs.

Neil ordered a whisky at the counter. One did not have to be psychic to guess that the glass the bartender handed to him was way overpriced by local standards, but he knew better than to run around looking for liquor stores in this city. It appeared that there were others who agreed with him: several more patrons hung around the lounge. Some were possibly reporters whilst others appeared to be contractors. They leisurely sipped their drinks as they typed on their laptops or scrolled through their phones.

Neil tasted his drink and immediately felt its strong flavour on his tongue. He made his way towards the flat-screen TV hanging on the back wall and sat down to watch. Naturally, an international news channel was running that moment. Another man was sat in a chair next to Neil's, holding a half-full glass as he dully listened to the anchor's speech.

Neil took a few more sips as the "drama" transported to the scene of an international economic summit and the faces of world leaders that had become familiar to billions around the world. There were shots of handshakes, group photos, and extracts from speeches—everything that knitted a report of this kind.

"Damn clowns," Neil voiced his dissatisfaction with that particular generation of politicians.

"I can recognise an American accent." The man in the nearby chair stirred. Lean, with strands of grey hair springing around his head, he turned to Neil. "Though I cannot distinguish which part you're from."

"I grew up in Oklahoma, but I am currently residing in New York," Neil said. "And where are you from?" he asked in return.

"Canada. Claude Faucon," he introduced himself, lightly bowing his head as he reached out to Neil for a handshake.

"Neil Feaver," was the reply as they shook hands.

"Let me guess—you're a reporter."

"Yes, I've had many years of experience in journalism," Neil said. "But on this occasion, I have come here in a somewhat different capacity: as a filmmaker."

"This country isn't really the safest place to shoot a blockbuster," Claude commented.

"I'm a documentary filmmaker."

"A documentary about the war, I assume."

"Indeed," Neil said, saluting with his glass.

"No surprise there."

"And what about you?" Neil asked.

"I'm a lecturer in Middle Eastern Studies at Harcourt University," Claude said. "It's in Canada's Ontario," he quickly clarified. "My main research interests are the manuscripts and official documents of the Arab world during the medieval and early modern periods. I am here to take part in a project aimed at digitising a number of Iraqi primary sources from that era."

Claude paused to sip a bit more of his drink.

"What drink are you having?" Neil asked.

"Rum. You should order one. It's nice."

Neil looked at his own mostly empty glass.

"Unfortunately, I am not familiar with your work," the academic confessed. "Is it centred on the Middle East?"

"Some of the instalments are. The series is called *Turmoil: In the World's Most Dangerous Places*, so, as the title suggests, my work takes me to different parts of the globe: the Middle East, Africa, Central America. For example, the most highly rated film in the series focused on the insurgency in the eastern regions of the Democratic Republic of Congo." Mentioning his magnum opus was a duty at this point.

"I'll make sure to watch some of them when I get the chance," Claude said. "But tell me something. Why do you choose to find the materials for your movies in the middle of war zones? I mean, there are different topics to explore and report on in this diverse world. You could have been going through the rubbish thrown out by Hollywood celebrities in search of their dirty secrets; tracking their old flames in order to find out some spicy details." He smirked. "Alternatively, you could be interviewing prisoners on death row, the prison guards and chaplains; exploring the themes of life and death, bad choices and circumstances, remorse, and narcissism. I'm talking about topics that can attract an equally large audience but keep you in a safe environment. Instead you come to a place like this, where if a stray bullet doesn't kill you, then a landmine will lie in wait for its turn."

"I hope you don't mind if I respond to your question with my own." Neil hit back. "Why did you choose to come do your research in this city? I know that Baghdad has historically been one of the biggest cultural centres of the Arab world, but why not go to Cairo? Why not go to Fez in Morocco? Cities with rich heritage which are actually safe."

The lecturer rubbed his chin in thought. "You have a point. I can't find a word to describe it. Not interest in its usual way, more like an urge."

"Something like a passion?"

"Something like that."

"Same with me. It calls out to you from deep inside. You know what needs to be done, and if you don't do it, perhaps nobody else will. To uncover something hidden under the surface, to give a platform to a story that would otherwise remain unheard. For you, it might be an agreement signed by two merchants three centuries ago that gives more information about the commerce of those days. For me, it might be the story of specific individuals behind a contemporary event that makes the news. Whatever the case, you're going to follow that call, no matter what pit or pedestal it leads you to."

"Yes, a passion." Claude shook his head thoughtfully. "You could even say an addiction."

"I wouldn't call it an addiction. Addictions enslave you; they make you lose control of your actions. Addictions are destructive by nature. Passions can be dangerous, but you're always free to make the choice to get out."

Their discussion was cut short by the news anchor introducing the next segment: a report from Baghdad. They both turned towards the screen immediately, finding themselves transported to the scene. It was a road in the middle of nowhere but as jammed as a big-city highway during rush hour.

"The long stream of refugees serves as a reminder that the war is coming closer to the Iraqi capital," the correspondent narrated grimly.

A multitude of cars kept slowly moving southwards. It did not matter if the car's owner was a labourer who barely made a living or an entrepreneur with investments in stocks and land. There and then, they were all one group swept together by fear and despair.

"Earlier today, the extremist Liwa al-Qadisiyyah militant group overran the city of Baqubah, about fifty kilometres to the north of the capital. The attack began at dawn. According to witness accounts, a brief battle quickly turned into a rout of the Iraqi army."

Neil heard the hiss of bullets and the thunder-like sounds of exploding shells when footage from the battle was presented.

The narration continued, talking about the insurgents' recent successes and the continuing demoralisation of the government's forces.

"Designated as a terrorist organisation by the UN, the United States, the EU, and a number of national governments, Liwa al-Qadisiyyah is a hardline Islamist militant group that seeks to reorganise the country along the lines of a fundamentalist Islamic theocracy."

A montage of scenes played out, highlighting the harbingers of fear. They showed pick-up trucks, the ever-present symbol of the region's armed conflicts, manned by people in dark uniforms, their heads and faces hidden under black balaclavas. A random fighter was then shown waving their banner, the white calligraphy on a black background radiating a sinister aura that could be felt even through the screen. The next scene showed several of the fighters jumping up and down as they brandished long knives; it felt like a dance, a dance mindless and maddened.

"A strict form of Sharia law has been imposed across the territories under the group's control. Women are no longer allowed outside unaccompanied by their male relatives. Punishments such as stoning and limb amputation have made a comeback. There have been various accounts of extrajudicial killings, forced disappearances, and torture taking place."

The report cut to an interview with a witness, originally a resident of one of the small towns to the west of Baqubah but now a refugee in Baghdad. The dark circles under his eyes were the aftermath of stressful days and sleepless nights.

"There was a man living down the street from me, a teacher at my son's school," the man spoke, voice trembling. "Several days after capturing the town, several militants came to his house. They claimed he committed blasphemy. They dragged him outside and shot him right in the middle of the road."

When the segment was over, Claude turned to Neil. "I don't want to sound cynical, but you've come to this country at the right time. You will be able to find plenty of new material. And I am sure there is more to come."

"Indeed," Neil said bluntly.

"Have you got any intentions of interviewing some of these jihadists?"

"I wouldn't mind. It would be intriguing to find out what is going on in their heads, but I doubt they're the types to open up to somebody they describe as a *kafir*."

"Speaking of Arabic terms, do you know what *Liwa al-Qadisiyyah* means?"

"The al-Qadisiyyah Brigade," Neil answered. "I'm a fluent speaker of Arabic."

"But what is an *al-Qadisiyyah*?" Claude was clearly testing him.

"I heard it was the location of a battle fought during the Crusades." It took Neil a bit of digging in his memory to bring that out.

"No, not the Crusades; the Crusaders never reached these parts. The Arab Conquests," Claude corrected him. "It was a place where the forces of the Arabs defeated the army of Persia's Sasanian dynasty in 636 AD. You could say that this event was a watershed moment that marked the end of ancient Mesopotamia and the beginning of Iraq." The academic was doing what he did best—lecturing.

"Still, a somewhat unusual name for an Islamist group," Neil said. "Typically, the names of these organisations are derived from various ideas of theological nature; like, for example, a *taliban* is a student at a madrassah."

"It actually gives a misleading nationalistic vibe," Claude said.

The call to the evening prayer made its way from outside. Traditional and mysterious, exotic and dangerous—Iraq greeted him.

CHAPTER THREE

"Camp Steadfast, the base I'm at, is one of one of the main American outposts in Iraq. It was set up in the Algaara area, a strategically important location that serves as a gateway to the south-eastern districts of Baghdad," Neil said into the camera as his tour of the compound continued.

He had spent the day behind the heavily-reinforced walls of the base, in the barracks and in the mess hall, as he held interviews with several of the soldiers stationed there. And the first batch of the voices of the war spoke out. They told him about their rotations, about their different upbringings and the diverse paths they had taken that ultimately brought them together at this location. They shared their dreams of a vague, distant day, their aspirations for the future. America's presence in the country throughout the last two decades had been a rollercoaster, an ever-churning cavalcade of troop surges followed by withdrawals followed by more surges.

The late afternoon sun blazing near the horizon was beginning to acquire reddish tints. Neil turned his head aside as he briefly looked at a guard who was walking the perimeter of the wall before starting a conversation with his latest interviewee.

Lieutenant Les Woodward adjusted his sunglasses as he waited for Jake to start filming. He was a hardened type who was on his third rotation in this country. Clad in armour and a helmet, he embodied the stereotype of a tough soldier. Though his sunglasses were covering his eyes that moment, it was easy to guess that his concealed gaze was a no-nonsense one.

"So what can you say about this area? What lies beyond these walls?" Neil asked as the camera focused on the officer.

"The short answer is: danger." Woodward's answer was brief but to the point. "This base has endured more shelling than rainfall. Just three weeks ago, several shells landed on the territory of the camp. Luckily, there were no casualties. Traditionally, different militant groups of different sectarian affiliations have operated in this area, ones that tend to fight each other when they are not fighting us. But in the last few months, it's Liwa al-Qadisiyyah that seems to be the one causing most of the trouble."

***

"Oh, God, not this again," Neil heard Jake complain behind his back.

Neil had just put a bulletproof vest on. He looked at the mirror; his reflection looked no different from a soldier serving at the base, in his military boots and fatigues. The only thing missing was the helmet, but he would be provided with one.

"What? You still haven't gotten used to it?" Neil smirked as he turned around. "This isn't your first stint in a war-torn country."

Jake's attire was identical to his own. The cameraman put his palms on the vest, trying to adjust it.

"It makes me feel like a steel-capped teddy bear," he said.

"Better to feel like a steel-capped teddy bear than become an eco-friendly substitute for a bear-skin rug at some warlord's house."

This type of personal protective equipment was compulsory on a trip like the one they were about to embark on.

***

The darkness of the night greeted Neil as he climbed out of the armoured personnel carrier. It was late, almost midnight, and in the rural area, the peculiar songs performed by nocturnal insects were the only sounds that his ears could catch. Everything around him was dyed black. Had he not had a pair of night-vision goggles with him, he would not have been able to tell if he was standing on the edge of a field or in the middle of a swamp.

He gave Jake the command to turn the camera on again. His subordinate did as told and pointed the device straight at the reporter.

"Tonight, we will get a chance to witness a raid as it happens," Neil said, almost whispering, whilst the soldiers that had come with them were readying themselves for what was to come.

"Coalition forces received a tip from an informer that an agent of Liwa al-Qadisiyyah militant group is residing in a nearby village. The aim of this operation is to have him captured in hopes of finding a trail that could lead to something bigger."

Lieutenant Woodward, the officer tasked with leading the raid, checked that everything was in order before giving the signal for the group to move out.

The locals who would have likely been out and about during daylight were tucked inside their houses; the night provided cover for the soldiers as they slowly advanced in their formation. They remained vigilant, holding their weapons with firm grips.

"It's a quiet, you could even say serene, night," Neil whispered. He leaned so close to the camera that his face eclipsed all of the background in the shot. "But you can just sense a feeling of intensity hovering around the group. There's uncertainty; it's impossible to say what awaits us."

They advanced from the fields into the village. They could see houses standing in front of them, but fences and darkness obscured all detail of the village dwellings.

Then a series of sounds ripped through the silence. Somewhere in the distance, a dog was barking, having heard their approach. Other dogs answered the canine's cry with barking of their own, rough and hostile.

"It appears that some of the dogs have noticed us," Neil commented to the camera.

"You know, there's one thing I never understood," Jake said. "If Muslims consider dogs unholy animals, why do they even keep them as pets?"

"They view them as unclean, not unholy. There's a difference between the two," Neil explained. "In these parts, dogs are kept as pets, but are usually kept in the yards or barns and not allowed to enter houses."

Neil silently swore to make sure that this conversation was taken out of the film during the editing process.

"The orchestra is welcoming the parade," Lieutenant Woodward whispered another one of his cynical one-liners.

The element of surprise kept dissolving further with every bark, but the group moved closer and closer. With the house in reach, Woodward gave orders to several members of the group: they were to form a perimeter around the dwelling in order to prevent anybody from escaping.

Then the formation pushed forth. Soon enough, the gun-wielding line surged through the gates of the house. No guard dog jumped to attack as they entered the courtyard, but weak lights appeared at the windows of the house. The inhabitants had caught the mutts' warning. The soldiers were not the ones who were to drop in with a surprise; they were now the ones expecting surprises. A rocket-propelled grenade could fly out of a dimly lit window at any moment. They could meet a barrel of a rifle point-blank. The intensity around them was boiling like water in a saucepan.

The first soldier to reach the front door kicked it open. Shrieks and screams erupted around the intruders as they stormed into the house.

Neil and Jake waited in what seemed to be the foyer as the soldiers searched through the rooms. Within minutes, the inhabitants of the house were gathered under guard in the modest, practically unfurnished living room.

The soldiers sent to inspect the rear garden soon came back with no detainees.

"Damn, he's not here," Woodward said. "The suspect is a man of fighting age."

And indeed, none of the inhabitants fit that description. There was an old man, a couple of teenagers, and four women of different ages shrouded in long black robes. Neil could read the fear and confusion on the faces of the men. Not only were they not of fighting age, none of them had engaged in military combat. Neil had interviewed countless people in different war zones; he could easily tell the difference between a seasoned fighter and a civilian.

"Sergeant, Sergeant," Woodward called out through the radio. "The suspect is not here. Did you manage to catch a glimpse of anyone?"

"No, Lieutenant, not a single soul," a voice responded.

"He probably pulled a quick one and fled through the back before we got here," the lieutenant said as he looked into the rolling camera, intentionally or not.

***

"A legend states that many years ago, when an enemy army laid siege to Rome and attempted to infiltrate the city under the cover of darkness, a flock of geese sensed their coming and honked vigorously, notifying the city's guards. In this case, it was the barking of dogs that warned the target of the raid," Neil commented, speaking into the camera.

The hunt for the suspect continued. The house the soldiers had raided stood close to the fringes of the village, so it was Woodward's order that the soldiers were to search the nearby grove. The soldiers split up to scour the wooded area. The film crew stuck with the lieutenant himself.

They walked slowly, their steps careful, for even the sound of a branch snapped under a heavy boot could notify the hiding suspect. Their night-vision goggles painted the nocturnal world around them in a green glow.

"I'll say one thing: a grove certainly looks different through these goggles," Neil whispered into the camera. "I'll keep this in mind next time I go strolling in the woods close to home during a leisurely evening." He tried adding some humour to the narration.

Woodward suddenly stopped, making the film crew do the same.

"Take cover," he hissed through gritted teeth, keeping his voice low. "I think I spotted movement behind that tree." He pointed the barrel of his rifle at a thick tree, a fig likely.

Getting the cue, Neil hid behind the closest tree, leaning against it. He looked sideways to where Jake had taken cover behind a nearby tree and was carefully trying to stick the camera lens out to catch the action. Woodward took cover nearby.

"You! Behind the tree!" the lieutenant shouted. "Step out! I know you're there!"

There was no evidence that the man the military was hunting knew even basic English, but often the right tone could convey meaning better than the most appropriate word.

Neil carefully peeked out from behind his hiding place. The goggles allowed him to spot a swift movement; something appeared from behind the fig tree, only to disappear instantly. Instinctively, he pulled back. For a fleeting second, the air beside him became unnaturally warm. He was certain a bullet had passed him by. He'd heard no gunshot—the suspect must have used a silencer.

Neil turned to Woodward just in time to see the officer dash from his cover, towards the fig. The darkness-clad figure of the militant briefly appeared from behind the tree, alerted by the officer's heavy-booted steps. The silent gun fired another round, but Woodward's agility turned into his lucky charm; he found cover behind another tree just in the nick of time, dodging the bullet.

The fugitive had bought himself a moment, and he used it to take flight. The bang of Woodward's rifle echoed in the grove, and the bullet struck a nearby tree. A bizarre, sinister game of tag ensued, with the militant on the run and Woodward in pursuit. The two ventured deeper into the woodlands, using the trees as cover when needed to avoid getting tagged by a bullet.

"I need support!" Woodward shouted into his radio, as he hid from another shot.

Neil heard somebody move through the grass and bushes. A moment later, a soldier swooped past him, the first to answer his commanding officer's call.

The odds kept stacking against the escapee as an entire posse went in pursuit. Rifle shots went flying into the night and, through his green-tinted lenses, Neil saw the militant drop heavily onto the ground.

"Got him!" one of the men shouted.

They watched for a couple of moments as the militant, lying on his side with his back to Neil, started making feeble movements.

"He's alive!" Woodward declared.

He moved towards the militant, who lay convulsing on the ground. Neil, Jake, and several soldiers, followed his lead. With the weapons of the soldiers pointed at the suspect in case he tried one last attack, Woodward knelt down and turned him onto his back.

And, indeed, the militant had one more trick up his sleeve. The night-vision goggles allowed the soldiers and film crew to see the grenade clutched in his hand...a grenade that already had its pin removed. The sight made goose bumps run down Neil's spine.

"Fall back and on the ground!" he heard Woodward shout.

Neil did not need instructions. He was already diving for cover when the grenade exploded behind him. The shockwave pushed him in the back like an angry man he'd had a verbal spat with. It was a hard landing as he hit his chin against the ground; luckily, there was grass, not stone. He tried flexing the muscles in his back, afraid he'd feel a shard of shrapnel implanted deep inside his flesh. He felt none; the deadly projectiles had avoided him.

He carefully lifted himself on his elbows and looked around. Jake was getting up, thankfully unscathed. Still shaken by the... explosive...encounter, Jake staggered to the camera that was lying nearby and picked it up.

"Still working," he said upon examining it.

Neil was back on his feet by the time Jake pointed the camera at him.

"Another close encounter with death," Neil said, looking at the camera as he gave an impression of a champion, basking in his confidence and good luck.

But inside, he was still shaking.

***

If the shootout had not killed the militant, the grenade explosion did. He would not be revealing anything, but his house might have some secrets hidden within its walls, secrets that could lead to a terror cell or reveal some plot.

Dawn snuck through the windows as Lieutenant Woodward stood in the middle of the living room. The spoils of the raid lay on the floor before him.

"A search of the house revealed the usual stuff," he said when Neil asked him to comment. "As you see here, there are guns. We've also found copies of pamphlets containing Wahhabi propaganda."

The sergeant entered the room, carrying a simple wooden box in his hands.

"Lieutenant, I think you ought to see this," he said. "We found it in the pantry."

He opened the box; Woodward peeked into it.

"Interesting." Woodward stepped back. "Lay it out beside the other items we found."

The sergeant did as told, carefully putting the objects inside the box on the floor one by one. Fascinated, Neil came closer and knelt to get a better look at them. These were items of metalwork: gold, copper, and bronze, plaques and medallions and other objects. Some bore engravings of different figures; others bore their shapes. Some appeared to be mythological beings, strange creatures that only human imagination could come up with. Others showed men in the middle of activities, whether the hunt or prayer. A few just had some symbols on them, signs that could have been taken from some script. Their curly style was reminiscent of Arabic script, but it was definitely something different.

"Jake," Neil said. "Zoom in on each of these items."

***

Neil did not bother to rest upon returning to the Jahwar Al-Tigris Hotel. Instead, he stood, laptop under his armpit, in front of a room marked with a number he had memorised. He knocked and heard a metallic screech as the door handle lowered and the door opened, revealing Dr Claude Faucon.

"Welcome back, Mister Feaver." The academic smiled. "Is there something I can help you with?"

"Hello, Dr Faucon," Neil said. "Actually, I could use your help."

"Then please come in."

Neil entered and heard the door close behind him.

"There is something I would like you to look at," he said as he put the laptop on the table. When the system loaded, he opened the file, and a series of images sprung up. "Perhaps you know what these are?"

"Hmm." Claude sat down on a chair and studied the images. "Where did you find these?" he asked.

Neil quickly retold the events of that night and the following morning.

"They seem to be old magic trinkets," Claude said, staring at the screen. "Very old ones."

"Strange. Why would they be in the possession of a jihadist?" Neil wondered. "As far as I'm aware, Wahhabis and Salafis oppose all forms of folk superstition."

"But here's the most interesting thing: these are not even Islamic. And I am certain they come from a time before the Arab Conquests."

"Well, yes, the imagery doesn't seem Islamic," Neil said, thinking it over.

"Some are Zoroastrian, like this one." Claude pointed at the screenshot of a coin-like object. The engraving was not very clear, but it appeared to depict a being with wings. The upper part of its body was that of a human, below the waist it was a bird. "It's called the Faravahar," Claude explained. "And it's one of the most famous images in the Zoroastrian tradition."

Neil listened intently.

"Here's another one. This might be an image of the god Mithra, an ancient solar deity," the scholar continued, pointing at another object. "See the rays extending from his figure? Only I'm not sure if this item is Zoroastrian or from the Cult of Mithra."

Neil had never considered himself a fan of antiques, but as he stood there, he felt a tingle inside his very essence. This discovery held the potential of a scoop, but perhaps...perhaps something more...

CHAPTER FOUR

The waves in the bay might have been light, yet were still enough to rock the boat. In the heart of the night, the stars and moon above offered the only guiding lights over the sea. A bay that would hear the screeches of a hundred seagulls during daytime was devoid of any sounds other than the pulsation of the waves, rhythmically accompanied by the drumming of the oars as they dipped beneath the water.

The lone rower sat on the bench, an oar in each hand. He had minimal experience in boating, yet he was doing his best, devoutly pressing on the oars. And in return, the vessel kept carrying him out into the open sea. The skyline of the small Djiboutian town he had departed from would have never impressed him. No single building appeared to be higher than two storeys, and the few lampposts on the street that ran parallel to the shore were not enough to prevent darkness from hiding most of it from view.

He took a momentary pause to wipe a drop of sweat that was slowly dripping down his forehead. He breathed deep, inhaling the refreshing maritime air with its unmistakeable salt and seaweed scents, and continued rowing with the same vigour further into the vast oceanic domain.

Yet he sought neither solitude nor inspiration. He sought escape.

I am not coming back to this godforsaken place, he thought bitterly. *Not even at the helm of an invading army that would overrun this country.*

His gaze stayed on his beacon, a distant object on the horizon: his mode of transport for the rest of his aquatic journey. And as he rowed closer, it grew bigger in size, the details clearer. Its appearance surprised him. He had not known what vessel he would find waiting for him. He'd thought it would be an old barge, leaking and creaking and barely able to stay afloat. Maybe a small but agile speedboat. Yet he beheld a yacht. It was not magnificent, but it was levels of luxury above a passenger like him.

The yacht had three decks. Likely silver in colour in sunshine, the dark camouflaged it in a steely shade. The side of the hull resembled a knife with the bow taking the place of the sharp tip.

Every stroke of the oars brought him closer to the vessel. Yet just as the yacht kept growing before his eyes, so did the suspense inside his mind. His handlers had let him know that a friend of the organisation he belonged to had volunteered to take him back to Iraq. Still, nobody had given a proper answer to one question: who was this friend? Perhaps they themselves had limited info. But such an opportunity was too good to decline. After all, what was the alternative? A multi-week journey involving crossing the land borders of about five different Middle Eastern states by walking through scorched deserts or getting a ride in the back of a lorry; a journey accompanied by the ever-strong possibility of being found during customs checks or running into a border patrol.

Three dark figures stood on the lowest deck of the ship. One lowered a rope ladder for him. The rower grabbed it and stood up. The boat rocked in response, almost as if it wished not to let go of its passenger, yet the man pulled himself free and up onto the deck. Two of the trio waiting for him could have been deckhands; the third one, the most rugged one, definitely had a different function. The automatic rifle hanging around his neck was there for a reason.

"You mustn't stay on deck longer than needed." Such was the greeting from one of the deckhands. "The boss will see you soon. Come with us for now." He spoke in English, and judging by their appearance, none of these crew members were Middle Easterners.

Sayid, for that was the rower's name, only nodded in agreement. They led him below the deck into a cabin as small as a prison cell. The interior was simplistic: only one bed bunk, which came with a pillow and a duvet. There was no window;

if he wanted light, he had to switch it on. The other door in the cabin led to an ensuite shower room, which promised to be the maximum amount of luxury his mystery host was willing to grant him.

He ran a hand through his long, messy beard. He wondered what his hair looked like after spending the last few weeks hiding out in dirt-filled basements and abandoned barns. But there would be a better time to find out. Weary after an entire day on the move, he just lay down on the bunk and closed his eyes. However, he did not have the chance to fall asleep. Whoever began banging on the door made sure of it.

Sayid got up to open the door, and found the same deckhand from earlier.

"The boss would like to meet you," the man said, as curt as before.

"Then let's go," Sayid responded.

When he arrived in the upper deck lounge, he felt like he had somehow crossed onto a different vessel. It was ten times more spacious than his cabin, with ocean views on two sides. There was no point in comparing the interior. There were chairs made out of high-quality wood. The floor had a carpet. Also included was a coffee table with a kettle, cups, and glasses. A large TV hung from the wall. And if all of that was not enough, the small bar counter implied that the owner wanted this room to incorporate as much as possible. The place emitted a sense of luxury that Sayid had never been familiar with.

The door opposite opened and a person walked in. A middle-aged man, he was well-trimmed and clean-shaven. His beige two-piece suit was flawlessly matched with a grey shirt and a pair of brown shoes. Clearly, this was a man of class and style—a representative of a type of people Sayid would usually be wary off.

"I have to apologise for not being able to greet you when you boarded this yacht; I was in the middle of an important phone call," the man said with a smile. "It might be well past midnight here at the Horn of Africa, but it is afternoon in certain parts of the world."

Sayid felt uneasy as he listened to him speak. He heard footsteps behind him as the deckhand walked away.

"So you are Sayid al-Buzali, a high-ranking commander of the Liwa al-Qadisiyyah militant group. I was told you would be the person joining me here tonight." The man spoke with an accent, and though Sayid was by no means a linguist, he'd have guessed German or Scandinavian.

"Indeed, it is I," Sayid confirmed. "I've been told that a friend would be picking me up to help get me back to Iraq. I assume you are that friend, yet I cannot recall meeting you before. Unfortunately, I do not even know your name."

"I do not reveal my name when I'm involved in such dealings. However, I am known under the alias of the Samnite. And we can say that I am a business partner of Liwa al-Qadisiyyah." A smile appeared on his face, a type that seemed pleasant and vulturous at the same time.

Sayid never understood why some people went to such lengths to come up with nicknames that were complex to the point that any symbolism was replaced with blatant farce.

"I am first and foremost, a military commander," Sayid told him. "I have had very limited involvement in the economic life of the territories our group controls."

"Fair enough. By the way, you are free to sit down." The Samnite pointed at one of the chairs.

Sayid did so.

"But you do know that being designated an international terrorist organisation, Liwa al-Qadisiyyah, like other similar entities, relies on different schemes to get financing. For example, Iraq is an oil-rich country, so pumping oil from the fields under your control and then smuggling it is one such enterprise."

"This I know."

"However, I am not involved with oil trading. I am an art dealer. It is through me that the artefacts and works of art your comrades have looted during their conquests end up on the black market. After all, Iraq is a treasure trove of ancient relics. Sumerian, Akkadian, Elamite, Assyrian, Babylonian, Arabic—sculptures, pottery, gold-work, and more."

Hands behind his back, the art dealer took a couple of steps forward.

"I was holidaying in the region when I found out about your escape from prison through one of my contacts in the Liwa, and that the group was thinking of a way of smuggling you back to Iraq. I volunteered to help out. After all, if anything, intelligence services would expect you to return by land. They do not expect your arrival by sea. Moreover, this way decreases your journey by many days."

"Yes, it does."

"I was surprised to find out that the CIA operates a rendition centre in Djibouti."

"Believe me, you wouldn't want to set foot there." Just remembering the year he had spent there made Sayid grit his teeth.

"And it appears Liwa al-Qadisiyyah has allies in this part of the world. Somebody had to harbour you whilst you were in hiding."

"The international jihadist movement is more intertwined than it might appear," Sayid explained. "Some of our warriors fight at our brothers' side across the Sahel region and vice versa. We've established contacts. I was imprisoned alongside a couple of Djibouti nationals who had been captured in Mali. They escaped with me, and the local cell they belonged to acted as my handlers."

"How did you manage to break out?"

"The prison inmates began a riot. We were able to overwhelm the guards, take some of them hostage, climb over the fencing, and disappear in the streets of the city."

"It sounds like security there was quite lacklustre. But I guess this is what happens when you outsource your detention centres to Third World cesspools," the Samnite commented with a shrug of his shoulders. "Were there any casualties?"

"Yes, a couple on our side and a couple on theirs." Sayid turned his hands and opened his palms. "I snapped the neck of one of the guards with these bare hands," he proudly declared as he raised them.

And as he spoke, he felt satisfaction, for this was his own small act of vengeance for enduring imprisonment in that rathole.

"Well, it's all in the past now. In a couple of days' time we will be in Iraqi waters. You shall disembark at a specified location in the vicinity of Umm Qasr where you will be met by the Liwa's agents. Then it will be up to them to take you northwards, past the front lines, into the areas controlled by the group. So this little boat trip is going to be the easiest part of the journey." The Samnite grinned.

Yet, even though Sayid chose to believe his host, the feeling of unease, falling on him like a shadow cast by a dagger aimed at his back, would simply not go away. He could not deny the possibility that this was just a set-up, that this smooth-talking stranger was an agent of some intelligence service. After all, secret services often had shady types on their payroll. For all he knew, the CIA, MI-6, Mossad, Interpol, Whatever, might have already had him on their radar. He had seen one armed man on the yacht. And if there was one, there were most likely more. And they could burst into the room, guns loaded, at any moment.

He tried to assess his host's physical prowess. The Samnite did not look much of a fighter and his mannerisms did not hint at being one, while Sayid had years of experience in combat. So, if a trap had indeed been set for him, he would at least make an attempt to break the traitor's neck before succumbing to a rain of bullets.

"By the way, you've got quite a nice yacht." He moved the conversation elsewhere.

"Thank you, although I must admit, it is second hand. An acquaintance of mine, quite a rich fellow, has recently bought a new, bigger yacht, so he sold it to me for a bargain price. Heck, had he gone for a lower price, the fee would have become largely symbolic!" The Samnite came up to his coffee table. "By the way, I seem to have forgotten to offer you any refreshments. Would you like some tea, or perhaps coffee?"

"No thanks, I'm fine," Sayid replied, unable to not imagine the teaspoons of poison that could be put into his beverage.

"I'm a scuba diving enthusiast," the Samnite continued. "So, now I know what it feels like to scuba dive from my own yacht." A bit more excitement in his voice would have made him sound like a child that had just got a gift. "Also, I prefer the Red Sea over the Mediterranean," he added.

"But shouldn't you be concerned?" This was a legitimate question. "Do you know what the waters we're sailing are known for?"

"You mean pirates?" the Samnite said with a grin. "I'm not worried about them. I've got connections in this area. Let these pirates raid this vessel! Just one phone call and the same pirates will later come crawling to me with an apology letter, a bouquet of flowers, and a box of chocolates." He sounded very confident.

Sayid chuckled; the host had a sense of humour.

"But since we're on the topic of money and power." The Samnite sat down opposite his guest. "My dealings with Liwa al-Qadisiyyah are not the sole reason I've agreed to help you out. I would like to request a favour in return."

Sayid discovered that he was able to breathe freely again. Treachery was unlikely in the works; ambition, however, was.

"And what is it?"

"I was intending to forward this request to your leader, Mullah Nishwari, and others involved in decision-making through the usual channels. And I still plan to do so. However, it would mean a lot to me if you could personally lobby this idea in front of the honourable mullah. Since you are a high-ranking commander, your word will give more value."

"Continue," Sayid said.

"It probably sounds a bit strange, but there is this person I play golf with, a billionaire, and he...wants to sponsor an expedition to carry out fieldwork in certain areas under your control."

This immediately made Sayid raise an eyebrow. "Is it supposed to be some sort of archaeological expedition?"

"He called it an anthropological expedition. He intends to send the people who will oversee it to Iraq soon enough. Aside from your permission, he asks the brigade to guarantee protection for this project. He is willing to pay Liwa al-Qadisiyyah for it."

"This is a very unusual request." Sayid stroked his beard lightly. "Why would he bother with something like this?"

"There are many ancient cities that could be found buried under the dust and sands of Iraq. My friend claims that he has memories of a past life...when he was an advisor to a Sumerian king ruling one such city-state. Certain beyond doubt that these 'memories' are true, he seeks to rediscover that city to prove it."

"I cannot recall hearing anything more stupid than this," Sayid told his host bluntly. "A simple explanation is that your friend is insane."

"I agree that this is the most likely explanation," the Samnite said with another of his smiles. "However, he is a billionaire;

he can spend lots of money playing these games without any burden on his finances. As his friend, I say: let him do it. I'm not losing anything and your group will get paid for it. Plus, in the unlikely event of this city being found, think of the treasures that might possibly be found there. We are talking about the level of Troy or the tomb of Tutankhamun. He can keep any clay tablets mentioning the reigns of long-forgotten Sumerian rulers, whilst we may turn a profit off everything else worthwhile that can be uncovered there. What do you think?"

"Personally, I have nothing against the expedition you are advocating. It does not harm the Liwa's functioning. And though it is born from your friend's misguided delusions, partaking in it is not blasphemy. Though I am not sure what conclusion Mullah Nishwari would come to."

"I'm sure we will come to an understanding."

"Why are you so certain?"

"Because business is the greatest equaliser," the Samnite said. "People can clash over differences in their beliefs and ideologies, and the ensuing confrontation can lead to some most gruesome outcomes. But what happens when parties with non-matching ideological doctrines come to realisation that they can achieve mutual economic benefit? They sit down and make a deal. Liwa al-Qadisiyyah needs finances to run its quasi-state and I need money to live the life. And we work together, contributing to each other's success. I know that there are things you and your comrades despise me for: the fact that I am not of the same faith as you is just one. And in turn, I have reasons to be disgusted by your organisation, such as your affinity for senseless carnage. Don't get me wrong, I do not disapprove of violence; I have no problem with resorting to it myself if I need to. But I fail to understand why you keep filling one mass grave after another."

You are not expected to understand, infidel. It's beyond you, Sayid reprimanded him in thought, but held his tongue.

"And let's be honest," the Samnite continued, "had I been of no use to you, you would have hung me from a crane in the middle of a city square if you had gotten your hands on me. And on my part, I would have celebrated every time a drone blasted any of your lot straight to whatever hell burns beneath Earth's crust."

Sayid suddenly burst into laughter: loud, long, and sincere. Many people he knew would have found this sight confusing, for it was so unlike him.

The Samnite just sat there, the corners of his lips curled into a grin as fiendish as his true self.

"You know what? You might be the only infidel I somewhat like!" Sayid declared. "I think I will have a cup of tea after all. A person who speaks so boldly right in my face would not sprinkle another man's drink with poison."

"I am delighted to hear this. Would you like any sugar with your tea?"

"No sugar."

The host got up and made his way to the counter.

"By the way, what if the coast guard stops your yacht for inspection?" Sayid asked.

"Don't worry about it. There is an authentic Ancient Egyptian sarcophagus in a glass case in one of the cabins on the lower deck. I have all the needed paperwork related to it. You can hide inside it. The coast guards will never look inside." The art dealer had his back turned as he prepared the beverage.

Certain images started coming to Sayid's mind, images of a centuries-old, bandaged corpse resting in its casket.

"There's no mummy inside, right?" He shuddered at the thought of sharing space with...that.

"So what if there is?"

***

Elliott was starting to come to the conclusion that the word "airport" had become somewhat misleading. If he were to propose a more accurate term, he'd go with "shopping mall with a landing strip outside". Once he passed security, he stepped into a seemingly endless department store. It was any shopaholic's dream. Turn to the left and you'll find glass displays of perfumes with their ever-present samples. Turn to the right and choose from a selection of confectionary. Forgot your bag at home? There's no point in worrying when a travel accessories shop is just a few feet away.

He passed through this labyrinth of merchandise and finally arrived at the departures area. He looked at his watch; he'd arrived about three hours before his flight. It felt too early, but he didn't want to take any chances. Not again. He recalled that time a few years back when he and a couple of friends decided to go on a one-week holiday to Ibiza. He'd thought then that he had everything planned out, that he would arrive at the last moment. But he got held up in traffic and, if that was not enough, the queue at the security check was enormous. He'd been the only one of the group to miss the flight.

He walked towards the seating area in search of a place to rest. He had come down from Bristol to London, and the journey was only beginning. The plane was bound to Amman; there he would switch flights and travel to Erbil.

As always, the airport was busy, but at that moment many spots in the seating area remained empty. When he saw who else was sitting there, he stopped in his tracks. Leonard Mergham sat flanked by two vacant airport chairs, a book in his hands and a backpack by his foot.

"Dr Mergham, is that you?" Elliott quietly asked as he approached the author.

"Yes." Mergham looked up at him.

"Hello, I'm Elliott Gildart. I'm—"

"One of the volunteers." Mergham cut him off and stood up to shake his hand. "Nice to meet you. So, are you looking forward to digging up stuff in the middle of nowhere?" he asked, jokingly but enthusiastically.

In real life, Mergham did not seem as imposing as he'd appeared on screen; he could have easily been compared to that type of neighbour who can always be found routinely watering flowers in his front yard.

"Can't wait." Elliott grinned.

"Oh, great to hear. I presume that's why you've arrived so early?"

"Well, let's just say that's one of the reasons," Elliot responded, perhaps somewhat sheepishly.

They both sat down.

"So, Elliott, what made you want to join this project?" Mergham asked.

"To be honest, it was your documentary film *Mysteries of the Ancient Gods*. It gave me this urge to..." He struggled to find the right expression. "Let's say, explore the unexplored?"

Yes, that was it. He still did not know what to think about Mergham's theses, but in its own hardly explainable way, that film had indeed inspired Elliott to make this choice.

"Splendid. Who knows, maybe you will choose to pursue this field further. I myself wasn't always a cryptoarchaeologist."

"You used to be a mathematician, right?" Elliott had familiarised himself with the author's biography.

"Correct, but then I had to prepare a university module on ancient mathematics. I went from studying the works of Euclid to the schematics of the Pyramids. Having found some oddities relating to the maths of their engineering, I began to dig deeper, and I've been digging ever since."

Mergham suddenly turned his head as though he had spotted something, or most likely someone, from the corner of his eye.

"Hello, Lauren!" he called out.

Elliott turned to see a red-haired young woman walking their way. Something seemed familiar about her, even though she had not appeared in Mergham's film.

Mergham stood up. "Lauren, I would like you to meet Elliott, one of our volunteers. "And Elliott, this is Lauren Border, my PA."

Lauren Border. This was indeed a familiar name. And suddenly, he felt like everything around him was revolving.

He looked at her, dumbstruck. "Does the name 'Simon Gildart' sound familiar to you?"

"Yes, he was my maternal grandfather." She sounded surprised.

This explained a lot.

"Elliott, Elliott Gildart..." she mumbled. "Oh my God!" she squealed.

"I guess this means you're related in some way," Mergham concluded.

"I think she might possibly be my cousin," Elliott said.

"You think? So you're not sure?" Mergham raised his brow.

"We haven't seen each other in many years," Lauren quickly explained. "Family problems," she added.

"Oh, I see. Well, the old saying is true: the Earth is indeed a small place. I'm sure you two have some catching up to do. In the meantime, I think I'll go and have a cup of mocha." With that, Mergham gave his assistant some instructions and left off, no doubt assuming that giving the cousins quality time was a good idea.

Elliott wished the author had stayed to maintain balance. He had never forgotten his cousin throughout the years. And even as he sat there, he remembered…remembered the bratty little girl who always wanted to be treated like a princess…remembered their constant quarrelling. The age difference between the two was not great: only one year, if Elliott's memory hadn't failed him. He was twenty-six; thus, Lauren had to be twenty-seven.

He doubted that her memories of him were fond. There really was no reason for them to be.

Lauren awkwardly sat down beside him. For the next several moments, there was only an uncomfortable silence between them.

"So." Lauren tried to start a conversation. "It's been a long time."

"It has, hasn't it?" Elliott responded. "So, Lauren, what's your life been like the last few years?"

"Well, I graduated uni with a BA in Geography and Archaeology. I held a couple of admin and secretarial jobs before moving on to work for Dr Mergham. And what do you do, in your life?"

"I work at a call centre, but I've taken a long holiday in order to take part in this excavation."

The rules of the universe dictated that something like this just had to happen. You go to great lengths to delve into something new to escape your reality and then get stuck with an apparition from the past. As he sat there, Elliott could have sworn that at that very moment, on a distant planet on the other side of the cosmos, Mergham's alien gods were laughing at him.

CHAPTER FIVE

"Reminds me of espresso," Neil commented, having sipped the coffee that room service had brought. The strong brew had immediately made itself known as he felt a stimulating rush through his body.

"This is how we make coffee in the Middle East," Massoud, seated in a chair, responded.

"So, yes, he tried to take us down with him as his last act," Neil finished, referring to the incident in the grove. The image of the primed grenade clutched in a convulsing hand once again formed before his eyes.

"Such is our line of work. You can never tell if there is a death trap awaiting you nearby—very exquisite ones at times," Massoud said, cup in hand. "Funnily, this reminds me of the times when I found myself under sniper fire whilst reporting from the frontlines."

"I've been under sniper fire before as well. But not in this country, in Libya."

It was strange to admit, but even memories of dreadful experiences and brushes with death were a way to bond when discussed over coffee.

"But since we're talking about different types of dangers..." Massoud stood up. "I might as well get this out of the way."

The fixer reached under his jacket and withdrew an object enveloped in a green rag. He carefully put it on the table.

"This is something you requested before you arrived in Iraq," he said, his voice serious.

Already anticipating what he was going to see, Neil stood up and slowly proceeded to unwrap the item. The rag came off, revealing a holster and the magazine of a handgun sticking out of it.

"I hope you have all the needed permits for it," Massoud commented.

Neil nodded. "Yes, of course." Many foreign reporters and documentary filmmakers obtain them when they carry out work in dangerous places. And I have no idea where this documentary might take me."

"Well, don't forget to keep it hidden unless needed," Massoud said, before smiling. "Especially when going out. The last thing you want is a member of the hotel's housekeeping staff entering the room and seeing it on the table."

"Definitely not."

Massoud took his phone out and looked at the screen. "Your driver should be arriving soon enough," he said.

He poured himself another cup of coffee before offering more to Neil, who accepted, although he'd already had his share. Then Massoud's phone rang. The fixer stood up to answer it. After saying a couple of words in Arabic, he put the device into his pocket.

"He has arrived and is waiting in the hotel lobby. Coffee time has come to an end," Massoud said before finishing his drink in one shot.

Neil did the same. "You can go there now," he said. "I'll get my cameraman."

Massoud nodded before disappearing through the doorway.

Having taken the fixer's advice into account, Neil put the gun in the safe; he, hopefully, had no use for it where he was going. He went to Jake's room and knocked. A couple of minutes later both were heading down to the hotel lobby in the lift. Passing by several other guests, they found Massoud standing just to the right of the hotel's revolving door in the company of a casually dressed man of similar height and built.

"Gentlemen, may I introduce you to Furqan. He will be your driver throughout the duration of your project," Massoud said.

Neil shook hands with the driver, then Jake did the same.

"And your vehicle is outside," Massoud added.

"I can't wait to see it," Neil said.

Furqan led them outside to where the vehicle was. It was exactly what Neil had requested. In appearance, the dark jeep looked heavy but still sleek. Its big wheels were a clear sign that this was a proper off-road vehicle that could handle any type of terrain in any type of weather.

"This looks like a powerful machine," Jake commented.

"That's because it is," Massoud responded. "You can cross an entire desert in it as long as you've got enough fuel."

"Are we gonna go on a desert safari?" Jake joked, turning to Neil.

"Whilst it's not part of the plan, I cannot deny the possibility that this documentary will take us somewhere remote." Neil paused before continuing. "I should remember to stock up on charcoal in case we end up having to spend a night in the desert."

"I see you are excited. Perhaps, you would like to go on a test drive around this part of the city?" Massoud said.

"Good idea."

***

They had no use for the car the following day when filming in Baghdad. Neil and Jake were crossing a bridge on foot, with the light sound of running water accompanying their every step. The river Tigris, more ancient than any empire that ever ruled this land, was running underneath them on its long journey to join with the Persian Gulf in the distant south.

Baghdad's old quarter awaited them on the other bank of the river, a maze of narrow streets and façades with honeycomb-shaped niches.

"You're right, Neil," Jake said as they took another turn and ended up on a different street. "This area is a great place to film some of the montage shots."

"Yes, it really does carry this...I don't know what would be the best word to use. Atmosphere, I guess. The Arabic East taken straight from the imagination."

He had to talk louder than usual, to avoid being overpowered by the clamouring of the crowds of locals around them. His gaze strayed towards the giant dome that rose above all the neighbouring rooftops. Perhaps it crowned a mosque, perhaps a palace—he didn't really know. But one thing was beyond doubt: Baghdad, with its complexes of shrines and libraries, palaces and fortifications, would have had the potential to become an intriguing destination for a cultural break had the history of the last several decades taken a different path.

"Wait." Jake stopped Neil and approached one of the coffee shops located on the side of the street.

Men, young and old, sat around the tables in the open-plan interior, watching a football game on the plasma TV fixed to a wall. They stared attentively at the action on the screen, watching a player make another frantic attempt to get the ball of out his opponent's possession as the announcer kept up a commentary in Arabic.

"Like you understand anything the announcer says," Neil teased him.

"I don't need to understand, I've got eyes," Jake said, still turned to the screen. "England is playing Belgium."

"So are we going to stand here until the match is over?"

"No, just hold on for a minute or two."

Neil had never been a fan of the game, so, having zero interest in whatever was transpiring on some football field countless miles away from them, he just gave the place another look-over. One person caught his attention. Sitting alone behind his table, he was one of the few others who did not seem to care about the game. Instead, he concentrated on a newspaper, occasionally scribbling something down with a pencil, likely solving a crossword puzzle. He was a man in his late thirties or early forties with longish dark hair and a short beard. Yet it was not his indifference to the game that drew attention but his outfit. Whilst everybody else wore jeans and shirts, he was clad in a navy tunic and brown trousers. Instead of sandals or trainers, he wore boots, the type a herder would wear whilst attending his flock in a remote rural area.

As if intuition told the man that he was being watched, he raised his eyes up and looked at the reporter. Their eyes met, and the stranger's look was so deep that Neil got the impression that this odd local was trying to extract information from him using his silent gaze. It felt a bit awkward. The man then looked back at his puzzle.

"Another goal for Belgium," Jake mumbled beside him.

"Can we go now?" Neil asked.

"Yeah, sure."

They wandered into another street. This one still had a few coffee shops, but books appeared to be its main theme. There were bookshops everywhere, and if that was not enough, then the booksellers' stalls lining the sides of the road took the cake.

Some tingling sense made Neil throw a swift look behind. There he was: the same man in the tunic. His gait was a leisurely one; he strolled around admiring the surroundings like a tourist who'd come to the city for the first time.

It seemed foolish to pay too much attention to this. After all, it was probably just a coincidence, and coincidences come in the most unusual varieties.

Neil and Jake proceeded like normal, eventually wandering into a crowded market. Again, Neil looked around, and again, he beheld the familiar figure. This time the man was standing beside a stall selling caps and headdresses, quietly observing the items as the merchant haggled with another customer. This was starting to look less and less like a coincidence.

Their path led them through several more streets to a square. Neil looked behind him and, not surprisingly, caught a glimpse of the stranger.

"Ah, Neil, what's up?" Jake asked him.

"I think some guy is following us. Look past my shoulder," Neil muttered. "See the guy in the navy tunic?"

"Yes, I do. He seems to be a bit disoriented, moving side to side," Jake observed. "Probably some bum with drug issues." The cameraman gave his verdict.

"A bum?" Neil raised an eyebrow. "This isn't San Francisco; we're in Baghdad. How should I put it best...the urban landscape in these parts is different...if you get what I mean. Plus, I saw him at the coffee shop earlier, solving a puzzle. That's not what bums typically do."

"Then maybe you're just making a mountain out of a molehill. He might be taking in the sights as well. I mean, the area we've covered since leaving that coffee shop isn't particularly big."

"I guess I might be looking at it the wrong way." Neil was practically forcing himself to admit it.

He hoped it was true.

***

Two types of sounds were swirling across the restaurant's spacious dining area. The first was the traditional Arabic music that was playing through the speakers. Laced with vibrant and exotic melodies, the tunes were brimming with energy that urged the listener to kick their chair back and whirl around in a frenzied dance. The second was the sound of chatter, but unlike the chaos of the squares and markets, this was simply the combination of many different casual discussions.

The aroma of grilled fish had filled Neil's nostrils even before the server placed his order on his table.

"Masgouf." The server mentioned the name of the dish before departing.

The carp, grilled and crispy, rested on an ellipsoid dish, surrounded by a wreath of salad and slices of lemon.

"So this is the national dish," Jake said, eyeing his own plate.

"Indeed. It's probably been around long before the foundation of Iraq," said Claude Faucon. "If the ancient Babylonians did not eat their own version of masgouf, they probably had something similar."

"Kinda reminds me of my home state, Maine," Jake commented. "Only our staple is haddock, not carp. And we prefer it battered and pan-fried rather than grilled."

Neil picked up his knife and fork and cut off a piece of the succulent carp. He tried it and savoured its crispy texture.

"This is pretty good," he said, taking a sip of juice to wash it down.

Both Jake and Claude agreed with him. There were three of them at the table; the academic was the only other foreigner the crew had become acquainted with, so it made sense to invite him to dine with them.

"And speaking about things that happened centuries ago, have you followed up on those artefacts you showed me?" Claude asked.

"Not yet," Neil answered. "But I do intend to feature them in the documentary. After all, it's a rather interesting discovery."

"Yes, you have jihadists collecting centuries-old magical artefacts." Jake got involved. "How's that for intrigue?!"

"As a scholar, you must have connections with local researchers in different academic fields," Neil said, looking at Claude. "Can you give any recommendations of people we could interview regarding this topic?"

"I can most certainly recommend a couple of names," Claude said, gently kneading a table napkin in his hand.

Neil cut off another piece of carp. He was about to tell the academic more about his itinerary for the upcoming days when an unexpected sound startled him.

It came as suddenly as thunder—only more surprising, given the clear skies—and ten times louder. The monstrous force of the sudden boom shattered the windows of the restaurant, making the glass cry as it broke.

Neil instinctively turned in the direction of the entrance. The windows that flanked the door had been reduced to empty frames, a painful but common sight he'd beheld whilst passing through towns caught in the middle of war zones.

The leisurely chattering in the restaurant gave way to squealing and commotion. And yet that still appeared trivial compared to whatever was transpiring outside where the wails of alarm sirens, the crack of gunfire, and screams of panic united into a chaotic concert.

"What the hell?" Jake uttered, catching his breath.

Claude just sat there, a lost expression on his face.

Not all of the guests at the restaurant remained sitting like the trio did. Some jumped up as if they were waiting for a signal to flee the establishment.

Then two men entered through the doorway. They burst in without reservations and they did not wait to be seated. They were not diners and they were not civilians looking for sanctuary. Each carried an automatic rifle. Wordlessly, they pointed the barrels of their weapons towards the restaurant's casual interior.

Dread hit Neil in the gut with full force. All the pieces snapped together into a single picture.

"Duck!"

Like a madman full of testosterone, he pushed the table onto its side. The dishes and napkins, the tablecloth and the grilled carp crashed to the ground, accompanied by the sounds of breaking porcelain and glass. Claude and Jake took refuge behind the giant wooden shield.

They'd made the right choice; shooting began the same moment. The roar of gunfire drowned out the noises coming from outside.

Neil's heartbeat hammered in his ears over the sound of bullets shattering cups and glasses, burrowing into chairs and walls. He heard the gasps of the diners and the heavy tumble of bodies collapsing on the floor. Once, twice, thrice... Shock did not allow him to keep counting further.

Some people ran past the trio's table, trying to make their way to the kitchen, and through it to the backdoor. Several fell before they could reach the bar.

The shooting stopped. Using the experience gained from reporting out of the trenches, Neil peeked round the side of the table. The floor was littered with dead bodies and scattered cutlery. He saw the two extremists slowly walk deeper into the restaurant, one following the other. They stopped at one of the tables. One roughly pulled the white tablecloth aside, revealing a server hiding underneath. The man let out a desperate plea in Arabic that fell on deaf ears. A bullet cut it short.

Neil had seen many horrendous things during his stints in war zones, but still his stomach churned. He fell back behind his rectangular cover when one of the terrorists began to turn his head in their direction. Neil looked at Jake and Claude crouched beside him, all three cramped together. If even a tip of a shoe stuck out, it would blow their cover.

Unless the terrorists left the place for their next target, only the swift arrival of the army and police could save the situation.

He peeked out again. The terrorists stood there, close together, eyeing the place, their backs turned to the front door. Neil's heart froze when one of them met his gaze.

Now there was only one option: scramble towards the kitchen and hope both terrorists missed.

But then, like an enchanted flower sprouting from a magical seed, the stranger from earlier rose up behind the perpetrators. Perhaps his towering form cast a shadow or perhaps the infernal intuition of the murderous duo gave them a warning, but the terrorists immediately turned around, fingers on the triggers of their weapons.

But the stranger's reflexes were swift. He grabbed the barrels of their rifles and pulled them upwards, pointing them away from him just before the weapons fired. Two rounds of bullets sang in unison and struck the ceiling, leaving two parallel trails of holes where the bullets hit. Small pieces of plaster fell on the combatants like hail.

The stranger delivered a kick straight to the chest of one of the terrorists. As the man stumbled backwards, letting go off his weapon, his companion tried to use the situation to his advantage. He tackled the stranger to the floor, crashing into a nearby table as they fell. They rolled around, trying to wrest control of the weapon. One of the assault rifles slid out of their clutches and spun away from them like a peg-top.

It was a chance that could not be missed. Neil dashed towards the rifle, but the other jihadist was not out of commission yet. He scrambled for the weapon as well.

Neil grabbed the rifle's barrel jacket but a strong punch in the face knocked him back to the floor. It took him a couple of seconds to shake off the pain, or a portion of it, at least. The next thing he knew was the sight of the terrorist towering over him, the wayward rifle back in his possession. Venom coursed in the extremist's eyes as he pointed the rifle at him.

"Neil!" He heard Jake's terrified voice behind him.

Neil wanted to shout back at him, to urge the cameraman to flee the facility. But one does not always retain the ability to speak when a gun is pointed at his head.

And then, like a leopard jumping an antelope, the stranger threw himself at the jihadist. He pinned him to the ground under his weight before head-butting him in the face.

Without losing a single moment, the stranger grabbed the rifle's magazine, ripped it off with inhuman force, and threw it into a distant corner.

"Run!" the stranger shouted at Neil in English as he jumped back to his feet.

In the meantime, the other jihadist had stood back up. With his weapon apparently neutralised as well, he withdrew a long knife he'd kept hidden under his coat. It came as no surprise to Neil—terrorists tended to carry cold weapons as back-up while carrying out their plots.

Keeping his eyes on the armed combatant, the stranger stepped back to a nearby table. He grabbed a large dinner plate and held it up in front of him.

At the same time, Neil dashed towards the restaurant's kitchen area, joined by Claude and Jake midway. However, he did not make his way towards the back door; the mind of a war correspondent made him take cover behind the counter and carefully peek out. The sound of another explosion outside roared through the shattered window.

The extremist went for the kill, swinging the knife. But the cold blade hit porcelain; the stranger was skilled enough to wield the plate as a type of shield. The jihadist stepped back and tried again, now aiming for his foe's stomach, and again the plate got in the way of the blade. The second extremist got up, drawing his own long knife. He joined the fight, uniting into a deadly tag-team with his comrade. The stranger swirled aside from his attack as if he was dancing, grabbing another plate in the process. He stood there, holding these two bizarre shields in front of him as if he was teasing his opponents.

The jihadists looked at him dumbstruck; they could have never anticipated getting involved in a fight like this. Though they had numerical advantage, it did not make up for skill. The stranger was much better than they were in this type of combat. Truth be told, he seemed to be a master in it. The jihadists kept trying, slashing and stabbing at him, but the stranger blocked every lethal blow and dodged the blades with grace. Step by step, he slowly retreated backwards as he fended off his adversaries. He seemed set to collide with a table, but leaped and cut through the air in a move that no known Olympic athlete would have been able to repeat. He landed on his feet on top of the table and sent a boot-clad foot straight into the face of the first jihadist to reach him. He jumped off the table in the same manner, letting go of one of the plates as he did.

As the other jihadist rounded the table, the stranger grabbed hold of a dining chair and swung it like a mace. He struck the man's hand, knocking the blade out of his grasp and sending it flying to the side. The jihadist let lose a wail of anguish as he grabbed his damaged wrist with his good hand.

The stranger retreated by a few steps; his gaze remained focused on his enemies. He brought the remaining plate down hard on the table, smashing it and reducing it to a jagged shard of porcelain.

The jihadist, the one that had punched Neil earlier, lunged at him. The stranger, in turn, went for an attack of his own. Like a serpent, he slithered past the terrorist. His agility allowed him to twist his body and avoid getting slashed whilst he sank the shard into his foe's neck, tearing his throat open. Gargling on his own blood, the extremist fell to the floor, face down. The long knife fell out of his lifeless hand. The stranger grabbed it from the floor.

He had only one opponent left. The jihadist stood some distance away from him, having retrieved his blade. He stood there clutching it in his left fist, unable to hold anything in his wounded right hand. But the stranger had zero intention of giving him time to recuperate. He charged. Their blades met, but the terrorist was not skilled with using his left hand in combat. A single blow knocked the long knife out of his grasp. A moment later, the stranger lunged and struck his blade right into the heart of his adversary, twisting it before roughly pushing the man to the ground.

He turned around and called out to those few who still remained in the restaurant hiding under the tables. "Everybody! You are safe here for now!"

And indeed, the restaurant seemed safe for the time being. But gunfire kept performing its tune outside.

CHAPTER SIX

At first glance, the drylands could have been mistaken for a desert. An arid and mostly lifeless landscape, they appeared to spread on and on with no end in sight. Yet when Elliott jumped out of the land cruiser, the crumbling feeling beneath his feet indicated that it was not sand but parched soil that he stood upon. He looked around the area. The terrain was uneven; many mounds of different sizes dotted the landscape, rising from the earth like boils on burnt skin.

And, of course, there was the heat. It might have been only February, but for somebody who hailed from lands of a significantly colder climate, it was unbearable. Elliott swore that had it not been for the baseball cap covering his blond head, the wall of heat would have brought him down on the ground unconscious. The door of one of the off-road vehicles opened. Mergham was the first to step out, followed by Lauren, who jumped out with her usual grace. They were then joined outside by another colleague: Mr Akhmad. A local of Iraqi Kurdistan who had met up with them in Erbil. He was some years younger than Mergham and noticeably bigger in muscle mass. He had been described as a local guide and logistics co-ordinator by Mergham, and this made him the third part of the triumvirate in charge of the dig alongside Lauren and the author himself.

Elliott was not a geography expert—he wasn't sure if these drylands even had an official name. Yet here he was, at the end of the known world, countless miles away from the perpetual dullness of urban life and the wretched call centre. Still, though their small fleet of four-wheel-drives had brought them to the middle of nowhere, they were not just left there in the wilderness. A small camp had already been set up. He could see the pointed shapes of two dozen tents about a hundred metres away. As he had been informed, a couple of people affiliated with the dig had arrived at the site some days beforehand.

"Ladies and gentlemen!" Dr Mergham spoke after summoning all the arrivals in a ring around him. "We've made it! This will be our camp for the next couple of months."

"Woo-hoo!" shouted one of the team members. This comical cry of joy was followed by a brief round of chuckling from a few others.

"Yes, I am sure you are all excited," Mergham continued, smiling himself, "but first please give a round of applause for the man without whom you would not be seeing this camp here." He gestured towards the man standing to his left. "Mr Akhmad!"

People clapped, and they clapped sincerely.

"Thank you," Akhmad said, his voice laced with a strong accent, lightly bowing his head. "Thank you."

"Perhaps you could give the team an orientation tour of this camp?" Mergham suggested.

"Of course."

The camp was not big, but neither was the group: there were just over twenty of them. The main operations tent, a fabric pavilion, was located in the centre of the encampment; it stood out amongst its neighbours in length, width, and height. Next to it was a gazebo used for the storage of equipment. Nearby was the one for supplies, and another chosen to store finds. One was set up as a kitchen. Other than that, the campsite did not have a special plan or layout; the individual tents were pitched at random. Shower tents as well as toilet tents could be found a short distance away from the main cluster. The team were introduced to the people who were already on-site: three assistant archaeologists and the cook.

Their guided walk ended back at their vehicles' location. Then their first assignment began; they had to unload the supplies they'd brought with them and bring them to the storage gazebo. Naturally, three people were exempt from it—it was not hard to guess who. And once this task was done, with everything out of the vehicles and sorted, they received payment...in the form of another excursion, now led by Mergham himself.

The sun was still shining far above them when they set out towards the archaeological site. Clutching a map in his hand, Leonard led them deeper into their new and unusual surroundings, this unexplored wilderness. They walked for about ten or so minutes, through flat land and mounds, until the site appeared before them.

"Here it is!" the author declared, extending his hand as he gripped the map even harder. "This is the place we'll be excavating."

The scene was not a particularly impressive one; there was no grandeur to strike awe into the beholder. The archaeological site took the form of a plain, as desiccated and dust-ridden as the rest of the landscape around them. There were signs that the colleagues who had arrived earlier had already done some preliminary work. Several markings had been placed and a couple of ditches dug out in different parts.

"Um, I thought this place would be...well...better preserved," Elliott commented.

"What were you expecting?" Lauren said. Her appearance startled him; it felt like she'd materialised out of mid-air like an apparition. "This isn't some Mayan city lost in the jungles of Central America."

"Indeed," Mergham said. "The peoples of ancient Mesopotamia used sun-dried mudbrick as their primary building material. And without proper maintenance, mudbricks do not last long. Only the foundations of the structures that once stood here remain, and they have been covered by layers of earth over many years." He spoke loudly so the whole group could hear, like a teacher on a school fieldtrip.

He took a quick peek at his map.

"Remember the mysterious platform I was talking about?" he continued. "We are standing just a few feet away from its edge. The temple was located to the north of it." He pointed the map in its direction. "There were other buildings around them, but you'll have to use your imagination to get a picture of this outpost during its heyday."

And Elliott tried, with little success. Whilst the image of a ziggurat did manifest, nothing else did. Such is the fact; many can imagine the marble-clad cities of the Greeks and the Romans, but few have any idea what a city in Mesopotamia looked like.

***

The sun set very quickly, and the arriving evening brought the impression that the seasons had changed as well. There was no reminder of daytime's heat left in the air. The same climate that had made sweat stream down Elliott's forehead hours before began causing light shivers. He threw a coat over his shoulders before exiting his miniature tent to go towards the meeting gazebo. The darkness of the night enveloped the lifeless surroundings, but the campfire beside the big gazebo was driving it away from the centre of the encampment, radiating a dreary orange-red tinge across the vicinity. Several others from the team were already seated around the flames. The crackling of the fire and the chatter of several voices became louder as Elliott drew closer.

He recognised Joe among the gathered. Joe was an average guy around Elliott's age. Quite simple in character and mannerisms, he was the type of guy you could find at the bar of any local pub on a weekend. He was the one Elliott had shared a room with when they stayed at the group's accommodation in Erbil. Joe, too, was a volunteer, though unlike Elliott, he really did buy into Mergham's conspiracy theories.

"Yo," Elliott said quietly as he sat down on the ground beside him.

"Hey, man. How are you?" Joe said.

"Coping. I've camped out before, but I guess doing this in the middle of a Middle Eastern desert takes time to adjust."

"We're not in a desert," Joe corrected. "It's the drylands."

He just had to act like a smart aleck; like Lauren alone was not enough.

More people joined them at the campfire. Even Akhmad tagged along, sitting down opposite the duo. From the corner of his eye, Elliott also noticed his redheaded cousin sitting further away.

The flap of the tent got pulled aside roughly, and the bright yellowish light of the oil lamps inside joined the glow of the fire. Leonard Mergham walked out, accompanied by one of the excavation supervisors.

"Hello again, guys!" he called to the group. "And welcome to our first evening together!

"Back in Britain, each one of us would have been doing their own thing at about this time. Some of you would have been watching some TV series, some might have been out clubbing," he continued, slowly walking in a circle around the fire and campers. "And yet here we are, in the middle of nowhere, where we'll be spending the next few months. I understand the importance of shared activities in bonding a team, especially on the first day." He finished his stroll, returning to his original place in front of the gazebo. "And I don't mean unloading the vehicles."

The last statement won a few chuckles.

"I'm talking about something more leisurely. I did receive a suggestion from one of you: karaoke."

A few people cheered.

"I hate to disappoint you, but we didn't bring any sound equipment, and for that matter, there's nowhere to plug it in."

According to Elliott, this would have been the right time for the crickets to sing their song...or make whatever noises crickets make. But there were none at that moment—the crickets had probably decided not to stick around without karaoke.

"So I hope roasting marshmallows is an acceptable substitute," Mergham finished.

It appeared that Mergham was a traditional type of camper, and in Elliott's book, there was nothing wrong with the idea... though it did feel somewhat lame.

"Marshmallows! Yay!"

Apparently, it did have its supporters.

There were enough skewers and treats for everybody, and soon the night air mixed with the aromas of melting sweets.

"By the way, does anybody still have any questions about the dig?" Dr Mergham still stood in his place, hands behind his back. "Perhaps there's something I forgot to address."

No questions were asked.

"Nothing?" His gaze went from person to person, scanning the party. "That's fine. Does anybody have any other questions? Any questions about anything?"

Elliott really had an urge to ask how much money he had made from his books, but he gave it a pass.

"I have a question!" Joe said, raising his skewer like a schoolboy would his hand during class.

"Yes?"

"But it's related to your research work in Egypt."

"Well, it is a related topic. So what's the question?"

"You have written about the evidence of extraterrestrial activities on Earth that can be found in Ancient Egyptian religious texts, and that the gods worshipped by the Egyptians were aliens. My question is this: How does the myth of Osiris, Set, and Horus—probably the most famous story to come out of Ancient Egypt—fit into all of this?"

"This is a very good question."

Mergham suddenly became more energetic; his eyes sparkled in the darkness. It was clear that any discussion about ancient civilisations and aliens had the same effect as a shot of adrenaline.

"For those of you who are not familiar with this myth, Ancient Egyptian texts state that many years ago the god Osiris was given rule over Egypt. Osiris was later treacherously murdered by his brother, Set, who usurped dominion over the land. Isis, Osiris' wife, posthumously gave birth to his son, Horus. When Horus grew up, he challenged his uncle's rule and, after defeating him in a series of duels and competitions, succeeded in overthrowing him. It was also said that Osiris was resurrected and given dominion over the underworld.

"Do I believe that this myth is based on something that happened in real life? I'm certain it was! But that's the thing: a myth can be based on a true event, but only to an extent. In this case, the extent is minimal. As time passed and dynasty succeeded dynasty, memories of these events became laced with anecdotal stories, fairytale motifs, and plain factual errors. I hypothesise that this myth is an incorrect reflection of a conflict between rival alien warlords who fought for control over Egypt, likely in the early days of the pre-dynastic period. How it really happened is a topic open to interpretation. Perhaps the real Set was not Osiris' brother by blood, but his right hand and confidant. Horus might have already been an adult, or at least an adolescent, when his father was murdered, and hostilities began soon after the event. The resurrection of Osiris is an intriguing element, but 'resurrection' might mean something else in this context; I wouldn't be surprised if it refers to the earliest case of cloning to take place on Earth."

Elliott's gaze slid to Akhmad. The Iraqi was sitting silently, listening to the archaeologist's hypotheses. The expression on his face stony and unimpressed; he kept slowly shaking his head as if was being made to listen to the blatant lies of his child or the paranoid gibberish of an insane sibling.

"All in all, how would people living in Egypt, say five thousand years ago, describe a war between two factions of extraterrestrials, using technologies millennia ahead of not just those of the Bronze Age but ours as well?" Mergham continued. "They would not have seen it in any way but as a supernatural occurrence.

"This is one of the reasons I've never really explored the myth of Horus and Set; it could serve as a subject for a separate book." He smirked. "Who knows, I might even write about it in the future."

He picked up a skewer and impaled a marshmallow.

***

The first night in the desert—no, the drylands, as Elliott had to constantly correct himself—was a thing to get used to. Several times during the night he woke up, his sleeping bag unable to prevent the nocturnal cold from pinching him. He would lie there on his side for some time, shivering occasionally. His tent was a small one; he only needed to stretch to find himself pushing into the tent's side with his feet. He would lie like this for some time before succumbing to sleep. Time would pass and the chills would give him another wake-up call. Then the same experience from earlier would repeat again and again, like a sort of time loop.

The scarlet disk of the sun rising over the horizon was the first thing that caught Elliott's attention when he crawled out of the tent. The trek towards the washing-up tent was noticeably longer and required more effort than his usual morning trip to the bathroom. Still bleary after an improper sleep, he walked towards the canteen gazebo.

It was early morning, just past 7 a.m., but the camp was getting up; after all, in climates like this, they needed to start early to do as much as possible before the midday heat arrived.

Elliott beheld several people getting out of their tents and saw a few more inside the gazebo.

The makeshift canteen was simple. Several tables joined together accommodated several thermoses and a modest buffet. There was a choice of porridge and cereal, scones accompanied by several types of jam and spreads, figs and dates. Toast and pancakes, a common feature of such tables, were absent, with flatbreads and hummus acting as substitutes. He chose cereal and coffee. Having picked his food up, his gaze scoured the tent in the search for a seat. There were several plastic tables, each with a set of matching chairs. For a second, his memory brought him back to the food court at the re-enactment event, making him wonder what Norm and Hollie were up to back in Britain.

It just so happened that none of the tables were completely free—a pity, for he preferred eating alone. The table closest to the buffet was taken, not surprisingly, by Lauren and her porridge.

What was surprising was the voice he heard behind him. "Good morning, Elliott."

He turned his head to see Leonard Mergham, who had just entered the tent and got a look at the breakfast options.

"Good morning, Dr Mergham."

"If you'd like, you could sit next to Lauren. I will join you two in a couple of moments."

Elliott did just that, exchanging greetings with his cousin. Mergham joined them with a plate of flatbreads and hummus.

"So, cousin," Lauren said, "how was your first night in the drylands?"

"Not that good," he confessed. "I'm not sure if I spent even half the time sleeping."

"Not used to sleeping in a tent?" Mergham asked.

"Not used to these local nights," Elliott corrected him.

"Yeah, they do get quite cold," Lauren said. "But don't worry, you'll get used to them after the first couple."

"In the meantime, drink some of your coffee," Mergham advised. "People in the Middle East like their brew to be very strong. It should help you wake up fully."

Elliott took a gulp and indeed felt as if a bolt of energy ran through his body.

They ate in silence for a bit. Elliott looked around but couldn't spot the group's guide among the people in the gazebo. Of course, breakfast time was not over yet, so he was probably yet to arrive. He remembered the look in Akhmad's eyes as he sat there, conjuring up silent damnations of Mergham's theses.

"I was wondering..." Elliott broke the silence. "Is Akhmad an archaeologist? Does he have the same research interests as you do?" he asked, though he was certain that was not the case.

"Not really," Mergham explained. "He's a nationalist historian."

"Nationalist historian?"

"A Kurdish nationalist historian, to be more precise," Mergham continued, his gaze deep and intelligent. "There's a thing called ethnogenesis, the process of the formation and development of ethnic groups. Such processes occur over the span of centuries, triggered by various events such as migrations, cultural transmissions, the collapse of empires, among others. So the ethnic groups of the Middle East in, say, 700 BC, were not the same as the ones inhabiting it now. However, nationalist historians tend to disregard any notion of ethnogenesis in favour of crafting nationalistic narratives, trying to establish direct continuity between ancient states and modern nations. In this case, Kurdish nationalists would try to present the ancient civilisations that flourished in the Near East during biblical times, like Medes, Mitanni, and Urartu, as Kurdish states. Naturally, this is just blatant revisionism that disregards many known basic facts, but it has its scholars and its audiences. Mind you, this is not just a local thing. You can find hardcore nationalists crafting faux historical narratives in any part of the world. But back to our guide—Akhmad is trying to prove that the Assyrian Empire too was a Kurdish state."

"But why would he join forces with an expedition that's looking for signs of ancient alien contact?" Elliott asked.

"Why wouldn't he? Archaeological digs aren't just about niche studies. Let's say we're excavating an ancient Roman site. What type of researchers do you think this dig would attract? There would certainly be Classical archaeologists, specialising in the material culture of the Romans. However, there might be some landscape archaeologists attached to the project as well, looking at the interaction between the settlement and its surroundings.

You might find paleopathologists, studying uncovered human remains for sign of diseases. These are just a few examples. So why wouldn't a cryptoarchaeologist like me and a nationalist historian like Akhmad cooperate for mutual benefit, if one does not necessarily contradict the other?"

There was a moral in this: just like love, archaeology could get very complex.

CHAPTER SEVEN

"Shaitan." Sayid cursed his enemies under his breath.

No doubt remained in his mind—he and his men were getting overwhelmed. He dashed through the debris-littered front yard of the cement factory, his eyes set on the five-storey building. In the past, this structure was most likely an economic lifeline of the nearby town. Now it was nothing more than a spectre, one of many lingering throughout the country after many years of war. Not a single window remained in place; his fighters were in position at the glassless frames. Chunks of its concrete walls had collapsed, mixing with various types of waste that had lain on the ground the day the factory shut its doors. If some patient man volunteered to count all the bullet holes drilled into the exterior, he would likely require several days. And so it stood there, a haunting reminder of better days.

He ran through the symphony of combat. The battle cries of his men melded with the clatter of gunfire. Several booming sounds entered the fray, indicating the arrival of rocket-propelled grenades.

He heard an ear-splitting whistling sound, and a fighter running in front of him fell down, another one lost to a stray bullet. Sayid made a leap for the entrance and the moment he passed through the doorway, he pulled himself to the side. A heated sensation tickled his skin as a bullet that would have otherwise gone through his neck scraped the collar of his jacket. He almost fell, but his legs did not give up on him. Several more of his men got inside before the heavy metal doors were closed behind them.

"Are you alright?" asked Hamza, his second-in-command, the last man to get in.

To an outsider, Hamza would have appeared little different from any other member of Sayid's group. Somewhat smaller than Sayid and younger by about a year, bearded and with a head of longish dark hair, he stood, eyes blazing with the look of a merciless killer.

"Yes, Allah decided that I should live to see dusk fall," Sayid answered as he tugged at his collar, displaying the hole left by the bullet.

They heard their men firing from the upper floors at the encroaching enemies.

"It will not take them long to break into this building," Sayid said, looking towards the door. It might have been thick and metallic, but they were in a war zone, and there were many ways to blast it open without trouble.

He hung his rifle over his shoulder by the strap, and Hamza did the same.

"That's not a problem. This whole building is defended well," Hamza said. "I've got men positioned on the rooftop and at every window. Even if the infidels break in, they will have to fight for every inch of this building, because we'll be waiting for them in every hallway and in every room."

"Let's hope that our brothers are close to launching a counter-attack and relieving us." Sayid started towards the bifurcated stairway leading to the upper floors. "Otherwise, this ruin is where we will make our final stand."

Without saying anything, Hamza followed him.

"Let's go to the windows upstairs," Sayid said. "I would like to get a glimpse of the situation outside."

The echoes of their boots clamping against the steps resonated around the spacious but unfurnished ground-floor lobby. The duo reached the landing where the stairway forked.

But before he could continue up the stairs, Sayid found his world turned upside down. First, there was a loud sound, one that could only be compared to the roar of an awoken monster. Before he could realise what was truly going on, a shockwave picked him up and threw him against the railing like a wrestler. Sayid let out a painful moan as his back hit against the staircase. He slid down, gritting his teeth, his eyes closed and watering, partly due to the physical anguish and partly because of the dust that had got under his eyelids. He blinked the pain away, only to see the room had undergone a radical change. The stairway landing now had a view of the outside, the wall blown away by something powerful. From his expertise, Sayid was more than certain that it had been a shell.

His gaze wandered to the side. Parts of the wall now lay scattered around the landing in a layer of dust and pieces of concrete. He shifted his head to observe the upper steps of the stairway. And then he saw his lieutenant lying there, as lifeless as the steps under his body.

Sayid should have felt pain when he bolted up. But he did not, for all his nervous system was concentrated on his fallen comrade.

"Hamza!"

Hamza was sprawled unnaturally, his hand thrown back as though he'd fallen whilst waving goodbye. His right leg was bent and pointed to the left. The back of his neck was pressing hard against the edge of the step, highlighting his Adam's apple. There was blood on his lips and a giant cut running across his forehead.

Carefully, trying to avoid slipping down the stairs, Sayid knelt and put his fingers on his friend's neck. Unsurprisingly, he felt no pulse.

The sound of another explosion made him turn and look at what was transpiring below him downstairs. The heavy door was obliterated, and before he could give any commands, a series of whistling sounds muted any words coming out of his mouth. A hail of bullets streamed into the foyer. One after the other, his fighters fell. Some joined Hamza in death, having been struck in their heads, necks, and chests. Others just plummeted to the floor, moaning, blood drizzling out of the wounds on their shoulders and legs, stomachs and wrists.

The moment this thunderstorm of lead ceased, men in helmets and fatigues swarmed the foyer, their rifles ready to summon another rain of bullets. There were two groups of men, both wearing badges with insignias of an eagle. But whilst one eagle had a red-white-black tricolour ornamenting its chest, the other clung to an olive branch in one talon and a stack of arrows in the other.

"Dogs and sons of dogs!" Sayid screamed out as he whipped out his rifle and began shooting in a fit of rage.

He stood in the open, exposed from all sides, but he did not care about his survival at all. A sharp gust of pain tore through the lower part of his left leg, ripping the rifle out of his hand. The weapon fell down, bouncing from step to step almost like a coin, the clanking sound reverberating across the foyer. Sayid looked down; there was blood sizzling down his leg just below the knee. He looked up to see the troopers closing in on him, and at that moment he regretted not wearing a suicide belt for the occasion.

***

The next thing Sayid heard was the sound of a running motor. He shook his head as he snapped out of sleep and found himself in a completely different setting. He was not restrained in any way, but riding in the backseat of a civilian vehicle. There were two people in the car with him: the driver and another man sitting by his side. Both had longish hair and beards, like him. He was not a prisoner; he was among his kin.

Many times had Sayid been in the midst of battle, from small skirmishes to full-scale urban fighting. And for every battle, he fought ten more in his dreams. Some were practically memories; others took him to new places. Some felt almost real, whilst some made practically no sense at all.

Sayid did not linger on this latest dream. There was not much substance to it. It was not a true recollection of the time he got captured before getting sent to Djibouti. For starters, he had not been captured at a cement factory; he could not remember if he'd ever found himself besieged inside one. In reality, he'd tried to find a hiding place in an abandoned barn after sustaining a bullet wound to the leg; that was where the coalition forces found him, as though they had tracked him via the smell of his blood like a pack of hounds.

As for Hamza, Sayid had not been present to witness his demise. He was occupied at a different part of the frontline when he received news that his lieutenant had been killed when his position was shelled by enemy forces. And that happened just minutes before his own began to collapse.

Sayid looked out the car window as the vehicle went past a billboard, a rare sight in these parts. But this one advertised no product. Giant graffiti had been written on it in black spray paint, a reminder of the new reality. "The glory of al-Qadisiyyah will live until Judgement Day", the sign read.

They were now deep in their territory, a large swathe of land where they could move freely—a relief after the last few days spent moving along backroads and little-known footpaths after the Samnite dropped him off at Umm Qasr. He'd changed escorts on several occasions as he traversed through enemy-controlled territories before crossing the frontlines. The city of Baiji, the powerbase of Liwa al-Qadisiyyah, was a couple of hours' drive away. Soon it would all be over.

Sayid brought his hand to his chin, almost mechanically, to curl a strand of his beard. He felt nothing between his fingers; he'd had to cut his beard prior to landing in Iraq, for a long beard had always been one of the most obvious attributes of a jihadist.

He found a newspaper lying discarded on the backseat and picked it up. It was a couple of days old, having somehow crossed the frontlines; after all, it was not the type of paper printed in the territory his group controlled. He passed the time by reading its various entries, getting up-to-date with the events transpiring in the country: another government reshuffle, another militant attack.

Ahead, the edges of the nearest residential complex could be seen through the car's front window. Just outside its boundaries, a checkpoint had been established. Three pick-up trucks stood by the curb. All three were dark grey in colour, as if the local commander wanted them to match. Several fatigue-clad men monitored the road underneath the scorching sun, their expressions serious and their rifles ever-ready. An anti-aircraft gun was mounted atop the pick-up in the middle, yet its thin, pipe-like barrels were facing the road, not the sky.

The man beside the driver rolled the window down and stuck his hand out as the vehicle slowed. In response, one of the members of the paramilitary patrol directed the others' attention towards the car.

Sayid had been notified that another companion would be joining his entourage, and it was safe to assume that this would be the place. The car stopped in front of the no-nonsense crew.

"Let's get out," the driver's helper said.

And so they did, out of the hot vehicle into the hot day.

"*As-salamu alaykum!*" the driver said as they got out of the car. "This is Sayid Buzali, a commander of the Liwa, and we are his companions."

Sayid greeted the guards. "I was told that another person would be joining us," he said. "Is he amongst you?"

"Yes, I am here!" another man proclaimed loudly as he opened the door of one of the pick-ups and hopped out.

Smaller in height but slightly more muscular in stature than Sayid, the man was without doubt another member of the Liwa, clad in fatigues and sporting a beard. And for a second, Sayid got an impression he was still dreaming.

"Ha-Hamza?" He was unable to utter the name without breaking off.

"What's the matter, Sayid?" The man grinned as he came up to him. "You look like you've realised that you died and ended up at the gates of Heaven!"

"Is that what's really happened?" Sayid said without showing emotion. Such an interpretation did not seem far-fetched to him.

"What do you think?" The man's grin was inerasable as the distance between the two shortened to just a couple of steps.

Sayid just stood there, trying to adjust to the earthquake rumbling through his inner world.

"But your time hasn't come yet," the man said. "We're still in Iraq."

Sayid was unresponsive.

"Are you not going to greet your old friend Hamza?" the man asked. "After everything that happened, the two of us meeting here is practically a miracle."

The step Sayid took towards his friend was as swift as a dash towards a finish line. Sayid's arms spread out on their own to wrap around his old comrade. He could not resist this sudden whirlwind of surprise and emotion, and burst into a fit of chuckling like a madman. Hamza's hand clasped his back, the strong gesture of a hardened soldier.

"The will of Allah directs everything that transpires," Sayid said as he stepped back.

"Such is the truth," Hamza responded.

There was another moment of tongue-tied silence, before Sayid uttered, "And I thought that we would only be able to meet again in Heaven. I was told that you were killed by a shell."

"I'll tell you this: you weren't the only one who thought so. A few media outlets also reported that I was dead. Can you imagine that? I've never even been a top-tier leader of the Liwa." A proud grin appeared on Hamza's face. "But they all forgot one important rule: notable jihadists often don't stay dead for long. The military releases a statement that so-and-so was killed in a strike some day, but after some time their claims will get proven false, one way or another. How many times have they declared you dead? Twice, if I am not mistaken. And if we are to believe reports then Jalil al-Quwaiti has already died five times. But as far as I'm aware, he's just fine."

"So did the shell miss?"

"Not really." Hamza grimaced. "I was struck by a few shards, in different parts of my torso. And trust me, a bullet wound feels like a small irritant in comparison. For a moment, it felt like I was struck and pierced by a dozen heavy metal bars. Then there was nothing. I was never interested in hearing the details, but I was told my body was a very unpleasant sight. I don't doubt it; I've personally seen exploding shells rip bodies into shreds. So, in a way, you could say that I was lucky. My wounds were grievous, but at least I was intact. Apparently, there was a point when I was on the brink of death due to my injuries. But don't forget—I am Hamza Saqqaf; my name means 'strong'. I am a survivor." He struck his chest with a fist in a display of bravado.

"So how did you get through?" Sayid asked.

"One of our doctors is a master of his trade. He used to work as a surgeon at some high-class private clinic in Australia. But unlike certain others who choose to lick the wounds of infidels— when they're not busy licking their feet, that is—in exchange for a comfy lifestyle, he heard the call of his faith and came to aid Liwa al-Qadisiyyah. Luckily, I ended up on the operating table in front of him."

"I believe we have a lot of catching up to do." Sayid smiled.

"Indeed, and I look forward to hearing the story of your detention at that rendition centre. I am certain you gave your captors hell." Hamza looked at the road, probably imagining the long journey still ahead of them. "But there will be enough time to exchange stories. Baiji is still a long way from here."

Hamza bid farewell to the militiamen at the checkpoint before getting into the car with Sayid and his entourage.

He sat next to Sayid on the backseat. "When I heard that you'd be going through these parts, I could not resist the urge to accompany you." His gaze fell on the newspaper that now lay between them. "I never thought you'd have an interest in reading this pro-government rag."

"I don't. I just keep it around to blow my nose in case of hay fever."

They heard the sound of the ignition as the driver turned the motor back on. Moments later, the checkpoint and the militiamen manning it were left behind as the car drove through the streets of the town. Though the houses either side of the road seemed to be in decent condition, only a few men could be seen wandering outside—a sight that some might have found tranquil, and some eerie.

"So, Hamza," Sayid broke the silence. "What have you been doing these last few months while I was..." He was not sure how best to finish that sentence. "...away. Leading raids against government checkpoints and military installations, no doubt?"

This is how he remembered Hamza Saqqaf, zealous and enthusiastic. Whenever the hour of attack came, Hamza would always be found on the frontline leading the charge.

"Unfortunately, not anymore," Hamza said with some remorse. "After the shelling incident, I spent several months recovering. Then certain high-ranking figures in the Liwa came to the conclusion that I will not fully recover and so I am not really fit to take part in fighting anymore. Maybe they have a point or maybe they're wrong; I'm not sure myself. So I have been given a new task."

"Which one?"

"I am now one of the tax collectors for the Liwa."

"A tax collector?" Sayid raised an eyebrow. "I never would've thought that would be something you would do."

"Neither did I. But you get used to it quickly."

"Ah yes, going door to door, charging farmers a percentage of their produce..." Though he had never done it himself, Sayid knew a thing or two about the group's economic strategy. "You must have had some memorable experiences," he said ironically.

"Of course." Hamza smirked.

***

The dining room at the mullah's dwelling was spacious but scarcely furnished. A low wooden table stood in the middle, surrounded by a circle of cushions that served as seats. Outside, evening had already darkened the sky like a smudge of spilt ink, but hand-crafted ornamented lanterns, adorned with traditional Arabic murals, illuminated the whole room.

Mullah Abdulaziz Nishwari stood up from his place at the head of the table the moment the guard let Sayid into the dining room. A man in his mid-fifties, the mullah seemed like a cross between a tribal sheikh and an imam from a small distant town. Sayid had not seen him in over a year, but the older man was not one to betray his choice of clothing style. The dark-brown bisht cloak kept most of his long thawb tunic hidden underneath, revealing the white garment only around the sleeves and in an inch of fabric at ankle level. There were more strands of grey in his beard than Sayid remembered; he was certain his hair had become greyer as well, though it was hard to tell for a kufiya headdress, fastened by an agal band, shielded his head from both heat and gaze.

"*As-salamu alaykum,*" the mullah greeted his guest.

"*Wa alaykumu s-salam,*" Sayid responded.

Nishwari walked towards Sayid as if he was on a stroll around a garden, and wrapped him in his embrace warmly, not like a commander, but a family member finally seeing his relative return home after a long war.

"Your blessing, honourable Mullah," Sayid whispered, bowing his head, the moment the older man stepped back.

"May the graces of Allah accompany you at all times," the mullah said.

They remained silent for a couple of moments before Nishwari put his arm over Sayid's shoulders and led him towards the table.

"The road you took was very long. Why don't we sit down?" the sheikh said. "Dinner will be brought soon."

"It is great to be back with the Liwa," Sayid stated, sitting down on the cushions.

"And it is even better to see you here again. It is a rare occurrence when a brother captured by the enemy manages to escape confinement. But for a brother to escape from imprisonment in a foreign land and then make his way back here… This is truly miraculous." A smile appeared on his face.

"Do you remember the day when your past superior introduced you to me and assigned you to be part of my entourage?" The mullah looked aside, recalling a distant memory. "I sensed your abilities and potential immediately. Now I am certain that an angel came down from Heaven and planted those thoughts in my head."

Sayid had never denied that it was at least partially Nishwari's favour that had helped him rise high among the ranks of the Liwa. Of course, all the attacks he'd led, all the blood he'd spilled, and all the bullets he'd dodged played a significant role as well. Yet the mullah's praise clearly had a role in it as well.

"I am not going to ask you about your experiences in detention over there," Nishwari said. "I am certain it is not a pleasant topic for a conversation."

"True, but I endured and I got out," Sayid said. "I wonder what my father would have said had he heard the story of my escape," he added, a sentimental thought that had somehow found a way to slip out. "If he was still alive."

Sayid felt a sting in his chest, more unpleasant than a slash with a knife. It had been five years, now, since his father succumbed to leukaemia.

"Alas. We never truly get over personal loss, do we?" the mullah said, as if he had read his disciple's mind. "But lighten your spirit up, my boy. He is at peace, surrounded by the bliss of Heaven's gardens."

They sat in silence for a few more moments as anticipation of the future overwhelmed the memories of the past.

"By the way, I have not told you something very important yet," Nishwari said, his tone now lighter and even…triumphant.

"What is it?" Sayid could not resist the urge to ask.

"You've arrived just in time."

His mysterious vagueness intrigued Sayid. "In time for what?"

"Our greatest military offensive yet." Nishwari grinned, his teeth as menacing as the fangs of a predator.

CHAPTER EIGHT

"Once again the streets of the Iraqi capital became a scene of gruesome terror attacks," the anchor's gloomy voice narrated the news segment.

Neil sat up straight in his chair, tense. As he watched the footage, he felt like he was reliving the previous day's dreadful events.

"According to the data made available by the Iraqi Ministry of Interior, the terrorist act claimed the lives of one hundred and seventy-eight people, one of the highest death tolls in recent years."

And as the anchor continued detailing the event to the audience, the station ran painful, soul-churning images: burnt cars and debris on the streets, the wounded being loaded into ambulances, police and the military securing different locations.

"The complex attack was carried out through a mix of shootings and suicide bombings. At this time, the police believe fourteen perpetrators were directly involved. Eight locations in the centre of Baghdad were targeted: shops, cafés, restaurants."

As though they had a mind of their own, Neil's fingers dug into the soft cushion of the chair.

"The Iraqi government has blamed the Liwa al-Qadisiyyah militant group for the atrocity. The group has so far neither accepted nor denied responsibility for the attack.

"And still, even amidst the carnage, there are stories of heroism."

Neil reached for the remote and turned up the volume.

A familiar image appeared on the screen: the stranger from earlier, standing at a spot close to the restaurant Neil and his companions were at when the attack unfolded.

"His name is Nouri Samir, originally from Hillah, a former security guard who has recently come to the Iraqi capital in search of new employment. According to eyewitness accounts, he was able to neutralise two armed terrorists single-handedly."

Neil made a note of the name in his mind. At least he now knew who the stranger was.

"I was startled when I heard the first explosion," Nouri told the reporter. His manner was unconfident, hinting that he was camera-shy. "At first, I could not understand what was going on. There was commotion everywhere. And then I saw those two men, armed, dashing towards the entrance of the restaurant. I knew I had to act."

Then the reporter described what had transpired within the walls of the restaurant. The account was spot on, as though Neil himself had given it.

"It is certainly beyond doubt that your act of bravery makes you a hero in the eyes of many Iraqis," the reporter on the scene told the man.

"I do not see it as an act of heroism. This was something I knew I had to do, regardless of any risk."

A shard of shame hit Neil for having thought that this man was some sort of stalker or low-life. Still, the origins of Nouri's fighting prowess remained an interesting mystery.

The news segment was soon over and the station began airing its next, unrelated report, this time from South-East Asia.

Neil turned the TV off but stayed sat down. After all that had happened, it was luck of the highest calibre that he had been able to get out of the restaurant practically unscratched.

And then he felt it. That awkward urge that kept kindling in him these last few days. He switched to the chair by the table and turned on his laptop. A couple of clicks brought up the now familiar images.

He was doing it again, looking at the photos of the mysterious artefacts found at the house of the jihadist agent. He would study their forms and the images that looked back at him from the depths of many centuries. The half-man and half-bird hybrids, the different deities, scenes of various rituals, inscriptions made in a script significantly different from the Arabic alphabet—he tried to study them like a scholar even whilst having no idea of what he was trying to work with.

He regretted the fact that he did not have the opportunity to hold some of these fascinating relics, to feel the ancient metalwork in his palm. He could not tell where this sense was coming from. Antiques were not his thing, nor did he have an interest in the occult. Yet here he was.

***

The hotel's revolving door led Neil and Jake outside into another humid day, the city's ancient quarter being their destination yet again. They walked alongside the busy road with its chaotic traffic. Cars and vans passed by them, each at their own speed, some moving steadily and some dashing as if it was a race. Every driver appeared to set their own rules.

They stopped at a crossing, waiting for the green light. And it was then that Neil beheld a familiar figure. Nouri Samir, the stranger, was walking along the other side of the road, approaching the crossing. The frantically passing cars made the sleeves of his tunic flap in the wind as the man went on his business.

He was mere feet away from the crossing when he looked their way. He stopped, calmly waiting.

"Hey, it's that guy again," Jake whispered.

"Ah, that guy," Neil said. "I saw him giving an interview on TV after the attack. I take back what I said earlier; he's not a dodgy type."

The two crossed the road when the opportunity arose, feeling somewhat tense as they approached the tunic-clad man.

"Fate keeps making us cross paths," he said, stopping them in their tracks. His English was infused with an accent, though not a particularly heavy one.

"Oh, hello there. How are you?" Neil could only respond with a generic greeting.

"I hope you were able to recover after the ordeal yesterday."

"Yes, I'm fine. We're both fine, thanks to you," Neil said sincerely. "I would like to express our gratitude for coming to our rescue. Without you there, neither of us would be standing here at this moment."

"Yes, we're definitely grateful for what you did," Jake said, bowing his head.

"I think of it as a duty," Nouri said humbly.

He raised his head and, for a quick moment, his gaze met Neil's. His deep brown eyes had a strange, mesmerising effect, as if they had the power to break a person's concentration and bind their will.

Nouri looked away. "I think I know who you are," he said. "You're a journalist. You also make documentary films."

"Yes, that's right," Neil said. "Only, I do not recall us meeting before yesterday."

"That's because we haven't. But my former employer is... how do you call them..." Nouri ran his fingers through his short beard. "A man of the world...I think that's the phrase. Watching documentary films and series of different kinds is one of his hobbies. I often used to watch with him. Some of your documentaries were among them. Unfortunately, I never memorised your name."

"Neil Feaver. And it appears I am more renowned than I thought I was."

"And my name is Nouri Samir."

"I know. You were on TV earlier today." He extended his hand towards Jake. "And this is Jake Parvis. You might not have seen him on screen, but he was the cameraman for some of my projects."

"I see." Nouri bowed his head.

"By the way, what you did at the restaurant. Those were quite impressive moves. What were they?" Neil asked.

"A form of old Arabic martial arts."

"Really?" Jake cut in. "What's it called?"

"This fighting style does not have a name. It's very difficult to learn and perfect, so the number of people able to master it has always been small. I happen to be one of the few masters that can be found in the Arab World—and the world in general. Nevertheless, this form of martial arts has a proud and ancient history. Some of the greatest rulers of the Middle East enlisted the services of its masters both for protection and to carry out important assignments. It is said Harun al-Rashid kept several as his bodyguards. Salah ad-Din made use of their services on a number of occasions." Nouri spoke with a sense of pride that was impossible to conceal.

"Interesting," Jake commented.

"I thought you looked familiar when I saw you peeking into the coffee shop," Nouri told Neil. "But I wasn't certain, so I decided to follow you around discreetly." He gave a lone chuckle. "Now that I think of it, I don't understand why I didn't just come up to you and clarify."

"And is there something we can help you with?" Neil asked, curious and somewhat suspicious.

"I assume you came to this country to make another documentary. Am I right?"

Neil said nothing, responding with a nod.

"You are well aware that this can be quite a dangerous place for foreigners, especially if you intend to venture into the depths of the country. Due to circumstances, I am jobless at the moment and have exhausted most of my savings. Hence, I am looking for temporary employment, so I was wondering if I could offer you my services."

"The news segment about you mentioned that you were a security guard," Neil said, thinking.

"More like a bodyguard. I am also an expert in cold weapons. And in case you are wondering, I know how to use firearms as well."

"That's quite a portfolio," Jake remarked.

"I used to work for a local businessman in the town of Al-Qasim, the same man who used to enjoy your shows. Another one of his hobbies was swordsmanship, so aside from being a guard, I was also his sword-fighting instructor and sparring partner. The salary was good, so I stayed with him for many years. However, having grown tired of the endless chaos, he recently left Iraq and migrated to France with his family. So I became unemployed. However, one of his business partners, based in Abu Dhabi, has expressed interest in giving me a similar opportunity at his household. He promised to arrange a visa and other matters, but it would take some time, and he did not offer any advance payments that I could use to sustain myself while all of this is being arranged. So I am in this situation. And people of my kind...masters of these martial arts...are simply too proud to work as general labourers or security guards at supermarkets for a miserly wage. Hence, I would choose short-term employment with a decent wage over those options."

"And how much do you charge for your services?" Neil asked.

"It depends on the duration," Nouri said. "And I am open to negotiations."

Neil took a deep breath as he thought over the proposal. If he was being honest, he did not need this strange though incredibly capable man. He had been in worse places—war zones, collapsed states, gang turfs—without additional security. Moreover, it would be the first time he'd ever picked up a guard from the street, literally. And yet, a sense of duty kept gnarling at his spirit. He owed this man his life.

"Perhaps we could discuss this further at a coffee shop," he said.

Nouri Samir smiled and nodded.

***

"Don't get me wrong, Neil—I have nothing against that Arabic ninja dude. I actually think he's cool," Jake said when the elevator doors opened and they stepped out into their hallway. "But are you sure there are enough funds in the project's budget to pay his salary?"

With a mechanical buzz, the lift doors closed behind them.

"There aren't," Neil said solemnly and paused. "I'm paying him out of my pocket."

***

Neil had thought that the office of the museum's finds expert would be some unusual study lined with shelves cluttered with archaeological fragments. Instead, it was little different from any other office: a computer, a printer, a desk, a filing cabinet. One could have thought it belonged to a manager or an accountant.

Ubaid Amin, the finds expert, adjusted his glasses as he looked at the screen of Neil's laptop. He carefully studied each picture, with Neil standing by his side, arms crossed over his chest.

"Yes, this is quite an interesting collection," he said eventually, turning to Neil.

"Just one moment, sir." Neil gave Jake the command, and moments later, the camera was on and pointed at the expert. "Whenever you're ready."

"The recovered artefacts originate from the pre-Islamic era," Ubaid said into the camera. "They appear to belong to different historical periods of Mesopotamian history. And not only that, they represent different cosmological models."

He enlarged one of the images, a plate-shaped brass relic. It bore the image of a cloaked man, his curly hair covered with a conical headdress. In his hand, the man held an item similar to a wand.

Ubaid turned the laptop towards the camera. Jake zoomed in to focus on it.

"The man depicted on this trinket is most likely a Persian magus. But note how he is depicted," Ubaid said. "It's almost as if he is looking back at you."

And indeed, the image could have been described as an ancient take on a profile picture.

"The ancient Persians used to show figures from the side. However, this frontal artistic style was common in the Parthian Kingdom. The Parthians, originally nomadic peoples from the steppes of Central Asia, ruled these lands between the second century BCE and the third century CE."

Even Nouri, standing beside his new employer, seemed to be following this presentation with interest.

Ubaid brought up a picture of another artefact on the laptop screen. This one was round, like a coin or medallion. Time and environment had not been kind to it, having partially worn away the engraving. Yet one could still distinguish bent lines, each running above the last. Neil had found himself curious about the symbolism; he'd thought it an incorrect depiction of a rainbow, the artist having added one additional line through some mistake or reason known only to him.

"I would say that this relic was made during Late Antiquity," the expert continued. "I believe it represents a feature of the Manichaean cosmological model. The eight lines engraved on it were probably meant to symbolise the eight layers of earth that existed according to Manichaean belief. Manichaeism was a dualistic religion of either Mesopotamian or Iranic origin, widespread across the Middle East and Central Asia during Late Antiquity and the Early Middle Ages."

He switched to a new image.

"This relic is not even metalwork. This is a clay cylinder," he said, emphasising its form. "And if you pay close attention, you can see writing in the cuneiform script on its sides. It appears to be Sumerian."

"So, in your opinion, do these relics have anything in common?" Neil asked.

"Yes. The overall theme: these were amulets, used by the ancient people of Mesopotamia as magic charms and trinkets."

***

Ubaid Amin was not the only expert Neil had arranged to meet. The following day he found himself in the office of Professor Suleimani, a lecturer at a local university, whose expertise lay in the field of social history.

His was truly the office of a scholar. The two large bookcases, filled with tomes, were the first things to catch Neil's gaze. But it appeared that even all these shelves were not enough, for there were a few more books placed on the desk in a neat stack.

Professor Suleimani was no doubt used to giving interviews on topics related to his field.

"Yes, in general, the tenets of Islam look negatively at anything related to magic, sorcery, charms, and superstition. There are verses in the Quran discouraging the use of such practices." Suleimani talked confidently, seated in his chair. "But at the same time, like with many other faiths, there has always been a distinction between 'organised' and 'folk' religion. The average preacher—imam, mullah, or mufti—would criticise a person if he found out that person, let's say, was using some charm to bring good luck. However, in folk religion, the version historically engrained in the minds of many common people, especially in rural and isolated areas, everything operates under different rules. For instance, in the past—and, for that matter, the not so distant one—it was not uncommon to find somebody akin to a shaman in practically any settlement in every part of the Islamic world, from the Maghreb to Malacca, Turkestan to Zanzibar. And of course, amulets meant to ward off the evil eye have widespread use even nowadays. After all, Islam arrived into a region where traditions related to magic and occultism had been flourishing throughout millennia. Think of the Middle East: the ancient traditions of the Egyptians and Phoenicians, Sumerians and Babylonians, Persians and Nabateans. Now add Gnosticism and mystic cults such as the Mithraic mysteries into the mix. Their practices were not forgotten. Instead, what happened was that folk Islam absorbed and incorporated parts of these superstitions, creating an unusual blend, a type of syncretism."

"But radical movements within Islam—Wahhabists, Salafis— they zealously oppose any form of superstition," Neil said.

"Yes, they see themselves as purists. They are bent on cleansing the religion of any outside influence," the professor responded before adding, "In any way possible."

"Then why would a member of the radical Liwa al-Qadisiyyah Islamist group hide an entire collection of magic trinkets under his bed?"

Suleimani let out a chuckle, leaning back into his chair.

"The eternal conflict between belief and money!" He clapped his hands together to emphasise the statement. "Jihadists hate everything related to the pre-Islamic cultures of the Middle East and want to see their remnants erased. But they also understand the monetary value of archaeological treasures. Hence, different Islamist groups have been caught running schemes smuggling ancient artefacts to be sold on the black market. But the main question is whether this character was working under the instruction of his superiors or whether he was...let's put it this way...trying to earn some money on the side."

***

Their jeep was waiting for them in the university's parking lot. Nouri opened the vehicle's back door for Neil and Jake, then closed the door behind them, like a faithful butler, before joining Furqan at the front of the car. The driver threw his employers a quick look before starting the vehicle.

The university complex soon disappeared behind them. Neil listened to the sounds of the motor running as the jeep took its place amidst the city's eccentric traffic. Their pace slowed until it was only slightly faster than that of a tortoise, before ceasing completely. A multitude of car horns was not an unfamiliar noise on the city's roads, but on this occasion, they wove together into a full orchestra. Furqan's annoyed swearing came from the front seat.

"This is going to take a while," Neil muttered as he peered out of the window, only to see a row of cars stretching beyond the limits of his sight.

To pass the time, he pulled his smartphone out of his pocket. A few quick taps, and he was looking at the familiar relics.

Time for my daily dose, he thought, smiling at the joke.

He swiped from the first image to the second to the tenth.

"Seriously, don't you think you're getting a bit carried away by all of this?" he heard Jake say, his tone both concerned and sarcastic.

Neil turned to Jake and found him looking over his shoulder.

"Yes, you do have a point." He couldn't disagree. "I need to take it easy. My last obsession led me into a disastrous four-year marriage."

He heard the ever-stoic Nouri Samir laugh at that.

"Please excuse me," the guard said, quickly regaining his usual serious self.

"It's alright," Neil said.

A series of scenes flashed before his eyes, mementos from a past that seemed both as distant as ancient history and as recent as the previous day. He wished they had not come like this on this occasion; he wished they would not come at all...

He put the smartphone back into his pocket.

"Don't get me wrong, Neil," Jake said, "I'm glad that you've found a new hobby. But are we actually going anywhere with this thing? Ever since we came back from the American base, these relics started stealing the spotlight. I mean, aren't we falling behind the original schedule?"

"You do make a good point," Neil agreed.

"I mean, the documentary is supposed to be called *The Voice of the Iraq War*. Right?" the cameraman continued. "These amulets can't talk and the guy who was hoarding them...um, he didn't get that chance."

"But I still think it can add some interesting stuff to the documentary," Neil said.

"I'm not arguing about it—just keep in mind that it shouldn't be the focus," Jake said. "Imagine what the network executives would think when instead of an insight into the lives of people caught in the conflict they get a set of theses about jihadi wizards."

***

The roads in this neighbourhood were quite rough and bumpy, which was no surprise, for the team was approaching the outskirts of the city. The area had more of a rural feel with simple houses standing in the shadows of trees.

In the front, Nouri was giving Furqan directions, for due to a lack of any street signs, it would otherwise be impossible to find their destination. The car eventually stopped beside one of the houses. The building, a compact two-storey house, was old and derelict. The outside layer of its walls had already begun crumbling into dust. On a brighter note, the windows were still intact.

"I guess this is your pad?" Jake asked Nouri, looking out of the car window.

"In a way. My uncle used to live here before he died. It stood vacant for years. I only started living here when I came to Baghdad recently."

Nouri opened the door and got out.

"It won't take long," he said, "I suggest you wait in the car in the meantime."

He went towards the gate and opened it with his key. He disappeared into the courtyard, the half-closed gate hiding him from view.

Nouri re-emerged about fifteen minutes later. On his back he carried a bag big enough to store golf equipment. He thoughtfully locked the gate and then put the bag into the back of the jeep.

"We can go now," he said, getting back in the car.

CHAPTER NINE

One basic fact needed to be admitted: a lot of professions get over-romanticised, and archaeology is probably the poster child of this. The reality Elliott had stepped into could not have been further from the fantasy images he had envisioned. Instead of well-preserved ruins, intact walls and porticos, there were barely distinguishable foundations of structures. You could stand in front of a site but, with an untrained eye, find it nearly impossible to tell where an interior room had been and what was backyard. Intact artefacts in the form of jewellery and weapons were scarce; if somebody unearthed something, that something was more likely to be a fragment of a terracotta object, small enough to become hidden in a clenched fist. And of course, in an ultimate case of bait and switch, a life of adventure was substituted for hard work amidst layers and layers of dirt.

Elliott's knees were crying after sustained contact with the hard surface beneath him as he used a trowel to clear the foundations of centuries-old dust, crevice after crevice. Sweat drenched his forehead, but that was nothing new. He put the trowel aside and, releasing a grumpy moan, stood up. Whilst the pain in his knees did not completely fade away, he felt relief nonetheless. He took a sip from his water bottle, barely resisting the urge to drink it all. He shot a look beyond the ditch he was working in; there, two of his colleagues were processing portion after portion of earth through a sieve in an attempt to find artefact fragments, like a pair of prospectors looking for gold nuggets.

The supervisor's call heralded the end of the day's work. It could not have come soon enough. Elliott picked up the trowel and climbed out of the ditch.

It was still daytime, and a short walk around allowed him to get a proper look at the place. The remains of the old Assyrian outpost resembled a construction site, with several ditches and trenches that had been dug across it during these last four weeks. The star attraction, the platform, had been cleared. It was a sight to behold: over a hundred metres in length and twenty in width, it was made out of perfectly cut limestone slabs that fit together so well that even after all these years it would have been impossible to stick a toothpick in the crevices between them. A geophysical survey also revealed that the blocks used in the construction were rather thick. And it was just sitting there, a limestone megalith surrounded by mud brick, amidst remote drylands. It was not hard to understand Mergham's obsession with it.

Hours later, Elliott was sitting in front of his tent, silently looking at the darkness-shrouded, star-littered sky. Prior to this trip, he had not been into stargazing, but with a lack of evening entertainment, it was becoming a more or less acceptable substitute.

"Yo, Elliott!" a voice called out to him; a voice that definitely did not belong to one of Mergham's ancient extraterrestrials.

He turned around to see Joe coming his way, accompanied by two more project participants, Frank and Mitch. The latter two were average diggers, and though both had more experience in excavations, neither particularly stood out among the rest. Aside from a few short chats, Elliott could not recall any other interactions with them.

"Whatcha doin'?" Joe asked when he reached Elliott's tent.

"Just chilling here with my new friend," Elliott said as he pointed his hand at the empty space beside him. "His name is Boredom."

Joe chuckled. "Do you want to hang out with us for a while?"

"Sure, of course." Elliott got up.

"Glad you're in. It's going to be an authentic Middle Eastern experience."

Whatever it was, it sounded unique. It sounded mysterious...

"Let me guess, you've hired a troupe of belly dancers to perform at the campfire?" Elliott asked sarcastically.

"I wish."

Then it had to be something different. How unfortunate.

Joe signalled the others to follow him, no doubt towards his tent. Elliott's hunch was right; they walked past several tents before their path led them to Joe's. The young man ducked into his fort of fabric, emerging a minute later with an object that looked like a cross between a vase and a trombone. Its base was made out of glass, whilst the stem was copper; at least it seemed like that in the dark.

"A hookah?" Frank said. "Good one!"

"Yep, and a proper one at that. I bought it when we were in Erbil."

Elliott had shared a room with Joe in Erbil, but he could not recall seeing this contraption before. He assumed his roommate went out and got it when he had dozed off whilst recuperating after the long flight.

"Good thing I bought one," Joe said. "All this marshmallow roasting and other things Mergham is into aren't my cup of tea."

"So are we gonna smoke it here?" Mitch asked.

"No, it's not really the right weather," Joe said, referring to the nightly chill. "Let's go to the meeting tent. Nobody will be using it at this time."

"Are we actually allowed to do that?" Frank asked.

"No idea. But if it's not outright banned—you know."

Another short walk took them inside the meeting tent, where they were surrounded by the glow of lamps that had been left burning in the night. Maintaining distance from the table Mergham used for administrative work, they sat on the floor. Joe took the duty of preparing the device and tobacco upon himself. Naturally, when everything was ready, it was Joe's honour to have the first go. Then it was Elliott's turn. He had never tried it before, and he barely restrained from coughing as the moist, vanilla-flavoured vapour filled his lungs. At the same time, it did have a soothing effect on the mind.

The four sat in a circle orbiting the contraption, passing the mouthpiece around as they talked about different things: job prospects and salaries, video games and new releases, dating advice and clever pick-up lines. It was hard to tell how much time had passed, but when it's a good time, it doesn't really matter. He couldn't speak on behalf of the others, but if they'd stayed up until dawn, Elliott would've been alright with that.

And then the tent's flap was roughly yanked to the side, letting fresh air into the smoke-filled room. From his position, Elliott beheld a dark silhouette at the entrance. The shade-clad figure stood regally, its hands on its hips, radiating an aura of power and anger. Elliott recalled some folktale he had heard somewhere on some occasion, a story that spoke of a night demon which, under the cover of darkness, wandered through the land in search of children to abduct and devour. Now it seemed it had found its way to their camp.

"What do you guys think you are doing here?!"

If this was truly a demon, it was a damn good impressionist.

"Hey Lauren!" Joe cheerfully called out, saluting her with the mouthpiece of the hookah.

Poor fool doesn't understand what we are about to get into, Elliott thought, slowly shaking his head.

"What's this smell?" Lauren said, having stepped inside the tent. "Have you been smoking in here?"

"Want to join us?" Mitch asked, though it was clear he was in damage control mode.

"Not really, because your little party is now over." Her furious gaze was fixed at them, blue eyes flashing amidst the glowing lamps. "Now put that thing out and go! This tent is supposed to be for operational purposes only!"

Lauren moved to the table and checked the documents and maps on its surface. "I swear, you better not have used any of the paperwork to roll joints or anything," she hissed.

"Chillax, Lauren, that's not how this thing works." Elliott gestured vaguely at the hookah. "You're thinking of something completely different."

She stepped away from the table, possibly swayed by his words, possibly having already checked everything. "Thank goodness for that." She gave him a look similar to the one a teacher gives to a scolded student. "But you're getting out of this tent right now. And I suggest you go to sleep. The dig resumes in the morning."

Supervised by the redhead's gaze, the four exited the tent, with the fateful hookah in Joe's hands. And as they retreated, in his mind, Elliott added a new entry to the list of fun events Lauren had ruined throughout her life.

***

Getting disciplined by Lauren led to a predictable outcome: there was no shisha party the following night. Elliott tried to go to sleep early but could not. He kept tossing and turning in his cubicle of a tent, his nose brushing against the flap.

"Darn it," he hissed as he clambered out of his sleeping bag. He crept out of the tent into the night.

Everything was quiet, too quiet, almost as if Lauren had taken control of the camp and imposed a curfew. He wandered around the camp, his path aimless until he reached its edge. And then he saw it: a lonely figure becoming smaller as it ventured further into the distance. This sight gave him an eerie feeling; after all, even after several weeks here, these lifeless landscapes still seemed foreign and otherworldly, the type of place where mystical things happened. Perhaps he'd found a lost soul roaming these lands, bound to this place by some tragedy many centuries before. However, when he focused, Elliott recognised the grey sleeveless jacket. It became clear that the shrinking figure was, more likely than not, Leonard Mergham. And it was probably no coincidence that he was walking in the direction of the archaeological site.

The identity of the figure was revealed, but another mystery formed. Why would he go there in the middle of the night? Curious, Elliott waited for Mergham to disappear behind the mound before going on the trail.

Elliott did not need to see Mergham to follow him; he had the way memorised. He kept his distance, making sure to stay concealed by the mounds. He climbed one commando-style, crawling on his stomach. The top of the small hillock gave a good view of the site lying below. Finding what he thought was the best spot, Elliott waited, still on his stomach, and observed.

It was no surprise that it was the mysterious platform calling out to the author in the night. Mergham now walked on top of it, stopping near its centre. He held a folder in his hand, no doubt filled with charts and papers.

Like a naturalist observing a bird in its habitat, Elliott watched how the conspiracy theorist approached the landmark that meant so much for his research. For a long while, Leonard just stood there, silently looking at the sky and stars, interrupting the viewing by throwing glances in different directions, as though he was anticipating someone's arrival. He walked towards different parts of the megalith, scribing something down in his papers, a calculation of some sort, no doubt. Several times, he bowed down and felt the unusual stones with his palm.

Elliott began to feel goose bumps running down his skin that had nothing to do with the cold night. During the day, this archaeological site was no different from the camp in atmosphere. But under the circle of the moon and the cloud of darkness, it acquired a sinister character. A couple of times, the notion arose that Elliott himself was being watched. No, not by Mergham—the author's attention was dedicated only to the platform—but by somebody else. Elliott looked around, left and right, but he saw no shape, heard no step or breath. And this only made the surroundings more disturbing, as if the shadows all over this place were, in fact, alive.

"Damn Gothic crap," he whispered.

Enough was enough. Mergham could prance around the platform as long as he wanted to, but Elliott was out. He carefully pulled back from the mound and began walking towards the campsite as fast as he could. He did not look back even once; the last thing he wanted to see were shadows walking around without anyone to cast them.

Stepping within the circle of the campsite automatically put him at ease; it was like swimming to a peaceful island in the middle of a raging sea. Yet he chose not to return to his tent. Instead, he staggered to Mergham's and sat down, leaning against it. He was going to find out what exactly the author was doing at the platform. He closed his eyes, intending to rest for a bit...

He was brought to his senses by somebody calling out his name. There was Mergham standing in front of him, the same folder in his hand.

"I say, lad, what are you doing here at this hour?"

"Well, I couldn't get any sleep, so I went for a stroll around the camp, but it seems like I was more tired than I thought I was, so I guess I dozed off." Elliott made up an excuse.

"Oh." It appeared that Mergham fell for it. "Well, for the future, be careful. The nights here are cold; this is actually a way to contract an illness."

"Sure thing, Dr Mergham." Elliott nodded. "And are you still doing paperwork so late at night?"

"No, I went down to the archaeological site." Mergham did not keep it a secret. "Doing some research in astroarchaeology. It's the study of the connection between heaven and earth. I was trying to figure out whether the platform there aligns with any of the constellations, or perhaps if the moonlight could reveal any hidden details when it falls on it."

"So I guess you're working night shift this time." Elliott chuckled; the mystery was solved and everything was back to normal.

"You could say that I work all shifts. I have studied the platform on location at sunrise and sunset as well."

"Any unusual discoveries?"

"Not yet."

CHAPTER TEN

"Back in its heyday, the city of Ctesiphon rivalled both Rome and Constantinople in splendour. It served as the seat of power for the Parthians and then the Sassanian dynasty of Persia. For over seven centuries, the decisions made within the palaces of the kings who ruled from this city shaped the fate of the entire Near East. But now, Taq Kasra, the arched façade of the royal palace, is all that remains of the once great capital."

Neil formulated the narration for the segment as he gazed at the crumbled monument. The regal arch rose above its surroundings. The astonishing sight made a person ponder about all the efforts and resources that needed to be put into its construction, as well as the vision that guided it. One could imagine an ancient Shah sitting atop his litter, right on the same spot Neil stood, observing the construction of the project. One could imagine a mason, his bare back tanned by the harsh sun, laying brick after brick under the cloudless sky.

Two millennia ago, many streets had ringed around it with buildings of all types: houses, workshops, temples. The eons had reduced the neighbouring structures to their foundations; dirt and sand had hidden them from the human eye. The palace itself, which the arch was meant to have been part of, too had turned into nothing.

Beside him, Jake put the camera down. "I think that's enough filming. Do you want to see what I have?"

"Show it."

Jake passed the camera to him, and Neil played the video.

"Good work." Neil gave the camera back to Jake.

To his other side, Nouri stood, looking at the site with an expression that revealed neither enthusiasm nor boredom.

Honestly, Neil," Jake complained. "We were headed towards Karbala, and yet you still made us take a detour so you could add more of this ancient Persian stuff to the documentary." He raised his foot and took his shoe of. "And just to make matters worse, I think I've got sand in my shoes." He flipped the shoe, letting sand flake towards the ground. "I've never even heard of this place before," he said as he put the shoe back on. "And frankly, I had no idea you knew of it."

Neil gave Taq Kasra one last, quick look. "I do," he said plainly. "Anyway, I think it's time we got going." He turned around and began to walk off, followed by Nouri.

"You know," Jake said, walking beside him, "I'm beginning to think you've developed an obsessive-compulsive disorder because of all these trinkets." He smiled. "You might want to see a professional once we get back to New York."

"Or, who knows, perhaps you are hearing an ancient call," Nouri suddenly said.

His statement immediately caught their attention. The rough and enigmatic guard, clad in his navy Bedouin-style outfit, did not talk much, so this felt like a sensationalist scoop, coming from him.

"What do you mean?" Neil asked.

"What I mean is perhaps you really did establish some sort of connection with..." Nouri paused, trying to find the right word. He looked back at Taq Kasra, which was shrinking into the distance. "All of this," he settled on, lacking a better choice. "Some claim that objects with mystical properties can absorb parts of the life force of their former owners. Perhaps you have managed to tap into it by some means. For all you know, an ancient ancestor of yours might have owned one of these artefacts. Also, some religious beliefs of the Middle East, like those of the Druze, for example, state that, after death, a person can be reborn in a new body over and over again."

"You're talking about reincarnation?" Jake asked.

"Yes." Nouri nodded.

"So it's like Buddhism," Neil said.

"Not really. Buddhists believe that a man can be reborn as an animal under certain conditions. The Druze, on the other hand, believe that man can only be reborn as a man."

"Interesting."

"Is the belief in reincarnation present in Islam?" Jake asked.

"No," Nouri answered coldly. "The Quran categorically contradicts this notion."

The trio soon reached their jeep. Neil climbed in, and before setting off, took his water bottle from his backpack for a drink. Behind him, Nouri and Jake were talking.

"Your martial arts are very impressive. So how good are your reflexes really?"

"Very good," Nouri said. "Imagine somebody pulls a gun out right in front of me, pointing it at me."

"Sure."

"I would be able to knock it out of his hand before he gets the chance to pull the trigger."

Jake whistled. "Wow."

"It sounds almost impossible," Neil said, turning around.

"But it's not," Nouri said. "We can even carry out a test to oust any scepticism."

"With a loaded gun?" Neil chuckled.

"Yes." Nouri did not laugh.

Neil was in possession of a gun, the one Massoud had given him a few days before. It was within reach, hidden in a compartment of his backpack. A curious part of him had an urge to accept the martial arts master's challenge. He wanted to witness this feat first hand; at the same time, he knew better than to try something so absurd, especially right in the open.

"And how good are you with using firearms?" Jake asked.

To his surprise, Neil realised that he had not asked Nouri this question before giving him the job.

"I've been trained, but I don't rely on firearms," was the man's answer. "This is how I was taught. A blade is a noble weapon. When you duel, you engage your opponent straight on, your face mere inches away from his; you read the thoughts in his eyes. Your enemy always has the opportunity to get your weapon out of your hands if he is skilful enough. This truly tests your abilities. There is no such honour in pressing the trigger of a gun whilst standing at a safe distance."

"I guess you don't need guns anyway," Jake said with a shrug. "You took those terrorist scumbags out at the restaurant without one."

"I've been through worse," Nouri said.

"How much worse?" Neil asked.

"Notably. My former employer was a prominent local businessman. And, as you know, competition in business can be very ruthless. A business rival of his ordered his death. So, one night, four thugs armed with pistols broke into his house with the intent of killing him. Armed only with my daggers, I took up to defend the house. I managed to kill all of the attackers, one by one."

"Wow." Jake could only repeat the exclamation from earlier.

"And what about your employer's rival? Did he get indicted for it?" Neil asked, curious as to how the story ended.

"No, he had good connections in different branches of the local administration, so he avoided arrest. However, he was found dead a couple of days later. The police came to the conclusion that he committed suicide." Nouri went quiet to let them draw their own conclusions.

"Quite a story," Neil said.

He pulled his phone out to look at the time. They would be back on the road in a matter of minutes.

***

"The population of this camp expanded quite rapidly, and it has become one of the biggest refugee camps in Iraq," the crew were told as they were led up something that could be compared to a street.

Luis Hofer was a Camp Management Officer working for the Refugee Agency of the United Nations. Due to the nature of his position, he seemed to have knowledge of every aspect of this refugee camp located near the city of Karbala, from the details about supply distribution to the leisure activities of the facility's inhabitants.

"There are more and more refugees arriving here every day. We have people from all over Iraq," Luis said as he looked around.

He wore a light blue T-shirt with the insignia of the organisation he worked for sewn on the chest. His identification badge hung from a lanyard around his neck, lightly hitting against his chest with every step he took.

Around him and the group he accompanied, life continued in the chaotic refugee camp. The camera on Jake's shoulder kept turning left and right, catching glimpses of its day-to-day realities.

The refugee camp had become a type of town. There had likely been no intent to it, but the layout of the camp, or at least portions of it, did remind Neil of streets. Most of the dwellings were tents of different sizes; many acted as a tragic parody of shared accommodation, housing multiple families under their polyester roofs. Some were more complex, appearing to be made from a mishmash of different materials, including but not limited to clay, cardboard, and sheet metal, probably brought by their inhabitants.

There were, of course, structures of a more stable nature. Made out of brick and rectangular in form, they resembled cottages. They played a major role in the functioning of the camp, serving as the base for the public services the inhabitants had access to. Each was furnished depending on its purpose: the school had desks and a blackboard; the clinic had hospital beds.

These services felt like a small spot of morning light amidst a dark sky. Like at any other camp of this kind, the atmosphere was that of utmost misery. Dirt and rubbish lay everywhere, and a peek into any of the tents provided a lot of insight into the unsanitary conditions of the place.

Still, the people seemed to make the best use of the limited things they had. At one point, Neil sensed a smell in the air, a pleasant change from the rot and filth that hung thick over the camp. He turned to the side and saw its source: a woman, her head veiled with a broad pink scarf, was sitting in front of a tent, baking bread on a small open-air hearth.

Children would occasionally run up to them, summoned by the sight of the rolling camera. In their innocent naivety, they would smile and wave hands whenever the lens turned towards their small shapes.

Naturally, a place like this was a hoard of life stories, and it was not hard to find people willing to share theirs. An entire extended family gathered outside beneath one of the trees that grew on the camp's territory. There were over ten of them, men and women, children and the elderly, the young and middle-aged. The patriarch sat in the middle of the congregation. He had long pushed beyond the age of seventy; life had worn him out, and he relied on the support of his sons just to get up.

"The family of my grandfather settled in the vicinity of Mosul when he was still a boy," he told the camera in his slow, low-toned voice.

Then the sudden echo of ferocious noises came from the distance, as unexpectedly as thunder in the middle of a heat wave, startling the old man into silence. It caught Neil's attention immediately. His ears were familiar with this noise; he had heard it many times during his stints in war zones.

He turned to Luis. "Do any of the inhabitants of the camp have access to firearms? There's a gunfight going on."

The Camp Management Officer looked severely disturbed by what he was hearing.

"No." He shook his head, his voice laced with worry. "It's an attack! Somebody is trying to break into the camp!"

Something clicked inside Neil's head, like a subliminal command had been given by an unseen puppeteer. He knew what he needed to do.

"Follow me, Jake!" he declared as he dashed forth in the direction of the shooting.

He threw a swift look behind him and spotted both his cameraman and his guard running behind him.

Many cities of the Arab world contain a place called a madina. Ever since the old days, these areas have served as the pulsing hearts of cities, the centres of social life. Neil had compared the refugee camp to a town earlier, and it was only natural that it would have a madina of its own, unique kind. A relatively large open space lay sprawled in the middle of a camp. One could not call it a square—no cobbles lined its surface—more a clearing. Tents stood all around it like houses in a historical district. One brick building used by the refugee agency stood out amongst its neighbours.

A large number of people had gathered there, listening to the gunshots. Then another sound reached their ears; the accompanying screeching hinted at its mechanical nature. Moments later, a bulbous vehicle stormed into the clearing at a speed so wild that anybody unfortunate enough to get in its way would have been crushed under its heavy tyres before even realising what was going on. Then it stopped just as suddenly.

Nouri clasped Neil's shoulder and yanked him to the side, pulling him into cover behind a tent. Jake bolted to hide behind the tent that stood on the other side of the 'street'.

The manufacturer of the vehicle had intended it to be a truck. All the modifications it had gone through later had made it unrecognisable, like the bastard spawn of an armoured personnel carrier and a bulldozer. On all sides, its exterior had been reinforced with large metallic plates. Its armoured hide was especially thick at the front. Neil had seen all sorts of vehicles get upgrades of this kind in war zones. He had no doubt that this was the siege weapon that was used to break through the gates of the camp.

About a dozen men, clad in fatigues and armed with automatic rifles, jumped out of the vehicle. One raised his weapon upwards.

"Everybody stay where you are! No movements!" he shouted with his wheezing voice. The authority he appeared to emit made it pretty clear that he was the commander.

He released a round of bullets into the air to illustrate the severity of his words. The crowd responded with gasps and screams as they got down. The militants dashed into different directions, ignoring the crouching people. Some went for the brick cottage. Whatever they'd come for was a mystery, but one thing was for sure: they had no interest in the refugees.

Neil's and Jake's hiding spots were some distance away from the clearing, but the intruders would only need moments to reach them if they chose. More shooting was coming from the distance, a sign that this was not the full force attacking the encampment.

"It's not wise to remain here," Nouri whispered. "We need to go back. It's too dangerous. The other side of the camp might have better defences."

Nouri tuned his attention to Jake, and conveyed the same to him through gestures, letting him know which direction to take: sideways and forward. Crossing the gap that separated them would come with a high risk of being noticed by the militants.

Jake nodded and, losing no time, disappeared amidst the tents.

"Let's go," Nouri whispered as he urged Neil to follow him in the opposite direction.

It felt like they were running through a madina quarter. The passages between rows of tents intimately pitched beside each other became alleyways, winding and bending as they led further and further towards unknown destinations. People came out of their shelters in confusion or curiosity, unaware of what was going on. A quick glance to the side, through the open flap of a tent, revealed a family cowering in the corner.

"You! Stop!"

Neil looked back to see one of the militants emerging from behind a tent. He was clutching his automatic rifle, and even though he stood quite a distance away from them, Neil could feel the menace radiating from him. Neil had no idea if the militant was part of that unit from the clearing or a different one.

"Go, damn it!" Nouri hissed, grabbing his employer by the hand to make sure he followed his advice. He quickened his pace as he turned to a different path.

They coursed from one alley to another, navigating through the maze of dirt and fabric. Neil could hear angry swearing in Arabic coming from behind them; the militant was giving chase.

"I'll shoot!" he shouted after them, but his threat did not come to pass.

Neil doubted that some moral value had kept their pursuer from sending a round of bullets into their backs. There had to be something else.

Suddenly, Nouri ducked into a random tent, taking Neil along with him. The flap swung back down behind them. The tent happened to be empty at the moment, though from the unmade cover, pillow, and mattress, it was not vacant. Articles of clothing and random personal items that lay around served as further proof.

"What...are we...doing here?" Neil asked. After a run like this, he could only talk in between heavy breaths. He felt he was suffocating.

"What is needed," Nouri said, looking away.

Nouri then pushed him, quite roughly, to the ground. The guard himself dropped down to a hunched crouch and grabbed his head with both hands.

A mere moment later, the flap got pulled aside. The militant stepped in with outright fury in his eyes as he looked down at his prey. Nouri began to snivel, rambling incomprehensible words in Arabic like a madman. His whole body shivered as if he had succumbed to a strong fever.

"Please, brother, please do not hurt me!" he cried, choking on his sobs. "I'm scared! I have lost everything! I don't even have a single dinar! Please!"

Their pursuer looked at him with contempt.

"Dog!" he spat out, kicking Nouri in the side. He then looked at Neil, who had propped himself up on his elbows, studying him. "You, foreigner!" he growled in Arabic. "Get up! You are coming with me!"

Many centuries ago, a wise man who had seen a lot in his life said these words of wisdom: "The most dangerous opponent is the one that seems defenceless." Perhaps the brigand had never heard this expression; perhaps he did not heed these words. And that proved to be a grave mistake. One moment, Nouri was as hunkered as a tree stump; the next, he swiftly swung his leg out and kicked the militant across the feet. The man fell on his back with a surprised yelp, releasing his hold on the rifle. At the same time, Nouri jumped back on his feet, blazing with confidence and power.

The brigand gritted his teeth in anger. He kept his eyes on Nouri and reached for his weapon. Nouri went for the attack and brought his foot down, striking the militant in the groin. The man screamed out in agony, his fist shooting open as part of the painful reflex, and the weapon again ended up outside his grasp. Nouri brought his foot down again, this time on his opponent's neck, making the thug gargle under the weight. Nouri just pressed harder, crushing the enemy's throat under his boot like a dry twig. The man's body went numb.

"Are you alright, Mister Feaver?" Nouri asked, watching his vanquished foe for any sign of life.

"I think so," Neil said as he got up.

Certain that the militant posed no threat, Nouri took his foot off the dead man's neck. He crept towards the entrance and peeked out. "At least none of them are outside this tent," he said.

Some shooting could still be heard in the distance.

"I'm still not completely sure why these bastards attacked this camp, but I think they are aiming at foreigners," Neil said, recalling the militant's command.

"It seems like it," Nouri agreed. "In any event, we need to exercise caution. I suggest we hide out in this tent for now. In the worst case scenario, if another one of them finds us, this tent will become a death-trap for him."

With that, he grabbed the corpse and dragged it into a corner before putting a blanket over it.

***

"Jake!" Neil called out.

A silent Nouri was walking beside him, his attentive gaze wandering side to side as the two roamed amidst the tents.

"Jake!" he shouted again. His voice was getting raspier with each shout. Every moment, he hoped that a familiar voice would call out to him from this sea of tents. But no such voice replied, and only the inhabitants of the camp, still shaken by the recent events, would come out to respond with their silence and confused looks in their eyes.

Concern was making Neil's heart beat hard. Like a child looking for their lost cat, he scoured every corner of this section of the camp in search of the cameraman, continually reminding himself that a lack of response was not necessarily a bad sign. Maybe Jake was sleeping, fully exhausted, hidden behind a flap in a different sector of the refugee camp.

Neil had spent quite some time hiding in a tent himself with Nouri as his guard, sharing company with the corpse of the militant. Only after the distant shooting had died out had they emerged from their hiding spot. By that time, the militants had withdrawn, having most likely got what they had come for.

Some time later, Neil was back at one of the camp's humble clinics. He leaned against the wall, feeling the rough bricks against the back of his head.

"I suggest we look for him around the southern section," Nouri said. The guard stood next to his employer, arms crossed over his chest, looking into the distance. "He might have made his way there."

An armed Iraqi soldier bearing the regalia of the nation's military passed by on patrol. A small military force had received the distress call and had come to stabilise the situation at camp. Unfortunately, they were too late.

"Mister Feaver!" Neil heard a familiar voice on his left...but not the one he was hoping for. "I'm glad you're safe."

Neil turned to find Luis Hofer coming up to him, holding an object that managed to instantly fill him with dread.

He had held this item in his hands many times, but on this occasion, he had an urge to step back like he was afraid to get jinxed by touching a cursed trinket.

"A security guard found it whilst on patrol," Luis explained.

It was Jake's camera.

Some dust and dirt had attached itself to it, but it appeared still intact. The undamaged lens was staring at Neil. "And Mister Parvis?" he asked, his chest trembling.

"We found no sign of him. He probably dropped or discarded the camera whilst trying to flee."

"Damned militants." Neil stomped his foot in anger, regretting he could not bring it down on the throat of one of the thugs the way Nouri had done. "Do we know anything about their motivations?" he asked.

"Yes: abduction. And it appears that they were specifically targeting foreigners. We already have witness accounts of them ignoring refugees and going straight for the aid workers. Several members of our staff working at this refugee camp have also gone missing."

Neil felt his head spin as a gut feeling whispered to him. They had taken Jake.

CHAPTER ELEVEN

Important figures from different towns and provinces kept arriving for the gathering. However, this occasion featured no group photos or intricately orchestrated greeting ceremonies. Every man who arrived was guided straight into the compound that had once served as a college for technical trades. Yet none of its teaching rooms or auditoriums, neither the library nor computer lab, had been converted into a meeting room. Instead, arrivals ventured further down, to where the school's basement, after many hours of work, had been turned into a system of underground tunnels. Like catacombs, the long, wide corridors flowed in different directions, leading to rooms, vaults, and hidden exits. A bombing raid could collapse the roof and walls of the former college onto anyone who made use of its empty hallways, but it would take much more effort to destroy the underground complex.

Sayid was already seated behind a long, rectangular table. He knew some of the arrivals from past encounters and recognised others from images he had seen. The highest echelon of Liwa al-Qadisiyyah was gathering in this place: the top military commanders and administrators, scholars and propagandists.

His eyes stayed focused on the entrance of the room as another man walked in. The oldest of the bunch, he appeared in his mid-seventies. Age had wrinkled his skin, and his long beard was white, matching his thawb robe and kufiyah headdress. Something about him felt old-fashioned and incredibly traditionalist, like he'd stepped out of a century-old photo of a madina or a souq. His name was Khaleed Awal, and among the ranks of the Liwa, only Abdulaziz Nishwari could rival his reputation in the field of religious scholarship.

Several more people walked in, but their arrival was quickly eclipsed by the appearance of another commander. Sayid himself was twenty-nine, and if he was not mistaken, this new arrival was about a decade older than he was. The expression on the newcomer's face was stone-cold; it always had been, as far as Sayid remembered. His name was Jalil, but Sayid could not recall his last name. His was primarily known under his alias that stemmed from his land of origin: al-Quwaiti. It was said that he used to be an officer in Kuwait's security services before he went to Iraq a decade ago, where he fought on the side of several militias before joining the Liwa. He was a formidable warlord, and many of his own comrades feared him, for the sheer ruthlessness of Jalil al-Quwaiti surpassed the cold-blooded infamy of the rest of Liwa al-Qadisiyyah. A subordinate that failed him had as little chance of survival as an infidel that crossed his path.

Silently, Jalil made his way to the nearest empty seat. Sayid turned to Mullah Nishwari, who had been peacefully sitting at the head of the table from the very beginning. The emir looked over the room, making sure everybody was in attendance. Sayid's gaze slid to the table and the big map of Iraq sprawled on it. Urban centres and strategic points, the frontlines and positions of the warring sides—all were reflected on the chart.

"Welcome, brothers!" Nishwari said as he stood up. "I have decided to invite all of you, the highest ranks of Liwa al-Qadisiyyah, to be present at the unveiling of our upcoming offensive. An offensive which, by the favour of Allah, will give us control of the capital."

"Are you sure this is a wise idea, Abdulaziz?" asked Amir Shamil, one of the assembled warlords. "Gathering the leadership of the Liwa in one place? What if the Americans have gotten word of this meeting through some spy or traitor? They could decapitate the whole organisation with one air strike."

"Are you afraid of death, Shamil?" the mullah asked, in the same manner as an ancient philosopher would have addressed his disciples.

"No, I am not—"

"If it is the will of Allah to take us to Heaven this very day, do you have a problem with that?" Nishwari continued. "After all, even if we are to be martyred, another flock of leaders will rise to pick up our banners.”

He gave his subordinate a couple of moments to respond, but the commander said nothing.

“Personally, I do not expect any air strikes on this compound today. And I promise you that all of us gathered here today will gather for prayer at the Baratha Mosque, the oldest mosque of Baghdad, the day true Islamic rule is restored over the city!” Nishwari proclaimed.

His eyes shone with jubilation. The triumph he was expecting might have seemed a distant image to most people seated around him, yet in the eyes of the mullah, it was a fully manifested apparition, hovering in the air within reach.

Some of the warlords, Nishwari’s solemn loyalists, cheered in response.

“But you have also been summoned to attend a little... presentation that will take place after this meeting’s end.”

That sparked curiosity. Sayid had overheard Nishwari mentioning the presentation earlier, but the nature of the event remained cloaked in mystery.

“Jalil.” The mullah turned in the direction of al-Quwaiti. “I have no doubts that you have spent many hours perfecting the strategic plans for the offensive. I would consider it a great honour if you could use this opportunity to share them with us.”

One fact was undisputed: as ruthless and unstable as Jalil was, he was a capable commander and a skilled tactician.

“I would be glad...most honourable Mullah,” Jalil said, bowing his head as he stood up.

Still, Sayid could catch the sarcasm peeking through the masquerade of courtesy.

When the other attendants joined him in getting up, the commander reached out to pick up a pointer that lay on the table beside the map.

“As you are all no doubt aware,” Jalil said, his voice becoming more authoritative, “through the favour of Allah, Liwa al-Qadisiyyah managed to acquire substantial gains in the central areas of the country, thus bringing the frontline closer to the capital.”

He brought the tip of the pointer down on the part of the map that outlined the boundaries of the city, holding the instrument against it like a medic holds a needle before injecting it into the bloodstream of a patient.

"Now the capital is within our reach," Jalil continued, marking the group's nearest positions. "The attack will be taking place from three directions simultaneously. Hence, the forces taking part in this offensive will need to be divided into three groups.

"The first group of units will strike from the north-east. The first objective is capturing the city of Baqubah." Jalil dragged the pointer's tip northwards, along the road leading to the aforementioned city. "It is the last notable urban settlement left standing on the way to Baghdad. Capturing it opens the road towards the capital, exposing the Sadr City district.

"The second group will establish a foothold in the area that lies in the vicinity of Taji." He pointed at a swath of mostly green terrain just to the north-west of the city. "I hold the view that this would be the quickest route to the Green Zone.

"The third group will move out of Al Anbar Governorate. They are positioned to the west of the capital and are our closest forces to it. The main objectives of this group are to capture the airport and cut the supply lines that run from the south.

"This battle will be fierce, and many amongst us will be martyred, but no other force in the last two decades has had a better chance of liberating the capital," Jalil concluded as he put the pointer down.

A certain amount of time passed in debate and deliberation as the warlords discussed the idea.

Jalil turned to his superior once this part was done with. "Mullah Nishwari."

"Thank you, Jalil." Nishwari nodded. "Now that all of you are acquainted with what is to come..." His voice rose as he addressed everybody in the room. "I would like to invite you to attend a special event."

***

It turned out that the event Nishwari was referring to was to take place at a different location. One by one, following precautions, the leaders of the group were led outside and driven there in plain cars in a bid to fool any watching drones.

Sayid was certain that they would be taken to one of the organisation's training camps in the vicinity of Baiji. Yet, when he stepped out of his vehicle, he found himself standing in the parking lot of one of the town's stadiums. From there, he, like the others who'd arrived at the place before him, was led to his seat by the group members acting as event assistants.

The stadium was a simple one. It had no special lounges, so the whole group was seated in one section, in the upper rows. Sayid was certain that no sports activities had taken place at the stadium since the city's takeover by the group, yet below them, the arena seemed well-maintained. Clearly some men had taken their time to sweep up any debris or rubbish that had littered the space.

Nishwari was the last to come in and sit down. Two more event assistants walked down the stairs towards the group's seats, like merchandise sellers would do during a match. Each of them carried a tray with a number of binoculars.

"I recommend using them if you want a more detailed view," Nishwari said, voice raised, his gaze fixed on the arena below.

Sayid picked up a pair of binoculars, his fingers gliding along the smooth, cold, metal frame. A mix of awkwardness and curiosity scratched his inner sense. He could not wait to find out what this mysterious event was about. Binoculars in hand, he almost felt like he was on some sort of bizarre bird-watching outing.

A plain-clothed individual entered the arena. He looked around it like an inspector seeking the smallest flaw. But, apparently, he did not find one, and saying no words, he looked towards the spectators. He then turned around; Sayid had a hunch he did so upon receiving a hand signal from the mullah. He disappeared through the same passage he had arrived from.

A minute later, another man walked into the arena through the same entrance, mirrored by a second man appearing from the opposite entrance. They were both men of fighting age, yet they did not wear fatigues or plain clothing like the average militant of Liwa al-Qadisiyyah did. Instead, green jumpsuits were their uniforms, and that came as a surprise to Sayid, for he had not seen any member of the group, fighter or administrator, ever wear something similar.

The plain-clothed man returned to the arena again. He made his way to the centre and gave a nod to each of the duo. Everything became relatively clear. This event was a type of tournament. The two were contestants, and the man in plain clothes, a referee.

Sayid wondered what type of match it was.

Perhaps, it's a wrestling match. The thought flashed in his mind. After all, wrestling was an ancient Arabic sport. What made little sense was the reason why Nishwari, not known for any affinity to sports, would throw an event of this nature.

Down below, the referee left the arena once more, this time climbing the steps to the first row of stadium seats.

"Begin!" he proclaimed.

The first contestant extended his hand. He said nothing and made no other move, yet, suddenly, a gout of fire burst out of his palm like a flame burning on the top of a gas oven. Surprised, Sayid adjusted the zoom of his binoculars for a more detailed view. There had to be a trick. The suits the contestants wore had to have had some mechanism built into them, unnoticeable from a distance. He was sure some compact flamethrower had to be incorporated into the suit, with small hoses that ran alongside the sides of the hand like miniature artificial veins carrying the fire to burst out of the sleeves. But even at maximum zoom, he was unable to spot these. Indeed, the flame appeared to be burning on the man's skin. And yet the man just stood there, posing, showing no response to a combustion that should have burnt his hand off.

Sayid heard some of his comrades whispering to each other in amazement. But the day's marvels were merely beginning. The contestant swung around and hurled that very same flame, no longer a cloud but shaped as an imperfect orb, like a sportsman would toss a baseball. As if this was a game of dodgeball, the other contestant evaded by jumping aside, and the fireball died upon hitting the stadium's concrete wall.

Then the hands of the other contestant lit up as well; a similar fire kindled in his grasp. Pushing his hands forward, he unleashed the fire on his adversary. The first contestant did not duck. Rather, he threw out his hand and another fireball flew out to parry the skin-scorching threat. The two fireballs collided in the middle of the arena and disappeared in tendrils of flame. This display of fireworks was as impressive as it was suspenseful.

And still this was not the end of the demonstration. The first contestant began launching fireballs in a frenzy, forcing his opponent to demonstrate the full scale of his agility and acrobatic skills. He dodged, he ducked, he flipped, avoiding strikes. He was able to hurl a few fireballs of his own in response; a couple of them extinguished the fiery projectiles. A few more flew towards his opponent, and it was now the first contestant's turn to respond to the heated assault. He swung his hand before falling to the ground to evade an attack, making several more fireballs manifest in the air and fly towards his adversary. Flames crackled as the fireballs hit the walls and the ground.

Then the two adversaries lunged at each other, their palms alight with unnatural flame, cradling growing fireballs. They each threw out their hands and shot each other from close range. The fireballs crashed together in an explosion of light, unleashing a shockwave that sent them both stumbling back.

The sound of a whistle blown by the referee stopped the duel. Having lowered their hands, both contestants turned to the row accommodating their high-ranking observers who sat in confused silence, neither cheering nor booing. In the meantime, a couple of assistants entered the arena, carrying human-sized dummies made out of twigs, straw, and rags, fixed on circular platforms. They placed them in the arena before withdrawing quietly.

Another whistle screeched through the air.

"And now let's show our honoured guests the finale!" the referee proclaimed.

The duo turned towards the practice dummies. Their hands lit up with the mystifying flames. Each brought his right hand forth and sent a fireball flying at their target. The projectiles collided with the mannequins, immediately igniting the lifeless figures.

Some of the warlords who sat and observed this unusual demonstration gasped as the fires crackled, consuming the dummies almost instantly. Sayid himself sat with his mouth wide open. In the back of his mind, he had initially considered the possibility that these flames were akin to Bengal fire: a trick, a form of whimsical entertainment, an illusion of a real conflagration. But he was wrong. Whatever this was had nothing to do with Bengal fire. If anything, it brought forth associations with the famed Greek fire: a dreaded weapon with a mystery-shrouded formula that burned entire Arabic fleets in Mediterranean harbours back in the Middle Ages.

With his long, dark-brown cloak almost sweeping the ground, Mullah Nishwari casually strolled towards the centre of the stadium. In surprise, Sayid glanced at the seat where he'd thought the man had been sitting, only to find it empty. Nishwari had managed to make his way down unnoticed amidst all of the excitement.

"Behold, brothers!" he proclaimed, raising both hands. "Behold the key to our victory!"

CHAPTER TWELVE

Not a single leader of the Liwa raised the topic of the extraordinary performance before the late afternoon prayer. But there was no doubt that as soon as praying time was over and they all went back to the winding underground compound, questions would be asked.

Sayid took a sip of cool water as the predictable debate began.

"Mullah Nishwari, are you going to tell us what exactly we saw earlier today?" asked Amir al-Baidun. "What type of gadget did those two use, and how did the Liwa manage to obtain it? I have never seen anything like it before."

"What makes you think it was a gadget?" Nishwari said with a calm smile.

"Are you implying that the fires they wielded were natural?" Shamil joined the conversation.

"Indeed, there was no technology involved in what you saw. There was no hidden device that generated that power. Their mastery over fire was achieved through seasons of training." The mullah spoke like he was explaining some basic fact, after stunning everybody else in the room with a miracle. "Think of the potential this has. Imagine the feats fighters who can manifest fireballs can achieve on the battlefield. The mere sight of them will throw our enemies into disarray, helping us secure victory after victory. And not only that! I can already see fire-wielding warriors of faith striking fear in the hearts of our enemies across the world. There will be no need to acquire weapons for bombings, shootings, or stabbings. No ploughing through pedestrians in hijacked vehicles. Just fireballs conjured out of thin air, spreading death around. Minimal resources will be spent, and preventing such an attack would be practically impossible."

"But first a detailed explanation is in order," said a grumpy voice.

Sayid turned in its direction. At the other end of the table, Sheikh Khaleed Awal sat with a heavy gaze. The look in his eyes could be compared to that of a school teacher during a disciplinary meeting with a failing student. And that gaze was clearly directed at Nishwari.

"Start from the beginning, Abdulaziz," Awal said.

"Very well." Nishwari stood up. "I showed it to you fully understanding that you would be curious about its origin. And here is the explanation: the technique for learning this power was detailed in a treatise written many centuries ago during the Golden Age of Islam, but later forgotten."

"How curious... Continue," said Amir Nayaub, another high-ranking figure.

"As you all know, I taught Islam at a madrasa in Baghdad decades ago," the mullah spoke. "At one point, I was tasked to do some work at the library of the madrasa, to help revise their catalogue of books. The library collection was quite big, and their catalogue did not account for every book held within its walls. This treatise was one of these. I found it piled among a number other books in a distant corner, covered in dust, unopened for many years. I am not sure if it was the original manuscript or a later copy, but I assure you, by the style and handwriting, it was centuries old. Naturally, it caught my interest due to its unusual content, so I kept returning to the library to read more and more of it. Mind you, this was taking place a couple of months before the American invasion began. Later, when Saddam's hold over the city dissolved days before the entry of American forces into Baghdad, I went back to the library and retrieved that treatise along with several more books. It has been in my possession ever since."

"So you stole that book from the madrasa?" Awal raised an eyebrow.

"No, I did not steal it. I saved it." Nishwari almost hissed the words. "Many of you are old enough to remember the wave of lootings and arson that took place in the anarchy that followed the city's fall. Unfortunately, the madrasa's library did not avoid becoming one of the targets."

"What happened next?" Sayid asked, unsure where all of this was going.

"I understood the potential of this fire-wielding craft and the advantage it could bring to our cause. After the founding of Liwa al-Qadisiyyah, I began work on bringing it back. However, there were some difficulties. First of all, I did not want any of our enemies, both inside Iraq and foreigners, to find out about the secrets of this ancient craft. Hence, the whole endeavour had to remain a secret until a certain point. I made sure only a small number of people, fighters hand-picked to learn these arts, were let in on it. All initiates were sworn to secrecy. These arts are not calligraphy and they are not gardening. They were not made for everybody. Not everyone is able to master them. One requires a lot of inner strength, a lot of concentration, a lot of mental balance to succeed in them," the mullah explained. "This made the selection of trainees even more difficult.

"There were no training camps. The initiates ventured into remote areas of the countryside, away from the eyes of our men and local peasants alike. There, in solitude, they spent weeks, months, learning and perfecting their skills."

"And how many initiates are there?" Baidun asked.

"Over two hundred at this point."

"And what is the percentage of failures?" Shamil enquired.

"About one in ten," Nishwari answered casually.

"And where did you reassign those who failed?"

"There were no reassignments. Those who learn this art learn mastery over fire. Failing means losing control of the fire you are trying to wield. This tends to be fatal. Not a single initiate that failed survived."

Some of the attendants began whispering among themselves upon hearing this revelation. The atmosphere in the room was getting colder and colder with Nishwari's every answer.

"So you chose to go and create your own version of the Mamluks within the Liwa, not only unaccountable to any structure within the group aside from you personally but unknown to all but a few?" Nayaub commented. "To be honest, what I have heard today does not present you in a good light as the leader of the organisation, Abdulaziz."

Everybody there had heard of the Mamluks before, one way or another, for they were a major part of the social and military history of the pre-modern Middle East. Slaves trained in the craft of military combat from a young age, they became a special warrior class obedient only to the rulers of Arabic states and local emirs. Their superiority over regular troops in the military field had a tendency to turn them into major players, the kingmakers deciding the policies and futures of Arabic states.

Sayid silently admitted that it was indeed a frightening thought that a group of fighters capable of using fire kindled through a snap of a finger could have such power. After all, in a world where might gave access to control, it was only a matter of time before they rose above the rest of the organisation.

"I do not think your comparison to the Mamluks is an appropriate one, Amir Nayaub," the mullah said. "And is this not why I have revealed them to you first? Because the time for secrecy is over, for no enemy can sabotage this programme anymore. The practitioners can now be properly integrated into the structures of the Liwa alongside any regular unit."

"Abdulaziz," Awal said, after sitting in silence for some time. "Do you have that book with you? I, and no doubt everybody else gathered here, would like to have a look at it."

"Unfortunately, it's not with me at the moment. I currently keep it at an undisclosed location in order to ensure it is safely preserved," Mullah Nishwari said. "But I assure you that all of you will get a chance to scroll through its pages when the right time comes."

"Very well, you've talked about the training your selected men have done in these 'arts', as you have called them. You described your discovery of this treatise. But you haven't said a word about the story behind this book," Awal said. "After all, there has to be a story behind a text that teaches such extraordinary things. And I suggest you try making it as detailed as possible."

"Naturally, you all have the right to know. But first tell me one thing. Have any one of you ever heard the name Abdal Qadir ibn Hatim al-Karwaini?" The mullah's gaze slowly travelled from one man to another and found only looks of concern and curiosity. "I thought so," he said. "He was a personal friend of Abu Yusuf al-Kindi, one of the greatest thinkers and scholars in the history of the Islamic world. Karwaini was an explorer, geographer, cartographer, and what is nowadays called an ethnographer, who travelled across the length and breadth of the Abbasid Caliphate in the first half of the ninth century. The first part of the treatise is an account of his exploration of remote areas of north-eastern Iran, where he met and befriended a secluded society of Persian magi, who knew the secrets of summoning and controlling fire the same way you saw today. Karwaini stayed with the magi for years and too managed to master these skills, the only outsider who had ever done so before, and the last one prior to now. The second part of the treatise details the techniques and methods he learned as he studied this power alongside the magi.

"This is the only written account that describes the study of this power, for the magi themselves handed down the secret through an oral tradition. Although the magi had their ignorant superstitious beliefs regarding the origins of this power, Karwaini speculated that they had learned it from the jinn. So he gave this mysterious craft a name: the Jinn Arts."

"Haram! Haram!" sounded the raspy groan of Khaleed Awal as the old sheikh stood up, drawing the room's attention. "You thought that introducing the Liwa to the sorcery of fire-worshipping pagans is a good idea? What has clouded your senses, Abdulaziz?! Shame on you!"

Another round of whispers spread among the leaders of the group. All of them were united by one theme: what seemed godly and what seemed sinful.

"Do you assume I did not think about this before I made the decision?" the mullah said in defence. "And I have to disagree with you, Khaleed. Sorcery is a superstition just like the false gods of those fire-worshippers. We all know that. But these arts are different; they are akin to a hidden skill."

"A skill learnt and adapted from polytheists!" Awal continued to rage.

"Have we never made use of the inventions made by our enemies? After all, Khaleed, you use the internet to transmit your preaching, and think how many people we recruited using this medium. But wouldn't a man who lived a thousand years ago consider the internet a form of sorcery, had he been introduced to it?"

The whispers around the two arguing scholars did not stop.

"You are trying to compare the incomparable! At no point have I ever gone against the natural order!" Awal declared as if he was giving an oath.

"And how can I go against the natural order? I am a mere mortal, in no way different from any other mortal in the eyes of Allah. I do not have the abilities to change anything even if I wanted to."

"You said it yourself: that explorer wrote that the fire-worshippers learned these arts from the jinn. Allah created humans out of mud; Allah created the jinn out of smokeless fire. One was never meant to benefit the other, even though many misguided men worshipped jinn as deities in the dark times before the coming of the Prophet."

"But are not the jinn children of Allah just like humans? And just like among humans, there are Muslims and infidels among the jinn. This is what the holy Quran teaches us."

"And after the Day of Judgement, Allah will fill Hell with both humans and jinn that disobeyed him! This is also one of the truths revealed in the Quran. So how many otherwise good men do you see yourself leading into the eternal fires, Abdulaziz?!" Awal was practically spitting in his zeal as he pointed a thin finger at the mullah.

"You are being overdramatic, Khaleed. You are being too categorical, and you have unintentionally taken some things out of context." The mullah maintained a calm tone. "Indeed, men and jinn were not meant to benefit each other. But how does the practice of the Jinn Arts benefit the jinn? After all, everybody who was taught them knows that there is only one God and only in Him can they find refuge. And as for the benefit of humanity... remember that Allah gave King Solomon authority over the jinn for the duration of his life."

"You are not King Solomon!" Awal proclaimed.

"Nor do I claim dominion over the jinn! Behold!" The mullah extended his hand, pointing at one of the glass water jugs standing on the table. "Jinn, bring me this jug!" His tone was as commanding as his stance.

Several moments passed, and yet the jug did not magically rise from the table and flow towards him.

"Do you see, Khaleed? Nothing happened." The mullah lowered his hand; his posture eased up. "For I am a nobody compared to King Solomon. Thousands of jinn built palaces and dug wells for the great king and prophet. I can't make a single one bring me water." He chuckled lightly.

"Still, everything in your plan is wrong. It was wrong from the very beginning. This should not be happening. This is un-Islamic," Awal hissed.

"Why can't you understand, Khaleed? A lot of things have changed since the Prophet united the tribes of Arabia. A lot of things changed since Caliph Umar captured Alexandria, Jerusalem, and Babylon. Nowadays, we have a better understanding of natural phenomena than Ibn Rushd did. Our knowledge of our anatomy is more correct than that of Ibn Sina. Karwaini might have thought that the magi learned these arts from the jinn, but perhaps those magi in their blindness still managed to uncover a hidden talent that Allah blessed men with. After all, all that happens transpires through the will of Allah."

Awal's gaze slid to the table. Seemingly defeated, he sighed deeply and picked up his still-full glass. He then calmly walked towards Nishwari.

"Many years ago, you earned the title of mullah," he said, walking closer. "And it happened for a reason. You are right: things do change." He stopped a few feet away from Nishwari.

The old man raised his glass in an obvious sign of reconciliation...only to swing it and splash its contents in the face of the mullah.

"You, Nishwari, are a deluded soul that wastes his days obsessing over the practices of long-dead fire worshippers instead of reading the Quran!" Awal screeched.

Water was dripping down Nishwari's face and beard like tears. The mullah's face twisted into a grimace of anger. Enraged, he swooped and grabbed his own glass from the table.

"And you, Awal, are a senile old fool who is trying to issue fatwas instead of playing with his grandchildren!" Nishwari hissed in return and mirrored the sheikh's move by splashing water in Awal's face.

Shocked by this scene, warlords and officials began jumping up from their places at the table.

"Awal is right! Nishwari has lost his mind! His is unfit to lead the Liwa!" one of the men declared.

"You are wrong! Nothing he said contradicts the principles of the Liwa!" another shouted back.

Chaos descended as most of the leaders quickly chose sides and began to argue amongst themselves.

And Sayid, along with a few others, continued to sit in the middle of the emerging bedlam, unsure what to make of the heated polemic between the two elders. The scene around him was beginning to resemble a hectic bazaar where the warlords were the merchants and buyers haggling for the price and the main commodity was death. All that was needed was for one of the quarrellers to get hotheaded enough to draw a gun and this would become a bloodbath.

"Enough!" Jalil al-Quwaiti's wrathful voice declared as he, one of the undecided, bolted up.

The room fell quiet.

"Look at yourselves!" Jalil spoke, teeth bared, fingers clenched. "Who gains from this ludicrous bickering among us? Heretics of all varieties? Crusaders? Zionists?"

He kept turning left and right as though he was suffering from anxiety, but the wild expression on his face displayed something else.

"I will tell you one thing for sure. We will contribute nothing to our cause if there is a civil war within the ranks of Liwa al-Qadisiyyah."

Ironically, it was Jalil, the most untamed commander of the group, who was making the most sense in this situation.

"We cannot unmake what has already been made. So I suggest a temporary compromise. The practitioners of these...Jinn Arts... will take part in the upcoming offensive, as was part of Nishwari's plan. However, afterwards, the Shura will be gathered to decide how well the Jinn Arts fit with Islamic teachings. If necessary, scholars from outside the Liwa can also be brought in to take part in the debate."

Everybody in the room remained silent.

Jalil suddenly grinned. "We've already had one demonstration today. Now I am going to entertain you with another one!" he said as he whipped out an army knife from his belt.

The blade danced in his hand, swirling around as the warlord passed it from one hand into another, treating it as casually as if it was a pen or a toothpick, showing why he was known as a master of cold weapons. He suddenly brought his hand down, stabbing the knife into the table.

"And I swear that if one of you starts arguing about this topic again now, I will slit his throat with this knife right in this very room. Does anybody doubt my words?!"

It felt like death itself was glaring at the assembled men through Jalil's eyes.

The warlords remained silent.

"Mullah Nishwari! Sheikh Awal!" Jalil looked at the two men. "Do we have an agreement?"

"I accept," Nishwari said, letting out a deep breath.

Awal lowered his gaze. "So do I."

The topic was closed—for the time being. Where arguments had achieved no compromise, threats had imposed one.

Chapter Thirteen

Neil continued to pace in circles inside his hotel room. In his current state, he was a boiling cauldron with anxiety as its contents, simmering to the point when the bubbly foam begins to drip beyond the edge.

Every now and then, he would throw a quick glance at his phone resting on the table, expecting a call from his contacts in Baghdad, the local authorities, the embassy—whoever.

His thoughts kept returning to Jake. The cameraman had been abducted, one of seven foreigners to go missing in the aftermath of the attack on the refugee camp. The kidnappers were yet to make their motives known and it was hard to guess what they would demand in exchange for the prisoners' release.

As often tended to happen in situations such as this, the worst-case scenario kept running through his head. He was starting to think that never again would Jake shoot another scene for Neil's documentary; never again would he question Neil's fixation on those ancient artefacts.

So many things could go wrong. The kidnappers' demands might not get fully met and the prisoners would pay with their lives. A rescue mission could succeed in locating them, yet the attempt to break them free could end with the prisoners meeting their doom. Many events in recent years served as tragic illustrations of such scenarios.

And somewhere deep inside, Neil blamed himself for all of this. If only he had stuck to his original plan, instead of doing all those interviews about a topic that had only a loose connection to the theme of the damned documentary, they would have done their filming at the refugee camp a couple of days prior. The whole ordeal would have been avoided.

Neil paced and paced and paced. An image of a man appeared before his eyes. The man was not Jake. His hair was also raven-black, but his complexion was darker, olive toned. The man stood silently as he looked back at Neil, then disappeared, as mysterious and otherworldly as a phantom.

And then Neil felt even worse.

"Damn it, Hector," he muttered, and gave a melancholic sigh. "You were always the type to arrive without warning."

But there was nobody in the room to respond.

It was unavoidable that memories of Hector would cross Neil's mind at a moment like this. Jake was a cameraman; Hector had been too. Jake had worked with Neil on his recent projects; Hector had worked with him when it all began. Jake got abducted recently; Hector was abducted years ago.

But unlike Jake, who, whilst rebellious at times, still chose to follow rather than lead, Hector had been full of ambition. After years of working together, he and Neil had parted ways when Hector went on to work on his own series. That project eventually brought him to Guatemala, where he had the misfortune of crossing one of the country's powerful drug cartels. From what Neil had heard, Hector was abducted in broad daylight whilst filming in one of the country's impoverished towns. No gang came out to demand a ransom for his release. He was never found, neither dead nor alive, once again proving a grim truth: if a cartel wanted somebody to disappear, they would do it so skilfully that a strand of hair in a sinkhole would be easier to find.

The metallic voice of a key turning in a lock screeched in the corridor. And before any more phantoms from the past had a chance to emerge before his eyes, Neil realised that it was the door to Jake's room. His pacing stopped, and he listened to the sounds coming from outside.

Hope was the biggest stimulant and, for a brief second, Neil's spirits were lifted—Jake must have got free and somehow found his way to the hotel. But his euphoria was short-lived; he knew how unrealistic that scenario was.

There was something suspicious about this situation. Whoever was making these sounds, it couldn't be the housekeeping staff; their visits were scheduled for mornings, not late evenings.

And whoever entered the room closed the door behind them very carefully, as if they sought to remain unnoticed. Just like a sensational claim, this required further investigation.

Before going, Neil took a certain item out of his bag, one he hoped he would not need to use in whatever situation he was about to step into: the gun.

Carefully, Neil slid into the hallway, holding the gun behind his back. He had not heard the click of the door locking again—it would still be open. Trying not to lose a single second, he turned the knob and swung the door open. The light in the room had already been turned on, so Neil saw the intruder straight away. The trespasser stood in the middle of the room, surprised by his sudden company.

"You?" Neil hissed out upon recognising the familiar features of Nouri Samir. "What are you doing here?!"

"Calm down, Mister Feaver."

"And how did you obtain the keys to this room?"

"A lot of things are for sale in this country these days," Nouri said, his voice shaded by sadness.

Neil did not require further elaboration. It was as clear as day: a member of staff at the reception had given him a copy of the keys in exchange for a bribe.

Neil stepped into the room and pointed the gun at the guard, finger on the trigger. He had front-row experience of Nouri's fighting skills and prowess; he could not afford to be careless.

"I don't think that's appropriate, Mister Feaver," Nouri said with a slight hint of snide amusement.

"You haven't answered my question." Neil tried to speak just as calmly. "Why are you in this room?"

"I am planning to go and search for Mister Parvis. But I need to collect something before I do." Nouri said it straight, like it was the natural answer.

"What are you talking about? How are you planning to search for him? We don't even know where that gang has taken him. He could be held inside some abandoned warehouse in Karbala or in a bush of reeds on some islet in the middle of the Hammar Marshes."

"I have my ways."

"And what are they?"

"I don't think you would agree with this method if I told you about it."

"Speak. I'm curious."

"I will rely on my psychic powers," Nouri said bluntly.

"What?"

Neil needed a moment to process the words he'd just heard. He stood there, staring at the guard like at some unnatural absurdity.

Nouri sighed. "This is why I didn't want to get you involved."

"You have psychic powers?" Neil mumbled, gun still in hand.

"Yes, I was born with them," Nouri said, like it was an everyday occurrence. "Even when I was still a small child, I was able to catch visions of events that were transpiring many miles away. I could guess the most secret parts of a person's biography. My psychic abilities are not particularly strong, but they can help me find Mister Parvis."

"You...can...do that?" Neil asked. This whole thing was downright strange, and he had no idea what to make of any of it.

"You might have heard stories of investigators enlisting the assistance of mediums in order to find leads and solve crimes," Nouri said.

Neil had heard such stories before, though he had always doubted the effectiveness—and even the authenticity—of these methods.

"So can you tell where they've taken him?" Neil asked as a ray of hope shone through the fog of troubles in his mind. He knew it was silly to rely on something like this, but he was desperate enough to work with whatever option was on the table.

"I might, but I will need to get my hands on one of his possessions in order to catch a trace of his life force," Nouri said. "The more intimate it is, the more personal value it has to him, the better."

"I'm sure this can be done." He finally lowered the gun.

No longer at risk of being shot, Nouri calmly stepped towards the wall, giving Neil more room to manoeuvre.

Neil immediately darted towards the luggage bag that Jake kept under the table. It took him a minute or so of rummaging through its contents—clothes, tea bags, a tube of toothpaste, aftershave—to find what he was looking for: a comic book that seemed in such good condition that it might as well have just come off the shelf. Nouri looked at the vividly illustrated cover upon which the fictional hero of Urban Ronin was in the process of delivering justice to some thug with a kung-fu kick.

"Jake's favourite graphic novel," Neil said. "That's probably the thing with the highest personal value that I'd be able to find here." After all, the cameraman had no family; hence, there were no cherished photos of a wife and children for him to keep.

"It should be fine."

Nouri took the comic and sat down in the nearby chair. He held it in his hands for a couple of moments, fingers gliding up and down the smooth cover like he was patting a house pet. Then his whole body froze, and only an empty gaze looked back at the stunned reporter.

***

Alice's whole body rocked as the vehicle abruptly came to a halt. Every moment of this journey had been filled with immense dread; several times she'd thought her heart came close to stopping. She had no idea where she was, or what type of vehicle she was in. The black blindfold hid the world away from view. A doctor by profession, she'd been treating another patient at one of the refugee camp's clinics when *they* arrived and dragged her away with them.

She heard familiar voices. There were more people held in the same vehicle, their hands no doubt bound by ropes, just like hers. The sound of the door opening came from behind her. If the reverberations on the floor were any hint, somebody had jumped into the vehicle. A rough hand yanked her up by the shoulder and pushed her towards the exit. Another person pulled her from the vehicle onto the ground. The surface underneath her shoes felt very soft; it had to be sand.

She stood there waiting as the others were taken out. It had been hot inside their transport, but only now did she understand how scorching the weather truly was.

Then somebody came up to untie the blindfold. The sharp brightness of the daylight overwhelmed her sight, and she shut her eyes tight, needing a couple of moments to adjust. Gradually, she opened her eyes, and saw they were in the desert; no road and not a single hut in sight. A trio of acacia trees stood a few metres in front of her. A blanket had been laid underneath one of them with an armed guard standing nearby.

"Go!" said one of the bandits that had got out of the vehicle, pointing at the blanket.

She looked back. There were six people with her. Alice immediately recognised five of them; they were aid workers at the same refugee camp, all wearing the same blue shirts. Mark, Nate, and Leah—Shawn and Caden, too, had got into this mess. The other one was a member of a film crew that she had seen on the camp's premises.

The captives were marched towards the shade of the acacia tree and sat down on the blanket.

"Get the headwear," the apparent commander of the small group of brigands told one of his subordinates. "The last thing we need is one of them getting heat stroke."

The militant obliged and went back to the gang's off-road truck. He soon came back with a collection of Arabic headdresses that he personally put on the prisoners.

They had to spend quite some time under the tree. Anxiety made the atmosphere feel heavy. The heat made things only worse. Luckily, their captors did serve them water on one occasion. Time was passing slowly; what felt like hours might have just been a span of twenty minutes.

"Damned idiots," said one of the militants, leaning against another acacia. "Couldn't they find a better rendezvous point?"

The commander said nothing and only looked at his watch. The comment made Alice wonder: who were these others that the gang was set to meet?

The group stayed at the site for some more time, until one of the militants pointed towards the horizon.

"It has to be them."

There, in the distance, five dark spots could be seen approaching at speed. As they got closer and closer, their shapes became more distinguishable. At first, they appeared to be horsemen. Then it became obvious that they were riding camels, which grunted as the riders made them halt.

Initially, Alice thought the men were Bedouin, but a closer look made her question this assumption. Four of them bore only some remote resemblance to the desert nomads when it came to their clothing. They wore long shrouds that fell to knee level. Black and crimson patterns on the fabric of their garments formed motifs that reminded her of the suit of diamonds in a pack of cards. The way the shrouds clung to their bodies hinted that the layer of clothing underneath was made out of a more solid material, likely metal: armour of some type. They wore high caps on their heads somewhat reminiscent of turbans.

The man at the head of this group was definitely not a Bedouin. He wore a tunic and trousers of a white so pure that it appeared that even the sand of the desert, which had a habit of getting practically everywhere, was unable to taint the fabric. A long yellow-gold cloak sprouted behind his back, matching his gloves and boots in colour. A copper helmet crowned his head; the most striking part about it was the mask. Though it hid the features of its wearer, the mask served as a grotesque imitation of a face, having a mouth and nose. Locks of long grey hair resting on the rider's shoulders looked like they were growing from the helmet itself.

"Greetings," the man said, his dry voice making its way through the helmet.

"It's great to see you again, sir," the militia's leader said humbly as he stepped forward. "We were starting to fear you would not be coming."

The Masked Man brought his camel closer to the party assembled under the acacia trees; his companions followed him. He then jumped down and took a few steps forward. This newcomer had a sinister aura to him; Alice felt like a gust of artic wind had suddenly hit her right in the middle of this scorching desert.

"I presume that you have fulfilled your end of the bargain," the Masked Man addressed the top militant.

"Yes, of course, sir. Seven foreigners; not one more, not one less," the commander responded with an anxious nod, like he was reciting a line he'd memorised.

"And none of them sustained any harm under your watch?" the Masked Man asked. Through the eyeholes of his mask, he studied every captive, paying special attention to the two women. He then turned to the brigand.

"Of course not," the militant said defensively. "I would rather lose my right hand than let anything bad happen to them. I made it clear to everybody."

Alice had no doubt that the rough militant had taken part in various atrocities—looting, torture, extrajudicial killings. Yet even he found his employer intimidating.

"Then you can get your reward," the Masked Man said and turned to one of his mounted companions.

The rider unfastened something from behind him and got off his steed with a briefcase in hand. Without uttering a single word, he opened the case, showing its contents to the commander.

"It is exactly what we've agreed on," the Masked Man said.

"Yes," the brigand mumbled, nodding.

The briefcase was then closed and handed to him.

"The captives will be under our watch as of this moment," his mysterious employer said. "You may depart."

"Of course, sir, thank you," the militant said, clinging to the briefcase like a child to their favourite toy. He quickly glanced at his subordinates before looking back at the man. "And if you need some task done in the future, you know we look forward to hearing from you."

He retreated back towards the militia's vehicle, and the rest of the gang followed. But the fates of Alice and her comrades in misfortune were still in the hands of captors—different, more mysterious ones.

***

Nouri only needed to blink in order to startle Neil, who had watched the guard sit in this peculiar coma-like condition for over an hour.

"I've done it," Nouri whispered. "I managed to establish a connection with Jake's life force."

"You did?"

"Yes, and I can tell that he's alive."

"Is he alright?"

"This is not something that I can find out through this method."

"So...what? Can you pinpoint his location on a map?" Neil asked.

"It doesn't work like that. Compare a life force to a scent," Nouri began to explain after a pause of several moments. "You pick up a scent when the wind blows in your direction, and you follow it. The wind turns direction and you lose it. The wind starts blowing your way again and you are back on track. Sometimes, the connection will start fading, so it will need to be...rejuvenated. But I guarantee you; I will be able to find him." He stood up. "I will need this in the search." He raised his hand and clutched the comic in his fist.

"Then make use of it if you need to," Neil said.

They both fell into a silence that Neil found somewhat awkward...in other words, little different from any of their discussions that day.

"So do we get the authorities involved?" Neil broke the brief silence. "Or, I don't know...the Navy Seals?"

"No," was Nouri's answer, as solid as a wall. "Any outside assistance will not only be counterproductive, but could jeopardise the mission. I'll do it myself. Moreover, there's no real practice of relying on psychics in this land."

He looked at his employer with piercing eyes. "I would also request that you give an advance on my salary. I will need it to rent out a horse or camel. There is a strong chance I will need to venture into the desert."

Neil sighed as he rubbed his chin, thinking deep. Saying that all of this seemed crazy was an understatement; it *was* crazy.

"Or there might be another option," Neil said.

CHAPTER FOURTEEN

Another week passed before Elliott was finally able to take part in a geophysical survey. Judging by its appearance, the mechanism he had been entrusted with was a relative of the lawnmower. They were at a plot of land about a mile away from the main excavation site, and there was certainly no grass to mow here; instead, the four-wheeled apparatus glided over dust and dry clay. Perhaps, many years ago, some craftsman had maintained a yard right at the same spot. Perhaps it was not a yard but a garden; maybe something else. Whatever it was, its remnants had been hidden under several layers of earth, and it was the purpose of the ground-penetrating radar installed in Elliott's machine to uncover the secrets hidden in the crust.

The supervisor walking beside Elliott and monitoring his performance sighed as he complained about the arid day. Once the designated area was ploughed through, the supervisor called it a day.

Dinner at the canteen gazebo was simple: rice with chicken, a staple during these two months of excavations. The entrance into the gazebo remained open, and from his place at the table, Elliott was able to absorb the dusk when the sun faded beyond the horizon.

Eventually, the camp retired for the night and Elliott did as well. He was able to get a bit of shuteye, but was soon awoken by a burst of turbulence that suddenly rocked his tent.

"Hey, dude!" He heard the familiar voice hiss through the cotton walls.

"I'm up! I'm up!" Elliott hissed, loud enough for the miscreant outside to hear him.

The quake ceased immediately. Moments later, Elliott was out of the tent and facing a smiling Joe.

"Hey, do you want some of that authentic Middle Eastern experience again?" Joe asked.

"Where? Right here in the great outdoors?"

"No, same place as last time."

"You're probably forgetting us getting busted when we did that last week," Elliott remarked.

"True, but hear this out. Mergham got word of that doomed party of ours. We had a brief talk about it and he said that he doesn't really mind us smoking shisha in the operations tent as long as we're careful and don't accidentally burn or misplace anything," Joe said. "Turns out he's quite a chill guy."

"Then, hell, what are we waiting for?" Elliott announced in celebration.

But first they needed to stop over at Joe's tent.

"Are Mitch and Frank going to join us?" Elliott asked as Joe got the hookah out along with the supplies.

"No. Not this time, they said." Joe led the way to the gazebo.

"Let me guess, they're afraid of Lauren?"

"It's possible."

"Wouldn't be surprised if she turns up to ruin the party again," Elliott muttered. "That would actually be her style."

Bad memories had a habit of coming back. He remembered that time when Lauren, much smaller but just as red-haired, nicked and hid the bubble-making kit he and another cousin had been playing with, no doubt for no other reason than some sort of sadistic pleasure. Now that he thought of it, Elliott realised he'd never managed to get that toy back.

Once they were inside the operations tent, Joe got straight to his task. Like an alchemist, he put the components in place and operated the apparatus by the dull light of the oil lamps surrounding them.

He put the mouthpiece to his lips and inhaled the aromatic vapour, then breathed out a stream of smoke like a dragon. He passed it to Elliott, who had his turn. They swapped it back and forth as they talked about life.

"So, there's this guy I know," Joe said, shaking the hose lightly. "He and his girlfriend had been together for a long time—from high school if I'm not mistaken. Yet it was quite a toxic relationship. He used to go out in public, in this, like, urban style. You know, ripped jeans and stuff like that. He liked his video games. She wanted him to change, become more...I don't know...formal, I guess. Not sure why she wanted to convert a bad boy into one of these more standard types instead of hooking up with one in the first place, but choices are choices and feelings are feelings. Anyway, he no doubt loved her but he couldn't live with this nagging. Eventually, he changed. Guess how?"

"How?" Elliott asked, having a smoke.

"He dumped her. Got his own motorhome and went out to live on the road, living off casual jobs he would find across the country. And you know what? I've talked to him. He's actually happy that way. If my information is up to date, he's somewhere in Snowdonia at the moment. See, everybody finds his own way eventually, even if it's not one you expected."

They continued their hookah smoking session. For a few moments, they sat amidst absolute serenity, which was soon interrupted by the sound of dry earth crunching underneath somebody's feet.

A shadow fell on the tent's side a few feet away from where they were sitting. They both noticed it, looking in its direction. Instinct said it was Lauren, but Elliott quickly dismissed that thought—whoever was casting the shadow was noticeably bulkier.

"I think it's one of the supervisors," Elliott said. "Probably going for a leak."

"I guess he didn't get the memo that Mergham gave us permission," Joe said. "Communication between the guys running this whole thing is actually rather poor."

Joe stepped closer to the screen of the tent. "Everything's fine here, man! We've got permits!" he declared, not forgetting to add some humour.

Then, in a swift move, a monstrous force ripped through the cotton wall. A hideous hairy muzzle pushed through the enormous tear with a vicious screech. Joe didn't even have the chance to jump back before the thing grabbed him by the neck with its strong jaws, pulling him out of the tent like a fox snatching a chicken from a coop. With his muscles frozen in shock, Elliott heard a short scream.

His thoughts as scrambled as eggs at breakfast, Elliott grabbed the hookah by its bowl and ran. He heard another scream as he jumped through the tear, all risks damned. He saw Joe, sprawled motionless on the ground, being mauled by the beast that had taken him. Elliott now had a better view of the creature. Clearly canine in nature, the beast had short grey fur that grew longer around its neck, ornamented by dark spots. Its pointy ears were facing up as it feasted on its victim.

With a bestial scream of his own, Elliott swung the hookah and hit the creature across the back with all his strength. The thing jumped back in pain, turning a blood-drenched muzzle to Elliott as it hissed at him. It was a hyena—a giant one, probably just slightly smaller than he was. Just as desperate as the moment before, Elliott used the hookah as a club, striking the animal right in the muzzle before it had the time to respond. He followed with a strike to the nose, which made the hyena squeal and run off.

Elliott ran to kneel beside his friend, but it became obvious that there was nothing he could do. Joe lay there, eyes empty. His mouth was open, frozen in the middle of his last scream. The wounds were horrifying. His throat had become a disfigured piece of meat, torn open by the creature's fangs. Blood had spilled on his green T-shirt and the ground below, painting them brown. Bite marks and claw trails marred his chest and shoulders.

Then Elliott realised that he was having trouble breathing himself. He gasped for air, taking in long gulps, still struggling to believe that this had just happened.

Then he heard screams. Some type of commotion was breaking out in the campsite. Clenching the hookah tightly, Elliott stood up. Further away, he saw a camper get out of his tent.

"What the hell is going on here?!" the awoken archaeologist asked loudly.

And that was all from him; another hyena skilfully pounced from behind a nearby tent, bringing the camper to the ground before biting into his neck.

Looking left and right, Elliott saw at least two more four-pawed shadows running between the tents. The campers were facing a pack out for their nocturnal hunt. Now he could hear it all, all the dread-filled screaming and the ripping of fabric. But the most terrifying segment of this racket took the form of chuckling. Low-pitched and never-ending, it assaulted the ears from every direction. He had no idea how many predators had come along, but one thing was certain: just standing there made him an easy target.

A tent was definitely no barrier for the predators, so he ran towards what he thought was the safest place: the four-by-fours. With luck, somebody with the keys would be there.

His survival instinct overwhelmed him. As he ran, he beheld several of the campers get pulled down, one after the other, by the monstrous scavengers. He wanted to help, but his fleeing legs had a mind of their own.

But it appeared that whatever benevolent spirit roamed this land was watching over him for a brief while, allowing him to get outside the ring of the camp. Elliott could see, not far away, the front lights of one of the vehicles blazing, a symbol of safe haven. Somebody had already made it there. He just needed to cross the short distance that separated them. But then he heard a revolting chuckle behind his back. Turning, he saw a hyena emerge from amidst the tents. He locked eyes with the beast as it stealthily moved towards him, having chosen him as its game. Elliott was in the open; turning his back on this thing could become a fatal mistake. He staggered backwards, but for every step he made, the hyena made at least one of its own.

The hyena crouched low, ready to pounce. The hookah had already become Elliott's weapon. The glass base touched the ground; he thudded it several times against the earthen crust like a baseball bat.

"You want me, you mangy piece of shit?!" he shouted, frantic enough to believe it could understand him.

"Run towards the car, boy! You're covered!" He heard Akhmad's accented voice.

He took the risk, perhaps foolishly, and glanced back. Akhmad now stood in front of the beckoning four-by-four with a gun in his hand; the lack of a clear shot was likely the only thing preventing the guide from pulling the trigger. Elliott turned back towards the monster, who growled at him in return.

But the hyena had a surprise in store for him. Instead of jumping, it used its front paws to push up...and stand up on its hind legs. Then it took a couple more steps towards him, like a human but more heavily.

"What the hell..." Elliott whispered.

The sight of a bipedal hyena was the last straw. He turned and ran, but, overwhelmed, his legs gave way. He fell, pain bursting in his knees and elbows as he collided with the ground.

The hyena chuckled again, as if his clumsiness amused it.

Blinking the dust specks out of his eyes, Elliott raised his face from the ground.

"*Ya Allah!*" Akhmad exclaimed, the gun shaking in his hand as he beheld the monstrous wonder of nature.

Elliott turned back to the monster. The furry abomination stood there, its feral eyes locked on him.

Akhmad shook off his earlier astonishment and stood poised to plant some lead in the thing before him. But he'd underestimated the threat. The most dangerous nocturnal predators know how to use the dark to their best advantage. They lurk in the shadows, and upon laying eyes on their prey, they follow it stealthily, careful to avoid making the slightest noise until the best chance to strike arrives.

Another hyena jumped on top of the four-by-four from behind and pounced on Akhmad. The beast's moves were swift; everything transpired in a few fleeting moments. Akhmad screamed out as the creature's claws dug into his back and pinned him to the ground. A gunshot echoed, but in the dark, it was hard to tell what path the bullet took. Still, one thing was clear: the bipedal hyena was left unscratched.

Unscratched, but infuriated. It dashed past Elliott, towards the person who posed the bigger risk to it.

Akhmad's blood-curdling scream pierced Elliott's ears as painfully as a needle when the two monstrosities began to rip him into pieces.

Acting on instinct, Elliott jumped to his feet and ran, away from both the camp and the vehicles. He did not know what the vast drylands had in store for him, but he had a chance out there, while only death and its spotted messengers remained in the campsite.

He ran into the night, one of those famed Arabian nights, a night arid and merciless, that mystical night where ancient marvels came to life alongside unspeakable nightmares.

CHAPTER FIFTEEN

Jake could not recall a time when he'd felt greater discomfort. All seven prisoners, their hands still bound, walked in a chain, enclosed on all sides by a new set of captors. Sand had got inside his shoes, irritating the soles and sides of his feet. The harsh environment left him drenched in sweat; his shirt stuck to his body. But worst of all was the feeling of uncertainty. Everything tended to be simpler with gangs—they wanted ransom in exchange for release. What these people sought was a complete mystery. They did not seem like talkative types; ever since their strange leader gave them the order to march, none of these men had said a word to their prisoners.

Jake still could not properly recall how he'd got into this predicament. One moment he was running through the chaotic refugee camp, then there was a blow that felt like it came from nowhere, a painful strike to the top of his head...

One of the prisoners started to slow, exhausted by the journey. The man riding to his left poked him with the haft of the halberd he was armed with, urging him on. Fortunately for the prisoners, their captors abstained from using whips.

The convoy kept moving for hours through this domain of sand, dunes, and thorn bushes. After some time, distant shapes, as crimson as a blood-soaked dress, manifested in the distance. At first, Jake thought it was a mere mirage. Yet this vision did not melt away as he drew nearer. On the contrary, the shapes only grew bigger, and soon took the form of tents—an encampment that stood hidden amidst the dunes of this remote place.

Soon enough, they crossed the camp's boundary. The encampment was not a large one, consisting of only a dozen or so tents, though each was quite large in size.

A small group of people had already gathered to meet them. Most of them were dressed the same as the four riders. One looked a bit different; though his outfit bore the same ornamentation, it looked like a proper robe rather than a shroud. A hood appeared to be his headdress.

The Masked Man barked out an order to that man, that... Hooded Host. Jake, who lacked fluency in Arabic, had no idea what he said. With that, the Masked Man got off his steed, and handed the captives over to the waiting group. The Hooded Host led the way to one of the tents that stood in the middle of the camp. Nearby, a banner fluttered in the dry desert wind. As he passed it by, Jake looked up at the standard. The fabric was white, like the Masked Man's tunic. It depicted something long and thin that curved near its tip. Due to the strange, archaic style, it was hard to tell what it was supposed to be. The stem of some plant was Jake's first guess, or maybe a cane.

But he did not have a chance to study the banner in detail, even though he was pushed into the tent last. It did not look like a camping tent, having a bigger resemblance to the pavilions used by ancient armies, with a very simple interior, having only a couple of rugs sprawled on the floor.

The captives were made to sit. The Hooded Host soon came in with a tray bearing seven glasses of water. He put it on the ground and personally went from prisoner to prisoner, letting each of them empty a glass, then left again.

The seven captives sat, anxious but quiet as they listened to the men discuss something outside for a minute or so before all talking ceased.

"Who the hell are these freaks?" Jake finally broke the silence. "And what the hell were they talking about? What do they want from us?"

"I don't know," said the woman that had been seated beside him.

Jake turned his head to look at her. The woman's name was Alice, if he remembered correctly; she was one of the aid workers he and Neil had met at the refugee camp. Blonde and slender and in her mid-thirties, she'd have been his type if, of course, they all had not been in this distressing predicament.

"And I have no idea what they were talking about," she continued, staring at the light coming into the tent through the semi-open flap. "The language they use to communicate with each other…that's not Arabic."

"It's not?" Jake asked.

"No, it's not," said another captive.

"It sounds like a language related to Arabic, but I have no clue what it is," Alice elaborated.

Jake sighed and closed his eyes, wishing that all of this was just a bizarre dream.

***

It was quite a bland picture: a dirt road cutting the sandy realm of the desert in two. It ran on and on, the only line that connected the green core of the country with the rare desert towns and villages that stood along its way.

This portion of the road was lifeless. It was empty of any other vehicles, and no animal crossed the track in front of them. Not a single house stood by either side; no tent had been pitched in its vicinity.

"Are you sure you want to go along with this?" Nouri asked, seated next to Neil. His left hand rested on the graphic novel that lay on his lap.

"Yes," Neil responded, hands on the steering wheel and eyes on the road. "This whole idea might be insane, and I might live to regret it…" He thought about Jake; about the times the cameraman was there by his side as shells landed mere metres away from them; about all the things Jake had told him, both useful advice and ridiculous claims. "…but what I'm really afraid of is living to see a moment when I regret sitting this one out."

"You are a valiant person, Mister Feaver. I commend you for this."

Neil remained quiet. He had left the driver, Furqan, at the hotel in Karbala; he could not gamble the well-being of another member of his crew on this frantic affair, so he had instructed the driver to wait for their return.

"You can turn left whenever you're ready," Nouri told him.

"Got it," Neil replied. "You know, I specifically requested an off-road vehicle. Thought we might have to drive through the desert at some point. But I never thought it would happen like this." He smiled sadly.

All of this was insane. The idea that two civilians would go off to save hostages from an armed militia, while relying on some enigmatic psychic sense of a recent employee he had recruited off the street... But was insanity not his thing? After all, he'd chosen a lifetime of stints in war zones as a career.

"Let's see what this baby can do," Neil said, and roughly turned the steering wheel left.

The jeep changed course, and in a matter of moments, the bumpy road gave way to a sea of sand. The vehicle endured and kept on towards the horizon. The desert awaited them, vast and mysterious.

***

Alice had begun to see the light that had broken through the tent flap as a distant ray of hope. Yet as the hours passed, the light dwindled, and her hope with it. Dusk took over the sky outside, and now only a reddish glimmer was slipping into the tent. The seven hostages had been sitting in silence for quite some time; the situation they were in did not beget any topics for conversation.

They were deep into another hour of silence when the tent flap was pulled aside and the Hooded Host entered, accompanied by a sword-bearing companion. Alice had come to speculate that the men's outfits symbolised their place in this mysterious organisation. The ones in shrouds and turban-like headdresses seemed to be guards and enforcers. The one in the hood had to hold some administrative role.

"All of you get up!" he declared in Arabic, then, to their surprise, repeated it in English.

All seven obeyed his order.

"What do you want?" Nate, another abducted aid worker, asked as he got to his feet.

"You will find out soon enough."

The hooded figure and the guard escorted the prisoners out of the tent. Outside, torches pitched into the sand all around the camp were blazing, reinforcing the feeble illumination of dusk with their own red hues. Over a dozen people were congregated in the centre of the camp. Alice thought she recognised the four riders from earlier. The Masked Man was present as well; he stood there in silence, arms crossed, as though he was a commuter waiting for a bus. Several guards held torches in their hands. Three more men in hoods were part of the gathering.

She noticed Jake gazing towards the side. Curious, she looked in the same direction and saw the Host enter a tent near the camp's hanging banner. He emerged a minute later, holding an object with both hands. Quasi-transparent, it looked like a crystal of some sort, big enough to be used as a blunt weapon if needed.

The Hooded Host walked up to the Masked Man and told him something in the mystery language. The white-clad man then placed his gloved hand on the crystal for a long moment. He said something to the hooded man, who immediately went back towards the tent.

The Masked Man turned and made a loud proclamation to his subordinates. Without delay, six of them went into formation, enclosing the group of captives, like they had done earlier that day.

A pair of guards handed torches over to two hooded men, who began to walk forward as if they were leading the way.

"The time has come," the Masked Man said in English, the gaze through the eyeholes of the helmet as emotionless as his mask. His golden cloak flapped in the air as he turned around and followed the guides.

Ushered by the guards' halberds, the prisoners had no choice but to follow.

***

"I am starting to lose the connection to Jake's life force again," Nouri said for the second time that day. "I will need to meditate again."

"Do what you must," Neil responded, his eyes on the path ahead.

They were in the middle of the desert of the southern part of Anbar Province. Night had descended on the area, plunging it into darkness. Only the headlights and stars allowed Neil to see what was there before them.

An unusual shape appeared in the distance.

"What is that?" Neil said.

He soon recognised it as a man-made structure, a building standing alone, coated in darkness.

"Interesting," Nouri uttered beside him.

"Should we see what it is?" Neil asked.

"Most certainly."

Neil drove up to the building, took out a flashlight and got out of the jeep. Nouri joined him.

Neil scanned the beam of light across the building's façade. The building was relatively small in size, rectangular or possibly square in form. An arch served as its entrance; a similar arch had been opened up in the back wall. The roof was topped with a dome that had partially crumbled over the eons. "Hmm."

Nouri came closer to the building. He had draped a long navy cloak around his shoulders that hung loose behind his back, making his outfit seem even more old-fashioned. Neil followed, letting the flashlight guide the way.

Soon enough, they passed through the arch. Once inside, Neil saw two more arched openings in the side walls, allowing moonlight to enter the structure from all directions. If some paintings had adorned the stone walls centuries before, no traces of them remained, nor a single decayed piece of furniture. The only exception was a large bronze vessel, reaching half of Neil's height, which stood at the heart of the room. It was ancient, displaying signs of corrosion, its whole surface encrusted in a coat of blue and green.

"I think I know what this is," Nouri said. "It's an ancient Zoroastrian fire temple." The place was giving his voice an eerie effect.

"Standing in the middle of nowhere?" Neil commented cynically, rocking the flashlight in his hand.

"It may be the middle of nowhere nowadays, but don't forget about the process of desertification. This fire temple is very old, possibly having stood here for two millennia. It's logical to assume that back then this area was much greener and there might be an entire town buried under the sands."

"I guess you make a good point."

They exited the sanctum. A melancholic howl of desert wind caught their attention. Far in the distance, clouds of sand were beginning to form.

"I think a sandstorm is coming," Nouri said. "It would be better if we stay here for now."

"I will utilise the time to get back in tune with Jake."

"Very well."

The night air sent a shiver running down Neil's spine. He shrugged. "Do you want me to make a fire? I've had a bag of coal in the jeep in case we needed to sleep under the stars during the filming of the documentary."

"No need. We can just stay in the car."

In the distance, the sands kept swirling.

Chapter Sixteen

The march from the camp lasted a couple of hours, but on this occasion, the biggest burden manifested not as insufferable heat but the chill of the night, so cold that it made every muscle in the body shiver.

The voice of one of the hooded men broke the long silence and stopped the convoy. The mysterious figures in front soon parted ways with the rest of the group, allowing Jake a view of the place they had arrived at. The spot had no natural landmarks that would have made it stand out among the vast lifeless landscape: no tree, no thorn bush, no rock formation. Everything that made it stand out had been wrought by human hands. Shallow ditches, wide as a human wrist, ran through the sand like irrigation channels through a garden. They stretched further and further into the distance, forming a shape that Jake could not fully distinguish in the dark. A few torches on long posts stood stuck in the sand at random locations. The first thing the hooded men did was light these torches using the flaming ones they had brought with them. They then pitched their torches into the ground as well.

The Masked Man told his enforcers something in the unfamiliar language as he pointed a gloved hand at a spot within the confines of the contours engraved in the sand. The shroud-wearing guards ushered their captives towards it and roughly pushed them down on the trodden surface. A metallic screech suddenly erupted as the six guards withdrew their swords from the scabbards they wore concealed under the ornamented shrouds.

"What is this? Why did you bring us here?!" another aid worker, Shawn, shouted frantically.

"You will see."

The voice belonged to the Masked Man himself, who was standing some distance away from the group, his back turned to them, as he stared deep into the desert.

Jake watched in fear and suspense as two of the hooded figures went down on their knees. They began to chant, and it became clear that they were praying. The sinister resonance of their words carried through the desert. Jake listened, even though he knew he would not understand a single word. Yet he quickly came to suspect that these incantations were whispered in another, completely different language, one that had no resemblance to Arabic whatsoever.

The three hooded men appeared to be priests of some kind. Whilst two of them kept praying, the third remained silent, standing motionless. After some time, he turned around and slowly stalked towards the prisoners. In the shadows and moonlight, he looked as terrifying as a phantom. Only a couple of steps separated him from the group of captives, and the mere proximity of this figure made them shudder. His eyes, sparkling in the shade of the hood, went from one prisoner to another as if he was studying them.

The priest then said something and pointed at one of the captives, Mark. One of the guards responded immediately, grabbing the man by his hair. He moaned in pain as he was yanked up and pulled aside. The priest stepped up to him and reached into his long robe. When his hand withdrew, he was clutching the hilt of a dagger. Moonlight danced on the blade. And then, with no prayer or explanation, he stuck the dagger into Mark's chest. The captives gasped. Mark groaned, staggering. The guard's grip was the only thing that kept him from tumbling to the ground.

But that was not all. The dark priest withdrew the dagger only to strike Mark again...and again...and again, seven blows to the abdomen. The guard finally let go of Mark, and he fell down. The odious chanting continued as the lifeless body lay on the ground, blood seeping onto the sand.

The priest looked at the captives and barked another order. Another poor prisoner, Caden, stood facing the murderous cultist mere moments later.

"No!" Alice screamed out. "Leave him alone! Why are you doing this?!"

"Such are the requirements of the ritual." The voice of the Masked Man was enough to divert the group's attention from the gruesome event that was about to transpire.

He turned around and, hands behind his back, casually walked towards the group. "For the summoning to be successful, seven sacrifices are required. Not one more, not one less. It was said that all seven need to be dignitaries. But the instructions are millennia old. Back then, it meant representatives of the aristocracy and priesthood. But perceptions change depending on time and place, so a question arises: who qualifies as a dignitary in today's world? And perhaps in this war-torn land, an aid worker is a dignitary of sorts." His blue eyes, as cold as the night, looked back at the captives through the eyeholes of his mask.

Summoning? Jake did not like the sound of that.

But any further questions disappeared the moment the priest swung the dagger and stabbed Caden seven times. The man fell beside the corpse of his colleague.

The cultists wasted no time as they chose their third victim. By that time, Jake began to see the situation for what it was, and the spirit of ultimate hopelessness took over him. As he sat there, the third victim, Shawn, met the same fate as Mark and Caden, succumbing to the seven wounds inflicted by the dagger.

The desert wind suddenly howled in the distance, and sand began to whirl through the air. The strange storm raged around them but did not encroach on the ritual site. It grew thicker and thicker, becoming more akin to a fog.

Then Leah fell to the life-devouring dagger. The row of bodies at the cultist's feet was becoming bigger, and yet that was not the most terrifying element of this deranged ritual. Jake actually began to understand the chants of the praying priests as if he had learnt that mysterious language through some unknown means.

"Mighty daevas!" the first priest chanted in his fervour. "Two and a half millennia ago, the Persian king Xerxes decreed that none should worship you or bring you offerings. But tonight, we go against his order. Accept these sacrifices, mighty daevas, and come to us in all your splendour!"

"Fury and sand! Fury and sand!" The second cultist kept repeating the same line over and over.

The golden cloak of the Masked Man was trembling in the wind whilst its wearer concentrated his attention on the sandstorm that surrounded them.

The dark priest looked at the three remaining captives, trying to decide who the next sacrifice would be. Fatalism rang its bell in Jake's head as a sickening gut sense told him to be ready...

"The older man," the cultist said as he pointed the blood-dripping dagger at Nate.

Nate was dragged towards the priest, who greeted him with a blow of the dagger, followed by another one and then more. Jake was not sure if Nate was still alive by the time the seventh strike descended into his chest.

And then another unsettling feeling overcame Jake, joining the already troubled flux of emotions. He felt like they were being watched. He turned his eyes and looked into the sandstorm rampaging around them. And there, in the sandy mist, he was able to distinguish a figure, similar to that of a human in both build and height. Another figure stood by its side. And there were more of them—at least a dozen. Their arrival had been unnoticed; it appeared like the sandstorm itself brought them to this destination.

"Oh my God," Alice whispered at the sight of the strange newcomers.

"They are here!" the Masked Man declared, turning to his minions.

The other cultists froze in their places; even the priests ceased their chants.

A voice came from within the cloud of sand. "We have heard your call. So we have come."

The sandstorm did not gradually die down as it should have. Instead, it ceased all of a sudden; the specks of sand that had been dancing in the air disappeared without a trace, like snowflakes melted in the sun.

The newcomers now stood before them, and in the moonlight, it was clear none of them were human. Height was probably the only feature they shared with the human race. The beings had pointed muzzles with longish noses, big eyes, and disproportionally large mouths. Their ears resembled those of mules, and their fingers ended with long claws, as did their toes. Muscular tails sprouted from behind their backs. All were dressed only in a simple loincloth of a navy colour.

The congregated creatures were indistinguishable from each other—sans one. So different was he that he seemed a different kind of being entirely. At least this one looked somewhat human...a human that had lain buried in the desert for centuries. Clad in bronze armour from neck to toes, he could have been mistaken for the dried husk of an ancient warrior that some archaeologist had dug out of the sand, a mummified corpse. And yet he stood there, a pair of unnatural yellow lights glowing in his sockets instead of eyes.

"We have noted your zeal. You may stop the ritual," this nightmarish, mummy-like being said, walking towards the humans. "We give you audience."

It spoke slowly, its voice as dry as the desert.

"Are you the chieftain of the tribe of daevas that dwells in this desert?" The Masked Man stepped forth.

"I am," said the creature, this daeva. Only a few paces now separated him from the leader of the mystics.

"And what is your name, daeva?" the Masked Man asked.

"Apaosha."

Just hearing this name made the cultist bend his knee immediately. No matter how much fear the Masked Man struck in the hearts of his prisoners and his mercenaries alike, he himself beheld this Apaosha with dread and awe. True was the old wisdom that said "there is always someone worse".

"You may stand up, mortal," Apaosha said, uncaring about the display of humility. "Now tell me this: who are you mortals and why are you calling out to us?"

"We belong to an ancient society known as Was Peraa," the Masked Man said as he got up. "Our organisation's story began in the distant past in Egypt."

"The name sounds familiar," the daeva uttered. "The desert winds can carry tales and rumours to the most remote places. Now tell me: why have you come to us?"

"We come with an offer of an alliance that will be beneficial to both of us."

"And how does it benefit us?"

"Look around, great Apaosha," the Masked Man said, as he spread his hand and gestured at the desert. "You and your daevas rule this section of the desert. But don't you want to expand your domain?"

Apaosha said nothing.

"Our plans and visions are grand. It will take some time to succeed, for our intentions will require several stages to progress through. But the spoils will be worth it. By joining our forces, we can achieve a lot: vanquish enemies both mortal and exalted."

"You utter words that the daevas want to hear. But do you have the means to make your plans come to be?"

"We have for the first stage."

"And what form do they come in?"

"Behold."

The Masked Man brought his hands forward, and a moment later, a diamond-like shape miraculously appeared in his hands. It was a perfect copy of the crystal Jake had noticed at the encampment. Yet it did not seem solid. It appeared to be ethereal, like some sort of hologram.

Jake had worked with electronics all of his adult life, in one way or another. He seriously doubted that the helmet-wearing mystic had conjured this up with technology...especially after seeming demons summoned through a dark ritual. It could not have been anything other than some sorcery.

"What is this?" Apaosha asked, looking at the projection with curiosity.

"A very rare mineral with magical properties that can only be found in the deserts of Egypt and Sudan," the Masked Man said. "So rare it is that the one currently in our possession is the only known example found in a millennium. The Ancient Egyptians called it the Tear of Set."

"The Tear of Set?"

"An ancient legend says that during one of their battles for dominion over Egypt, the god Horus was able to damage Set's eye. And as Set retreated, the tears streaming from his damaged eye fell on the desert, where they calcified."

The image of the crystal dissolved in the night air.

"Think about it. Set was the god of droughts and deserts, and you daevas are the demons that cause droughts and dwell in deserts."

"The daevas are not the minions of Set, nor have we ever been!" Apaosha declared in irritation. "This is not Egypt! Set never had any authority in these parts!"

Had the demon not been a dry husk, he would have probably spat on the sorcerer. Behind him, some of the daevas snarled in defiance.

"Nor have I ever claimed so!" The Masked Man raised his voice for the first time. "What I am trying to say is that deserts are your element, just as they were Set's."

"Continue," Apaosha said, having regained his emotionless calm.

"This crystal has magical qualities. It is of divine nature and contains traces of a deity's essence. If harnessed properly, it can be used to increase the daevas' power, even if temporarily."

Apaosha's gaze slowly wandered towards his hideous kinsmen, then back to the Masked Man.

"There are more details about all of this that you wish to share with us."

"Much more," the sorcerer said.

"Then this desert is not the best place to discuss complex topics. As the chieftain of the tribe, I would like to invite you and your companions to our abode for further negotiations."

"And we accept your invitation."

"Then prepare to step into our domain," Apaosha said.

"And what about the remaining two captives?" The Masked Man threw a quick look at Jake and Alice. "What should we do with them?"

The cameraman and the medic sat on the sand, still bound, their grip on sanity slipping after the events of the night.

"There is no need for you to claim their lives," Apaosha replied. "The daevas can always make use of such offerings."

The demon raised his clawed hand. Enormous quantities of sand began to swirl around in the air, but this time no invisible barrier kept it away from the ritual site. Jake heard Alice yelp as the sands covered them like a tidal wave.

CHAPTER SEVENTEEN

Elliott could barely move his feet, yet he continued on his path. A strong shot of pain in his joints followed every step he made, but he went on and on. The whisper of the light wind, so weak that he could barely feel it on his skin, was all he could hear, other than the sound of his breath, heavy but out of rhythm. The wild heat had soaked his whole body in sweat, which drenched the shirt on his back, making him feel like he had just pulled it out of a puddle.

He walked through the dull landscape, which seemed to consist of nothing but cracked earth, occasional enclaves of vegetation that were strong enough to endure the local climate, and random mounds that popped up every once in a while, as dry as the flat ground. The heat had kept rising and now seemed at its strongest, making Elliott assume it was around noon. He had been walking for hours, ever since his legs gave up on running, long before the break of dawn.

The journey was long and aimless. Elliott had no idea where his final destination lay. There was no logic behind any decision to turn left or right. He did not keep count of the number of times he'd changed direction. He did not memorise any landmarks that could help him trace his way back; it would have been an impossible task anyway, for everything in these accursed drylands looked the same. His mind was in complete disarray. His memory kept flashing back to the events of the previous night. He could see the feral monstrosities that had stepped out of nightmares to go on their savage hunt under the cover of darkness. He could still hear the shrieks of the campers, the same people he had roasted marshmallows with just days before, as they were pulled down by the vicious predators. He could visualise bloodstains on the flaps of tents and in the cracks in the earth. And though the weather was hot, he could only shiver at the realisation that the creatures that had attacked them were no usual desert predators. A normal hyena would not be able to stand on its hind legs, let alone walk confidently on them.

Whatever fragments of sanity that were left kept scolding him for his wayward desire to come to this forsaken place. He had been bored by the mundane, but got more than he bargained for, much more, when the extraordinary had paid a cruel visit to his reality.

Elliott did not know what he could do next. There was no road ahead, not even a footpath; he was walking through the wilderness, and it was impossible to estimate how far it stretched.

He suddenly stopped and turned around. Deep inside, he wanted to get back to the camp, meet up with any survivors, and use the group's vehicles to get back to Erbil. However, overwhelmed by panic, he'd ventured too far, and had no clue how to get back. The scene ahead was almost undistinguishable from the scene behind. And so, he just went on. But with every ten steps, the burden inside his chest became heavier. Walking was already taking a lot of effort, and it was only becoming harder.

Further ahead, a lonely thorn bush stood like a signpost. Dwarfing the sprouts of dry grass that grew around it, the bush's branches pointed at the cloudless sky, the sharp spikes exposed.

His body now moving with autonomy from his mind, Elliott staggered to the hostile-looking plant. Then his feet finally gave out and he collapsed on the thin grass.

He lay there, his throat as dry as the landscape around him. From the corner of his eye, he noticed that underneath the lowest-hanging branches of the thorn bush, there was probably just enough space to fit a person lying on his side. Impulsively, he rolled into it. The thorn-armed branches did not cast enough shade to protect him from the sun entirely, but he had to make use of what he had.

***

It became obvious that he had passed out from exhaustion at some point, but he was coming back to his senses. There was darkness all around him, and he began feeling his surroundings. Something did not add up. His bedding should have been much rougher, made out of grass and earth. Instead, he felt bed sheets underneath him. The scorching sunrays that were supposed to burn without pause had gone away.

He opened his eyes to a world so blurred he could not tell what was what. It took a minute for his sight to adjust. He was lying on his back, but instead of seeing branches above him, he was staring at a ceiling.

"What?" he mumbled.

Immediately, he sat up in surprise. Still confused, he kept his gaze fixed on the ceiling, wondering what miracle had transformed the thorn branches.

Then he heard a voice behind him, saying something in an unfamiliar language. Elliott turned and saw a young man, even younger than him, sitting on a stool in the corner. The long blue cloak that the stranger was clad in, a type Elliott had never seen before, gave out a very traditional vibe. Elliott had no doubt that the man was a native of these parts.

"Hello?" Elliott said.

The young man stood up and responded in his language. Elliott did not understand a single word.

"Can...you understand...what I'm saying?" Elliott spoke slowly.

Again, the young man said something in his language. He made a gesture, holding his hand out, palm first. It appeared that he wanted his guest to wait. Elliott nodded slowly. The host gave him one last look before he left the room, closing the door behind him.

"I guess he wants me to wait here until he comes back," Elliott said to himself.

Still sitting on the bed, he examined his surroundings. The room was small and the interior simple, but not the type he would have found at home in Britain. Aside from the bed and the stool, the room had only one other piece of furniture: a simple wooden trunk, which was likely a substitute for a closet. Close to the bed, a bowl and a jug stood on the floor, no doubt used for washing up. He turned to the side and saw the shutters were open, baring a window with no glass or plastic frame. Whoever owned this house appeared to be very old-fashioned.

He waited alone for about half an hour before the door opened again. But the attendant from earlier did not return; instead, two men entered the room, notably more advanced in age. The first one to enter seemed to be at least seventy. His face and hands were wrinkled; his short beard was white. The second man appeared to be in his fifties, and grey hair was already sprouting in his beard, which was styled in the same manner as the old man's. Both wore cloaks of the same length and colour as the young man; the fringes of a second, white garment were peeking out from beyond the edges. Conical grey felt hats crowned their heads. An invisible radiance of wisdom and insight exuded from the two men.

"English? Français? Deustch?" the younger of them asked.

"English," Elliott responded, genuinely happy to find out that somebody in this unknown area was able to understand him.

"Perfect," said the elder man as he sat down on the stool.

The second man closed the door but continued to stand.

"This means there should be no problems with communication." The old man's accent was thick, but he was clearly fluent. "There are only two people in this community who can speak a language other than Arabic or Kurdish. That language is English, and we are these two people." He paused to smile. "But of course, an introduction is in order. My name is Ismail; I am the sheikh of this community. And the man beside me is Yussuf, the Master of Service."

Hearing this title sparked a flame of curiosity inside Elliott's mind. The term 'Master of Service' sounded fairytale-ish, something taken straight out of a roleplaying game.

"And I am Elliott Gildart. I'm from Britain," he said, still weak after his earlier experiences. "Can you tell me where I am?"

"You are in Tubsir, a small oasis town," Yussuf answered.

"How did I get here? The last thing I remember is falling down in the middle of the drylands." Elliott put a hand to his pounding head.

"And that is where one of the townsfolk found you whilst he was herding his camels," Ismail explained. "You should thank Allah, for he had pity on you. Heat is cruel to those unprepared for it. Had you lain there for a few more hours, you would have likely died."

"You were brought in here yesterday," Yussuf added.

"But here is the most interesting question," Ismail continued. "How did you end up in the middle of the drylands? This oasis stands in a very secluded location. We haven't had outsiders visiting this place in many years."

"I was part of an archaeological expedition that was excavating an ancient outpost in the drylands." Elliott began his account. "Everything was fine at first. But then one night—I don't know how long ago it happened. Two nights ago, maybe? Three nights?" His voice acquired a cold, mesmerised tone. "Our camp was attacked."

"Attacked by whom?" Yussuf asked with concern. "Brigands? Militants?"

"No, hyenas," Elliott said, his expression blank as he relived the carnage of that night. "I saw many of my colleagues get mauled by these beasts."

And among these images, one stood out in particular: that demonic hyena rising up and walking. Elliott had an urge to mention this detail, yet a pragmatic voice that still somehow lingered in his head told him not to. It would have sounded so outlandish that his two hosts would have likely assumed that he had lost his mind. And perhaps they would have a point. He was starting to believe that he had imagined that particular scene under stress and terror.

"I ran and managed to flee," he concluded.

The sheikh and the Master of Service exchanged quick worrying glances.

"This is horrifying news," Yussuf said. "Do you know if anybody else survived?"

"I don't know."

"Then there might be more survivors."

"If we show you a map of the area, young man, would you be able to point out the estimated location of the camp?" Ismail asked.

"I don't think I can," Elliott said. "To be honest, I've never seen the camp's location on any maps. But it was close to the ruins of the old Assyrian outpost."

"This information is not particularly useful. Our people are either farmers or clerics, not prospectors," the sheikh said. "We never searched for ancient ruins hidden under the drylands."

"And were there any women as part of your expedition?" Yussuf asked. "Women with red hair, in particular?"

The question took Elliott aback.

"Yes, there was one woman... She had red hair. Lauren, my cousin."

A quake rumbled in his mind. He had forgotten—he had forgotten about her in the frenzy.

"How do you know?" he gasped. "Have you seen her?"

Time froze as he waited for the answer, fearing the most horrifying explanation.

"After you were brought in, I sent scouts to look around the vicinity of the oasis for any other outsiders," Ismail explained. "One found her; she was unconscious. She is currently in Tubsir, but unlike you, she has not yet regained her senses. One of the local women has been tasked with attending her."

Elliott sighed in relief.

"So she's your cousin?" Ismail said.

"Yes. Can I see her?"

***

Many years ago, back in his childhood, Elliott had, after watching one of those slapstick cartoons, wished to see an anvil fall on Lauren's head. But now, as he sat there by her bedside, all these old quarrels and the bitter aftertastes they once left seemed irrelevant.

Lauren lay in bed, unconscious but peaceful. Elliott leaned back against the wall. He had been sitting in this room on the small stool for a couple of hours. He was still tired, but he was ready to endure many sleepless hours if needed.

To pass the time, he kept looking around the room, studying his surroundings. After all, what else could he do? He had no gadgets with him. Even his phone lay lost somewhere in the remnants of the camp. The room was practically identical to the one he got: bed, stool, trunk, jug and bowl. He had them all memorised.

His gaze slid to the stone floor as he tried to think about the things the next day would bring.

"Elliott? Is that you?" He heard a weak voice.

He looked at his cousin and saw her lying there, head turned and eyes half-open.

"It's me," he said, moving to sit on the bed next to her.

She sat up, and upon noticing her unfamiliar surroundings, began frantically looking around.

"Where are we?" she asked, her blue eyes wide.

"In a safe place," he said. "Safer than the drylands."

"The drylands," she whispered, memories starting to come back to her. "The camp... Elliott, the camp!" she screamed out. Her body began to shake.

"Calm down, Lauren." He placed his hands on her shoulders. "Calm down."

And perhaps for the first time in her life, she actually followed his instructions.

"Those things, what were they?" she asked.

"I don't know. They looked like hyenas to me," he said, not mentioning the bipedal canine.

"Where are the others? Mergham, Akhmad, everybody else?"

"I don't know, but we're the only two people from the group here at the moment."

He was lying about Akhmad, of course, having seen his grisly demise with his own eyes. But Lauren did not need to know that for the time being.

"How did you survive that night?" Elliott asked.

"I'm not sure if I remember everything the way it really was, due to all the shock and fear. But I think it went like this," she started. "I was woken up by screaming and commotion. I got out of the tent and the first thing I saw..." Her face twisted in disgust. "I saw one of those...things...gnawing at the body of one of the archaeologists...Gus, I think."

Elliott had never really interacted with Gus, but naturally, he was saddened that the number of potential survivors kept on shrinking.

"I froze in place when I saw it," Lauren continued. "That thing...that hyena was huge. Then it looked at me and snarled. I lost it and ran. I doubt it pursued, it was probably too busy stuffing itself. And I doubt I would have been able to outrun it if it tried." Her voice trembled. "And as I ran, I could hear more of these things rampaging through the camp. Then I remember walking senselessly around the drylands. And I don't remember much after that."

Guess it runs in the family, Elliott thought sadly.

He then told her his account of the night's events, though with some parts omitted, as well as everything he knew about their present situation.

"So now what?" Lauren asked.

"Well, our hosts said they would like to talk to both of us in the evening if you regained your senses," Elliott said. "And since you have, it would be rude to disappoint them."

"Um, ok," she said.

"Then perhaps you should rest for now," Elliott said as he stood up. "I'll come get you in the evening."

"Perhaps I really should. I still feel weak."

Elliott turned to the trunk and the garment that neatly rested on top of it.

"Oh, I almost forgot. There's one important thing." He picked the item up, his fingers sinking into the soft material. "You know the expression 'When in Rome, do as the Roman do'?"

"Yes, so?"

"This appears to be quite a traditional, conservative place. And women around here are expected to cover their heads with scarves when they're in public."

He handed it to her, certain she would not like this arrangement. Though he had not known her adult version for long, she clearly tried to maintain the image of a strong independent woman.

"You might wanna try it on first." He just could not resist making a witty remark.

***

As it turned out, Lauren was ready, at least sometimes, even if begrudgingly, to accept rules made by others. She exited the room with the silk scarf covering her flaming tresses.

"Where are the hosts?" she asked.

"Downstairs, probably," Elliott said, thinking of the room the Master of Service showed him earlier.

The stone floor of the gallery echoed their footsteps as they made their way towards the stairway, passing arched openings that gave a good view of the small yard. Such a walk allowed for a good understanding of the building's plan. It was a two-storey structure built around the courtyard. A couple of trees and bushes grew in the enclosed space, a miniature garden.

Elliott led his cousin towards one of the ground floor rooms on the left. It was the only one open at that moment, and lights shone inside as a reminder in case he had forgotten which room it was.

The room itself appeared to be a dining area. There was a table in the middle, accompanied by several stools. A couple of ornamented lanterns were burning on top of the table; a couple more had been fixed to the walls. All in all, just like with the bedrooms, décor was very simple.

The sheikh and the Master of Service were already waiting inside, standing by the table. But they had not come for dinner. A map was sprawled on the table, an old map that would have felt at home in a museum collection.

"Good evening, Lauren. How are you feeling?" the sheikh asked.

"I'm fine," she answered. "I would like to thank you for everything you did."

"We only did what was right," the old man responded.

He again introduced himself and his companion.

"We found out what happened from your cousin," he continued. "I am planning to send a party to inspect the scene and hopefully find more survivors. Unfortunately, the young man here does not know the estimated location. But, as we were told, you had an important role in the operation. So can you show us where it is?"

"Of course." Lauren nodded.

She came closer to the table and looked at the map that depicted the drylands and the outlying areas.

"This is Erbil." Yussuf pointed at the map. "And here is our town."

"Hmm, interesting. The maps we had did not have your town on it," Lauren said, her eyes locked on the contours of the oasis and the dwellings within it.

"That is no surprise. This is a remote, isolated area. Cartographers probably don't know that this town still exists."

"It's around this area." She brought a slender finger to a point to the east of Erbil and drew an invisible circle around it.

"I see." Ismail nodded. "Quite a way from here." He then turned to Elliott. "Young man, I hope you don't mind accompanying our group tomorrow. We will need you on location."

"I will."

"Well, this is all we need for now. We will arrive in the morning to pick you up," Ismail said and turned to his companion. "Yussuf."

The Master of Service rolled the map up.

"We will be retiring now," Ismail said. "Dinner will be brought for you to this dining area shortly. In the morning, breakfast will be brought here soon after Morning Prayer. Goodnight."

The hosts bowed their heads and proceeded to leave.

"Wait, may I ask something?" Elliott called out.

"Yes?" Yussuf responded.

"Is one of you the owner of this residence?"

"This is not a residence." Yussuf smiled. "This something called a *han*, a type of guesthouse that was once common across the Middle East. This might actually be the last functioning example of the old traditional variety left in Iraq."

Chapter Eighteen

The thin walls of the small, elegant glass could not prevent the heat of the tea from burning Sayid's fingers. He carefully picked up the small silver plate that it stood on. His gaze, distant and emotionless, was fixed at the calm surface of the tea and the barely visible steam emanating from it. At the other side of the small coffee table, Mullah Nishwari sat atop a cushion identical to the one Sayid was sitting on, as he described the group's plans for the near future.

Baghdad was not the end of the road. Nishwari went on to describe the administrative divisions—the wilayahs—that would be formed in the southern part of Iraq after their victory. He also raised the possibility of expanding beyond the borders of Iraq, mentioning that several groups in Syria and Yemen had declared their allegiance to Liwa al-Qadisiyyah while Sayid was still imprisoned.

Sayid listened, but though the mullah was sitting opposite him, his words sounded as distant as a radio programme playing in a different room. They were just a noise in the background of his own thoughts, thoughts of mystical arts and jinn, the miraculous and the Islamic way of life.

"Is something wrong, Sayid?" Nishwari asked.

Sayid looked up. "In what sense?"

"You haven't sipped your tea once."

And indeed, he was still holding on to the plate. Tea was Sayid's favourite beverage. He would choose it over coffee any day of the week, any season of the year. Nishwari knew this.

"Ah, yes." Sayid drank a bit, letting the beverage tickle his lips.

"You don't look like your usual self today," the mullah said. "It seems you are drained and exhausted from something. Perhaps you're coming down with a fever?" His voice was laced with genuine concern.

"No, no, I'm not ill. It's just that my mind keeps wandering off elsewhere."

"Are you thinking about the upcoming offensive?"

"Naturally."

It was no lie; he was thinking about the battles that were due to begin in a few days' time. He had taken part in a number of offensives, he was experienced and used to them, yet a strange sense of anxiety was always present. But it was not the full truth.

"But there's something bigger than that, right?" Nishwari said, calmly but assertively, as if he was able to read his mind.

For a moment, Sayid hesitated, thinking over what to say.

"Is it related to the Jinn Arts?" Nishwari asked before Sayid got a chance to speak.

"Y-e-s." Sayid stretched out his answer, feeling uncomfortable.

It was bizarre. He had issues with this whole thing—major issues, for that matter. At the same time, he did not want to hurt Nishwari's feelings. Sayid had noticed how emotionally invested the mullah was in this idea. Rebuking him for it felt as bad as upsetting an elderly relative.

"What are your concerns?" Nishwari asked gently.

"I don't think you'll like what I'll say."

"I am the emir of the Liwa," Nishwari said. "And a good leader ought to listen to the concerns of those under his command. It does not matter if the words he hears make him smile or frown; they ought to be heard. Moreover, you, Sayid, are one of my best and dearest followers, so the weight of these concerns doubles when you raise them." Surprisingly, the mullah smiled. "So, don't be afraid, my boy. Speak your mind."

"Very well," Sayid said, putting the glass on the table, somewhat feebly.

"You have taught thousands of men the Quran throughout the decades. Only a fool can deny that you are pious and follow the teachings of the Prophet. And I am honest when I say that I think you are sincere when you say that the Jinn Arts, in their nature, are not necessarily un-Islamic."

Nishwari kept looking at Sayid intently, revealing no emotion. The younger man took a pause and a deep but quiet breath to stop his maddened heartbeat.

"But even the greatest and well-versed minds are prone to occasional errors in judgement. The debate during the assembly a few days back shows that we appear to be walking on a thin line by endorsing the Jinn Arts. This might be one of your rare mistakes. Surely you understand that if you are indeed wrong, this mistake will have negative consequences for the souls of countless thousands of people."

"Naturally, this is a legitimate concern." Nishwari nodded. "And believe me; it took me years of pondering to come to my conclusions. During that time, I have reread the Quran many times and thought about every verse that might contradict this idea. I only went ahead when it became certain that no verse really opposes this endeavour."

"But on the other hand, Khaleed Awal too is a renowned preacher, and his stance on this issue is the direct opposite to yours."

"Ah, yes, Sheikh Awal." Nishwari slowly shook his head in a melancholic manner. "I must admit, that spat I had with Khaleed during the meeting was a shattering experience. I used to think that Awal was a wise man. But it appears that my perception of him was wrong. If anything, he is akin to a Bedouin who thinks that the world is limited to his caravan, the desert he roams, and the oases he stops at during his wanderings, and is too naïve to understand that so much lies beyond his narrow horizon.

"Just because the Quran does not mention something does not mean it denies or opposes its existence," he continued, talking like he was delivering a sermon. "It was left out for a reason, but I am in no position to assume why Allah chose it to be so."

"But did not the Prophet speak out against magic?" Sayid asked. "Did he not equate the use of magic to sins such as blasphemy?"

"He did!" Nishwari declared, nodding. He sounded excited, and sparks of the same excitement flashed in his eyes. "I am not denying it!"

Sayid was not sure what to make of this sudden enthusiasm.

"But now answer this question, Sayid. What is magic? How do you define it?"

"Um, I'm not sure what words are best to describe such an unusual phenomenon..."

"Actually, I'll ask a different question. What was primarily seen as magic in the times of the Prophet?" Nishwari said. "After all, many words have changed and acquired new meanings throughout the centuries."

"History has never been my strong point," Sayid said. "Not to mention the history of languages."

"Would you like me to answer this question?"

"Please do."

"So, what did the ancient Arabs see as magic?" the mullah began. "Imagine a soothsayer who carves an animal up with the intention of reading the future in its organs. This is magic, for, as we know, only Allah can know the future.

"Now imagine a bitter old woman. She is angry and jealous that a good man she wanted as a husband chose a younger, more beautiful maiden. And she has nothing: no husband, no children. So, what does she do? She tries to put a hex on that maiden, a curse that would cause infertility. She calls out to the dark jinn and they answer her call.

"So, what is magic according to our ancient ancestors? Magic is an illusion, a ploy to lead people into disbelief. The soothsayer trying to see the future equates himself to God in this aspect. He assumes he can do what God can, which is both a delusion and a transgression, for a mortal is nothing compared to God in absolutely everything. As for the jealous old woman: not only does she seek to cause harm to a person that did no wrong to her, but she substitutes the worship of God, who created her, with the worship of jinn that were willing to aid her in her act of petty villainy."

Sayid rubbed his chin, pondering. He had never looked at it this way.

"Now ask yourself a question, Sayid!" Nishwari spoke louder. "What is the purpose of Liwa al-Qadisiyyah? For what reason does it exist?"

The mullah went on to answer that question himself. "We fight to impose the laws established by God, not subvert them. And this makes us different from the examples I mentioned: the soothsayer and the bitter woman. Maybe the ancient cartographer al-Karwaini was right, and it was indeed a jinn who taught the magi what we call the Jinn Arts. But just as likely, he might have been mistaken. Either way, we praise no jinn, for we only praise Allah. And even though the fire-worshipping ancient Persian magi were the first to practice this craft, not a single member of the Liwa would ever pray at their derelict shrines or bring offerings to their crumbling idols."

Sayid felt a sense of relief in his chest, like a child who had thought he had done something bad, but was assured by an adult that no fault was his.

"I hope my explanation makes my perspective more understandable." The mullah's tone became softer.

"It does."

"But anyway, Jalil al-Quwaiti...mediated...a temporary compromise that day...in his own way. And I intend to stay true to it. Eventually, the Shura will assemble, and if it is decided that the Jinn Arts have no place in Liwa al-Qadisiyyah, the practice will be discarded and forgotten."

There was a sadness in his voice that he could not conceal despite his best efforts, the sadness of an inventor forced to set fire to a model he had built.

"But enough about this grim topic; it will be debated again on a different day." Nishwari raised his hand to adjust his headdress. "Let's talk about a topic much lighter but just as unusual: the Samnite's request."

Sayid blinked at the mention of a name he had practically forgotten. "So?" he urged the leader to continue.

"I must say that I was very much surprised by his proposal. Organising excavation works and sending supervisors to oversee them? It sounds just as strange as it reads."

"Do you think he might be up to something?" Sayid asked. "For all we know, he might be working for the CIA."

"He could be. Yet he smuggled you back into Iraq instead of turning you over to the Americans or Djiboutian authorities. Moreover, he did not need to help you out in order to pass his request on. You've never had any involvement in these activities."

"But still, he seemed like a sleazy type." Though Sayid respected the art dealer's boldness, this was an undeniable fact.

"I'm sure he is," the mullah said, "but he's good at what he does. The Liwa has benefited from collaborating with him in the past."

"So, what is the decision on the expedition he was proposing?"

"After some consultation, we decided that it can take place. Naturally, the details will be agreed on through our channels. But it is also natural that we are going to keep a close eye on the people he sends here and their work."

Sayid leaned forward to pick his tea up from the table. He could now hold the glass with his fingers; the beverage was getting cold.

***

This is way too easy, Sayid thought as he rode down the street atop a pick-up truck.

He had been expecting more of a fight. Yet from the first hour of the offensive, they had met only meek resistance from the Iraqi military. Under-equipped and demoralised by the never-ending dangers, corruption, and mismanagement, conscripts abandoned their positions, turning their retreat into a chaotic flight. Whole military bases and towns alike fell into the hands of the Liwa with minimal if any fighting.

Hisad al-Shaeir was a small town to the north-west of Baghdad. It was the type of town that had nothing of renown; the name rarely, if ever, featured in the news or in discussions. Personally, Sayid had never known anybody who had visited it before this day. And as he rode through its streets, he could understand why. It was a typical backwater small town.

Not a single street saw fighting; Hisad al-Shaeir fell without a shot. All they'd needed to do was overrun the army's positions to the north of the town; that had not been a hard task.

The black and white banners fluttered in the wind, the sound of them flapping intermixed with celebratory cries from the victorious fighters. Not a single local could be seen on the street, making the town feel abandoned. And it likely was. Half the population had fled; the other half was in hiding. Sayid knew from experience that these would start coming out once the dust settled.

Making a final sweep and securing the town did not take long, but the day was already in its third quarter when Sayid's pick-up truck reached the town square. Like everything else in Hisad al-Shaeir, the main square was small; comparing it to the central squares found in the country's notable cities would have been as outrageous as comparing a puddle to a lake. At the other end of the square stood the local administration building, a two-storey-structure with walls painted a pleasant honey colour adorned with balconies and arched windows.

The vehicle stopped in the middle of the square, as did the pick-up tailing it. Having checked the gun fastened to his belt, Sayid hopped out of the truck onto the paved surface of the square. Following his example, men began to emerge from both vehicles.

With a wave of a hand, he led them towards the building.

"Group One will follow me!" He turned around to face his subordinates before he set foot on the stairs leading towards the entrance. "Group Two will stand guard outside."

He entered the building, followed by half a dozen men. They went from room to room as they explored it. The place had been abandoned hastily, if the fallen office chairs and paperwork scattered on the floor were anything to go by. Some of the folders were open and empty; some of the civil servants who'd fled had managed to take or destroy the documents they did not want the Liwa to see. But at least some of the computers were still present and intact. Later, he would pass them on to the...right people. Perhaps, among the files hidden within them, they would find information that could prove very useful in the future.

On the top floor, he found what he assumed was the office of the local mayor. The biggest hint was the portrait of the president that was hanging on the wall behind the desk. A spark of anger lit inside Sayid. He did not simply dislike this tradition that was commonplace at government institutions: he outright hated it.

"Look at this, lads!" Sayid glanced at his entourage. "How low can these people stoop? They hang pictures of politicians and revere them knowing full well that the Prophet explicitly forbade the worship of idols."

Calmly, as if he was strolling through a meadow, he walked up to the portrait. The framed image was hanging rather high, so Sayid had to get on his tiptoes to take it down. He tucked it under his arm and went towards the window, carrying it as carelessly as renovator would a discarded piece of interior. He stepped onto the balcony and looked down on the square.

"Hey, boys!"

The sound of his voice made the men look upwards. There on the balcony, Sayid now stood, holding the portrait over his head with both hands.

"You see the Kurd?!" he asked, referring to another political tradition, one specific to Iraq: every President of Iraq in the last two decades was of Kurdish background. "He's about to fly!" he declared with predatory glee. "Catch the Kurd!"

Sayid chuckled as he threw the portrait down.

"Catch the Kurd! Catch the Kurd!" some of his men shouted in excitement, almost like children playing a game.

And yet they all pulled back; after all, not a single one of them wanted the portrait to fall on his head. So when the portrait fell to the ground, it heavily hit against the pavement with a crash that reached the balcony.

Then the jihadists bolted towards it, shouting. Any of the frame that survived the collision was smashed, the photo torn into pieces.

Above them, Sayid stood and watched, smirking.

***

Sayid spent the night in that building; he was confident enough to assume that no nocturnal bombing raid or drone strike would target the structure. After all, who would expect him to linger inside it?

He leaned back into the mayor's chair, thinking about all that had happened and what was still to come. The morning's pinkish hues were breaking through the window, brightening the room. The sound of footsteps on the stairway brought his attention to the open doorway. A few moments later, one of his men appeared into view with a somewhat puzzled expression on his face.

"Commander."

"What is it?" Sayid asked.

"There is a man asking for an audience with you."

The awkward announcement made Sayid sit up straight in the chair immediately.

"A man? Asking for me?" His brow rose.

"He claims that he is a local imam."

"I see. How did he find out that I am here?"

"He came up to the men patrolling the perimeter of the square shortly after Morning Prayer. The men did not reveal your whereabouts but agreed to deliver his request to you. How should we respond to him?"

"An imam..." Sayid ran his fingers through his messy beard whilst thinking. "I guess I cannot turn down a preacher. You can escort him to me."

The fighter nodded and turned around, about to walk out of the office.

"But search him first!" Sayid called after him.

"Yes, commander," the man said before disappearing in the doorway.

Imam or not, Sayid was not willing to take risks. Something about this whole request bugged him. This situation made him recall the fate of Akhmad Shah Massoud, an infamous warlord from the Afghan Civil War. His story ended when two Taliban agents got an audience with him under the guise of journalists... hiding suicide belts underneath their clothes.

Different militias and factions were operating across Iraq's vast and often uncontrollable territory. Each had its own ideology, its own vision of the future, its own methods and tactics for dealing with foes, and many disagreed with those of the Liwa. Sayid was not the leader of the Liwa, but he was a high-ranking commander. Still, even if taking one piece out of a house of cards did not make it fall, it would weaken it nonetheless.

Some time later, footsteps once again sounded on the stairway; Sayid was certain he was able to distinguish two sets. Sure enough, the same fighter entered the room in the company of another man. Dressed in a white robe and headdress, the newcomer was short in height. Had they been standing side by side, the top of his head, sans his headwear, would have been level with Sayid's chest. He was an ageing man; not as old as Awal but certainly older than Nishwari.

"Peace be upon you," the newcomer graciously greeted his somewhat reluctant host.

Sayid responded with his own greeting.

"Your men are very humble," the man said with a warm smile, quickly turning to the fighter and then looking back at Sayid. "And no doubt equally pious."

"They are most certainly are," Sayid replied, his tone formal. "You may leave, brother," he then told the fighter.

The militant was gone a moment later.

"You have requested an audience," Sayid said to the newcomer, resting his hands on the desk. "I was told that you are an imam."

"That is true. My name is Ibrahim Falai and, indeed, I am an imam. If you walk out of this building and turn right, you will see a minaret. It is part of the mosque I preach at."

"So how may I help you?"

"I did not come here for help. I am here because of a promise I once made," Ibrahim said.

"And what is this promise?" Sayid had to admit: this stranger was making him more curious with every statement he made.

"That as soon as the warriors of faith liberate this town, I will personally come to pay respect to the commander leading them." He bowed.

This act brightened Sayid's day. It was always nice to be admired.

"And what is your name, commander?" the imam asked.

"Sayid al-Buzali."

"Ah, yes, I have heard of you."

"Are you a member of Liwa al-Qadisiyyah?" Sayid asked. The man standing before him seemed to be a sympathiser, but whether he was an agent of the Liwa was a different question.

"Oh, no, I have never been a part of any organisation: not Al-Qaeda or DAISH or any other. However, just like you, I follow the Salafist teachings. And quite a few of my protégés, the people I influenced, have gone out to fight under the banners of similar groups. Because of this, security forces have raided my house more than once."

"I see." Sayid nodded. "Maybe this time you would be interested in becoming a part of a bigger group?"

"I will most certainly think about it, but to be honest, I am not sure about formally joining a specific organisation. I have always been somewhat of a loner, an independent preacher," Ibrahim continued in his courteous manner. "I am sure you can understand this, commander."

"Yes, of course."

"I would also like to use this occasion to invite you to come and pray at our mosque. Today is Thursday; tomorrow is Friday. It would delightful to see you and your men during Friday Prayer."

"There's nothing preventing me," Sayid said.

"Excellent, I look forward to your visit." Ibrahim smiled.

CHAPTER NINETEEN

The mosque was not large, but the atmosphere of bygone ages lingered within, implying that this place of worship had been standing on this spot for centuries. Whoever entered immediately saw the calligraphy that adorned the building. It swirled on the walls like a trail, elegantly bending from symbol to symbol. The patterning on the enormous carpet on the floor twisted into unusual geometric figures. Perhaps they were meant as a challenge to the wall murals, to see who had more skill in his trade, the painter or the carpet-weaver.

Friday Prayer was already mid-way and the imam's voice reverberated through the colonnaded room. Sayid knelt as he repeated the prayers chanted by the old preacher. He did not know how many people came to this mosque for Friday Prayer under the usual circumstances, but on this occasion, there were few attendees, so the prayer hall seemed bigger than it truly was. Ibrahim Falai stood atop the elevated dais of the minbar, the imam's traditional place near the far wall of the mosque.

"Brothers, do not concern yourselves with the ultimate fates of disbelievers!" He spoke with his full charisma, his voice raised in order to make sure every word reached the audience. "Remember, there is no greater source of wisdom than the Quran. And I gladly repeat what the Quran says: 'They have become lost and are failing to find a way.' But this is not the result of unfortunate circumstances. Each of them had dozens, hundreds of opportunities. They got them from their relatives, from their acquaintances, from the imams. And yet instead of heeding sincere and godly advice, they prefer to lose themselves by choosing comfort and entertainment."

Sayid listened to the imam intently. Yet at the same time, he tried to keep his ears out for any suspicious movements. He was in an unfamiliar town, invited to be present at a new location. It was often the case that when it comes down to power struggles, all methods come into play, even the most treacherous ones. He kept recalling a story he'd once heard about an Ottoman sultan who was assassinated during prayer at one mosque centuries ago. He was intent on avoiding a similar fate.

"Brothers, it is unfortunate that sometimes, no matter how hard we try, some things are simply unchangeable." The imam's tone shifted to a calmer one. "And indeed the Night Journey said wisely: 'We tried teaching them the Quran in many different manners so they would finally understand, yet it only increases their urge to rebel.' Well, they have made their choice! And this applies to some of our very own townsfolk, our very neighbours. They are not here praying alongside you, for they have chosen to flee the town rather than live under the edicts of the just and godly Sharia law!"

The imam's speech was making Sayid relive his own past. Almost a decade before, as an impoverished student away from home in Baghdad, he went to a mosque he had never been to before. It, too, had a preacher, one that differed little from Ibrahim. The messages he delivered during his prayer were uncompromising, yet his charisma attracted people from all walks of life. It was there that Sayid had met some new friends, through whom he began attending private groups to study the doctrines of faith, presided over by the same imam.

"And so the Quran tells us that those who are guided are guided for their own good and those who lose their way lose it to their own harm! No mortal soul should take up the weight of another!" the imam continued, more aggravated this time. "If they are destined to find their way, they will do it themselves, through their own will and their own intention!"

Sayid could see right through this preacher. The Liwa's presence was giving Ibrahim the bravado to speak so boldly in public. When the town was still in the government's hands, Ibrahim most likely preached his teachings in more subtle ways. And if the army one day managed to retake the town, Ibrahim would have his defence ready; portray his war-like preaching as a means of survival, a way to please the Liwa and its commanders. And no doubt, he'd manage to get off the hook.

"Brothers and sisters, before you go back to your households, I would like to remind you of a story from the past," Ibrahim said as he gazed down on the faithful from the minbar. "Many years ago, Prophet Mohammed led an army, ten-thousand men in its ranks, to liberate Mecca from the pagan Quraysh tribe. The enemies of Islam gathered all the forces they could muster to defend the city, yet their efforts were in vain. There was no battle and there was no siege. The Quraysh forces lost their will to fight when the time to confront the faithful arrived. The Prophet and his army entered the city facing minimal resistance. Mecca was cleansed of the tainting influence of the pagans who had ruled it before.

"Two days ago, the army along with the local authorities abandoned this very town, and this event is a reason for some deep, thoughtful reflection. So as we praise the remarkable deeds and achievements of the Prophet that were made possible by the will of the Almighty, let us also be grateful for the efforts the warriors of faith made in order to free our town from the darkness of the apostate Shias that dominate the government in Baghdad!"

"*Allahu Akbar!*" a voice rang out from among the audience.

Sayid thought he recognised this voice; he was certain it belonged to one of his fighters who had come for prayer with him.

"*Allahu Akbar!*" Several more voices, both familiar and unknown, repeated the chant.

"*Allahu Akbar! Allahu Akbar!*" The chants began coming from different directions.

Yet in these moments, Sayid could not help but wonder how many of these declarations of praise were truly sincere and how many of those gathered were just playing it safe.

When Friday Prayer was over, Sayid slowly rose to his feet. He had reached the shoe stands at the mosque's entrance when he heard a rasping voice behind him.

"Ah, commander."

Sayid turned around upon hearing the imam's voice.

"Seeing you here within the walls of this mosque brought me great joy," Ibrahim told him.

"And attending this Friday Prayer felt very fulfilling," Sayid responded courteously.

"I am delighted to hear this. Hopefully, this is not the last time you come here."

"I will be coming to pray here whenever opportunity allows me."

"Marvellous." Ibrahim nodded. "We live in tough times when even the most devout and pious adherents of Islam start losing their way and indulging in nonsense of all kinds. It is prayer that helps your soul stay strong and remain on course into the Hereafter."

***

It was close to midday when Sayid walked out into the courtyard of his new base of operations. Lingering in the local administration building for too long would have turned out to be a bad decision in the long run, due to the risk of potential aerial bombings after the Liwa had fully established control. And he had to admit, the new place was much better when it came to taste. Before the city's fall, it used to be a private house, and a fine one for that matter. It was enclosed by a wall, and the front entrance led into a small courtyard. Whoever had lived there seemed to have abandoned the town in a hurry, having left all the furnishings inside, to Sayid's further convenience.

He was starting to get annoyed, impatiently tapping at the ground with his foot as he waited for the dignitary that was supposed to arrive. He knew the value of timing and strongly disliked tardiness. It stemmed from his experience on the battlefield. After all, on the frontlines, a delay in the arrival of reinforcements could spell certain doom for an entire battalion.

After some more waiting, and some more tapping, a vehicle drove through the gates of the complex. There was nothing special about it: an average car, clearly of high mileage, with crimson paint that had begun to peel.

The door opened and the dignitary stepped out. Sayid had to use a great amount of willpower in order to avoid bursting into a chuckle.

"Hamza?!" he exclaimed upon seeing his old friend.

"*Ahlan*, brother!" Hamza Saqqaf bid him an informal greeting.

"*Halaa!*" Sayid responded with a greeting of his own, and the two shared a brief but friendly embrace.

"You really should start letting me know of your coming in advance—I would have ordered your favourite food prepared for the occasion," Sayid joked, gesturing towards the entrance.

He led Hamza through the foyer and into the living room, where they both sat down on the sofa.

"I assume you have come here as part of your new work as tax collector." Sayid leaned against the soft back of the couch. "Well, you seemed to have arrived too soon. The town has only been in the hands of the Liwa for a few days. Moreover, it is spring; the harvest hasn't come yet, so it's a bit too early to make the farmers in the town's vicinity pay their dues." He smirked.

"You don't have to lecture me about things I know," Hamza said, both friendly and sarcastic. "My father is farmer. As a small boy, I was gathering dates from our family's trees whilst you were playing ball games with your friends on the streets of your neighbourhood.

"Moreover, every town has small businesses, and their owners need to know when and how they are expected to pay taxes to the new authorities. But this is not the reason I came here," he added, smiling.

"Then what is it?" Sayid asked, curious.

"Let's just say that I received a promotion," Hamza said. "As of today, I'll be running the civic life of this town as the head of the local authorities."

"This is the second surprise from you today! Congratulations."

"Thank you, brother. I had a couple of options before me. But I specifically chose this place once I found out you're the one commanding the Liwa's forces in the area."

"But frankly, this is a small town, insignificant when it comes to any strategic purpose," Sayid said. "Don't be surprised if you start seeing it as a place of exile after some point."

"Actually, it's not just this town, but several more towns in the area that your men captured since the start of the offensive. And it's a temporary arrangement. Part of the population has fled, so running a batch of half-empty towns should not be that difficult," Hamza said. "Plus, with you around, it is the perfect setting. I run the civilian matters; you run security. There's no way we can fail."

"Sounds good to me. So I guess you'll be setting up a new administration centre in this town?"

"Sort of, since I'll have to stay at different towns depending on occasion." Hamza looked at his friend. "The Liwa is not just about waging jihad. We are here to stay. We need to let the locals know that there is a new power here and that Baghdad has no sway on anything that happens here from now on. It's all just beginning: setting up new institutions, maintaining order, winning hearts and minds..."

Sayid placed his elbow on the sofa's back. He knew how enthusiastic Hamza could be at times. This was promising to be a long monologue.

***

Several days later, Sayid had once again walked up the steps of the local administration building. But this time he did not go inside. Instead, he turned around to face the small square. The atmosphere that reigned in the square was a blend of contrasting feelings: fury and anxiety, tension and excitement. Every man that came to the scene added another tone to this elaborate painting. There were not that many people, but it was enough to fill the small square. Several of Sayid's fighters had already taken their positions at different ends of the square. Beside him, he heard Hamza mumble something under his breath as they both stood in the rays of the sun.

The main event was heralded by two more fighters who proceeded to shoo people away towards the sides whilst clearing a corridor leading towards the centre of the square. It took several long minutes of standing still before the corridor was put into use. Sayid's position allowed him to look straight at the head of the convoy arriving at the square. In the middle, there was an older man with his hands behind his back, his wrists tied; two men, each a decade younger than their captive, were by his side, ushering him towards the square with the occasional push of their elbows. There were more people in the convoy, both captives and their captors.

Once they reached the square's centre, the convoy's head ordered the captives put in a line. Soon, all eight of them were facing the group's leaders, with an equal number of guards an intimidating presence behind them. The frozen and lost expressions on the visages of the prisoners made it clear they were absolutely shattered, left abandoned without hope or any speck of comfort granted by their emotionless captors.

The rustle of a long robe sounded behind Sayid. He turned his head slightly to see one more man joining them. The newcomer was one of the Liwa's qadis—judges with the authority to implement Sharia law—sent to this newest part of the group's domain. He looked at the captives with cold eyes that showed nothing but disdain. Yet he did not come today to judge; the trial had taken place the day before. He was present to witness the verdicts getting carried out.

Sayid himself had not been present at the trial, having gone to the frontline to observe the situation there, but he had been filled-in on the situation. Not all of the prisoners were from Hisad al-Shaeir. In fact, most of them were not, having been rounded up across the recently captured territories. One of these men was a retired policeman; another was a civil servant who did not take his chance to flee when the time was still right; a third one had been accused of apostasy by one of his neighbours. But in truth, Sayid did not care who was who and which crime each individual had been charged with. He was here to preside over the execution.

"Behold!" the qadi proclaimed. The wide sleeves of his robe slid back as he raised his hands. "These people before you have been judged and found guilty of their crimes against the faith! So today you will see justice delivered onto them!"

From the corner of his eye, Sayid spotted a familiar figure in the crowd. Ibrahim was there, watching it like it was a performance by a troupe of acrobats; Sayid had expected little else from him.

"Governor, Commander," the judge said quietly as he nodded to Hamza and Sayid.

Sayid looked back at the square and caught the gaze of the convoy's head. He then gave a single nod. In contrast, his subordinate's order was loud; the militants responded by pushing the captives to their knees. Then they drew their weapons, which seemed somewhat antiquated: swords not much dissimilar to the ones their ancestors had used to fight their enemies, centuries before.

"Execute them!" Hamza, as the most senior figure of civilian authority present, declared.

Some of the captives lowered their heads for their last prayers. A few others just remained on their knees, too broken for any type of action.

The sun's rays reflected off the polished blades, making the weapons shine like mirrors. The swords whooshed through the air like serpents attacking their prey. They sang their deadly song as they cut through everything in their path: skin, muscle, and bone. Blood splattered on the pavement and on the clothes of the executioners.

Gasps rose from amongst the crowd. For the townsfolk, both the supporters of these new ways and the secret opponents, this was likely the first time they had witnessed something like this happen.

However, this was nothing new for Sayid; he could not remember how many times he had seen such scenes play out in different cities, in different squares.

***

The football rose up in the air, kicked by a bored militant. He bounced the ball a couple of times before sending it towards his five comrades. Sayid doubted that any of them noticed their commander watching from the corner with his two bodyguards. Beside him, Hamza leaned against the wall, arms crossed over his chest.

Sayid had been surprised to discover a small football field relatively close to his new headquarters. It immediately brought back memories of childhood days wasted away on different fields not too dissimilar to this one.

The sun above him had reddened as the day moved into late afternoon. He threw a glance at his guards and ordered them to follow him with a nod.

"Commander!" one of the football-playing militants called as he spotted him.

The group's leisure was cut short. All were now standing straight, and the ball fell to the ground. It slowly rolled towards Sayid before bumping into his boot.

"Where did you guys get the ball?" Sayid asked.

"I found it lying on the side of a nearby street," one of the fighters said.

"I see." Sayid softly kicked the ball, flipping it in the air. Before it hit the ground, he gave it another light kick, keeping it airborne.

"It's a non-eventful day, isn't it, guys?" he said as he kept bouncing the ball. "So I suggest a game of football, right here and right now." He caught the ball from the air with both hands. "Who's interested?"

Via word or gesture, all six men expressed their interest. Sayid looked back at his guards; both nodded in agreement.

Hamza just stood still. It was no surprise to Sayid, considering the injuries his former lieutenant had suffered during the shelling. It was a pity, for as far as Sayid could remember, Hamza, whilst not necessarily a lover of the game, was always keen on playing with him.

Already, Sayid could see a little problem. Nine men had expressed their interest: an uneven number. Each team would have three strikers and one goalkeeper. One man was surplus.

"Ok, guys, there's currently an uneven number of us!" Sayid proclaimed. "Does anybody want to be the referee?" *Because otherwise I'll have to,* he grumpily added in his mind. He wanted to play, not invigilate from the sideline.

"Why do you even need a referee?" Hamza asked.

"How else can you have two teams of the same size when you have nine players?" Sayid asked rhetorically.

"I guess you didn't count me in," Hamza said.

"You want to play too?" said Sayid, surprised. "But I thought you no longer could after...um...well...your wounds."

"The shards went through my abdomen." Hamza cringed at the unpleasant memories as he explained. "My legs were left intact. I can still play this game."

"Then excellent!" Sayid exclaimed. "You can be the captain of the opposing team."

The group split into two teams. Sayid made the first move as he dribbled the ball towards the adversary's goal. His opponents rushed out to stop him, but manoeuvring was Sayid's talent. He passed the ball to one of his teammates. That man then had to go up against Hamza, who tackled the ball away from him, his movements revealing no hint of injuries. Sayid had to admit that he had indeed underestimated him. With that, he smiled and dashed back; there was no way he would allow Hamza's team to score the first goal.

Chapter Twenty

In some twisted way, the latest part of this odyssey felt like a private tour. Nouri, with the graphic novel in his hand, took on the role of a guide as he led Neil further into the desert. The guard-medium thought it best to proceed on foot, for he could sense that the cameraman and his captors were not that far away. They needed to be stealthy if they wanted the element of surprise, so the jeep was left hidden behind a dune.

They had been walking for about thirty minutes in the roughest conditions. The sun above the reporter's head was blazing wrathfully, as if punishing him for forgetting his cap at the hotel. Sometimes, he got the impression that the sand beneath was hot enough to burn through the soles of his shoes.

"Oh my," he heard Nouri whisper in front of him.

"What is it?" Neil asked as he stepped past him.

Some distance away, several shapes lay scattered on the sands in an uncanny scene. At first Neil thought that the desert and its mischievous mirages were playing a deceitful game with his senses, morphing the carcasses of camels that had succumbed to some malady into human shapes.

"Bodies," Nouri finally responded.

Vigilant, the duo approached, and as the distance shortened, it became obvious that no illusion was at play and the row of sprawled corpses was not of camels. Neil instinctively checked the gun holstered at his belt.

He darted towards the massacre site, both expecting and fearing the worst. He heard the sound of Nouri's feet running behind him as he fell to his knees before the closest corpse. He looked into the eyes of the dead man, but did not recognise the life-drained features. He studied every face, going as far as examining wrinkles and birth marks. Four of the bodies belonged to men; one was female. One looked vaguely familiar; Neil was certain he had come across him at the refugee camp. Yet Jake was not among them.

"He's not here," Nouri stated, having done similar observations of his own.

"But these are the aid workers abducted from the camp. You can tell by the uniforms," Neil said, referring to the shirts worn by the unfortunate people.

Blood had soaked their outfits, leaving blots and trails of crimson on the fabric, but it was clear the material was originally of a sea-blue.

"And I recognise one of them," Neil added. "God," he whispered as he stood up. "What is this?"

He threw a quick look at Nouri, who stood there looking at the ground, serious and thoughtful.

"Look at their wounds," Nouri said, studying the bodies. "These are not bullet wounds. They were stabbed to death. If this was a group execution, why did they not shoot them? And why drag them all the way to this remote part of the desert just for that?"

Nouri lowered down to inspect the soft, hot ground. He brushed a layer of sand away using his gloved hand and picked up an object he uncovered.

"Is that a torch?" Neil asked, looking at the object's long pole and bulbous head.

"Yes," Nouri said, getting back up. He then cast the item aside with a sour grimace, as if it was contaminated. "I believe they were sacrificed."

"But why would militants carry out human sacrifices?"

"There might have been another party involved."

"Perhaps you're right. But none of this answers our main question. Where's Jake? And if I'm not mistaken, six aid workers were abducted along with him, so one more remains missing."

"I don't know." Nouri turned around and walked away from the bodies. "I lost connection to his life force once we reached this site. I'll need to meditate again."

Neil caught up to him. A sudden, unpleasant gust of dry wind blew in his face.

"God damn this forsaken place," he cursed as he kicked at the sand.

"Which god do you pray to?" Nouri suddenly asked, his navy cloak flapping in the sudden blast of wind.

The question seemed so out of nowhere that Neil raised an eyebrow as he looked at guard in surprise. And the way Nouri looked at that moment made him wonder if something was wrong with the man. The expression on his face was one of tight concentration; his eyes were looking into the distance, somewhere past Neil.

"What do you mean?" Neil asked.

"Who is the prophet of your faith? Nouri asked, elaborating. "Christ? Mohammed? Zoroaster? Mani?"

But this did not make the question fit the moment.

The desert wind became stronger as it played with the sand, lifting countless specks off the ground.

"I've been an atheist all my adult life," Neil told him. "And why are you even asking?"

"I can feel an evil presence lingering in the air," the guard said, his voice cold. The irises of his eyes slowly scanned the landscape, as if he was a cat that had gone on alert upon sensing a rodent.

Neil wanted to say something in response to this awkward comment. He opened his mouth...

"Try to remember any prayer you have ever learned and slowly recite it in your mind," Nouri said.

Carefully, like he was in the presence of a dangerous predator, Nouri began to back away, one step at a time.

"Do it as authentically as you can." The guard continued to utter his bizarre instructions. "Repeat it over and over again if you have to. And most importantly, do not move a muscle until I say so."

There was now more than twenty feet of distance between them. Nouri's hand slipped under his cloak and whipped out a sword that he had kept concealed. The weapon had been one of the items hidden in the mysterious bag Nouri had taken out of his derelict house, but this was the first time Neil had seen the antique blade clutched in the guard's hand. And this was another unforeseen occurrence. Unlike typical Arabic swords, which are curved in such a way that make them look like sickles, this blade was straight.

"I don't understand any of this," Neil protested.

"Just do it!" Nouri raised his voice. And then he froze in place. His position fixed in a battle-ready stance, sword in hand, he resembled a marble statue chiselled by an ancient sculptor that had retained its colourful plaster coating.

Neil's intuition, that thoughtful inner voice inside his being, suddenly advised him to go along with it. He scoured his mind in search of a prayer.

Our Father in Heaven. Silently, as instructed, he began to recite the first one he remembered.

Hallowed be your name...

The desert wind kept blowing in their direction, now bringing foreign sounds, low and distant, with it. They reminded him of the hissing of a snake. After all, what else could it be but the venomous song of a lonely cobra or asp?

Your kingdom come...

It took a few seconds to realise that these sounds were too complex to be a serpentine hiss. He could make out words, albeit whispered in a language he could not understand. The atmosphere was getting eerier.

Your will be done...

Nearby, a cloud of sand blew up in the air. Yet it did not come from afar like a sandstorm—it rose and came together like a fog.

On Earth and in Heaven...

And then, in a blink of an eye, the sandy cloud disappeared, replaced by an unexpected figure. Neil had no idea what specimen of fauna stood before him. A kangaroo was the first thing he could compare it to. A massive tail, muscular legs, crooked hands—but it was furless. And both its muzzle and frame bore recognisably humanoid features. Combined, these traits made this creature grotesque and dreadful: a stark contrast to the cute marsupial... that was not even native to the Arabian Desert.

The creature opened its mouth as it hissed, revealing a set of short but sharp fangs. Tilting its head, it made use of its broad nose to sniff the air like a dog on a scent.

And, as part of the most blood-curdling experience of the day, the thing looked straight at Neil.

Forgive us our sins...

He continued with the recital as the monster—for it could not be called anything else—began to walk towards him, sand crunching under its bare feet.

Neil fought the urge to run, drawing on all of his willpower. Soon enough, mere inches were all that remained between him and the ghoulish being. The thing was looking at him, its stare accompanied by hisses.

Do not lead us to temptation...

The being stood there like it was waiting for something.

But deliver us from evil...

The hiss gave way to a grunt as the thing turned around and began to stagger towards an immobile Nouri. And Neil could do nothing else but start reciting the prayer over again. The thing came up to Nouri and looked at him intently, as if it could not tell whether the figure before its hideous maw was of flesh or stone.

Nouri could have rivalled any desert predator in skill. The sun's rays danced off the finely polished steel as he swung his sword, aiming for the creature's neck. And yet, at least in agility, the humanoid monster was a formidable opponent. It fell back, managing to dodge the blow and keep its head. But Nouri had no intention of giving it even a moment's break. He charged and swung the blade again, and again. Heavily and fanatically, Nouri kept swinging his sword left and right, yet the creature's reflexes were unquestionably good. It sustained no wound—not even a scratch—as Nouri drove it further and further away from Neil.

A light gust of dry wind blew in the creature's direction. And even though the monster was as tall as a human and no doubt at least as heavy, the wind picked it up and hurled it away like a leaf. The thing fell to the ground some feet away from the menacing blade. The monster lifted its bony hand and a weapon materialised in its grasp: a heavy-headed mace. Any vestiges of normality that had endured thus far in the desert were now completely dashed. Neil could not think of a single law of physics that allowed turning aether into metal.

Releasing a cry, Nouri lunged at the being, but now the thing had a weapon of its own. Sword and mace clashed over the creature's head. Putting its strength behind its weapon, the monster pushed the blade away.

Now the creature was on the offensive. It charged, swinging the deadly mace. Nouri brought his weapon forth to block the heavy blow. The beast tried again and again with monstrous fervour. It forced Nouri to go on full defence; the man staggered back as he parried blow after blow.

Sword and mace clashed once more as the two opponents glared at each other with rage-filled grimaces, their teeth gritted. Then the creature suddenly rotated in a circle, almost like a pirouette, swinging its mighty tail like a second weapon. The long, strong appendage hit Nouri across the abdomen and knocked him off his feet, propelling him backwards as if he was not a living human but a practice dummy full of straw.

Even though he had stayed out of this surreal confrontation up to this point, Neil knew that the time to get involved had arrived. The guard did not seem savvy enough to take this creature on by himself. Neil swiftly drew his gun and pointed it at the beast. He pulled the trigger and the gunshot echoed amidst the sand and dunes.

He missed his target, but drew the attention of the nightmarish being. Immediately, Neil fired again. He was certain he'd got it right this time. He had enough experience at the shooting range, and he had been aiming at an immobile target. And yet it appeared he had somehow missed again.

The monster hissed and, ignoring the overpowered Nouri, moved against the newest threat, brandishing its mace.

Neil shot again. The bullet hit the monster square in its bare chest but passed straight through the grotesque figure without a single drop of blood appearing.

Panic shot through him. He fired again, again, and again. But no matter which part of the body the bullets hit—chest, stomach, head—they only stopped the beast for a couple of moments. With horror, he realised: the monster was immune to bullets. A squirt gun would have had the same effect. Neil stood there, watching the nightmare step closer and closer.

Just then, something sparkled as it whirled above the head of the beast—something like a noose or a lasso, which tightened around the monster's torso, stopping it in its tracks. The cord shone in the sun; more so, it appeared that it had been woven out of light itself, so bright and ethereal it seemed. An unseen force pulled the creature back and hurled it to the ground. For a brief moment, Neil saw Nouri holding the lasso before the strange instrument dissolved in the air.

Neil was at loss for words. Absolutely nothing was making sense anymore.

"I told you to pray!" Nouri shouted as he ducked and picked his sword up. "Do not get involved in this!"

With that, the guard charged at the monster, which was getting back on its feet some distance away from him. The creature did not raise its mace—instead, it rose in the air. Nouri stopped as he watched his opponent levitating far above him, trying to anticipate its next move.

The harsh desert wind began blowing again, stronger and more ruthless. It felt like the wild currents came from all sides: north and east, south and west. They congregated around the floating creature, circling around it.

And the sands rose to swirl with the winds, blasting up like geysers. Nouri's dark-blue mantle was flapping insanely amidst this magical storm. Clutching his sword as tightly as he could, he bent his knees, bracing himself, like he was preparing to run a marathon.

The monster threw its free hand forward, turning an open palm towards Nouri. A long tendril of sand shot out of the cloud, thick enough to bury anybody under its weight.

But before the sandy tendril hit the ground, Nouri jumped up and forth. Next thing Neil knew, the guard was running up the moving mass like it was the slope of a dune. Nouri launched himself off and, just like his opponent, hung in mid-air as if the cloak that was flapping behind him was a pair of wings.

With another gesture, the creature sent a bolt of sand the man's way, but Nouri dodged it, levitating to the right.

Down below, Neil found himself not even remotely sure what condition he was in. Was he really a witness to such an extraordinary spectacle? Was this a mirage born out of the games the desert's heat and landscape were playing with him? Perhaps he had lost consciousness and this was all a deranged dream? Or maybe he himself was deranged: hallucinating all of this in a fit of insanity?

And above, where sand and winds raged, Nouri kept on hopping and whirling in mid-air like a dragonfly. The wrathful creature continued to throw more bolts and tendrils of sand his way, but whenever Nouri did not evade the magical projectiles, he used them as stepping-stones to get closer to his enemy. It was as if he had somehow managed to tap into the sorcery of the mysterious being and use it to his advantage.

Sword and mace clashed again. The creature threw its free hand forward once more and a sudden blast of wind hurled Nouri back. The guard reached for his belt and threw a knife at his enemy. The short blade defied the storm as it flew forward and cut the monster's side, making the fiend shriek in rage and pain. Nouri recuperated fast and, clutching the sword with both hands, flew forward, head first. The blade slashed the monster across the chest, and with a move of a hand that mimicked the one the beast made earlier, Nouri blasted his adversary towards the ground.

However, at the last moment, the creature wrapped its long tail around Nouri's foot, ensnaring him. Plummeting towards the ground along with his foe, Nouri slashed at the tail until the fleshy noose let go of him. The creature tumbled to the ground on its back, but Nouri landed catlike on his feet beside it. He immediately continued his attack, thrusting the blade into the monster's chest.

At that moment, the mass of sand that had been circling above their heads fell down. Yet the two were not buried. Instead, the sandstorm began to revolve around them, making both disappear from sight behind this newly formed wall.

"Samir!" Neil called to the guard, using his surname.

But nobody shouted back.

Disregarding any common sense, Neil dashed towards the wall of sand, but could not break through. The sandy tempest expanded, catching him within its confines. Tears began to stream down his cheeks as sand lashed at his eyes. Distinguishing any form—human or monstrous—became impossible. The world was spinning around him, dyed in brown-yellow.

CHAPTER TWENTY-ONE

The call to Morning Prayer woke Elliott up as the sun was beginning to rise over the oasis. Some time after, an attendant's shout from the courtyard let the guests know that breakfast was ready. There was no diversity of choice for their morning meal; it consisted of bread, cheese, yoghurt, and tea.

The cousins lingered around the courtyard for the next hour or so, until the whinnying of horses and the clanking of hooves against the ground notified them of the arrival of a new group.

Ismail and Yussuf walked through the gates of the guesthouse, followed by two cloaked men. They exchanged greetings.

"Ready?" Yussuf said, looking at Elliott.

"Yes, we're ready," Lauren said, stepping forth.

Their hosts exchanged somewhat uncomfortable looks, then turned back to the redhead as if she were some unexplainable oddity.

"With all respect, we do not think that a massacre site is a place for a woman," Ismail said. "It would be much better if you stay here."

"What do you mean?" Lauren began to protest, but whatever argument she might have given was cut short by Elliott grabbing her by the elbow.

"Sorry, gentlemen, can you give us a minute?" He forced a smile before pulling her to the side.

"Please, Lauren, don't show any attitude," he whispered to her.

"But this is—"

"Remember: when in Rome..." he reminded her. "This is certainly not the time and place to debate gender roles."

"Fine, don't sweat about it," she said. "I'll try a different approach."

She looked at him and, under the influence of her commanding gaze, Elliott let go. Lauren turned around and rejoined the locals.

"I implore you to reconsider your stance," she said humbly. "I *need* to be there. I know everything about the camp, all the people that were there, everything. My presence there would be useful."

"We understand," Yussuf said. "But we are going there on horseback. This involves quite a lot of..." He paused, thinking of a word. "Closeness and physical contact...between the horseman and the passenger. And men around these parts don't ride with women from outside their households. It's not the norm."

"But I can ride a horse!"

"You can?" Elliott asked, surprised.

"Yes, I can. I was very into active sports a few years back. Aside from horse riding, I've also done scuba diving."

Seems like I've got a lot of catching up to do, Elliott thought.

Yussuf looked at the sheikh, awaiting his decision.

"I guess it is alright," Ismail said. "I will request one more horse. Now let's go."

His cloak flared behind him as he turned around and walked out through the gates, followed by his men and guests.

***

Elliott had learned to despise the drylands. The inhospitable landscape brought back memories of his torturous trek. Mere days later, he was back in same terrain—this time, riding atop a cantering steed, clinging to the horseman. The sun could not bake the top of his head like last time; a headdress protected him.

Their journey took them several hours. Aside from the elders and the foreigners, there were eight more men along with their horses. Several times the party stopped at the sheikh's command, and Ismail would pull out the same old map, study it, and go forth once more.

Eventually, they found what they were looking for. When a cluster of tents appeared in the distance, the group set their course towards them.

Elliott remembered the camp as neatly organised, but there was no trace of that now. Signs of a rampage could be spotted even from a distance. Tent walls were torn, strips of fabric flying in the arid wind like flags. Then there was the smell of death that infused the air, making Elliott feel a sickening lurch in his stomach.

At the sheikh's command, the group dismounted at the edge of the camp. Ismail then addressed his men in Arabic. Whilst he was doing so, Lauren got off her horse and, as if she was sleepwalking, ventured forth into the camp. The eerie atmosphere of the ravaged camp and its ripped tents made her seem like a phantom wandering around a haunted site.

Soon enough, Elliott, too, was roaming among the tents. He had thought that getting caught in the hyenas' vicious manhunt during the night was terrifying, but seeing the aftermath of their game in daylight was truly nightmarish. Any step offered the potential to come across dead bodies, corpses of familiar people. Some lay on the ground exposed to sun and dust. Some could be found by peeking into the slashed tents. And it was the state the corpses were in that made the scene so gruesome. Large chunks of flesh were missing: from chests and stomachs, thighs and shoulders. Some had their faces torn. Seeing exposed ribs and pelvis bones almost made Elliott throw up.

His path led him to the very centre of the camp, right to the operations gazebo.

He already knew what he would find there. Joe's savaged body lay sprawled in the same position it was left on that horrible night. His chest pressed hard by sorrow and guilt, Elliott knelt down next to him; even the smell of rot emanating from the body could not stop him.

"Well, bro, I'm back," he whispered mournfully.

Joe's open but emotionless eyes just continued to stare at the blue skies above.

The sound of footsteps made Elliott turn around. Ismail approached the giant gazebo, his attention drawn to the long vertical tear in the gazebo's wall. He ran his fingers down the side of the tear.

"Was this done by one of the beasts?" he asked, still looking at it.

"Yes," Elliott answered.

"Hmm." The sheikh lightly stroked his beard before moving on.

Elliott later found him near the parked four-wheelers. The scene here was just as gruesome. The hyenas had not been content with the destruction at the campsite; they had taken their fury out on the vehicles as well. The wheels had been bitten and clawed at, as if the monsters mistook rubber for flesh. A trail of claw marks ran across one of the car doors. The vehicle that Akhmad had attempted to use to escape that fatal night still stood there, door wide open. The steering wheel lay on the dusty ground next to it; one of the beasts had actually taken the effort to rip it off. Elliott turned around immediately when he saw what was left of Akhmad—that was just too much to bear.

"It is as if the ferocity of these beasts was fuelled by the Shaitan himself," Ismail said as he and Elliott walked back towards the camp.

Lauren emerged from the midst of the tents. Upon a closer look, it became clear she was in anguish. Her eyes were red; she used the corner of the headscarf to wipe away a tear that slid down her cheek.

Yussuf joined them.

"There was an armed guard at this camp, correct?" he asked.

"Yes, some of the supervisors were armed," Lauren said, looking sorrowfully aside.

"I found one lying on his stomach, the gun beside him," Yussuf said. "I assume that one of the hyenas was able to sneak up on him from behind. These creatures appear to be very cunning."

Ismail nodded in silence.

Soon, the sheikh's men began to bring their grim findings out of the site and carefully line up the bodies on the edge of the camp, like workers on a humanitarian mission.

"That's all of them," Ismail sighed, having received an update from one the cloaked men. "Twenty-three. Does this account for everybody?" he asked Elliott.

"No, there was one more," Lauren said.

It was hard for her to be here; her gaze had constantly been wandering off into the brown-yellow distance.

"Dr Mergham." She gasped. "Mergham isn't here!"

She was right. Even the most savaged corpse could not have belonged to the archaeologist; none bore a resemblance to him.

"Well, all the cars are on location," Elliott said. "So he couldn't have driven off."

"He probably was able to flee the camp and wandered off into the drylands," Yussuf speculated.

"He might still be alive!" Lauren's voice vibrated with hope.

"He might have been at the archaeological site when the attack happened," Elliott said. "He once told me he had a habit of going there at night time to study any possible astronomic alignments." He remembered the time he saw the author at the platform. "We might find...traces...of him there."

He knew very well that if Mergham really was at the platform when everything happened, those accursed hyenas probably found him there.

"Take us to that site," the sheikh said.

Lauren took the role of guide. She led them towards the site where the group had spent weeks working. They climbed up the mound, the same mound Elliott had observed Mergham from that one eerie night. Daylight revealed a good panorama of the area, offering a view of the dig.

"By the Prophet," Ismail gasped, his attention concentrated on the megalithic platform.

Elliott saw no human figure among the pits and enclosures; if Mergham had been there that night, he certainly was not anymore.

They climbed down the mound with the old sheikh at the front, leading them straight towards the platform.

"What is this?" Ismail asked, stopping the group in front of it.

"The centrepiece of our study," Lauren said. "Leonard believed that the gods worshipped in ancient Assyria and Babylon were in fact aliens from other worlds. He thought that platforms like this were where they landed their vessels when they came down from the skies."

"If this platform is related to Heaven, why does it feel like a tombstone?" Ismail asked grimly.

He took several steps along the megalith's length, his full attention on the mysterious stones. He walked like he was mesmerised, not just at looking at the megalith but actually trying to listen to it.

"Yussuf, please lead everybody to the camp," Ismail said and turned his back to the others. "I would like to stay here for a bit."

The Master of Service responded by urging the others to follow him. As the group made their retreat, the winds picked up melodious words in a foreign tongue. Elliott turned around and saw the old sheikh standing there, facing the platform, chanting what appeared to be a prayer.

The sheikh rejoined the rest of the group at the destroyed camp shortly after. He gave two of the horsemen the order to scour the site's surroundings in search of any sign of the missing man. In the meantime, the elder presided over the ceremony in which the victims were laid to rest—at least to a temporary one—in a common grave.

They spent the rest of the afternoon on the ride back to the oasis. Before parting at the gates of the guesthouse, Ismail let his guests know that he would be paying them a visit after the Evening Prayer.

***

Elliott and Lauren were sitting in silence in the brightly lit dining area, recollections of the hard day pushing any thoughts of conversation away. Ismail arrived as promised, once again accompanied by Yussuf. The Master of Service walked in, carrying another antique, this time, a manuscript.

"I intend to send a messenger to Erbil in order to notify the authorities of the tragedy," Ismail said as they sat down. "They should do what is needed.

"As for you," he continued. "I believe it would be for the best if you stayed here for a few days to recuperate. Then I will gather an entourage to take you to Erbil."

"I don't know how to thank you for everything you have done," Lauren said.

"Please, you are our guests," Yussuf said. "And hospitality has always been a sacred tradition in the Middle East."

"But this is not the only reason we are here this evening," Ismail said. "I know it's hard to talk about, but we would like to hear more details about what happened that night. And we will mention something ourselves.

"Our people have lived in this oasis for around a millennium, since the time of the Seljuks. Our cemeteries are located at the edge of the oasis, with many ancient graves going back centuries."

This narration sounded like a prologue to a true horror story.

"A couple of days before your appearance, it came to my attention that somebody had been frequenting the cemeteries at night, digging up graves, and feasting on the remains of our ancestors."

Elliott could feel goose bumps on the back of his neck.

"It was a mystery. I have lived in this area all my life. I used to play in the drylands when I was a child. But never, throughout all these years, have I seen a single hyena in these parts. And when I saw the scale of destruction they wrought on your camp, I was shocked; I could not believe that an animal could do something like this," Ismail said. "So try to remember. Did you notice anything unusual about those hyenas?"

"They were definitely bigger than the ones you see on television," Elliott answered. "They were about the size of a human."

"Was there anything even stranger?"

"What do you mean?" Lauren asked.

"For example, did any of the noises that they made vaguely resemble a human tongue?" Yussuf asked, his question unusual and disturbing.

Lauren just shook her head.

"I was probably hallucinating because of the terror," Elliott said, his voice cold, "but I could have sworn that I saw one of them get up on its hind legs and walk."

A sudden feeling of dread overcame him, as though some hidden sense was trying to warn him that the same bipedal abomination lay in wait for him in the shadows outside the dining room.

The sheikh threw a look at his subordinate. Yussuf opened the book, and after flipping a number of pages, pushed it across the table.

"Like this?" he asked.

Elliott and Lauren peeked into the book. The right-hand page contained only text, handwritten in Arabic script, but a picture took over the whole page to the left: a picture of a grotesque creature that stood on its hind legs, its claws extended, as it staggered towards a terrified kneeling man. It did not resemble a hyena, being more akin to a dog. But the picture brought back a familiar sense of terror.

"Something like that." A wide-eyed Elliott looked back at the elders.

"Then the things that attacked your camp were not hyenas. Your attackers were not even animals. Those were ghuls," Ismail said.

"Ghouls?" Lauren parroted a familiar-sounding word.

"The folklore of the Middle East tells stories about beings that live alongside humans: the jinn. There are many varieties of jinn, and the most vicious among them are the ghuls. They are predators and scavengers that stalk travellers and raid graveyards under the cover of the night," Ismail explained.

"So they're supernatural?" Lauren uttered, her expression baffled.

Ismail nodded.

"What kind of cursed place are these drylands?" Elliott could only shake his head, giving up on any semblance of rationality.

"Old women tell stories about the ghuls to frighten their grandchildren. But again, there had never been any sightings of them here before. There is a reason why an old wisdom instructs travellers not to make a mess in the middle of nowhere in order not to anger the jinn that might reside there," the sheikh said. "I do not know what that giant platform was meant for, but I believe that its unearthing is connected to their appearance. I could sense something odd radiating from those stones as I stood beside it. I have read a prayer over it; this should be enough to vanquish the ghuls."

Then there was utter silence: uncanny, utter silence.

CHAPTER TWENTY-TWO

As Neil struggled in the sandy haze, he felt the ground underneath his feet dissolve. He found himself falling, plunging into this strange sinkhole. Sand irritated his eyes, and tears blurred his vision. The continuing plunge made his heart race at an impossible rate, subjected to pressure that felt strong enough to rip it into pieces before he hit the bottom of this enormous pit.

Then a hand clasped his wrist in a grip as solid as that of a handcuff. Neil's whole body jerked as his fall suddenly ceased.

"Got you!" a familiar voice sounded from nearby.

Neil blinked intensively until his vision recovered. He gave his surroundings a brief look. What he saw left him shocked and trembling. He was dangling in the air with Nouri's grasp being all that that kept him from continuing his fall. The guard's grip was tight and solid, but his position was as precarious as Neil's. He'd braced himself against the wall of the pit, clinging to a dagger he'd implanted in the rock. The situation was dire. The dagger was not planted strongly enough to bear the weight of two men. Tremors ran through Neil's body as the blade slid out of the wall bit by bit. He looked down; he could see the bottom of the pit far below. Not even the luckiest man in the world would survive a fall from such a height.

"What are we going to do?" Neil called out to Nouri, his raised voice edging on hysterical.

"I am going to try to make our landing as safe as possible," the guard responded.

"How?!"

"Have faith. And don't make any sudden movements."

Nouri pushed back against the wall with his foot. The movement tore the blade out, sending the duo falling.

Nouri's grasp on Neil's wrist remained just as strong, but that brought the reporter zero comfort. He shut his eyes tightly, his heart pounding. Neil was certain that this second plunge lasted mere moments. But his mind mistook every second for a minute. He was sure that he would smash against the pit's floor head first, yet some unknown force flipped him in the air, making him land on his feet like a cat. Still, the impact was hard. He gritted his teeth as his feet cried out in pain. Nouri's supportive grip kept him from collapsing.

"Are you alright?" the guard asked.

"Yes," Neil hissed through still-gritted teeth before letting go of his hand.

It took him a few more moments to steady himself. Then his gaze began to wander around the place. The pit was wide; three or four university lecture rooms would have fitted in easily. Looking above, he could not see the crack they had fallen through; it was as if the crevice that had swallowed them had been sealed again. No sunrays appeared to reach the bottom of the pit from above, yet there had to be some source of light slithering into this underground cavern through some unnoticeable holes, keeping the space relatively well illuminated.

It was bright enough to allow Neil to recognise the grotesque figure a few feet away from the duo. The thing lay sprawled on the ground. Nouri's sword stuck out of its body in a sign of victory, but Neil found it hard to overcome the disturbing feeling that this monster might suddenly get back on its feet. He kept watching it for a while to drive away his doubts. The body did not convulse a single time, and relief washed over him.

Neil looked to the left, and what he saw astonished him. The façade of a building stood there underneath countless layers of sand, dirt, and gravel, built out of large stone slabs. The entranceway was wide enough for two people to walk in side by side; if a grown man had sat on the shoulders of one of them, a few inches would have still separated his head from the large stone block that served as the entrance's lintel. It stood there, pulsing with enigmas. The identity of the builders, the way it had ended up deep below ground—questions kept popping up in his mind.

Nouri walked towards his vanquished foe, grabbed the sword by the hilt, and pulled it out of the corpse. On any other occasion, the blade would have been stained crimson with blood, but the steel remained spotless, as if it had just been taken out of an armoury. Neil had stopped being amazed by this point; the cavalcade of miracles that day had proven that nothing was impossible.

Within moments, the creature's hideous form began to undergo its own type of decomposition. Flesh quickly turned into sand, and the sand evaporated into air right before Neil's eyes.

Sword in hand, Nouri stood tense, looking in every direction, searching the place for something...or someone.

"What...the hell...was that...thing?" Neil said between breaths, pointing at the empty space where the corpse had lain.

"A daeva." Nouri turned to him. "Or, more specifically, a desert daeva."

"Ok." Neil nodded slowly. "I also have at least ten more questions that I would like to ask."

"And I will answer most if not all of them. But this is not the right time," Nouri said, still on alert. "We should not stay like this in the open. One daeva is bad enough; the last thing we need is to get ambushed by several of them."

"You're right," Neil agreed. "What do you propose?"

"I don't think we can get out the same way we got here." Nouri looked upwards into the dark. "We have no choice but to go in there." He pointed his sword at the entrance to the strange structure. "There we might find some sort of means of getting back to the surface." Nouri brought the blade closer to him, ready to defend against any attacker. "Follow me, and always watch your back."

Neil followed after him and slowly walked towards the mysterious structure, caution accompanying every step he took. He stopped right in front of the entrance and peered into its unexplored interior. Neil waited in frightful suspense, sure some potential threat would burst out from inside. Yet nothing emerged to offer them greeting, neither warm nor grisly.

Cautiously, Nouri walked through the entrance, and Neil followed.

The building's vestibule lacked any furnishing. The inner walls had been erected out of stones much smaller than the slabs outside, each roughly the size of a brick. Not a single painting or bas-relief adorned the walls, and yet the blandness only added to the mysterious atmosphere of the place. From the vestibule, another archway led further into the complex.

The following room was a gallery of sorts. Though narrow, it was rather long. It ran on and on, a number of doorways located on each side.

Neil wondered at the presence of natural light in this underground structure. Not only had daylight passed through to a place buried deep under sand, but it had also found its way through the windowless walls. Neil had never thought that anything relatively bright could still feel so creepy.

Nouri, with Neil on his heels, crossed the room and peeked through the doorway before moving on and looking into the next one. With a gesture of his hand, he motioned for Neil to follow him. They ended up in a chamber about the size of an average living room. Just like the vestibule, it stood completely empty and unfurnished.

"Stand next to the wall in order to avoid being noticed from the gallery," Nouri said quietly as he did the exact same thing.

He did not have to repeat his recommendation in order for Neil to join him by the wall.

"Let's take a short break here," the guard said, lowering his sword.

"Can I ask at least some of the questions I have?" Neil said quietly.

"Yes."

"What is this place, for starters?"

"I'm not sure. There is no doubt that this structure is of some use to the daevas."

"And what exactly are these...daevas?"

"Tales about the daevas are present in Middle Eastern folklore. They are classed as a type of jinn. However, whether the daevas can be considered jinn is, in my view, debatable. After all, locals feared the daevas long before stories about jinn arrived to these lands. They're vile demons that seek to bring harm to mortals. They can be found dwelling among different landscapes. This part of the desert appears to be the domain of one of the tribes of daevas."

"I assume you've dealt with these demons before."

"No," Nouri said bluntly. "This was my first encounter with a daeva. Although I have...read studies about them." The pause he left in the middle of the sentence gave Neil a clue that the guard was going to withhold at least some information.

"Fine, now tell me this. I observed your fight with that demon. I saw you not only levitate in mid-air but actually fly. You were able to make us land safely on the bottom of the pit even though we should have been killed by the fall. How do you manage to perform all these miracles?" The fear of being overheard by any demons that might have been strolling through the long corridors was the only thing keeping Neil's voice low whilst confusion rushed through his mind.

"Mister Feaver, you are a decent man, so I will tell you something only a few people know about me. I hope you can keep a secret," Nouri said as he looked at his employer.

Neil responded with a silent nod.

"I can wield magic."

Neil wanted to be surprised by this statement. On any normal day, he would have been. But this day was not normal, so he responded with nothing whatsoever. The bizarre was promising to become the new normal.

"Now let's see. You can use magic. You have psychic powers. You can fight like no man I have ever come across. These are quite unusual skills for a security guard. Where did you learn all of this?"

Nouri stood just a few feet away from Neil. He was clearly as human as Neil was, and yet his eyes had started to acquire a strange quality that made him appear just as otherworldly as the demon he had slain.

"I hope you will not be upset if I do not answer your question on this occasion," Nouri responded. "But I will tell you this. The same crafts I have learnt were studied long before the times of the old Arabic rulers. They are very ancient; they go back many millennia, to a time when there was no Iraq, only Mesopotamia. They predate Hammurabi of Babylon, Sargon of Akkad, and even Gilgamesh of Uruk."

Neil wanted to know more about it, but he knew this was all he would hear on the topic, at least for the day.

"Very well," he accepted reluctantly. "But just one more thing. How is this possible? You slew that creature with your sword, but I fired a round of bullets through it to absolutely no effect." He would have been content with at least knowing the answer to this question.

"Because my sword was blessed whilst your gun and bullets aren't." Nouri dropped another extraordinary fact. The guard seemed to have a talent for doing this.

"Not everything that is solid is made out flesh and blood," he continued. "The daevas are beings made out of unholy power. Average metal might not be enough to kill one of them, though it can inflict harm of various degrees. However, everything depends on location. For instance, the daeva we faced was in its territory; you can say it drew its power from the surroundings, so your weapon was absolutely useless. But the holy can tackle the unholy. This is why I told you to recite a prayer. It does not matter what kind of prayer it is: when sincere, it produces holy energy that makes a daeva disoriented for some time. This is why that particular specimen was unable to lay a hand on you while you were praying. My sword, on the other hand, was blessed during a special ritual, specifically to slay beings like that."

Neil really wished he had an opportunity to sit down with this mysterious man and have a lengthy interview about all the things he had mentioned and implied. He was certain he would get enough material to write a whole series of articles, if not an entire book. Surely it would be an overnight sensation. But that day was yet to come; and for that to happen, he first needed to see the light of any day.

"We need to find a way back," Neil said.

"My thoughts exactly. And this is another reason I chose to come inside this structure. For all we know, there might be a way to get back up from here. Perhaps this place has some stairway or portal that leads to the surface."

Portal. Neil barely hid a smile as he thought about it. The idea did not sound absurd at all—and that was the most disturbing part about it.

"And what if there is no exit route?" he asked.

"Then we will try the other option. Only, the alternative carries a much greater risk." The guard's voice was cold.

"So shall we get going?"

"Just one more thing," Nouri said, placing the sword against the wall.

He reached beneath his cloak and withdrew the graphic novel.

"I'll try to connect to Mister Parvis' life force. He might have been here."

Nouri sat down on the floor, placing the comic on his lap and pressing his palm against it. His expression turned blank again. Neil feared that the guard would remain in this catatonic state for hours, leaving him to watch over his unconscious form in this dark corner of this accursed structure. But his daze was brief. Less than a minute later, Nouri feverously shook his head.

"I caught it," he said, looking at Neil. "He should be somewhere in this building."

Hope lightened Neil's spirit.

***

At first, Jake could not tell what was going on. One moment, he felt like he was taking a nap, having been overcome with exhaustion. That was before somebody got the idea that he was some sort of swing or rocking chair and pushed him roughly on the shoulder.

"Hey! Hey! Are you alright?" a feminine voice said.

He opened his eyes to a scene where rock was the main element—stone walls grew out of a stone floor. The hand on his shoulder, soft and warm, served as a strong contrast to what lay beneath him. It appeared that he had been taking a nap on a bare stone floor devoid of even the thinnest mattress.

"I am," he mumbled as he slowly sat up.

Then he began to feel the consequences of sleeping on bare stone: the muscles of his back, shoulders, and right hand howled underneath his skin, convulsing in pain.

A woman stepped into view. He recognised her immediately: Alice. Seeing her triggered a flood of other memories, each weirder than the one that preceded it: deranged cultists, human sacrifices, demons... It reminded him far too much of an acid trip he had back in his college years when he and some of his friends were fooling around with LSD...

"Holy hell," he mumbled and looked at Alice. "Tell me something. Was I tripping on some drug? The things I remember are just…" he paused as he tried to find the right description "…unbelievable."

Alice slowly shook her head, her expression just as stony as the floor beneath them. "I don't think that was a hallucination," she said. "We had the same experience."

"What were those creepy things? Demons?" Jake asked. The pain in his joints was starting to die down.

"I can't even imagine what else they could have been. But the bigger question is—where are we?"

Jake's gaze circled around the room like a periscope. They appeared to be in some sort of chamber. But no matter which direction he looked in, there were only walls. There was no door, not even a cat flap.

"I have no clue," Jake said. "The last thing I remember is being covered by a tsunami of sand."

For all he knew, they could literally be in Hell.

"Can you remember anything that happened after?" he asked.

Again, Alice shook her head.

"This place doesn't have a door or a window," Jake grunted.

"Not even an access door," Alice said, examining the ceiling.

Jake tried to get up. Alice extended a hand, which he took. Moments later, he was back on his feet.

"Thanks," he said, letting go. "Great predicament we're in. Absolutely marvellous. What should we do now?"

"Maybe there is a way out," Alice walked up to the wall and looked at it like an architectural expert.

Jake came up beside her. Yet a closer look still did not reveal an exit.

"Even if there is, what do you think is there on the other side?" Jake wondered.

"I don't know," Alice said.

Neither did he. There could have been anything on the other side of that wall, perhaps even something completely unimaginable. And that was the most horrifying thing about it.

***

Neil had no idea how much time they'd spent exploring the eerie building. They had gone through several more galleries and looked through every doorway they found. Some led into other adjoining galleries, others to chambers akin to the one they had taken rest in before.

"This whole place is teeming with energies that are not just dark but demonic," Nouri told him, explaining why he could not sense Jake's exact location in this complex.

The cameraman could have been in any chamber. They might find him tied and gagged, or enchanted by some dark spell.

They were moving stealthily up and down the long corridors, constantly checking over their shoulders. They kept their ears open for any sound of movement.

"There's one thing that I can't get off my mind," Neil said when they stepped into another chamber, which, too, turned out to be empty. "Where is all this light coming from? We're deep underground."

"Don't apply the laws of physics that you have been taught to this place," Nouri said. "According to Islamic beliefs, the jinn live side by side with humans, and yet their world is detached from ours. This domain is underground but it's not fully a part of our reality."

"I don't get it."

"Think of the world we live in as shirt. A shirt can have a number of inner pockets, each filled with contents. These are the domain of the jinn. This underground realm is one of these pockets."

"So it's a type of pocket universe," Neil said, vaguely recalling hearing about a somewhat similar concept.

"You could call it that."

They checked chamber after chamber, finding each of them empty. But, of course, there was bound to be an exception. One was notably larger. While the others were comparable to bedrooms in terms of size, this one was as large as a reception area of a big company. Even from the entryway, it was possible to see that it was in use. Neil distinguished the shapes of several heaps, standing there like haystacks.

"Curious," Nouri said as they stepped inside.

A closer inspection revealed that these stacks were made out of various types of items carelessly thrown into piles. The objects were not just old but ancient. Neil saw shields and daggers, pots and beads, ploughs of farmers and the tools of blacksmiths. It almost seemed as if some museum had rented this room as storage for the objects they had removed from display.

By Neil's side, Nouri studied these finds intently, like an antiques shop owner offered a look at potential merchandise.

"These objects." Neil crouched before one of the stacks. "They're ancient."

"They indeed are," Nouri agreed. "Only, I'm not sure if they all hail from the same historic period."

"Were they made by the daevas?" Neil asked as his recently-acquired fascination with ancient artefacts began to play its mesmerising melody inside his soul.

"No, they were made by humans. You don't have to be afraid of them."

That was a relief, for Neil had no idea what type of infernal taint one could catch upon touching an item of demonic origin.

His gaze fell on a clay object resting on the uneven slope of the pile. It appeared to be a bowl; its humble size would have only allowed room for one small appetiser. Its curved interior was decorated with engravings in a cursive script. It resembled Arabic calligraphy at first glance, but even though the script was similar, Arabic it was not.

"What's that item?" Neil asked.

"Which one exactly?" Nouri asked from behind him.

"The tiny bowl." Neil pointed it out.

"An incantation bowl," Nouri said. He briefly picked the object up only to put it down moments later. "The people of ancient Mesopotamia and some other parts of the ancient Near East used these as protective charms to ward off evil spirits."

"Ward off evil spirits?" Neil parroted the phrase. "Then what is it doing here in the possession of the daevas?"

"A trophy, no doubt," Nouri said grimly. "I believe that all the items stored here are spoils of the daeva campaigns against the human settlers that might have once lived on the edges of their territory. An incantation bowl is a magic charm, but protective magic might not help when countered by a more powerful spell. I do not know what exactly happened nor how all these objects made their way here, but the forgotten tale behind it is likely quite dreadful."

Chills ran down Neil's spine, and Nouri stepped away to look at another heap. Neil moved clockwise to study the artefacts that made up the left side of the stack. He took a step, and the stone beneath his shoe pressed deeper into the floor under his weight. A loud rumble sounded from behind. Neil turned around and saw that the opening that led into the chamber was actually a doorway. He could see the door, made out of the same stone as everything else, descending from the lintel.

"A trap!" Nouri shouted, having forsaken any notion of remaining stealthy. "Get out! Move!" He dashed towards the closing exit.

Neil ran, but the door was descending at a rather fast rate; the opening had gotten significantly smaller. Nouri leaped and managed to slide through the shrinking exit like a paper soldier pushed by a gust of wind.

Neil could have gone for a similar move—at least, an amateur imitation of it—but he could imagine only one result: getting stuck under the heavy door with a crushed spine.

He was almost there when the door hit the floor with a thud. What had been an opening became just another section of the wall.

Frustrated, he slammed an open palm against the devious snare. He was trapped. Bricked up.

CHAPTER TWENTY-THREE

The farther a nomad journeys into the desert, the harsher the surroundings become. The closer Sayid's forces drew to Baghdad, the fiercer the resistance became. The practically effortless takeover of Hisad al-Shaeir was starting to become a fond memory as Sayid spent his days on the frontlines. He'd grown used to the bitter taste of the dust in this scarred area as he dodged bullets, shells, and bombs. The offensive continued, and he could still report that despite the obstacles, his fighters succeeded in capturing more settlements and strategic locations.

He did not particularly like that backwater town behind the frontline, but it had somewhat grown on him. And whenever his duties sent him there for whatever purpose, he went with keenness.

The kitchen of the house Hamza was staying in in Hisad al-Shaeir was relatively modest in size; the table was more akin to a stall. The small kettle on the stove sang its whistling tune as its contents reached boiling point. Hamza came up to the table and placed two cups atop it before sitting on a nearby stool.

"So, everything on the frontline is going well," Hamza said as he listened to some of the stories Sayid was telling.

"More or less," Sayid said, putting an elbow on the table. "We've been able to push into the Taji area, quite a big development. It's the north-western gateway to Baghdad. Just a bit more and I'll be able to see the city's fringes through my binoculars."

"God willing," Hamza said.

"God willing," Sayid responded. "But I anticipate tougher resistance down the road. The army brought in some friends to help them: the Shia militias. I've seen their banners and insignia back there on the frontline."

He paused and looked at Hamza, whose expression was stone solid. They had both fought against these clerical paramilitary groups in the past, and they had proved to be some of the fiercest and most enduring adversaries they had ever faced.

"The tea should be ready by now," Hamza said when the kettle whistled more vigorously.

He got up and took the kettle off the stove. He poured tea into the cup of his guest before filling his own. Sayid took hold of the cup and sipped. The strong mint flavour overwhelmed his taste buds with its refreshing tang.

"How is it?" Hamza asked after drinking some himself.

"This is pretty good," Sayid answered.

"I'm glad to hear it." Hamza fell silent for a moment. "Do you remember Areeb?" he suddenly asked.

It took Sayid a mere second to conjure up a familiar face before his eyes, one belonging to another of his subordinates.

"Yes, of course I do," he said.

"Do you remember the teas he used to make?"

"Yes."

And Sayid suddenly felt an urge to have one of those beverages made by his tea-savvy lieutenant. If not mint tea, then sage tea; if not sage tea, then cardamom tea. But he knew he would not get that chance.

"That damned sniper killed one of my best men," Sayid mumbled as he remembered the day of Areeb's demise.

"He really had a skill at tea-making," Hamza said as he sipped more of his drink. "Who knows, if it had been Allah's will, Areeb might have become the most sought-after tea master of Kirkuk."

"Kirkuk?" Sayid raised an eyebrow at the mention of the northern city. "Areeb was not from Kirkuk."

"He wasn't?" Hamza looked confused.

"No." Sayid put the cup down. "Areeb wasn't even Iraqi. He was a foreign recruit from Libya. His hometown was Derna, in the east of that country."

"I guess I forgot after all this time."

"He died two years ago," Sayid said. Perhaps he and Hamza had different perceptions of time, for two years did not seem that long ago.

"Why then did I think of Kirkuk?" Hamza asked himself aloud.

"You probably got him confused with Faarez, another one of my aides. He was from Kirkuk," Sayid theorised. "But he was martyred in an American air raid on one of our camps."

"I guess so."

Their small chat went on as they drank tea. Matters both recent and old were raised and dropped as they continued to talk.

"And how are you handling your new duties?" Sayid asked.

"I want to believe that I'm handling them fine. After all, I've been tasked with running several towns, so I have to alternate my time between them."

"Well, do your job and, who knows, maybe one day they'll appoint you to run Basra," Sayid joked.

"Maybe they will." Hamza chuckled lightly.

"Only, we'll need to capture it first."

And that's going to take quite a while, Sayid added in his thoughts. Basra was the country's second-biggest city, located in the southern part of Iraq, close to the coast. Just getting there would require overcoming many lines of defence.

"You know, since we're on this topic, there's something I'd like to share with you." Hamza's tone became more serious. "I recently had to go north to settle something. That's where I heard something strange."

"What exactly?"

"About something…I'm not even sure how to properly describe it…called the Jinn Arts."

Even hearing the term made Sayid tense.

"And?" Sayid urged him to continue.

"I was told that those who practice them are the key to winning this war. I've never seen one in person, but, apparently they will be deployed to the frontlines soon enough." Hamza looked at him. "I heard they learned of a way to create fire out of thin air."

Apparently, the Jinn Arts were no longer a secret known only by the upper rank of the group. The fact that Hamza had somehow heard of them did not come as a surprise; after all, rumours were bound to spread.

"It's true." Sayid nodded. "I've seen a demonstration of their skills."

He described the unusual duel between the practitioners he'd seen back at the stadium in Baiji.

Hamza almost gasped. "By the Prophet, it sounds like a fairytale!"

"Only, I saw it with my own eyes."

"But..." Hamza went quiet, looking somewhat uncomfortable. "Do you think this is a good idea?"

"It is without doubt a complex topic."

Sayid let him in on the heated debate that had followed the demonstration, Nishwari's arguments, and the way it was resolved. He wanted to assure his friend not to worry about this topic, that everything was going to be fine. And yet he felt like he was, first and foremost, trying to assure himself.

"I heard the arguments in support of these Jinn Arts," Hamza said. "But you know that information can spread quite quickly across large swaths of territory, mixing with speculation and rumours along the way. It has already reached this town. I've done some investigating. And as I have found out, a lot of men in the Liwa are concerned about this practice."

This was no surprise to Sayid.

***

Sayid noticed that more people turned up for Friday Prayer on this occasion. A couple of weeks had passed since the group took over the town, and it was about time that the town's remaining inhabitants started to get out of their homes.

He was back at the town's mosque, kneeling on its intricate carpet. To his left and to his right, in front of him and behind his back, his men and the locals mixed into one as they recited Quranic verses. The next part of the prayer, the sermon, was soon to start, and ahead at the minbar, Ibrahim Falai stood up after taking rest between the two parts.

"My brothers and sisters!" The imam began his sermon. "All of you gathered here know that we live in times of troubles. Once again, like many times before, we, the faithful, those who follow the word of Allah that his angels conveyed to the Prophet, have to defend the World of Islam from the enemies that seek to unravel its very foundations!

"Both the infidels and the apostates are enemies to us," Ibrahim continued. "And our souls and minds are their primary targets, for if they make us go astray, make us forget the true teachings of the Prophet, they will break us, reducing us to the status of slaves who will find delight in serving them! And whenever their attempts at this fail, they go for the second target: our lives! Do not doubt that they would kill you like they would kill me, your family and mine, without a second thought! They have massacred many Muslims in Iraq and many more across the Islamic world. Our enemies seek to stop our commitment to the truth, and when they see they fail to achieve it through spiritual corruption, they try physical destruction!

"So, what I'm trying to tell you, brothers and sisters, is that the main battle is not waged for our lives! It never has been! It is fought for our souls! Lives are expendable; lives are discardable! For what is life but a short passage of time before the Hereafter? And can a life's turbulence, its ups and its downs, really be preferable to the eternal bliss of Heaven that Allah has in store for the faithful?"

Ibrahim went quiet for a moment as he eyed his congregation from the minbar.

"I have talked of our enemies. I have talked about infidels and the apostates. But there is another kind of enemy I would like to remind you of: the most cunning and terrifying one. The acts of the infidels and apostates are there for all to see. But the ones I intend to talk about work in different ways.

"Praised be Allah, for HE is the Almighty, the Creator of all life!" Ibrahim proclaimed with exaltation. "He made angels out of light. He made jinn out of smokeless flame. He made Man out of clay. And Man was his most beloved creation. So when He gave life to Adam, all the residents of Heaven were told to prostrate themselves before the first man. Everybody did, aside from one: the jinn Iblis, the Shaitan."

As the imam began to tell this story, one that everybody in attendance certainly knew, a troubling feeling began to stir in Sayid's gut.

"The Shaitan refused and for his disobedience Allah banished him to Hell. And from that day and until the Day of Judgement, he and the wicked jinn he commands have made harming men the main purpose of their existence."

Sayid did not like the direction this sermon was beginning to take.

"For countless eons, they have done their dark deeds in every corner of the world. They are doing it now, in different places at once. They can because their numbers are enormous. It is said that for every man there is an evil jinn watching him behind his back. They cast jinxes and cause illnesses. They can start a drought as easily as they can cause a flood or any other calamity. Yet their main strength is their cunning, and they excel at leading people astray. Always remember that even the most devout Muslims can fall for their deception!

"Evil jinn can find ways to exploit a man's weakness. They listen when you cry about your troubles. And then, standing beside you but invisible to the naked eye, they will whisper their suggestions into your ear, thus planting dark thoughts in your minds. They can come to you in the guise of man or animal and help you with your goal. They can make the wildest dream come true. They can make the unimaginable possible. But all of this comes with the heaviest price.

"When the Day of Judgement comes, Allah will bring you forth to answer for the wrongful deeds and choices you made in life. And then it will be too late for you to put blame on the Shaitan, for the Shaitan himself will step forth and respond by saying: 'You called and I answered.' The Holy Quran warns us about situations like this, but still there are those who fail to heed these warnings.

"Allah banished the Shaitan to rule over Hell for refusing to bow to Man, and the Shaitan, unable to challenge Allah in any way, fulfils his thirst for vengeance against men by directing them to paths that lead straight to Hell. And must I remind you of the torments that await the wicked and the misguided in Hell? Flames will become their shrouds and boiling water will pour on their heads like thick rain! And torment will stretch for eternity! The depths of Hell are vast, and there is always space to take in new souls, for it is said that if a stone gets cast into its abyss, it will not hit its bottom even after the passing of seventy years!

"So remember, brothers and sisters! Do not allow the wicked jinn to make you lose sight of the right path. Remember the verses from Surah Al-Jinn, where the good jinn, those jinn that are devout followers of Allah, warn you: 'There are the Right Ones and the Stray Ones, and the Stray Ones will become the twigs that will forever fuel the fires of Hell.' Remember this!

"So whenever you notice delusions beginning to fog your mind, rely on the advice the Holy Quran offers you: 'Against the whispers of wicked jinn, find solace by praying to Allah'!"

The sermon and prayer were soon over, and the mosque's colonnaded hall started to empty as the worshippers went back to their households. Sayid stood up and made his way towards the exit, where he picked his boots up from the shoe stand beside the doorway.

"So, how did you find the sermon?" Sayid heard Hamza's voice behind him.

Holding his boots in his hands, he turned around to face his friend.

"I am not sure whether I will be coming to this mosque for Friday Prayer again," he told him. "I cannot say that I find the imam's sermons spiritually fulfilling."

Instead of strengthening his will, the imam's speech did little more than fill Sayid's head with troubling imagery and more insecurity.

"It did seem like an odd topic, considering the timing," Hamza said, looking around like he was searching for eavesdroppers.

Everybody else had already left. Sayid's and Hamza's guards were the only other attendants remaining, standing some distance away.

"Quite a coincidence, isn't it?" Sayid said. He was not sure if he was being genuine or sarcastic. He stepped closer to Hamza. "Especially in light of the Jinn Arts controversy," he practically whispered into his ear. "Can you imagine how this might affect the morale of my fighters? The last thing we need is a mutiny on the frontline."

Sayid put his boots back on the stand. "You know what? I would like to talk to him. Right now. You can join us if you want."

Hamza nodded. Sayid then walked up to the guards and gave them the order to wait outside. The guards obeyed his command and disappeared. Sayid and Hamza then headed towards the heart of the mosque, where the imam was standing by the minbar in the company of his young assistant, the muezzin.

"Ah, Commander Buzali, Governor Saqqaf," Ibrahim called out to them. "It is always a delight to see you here," he said, as courteous as always.

"Imam Falai, may we talk to you?" Sayid asked. "In private?" he added.

"Of course," the imam said and shot the muezzin a deep, commanding look.

His assistant said nothing, merely nodding before making his exit.

"I am sure I am right to assume that today's sermon heartened your already strong devotion to Allah," Ibrahim said rather casually.

"This is actually what I wanted to talk to you about." Sayid wanted to get straight to the point. "The topic you chose for today's sermon—"

"Is rather relevant in today's world." The imam cut him off. A mysterious smile appeared on his face.

He knows something, Sayid realised. "Would you like to elaborate on this?" he asked in full seriousness.

The matter was indeed a serious one, and he hoped Ibrahim realised it. Otherwise, nothing would stop him from ordering the imam's detention the moment the old man walked out of the mosque.

"Sayid." Ibrahim chose to address him by his first name. "I have been an imam at this mosque for over three decades. I suppose I was already preaching here at the time you came into this world. Listening to concerns and offering spiritual advice to the followers of the Prophet is one of the duties of an imam. Recently, one of your fighters came to me with his concerns. And I must say, what I heard sounded like a tale from *One Thousand and One Nights*."

Sayid had to admit that it was a great comparison, but it could only mean that the imam had heard of the Jinn Arts. This was a bad sign; the rumours were spreading outside the ranks of the Liwa.

"Did the fighter have a name?" Sayid asked. There would be consequences for carelessly spreading information to outsiders.

"I do not ask for names unless it is necessary," Ibrahim said, strict. "And even if I knew it, I would not share it with anybody, not even if you threatened me. I am a preacher of the Holy Quran; I am expected to serve as a pillar to devout Muslims that seek guidance. How can I be one if they cannot trust me?"

Sayid never particularly liked Ibrahim, but on this matter, he had nothing but respect for the old imam for standing up for his principles.

"But let me put your heart at ease," Ibrahim continued. "I advised him to find refuge in Allah through prayer; the Almighty will make everything clear in due time."

At least it seemed the imam sincerely sought to deescalate the situation.

"And now that we are alone, I hope you do not mind listening to my concerns about these...Jinn Arts." The imam said the last two words with barely concealed disgust. "I heard of Mullah Nishwari long before the appearance of Liwa al-Qadisiyyah. I know he is a renowned scholar of the Quran and I do not doubt that he is a devout servant of Allah, but even the wisest men sometimes heed bad counsel. So I implore you, Commander Buzali, Governor Saqqaf, to use your high positions to have the advisor that suggested this madness to the mullah removed."

"It's more complex than that," Sayid said. "But the Shura will later convene to make a decision on the use of these Jinn Arts."

Sayid's tongue was not loose; he was not going to tell the man that the whole project was the mullah's idea.

"But why was it not convened before all of this was set in motion?"

Damn. It was a legitimate question, and one he himself had overlooked.

"Let's say the Shura convenes and they find it unquestionably un-Islamic, then what?" Ibrahim pressed on.

"Then this practice will be discontinued."

"By that time, the damage will already have been done and it will become irreversible. Can you imagine the rift it could cause among the followers of the Prophet?"

Sayid preferred not to think about it, but that did not make the imam's words any less truthful.

"Can I find out where this concept of the Jinn Arts was learnt from?" Ibrahim asked. "By the Prophet, I swear I will not tell anybody else of it."

The imam did appear to be quite reliable in this respect.

"From an ancient manuscript written over a millennium ago by a Muslim explorer who spent years studying the ways of a group of Persian magi," Sayid explained.

The answer seemed to plunge the imam into a state of despair. His hands shot up to grip the sides of his head as he began to pace in small circles, as though he was suffering from a strong migraine.

"Haram! Haram!" he repeated as he walked circle after circle. "This is madness of an unbelievable scale! Relying on the sorcery of ancient pagans—haram! Haram!"

"But you cannot really call it sorcery," Sayid protested. "Magic is an illusion meant to lead people into disbelief." He repeated Nishwari's thesis. "But this is not an illusion. I've seen its effects. For all we know, the Jinn Arts could indeed be what they are called...an art...a skill...a hidden talent." The sentence kept breaking off. Unlike his superior, Sayid found it harder to defend his position. Or perhaps he had trouble believing it himself. "We've discovered more about natural phenomena since the times of the great thinkers of the past." He parroted another one of the mullah's statements.

Like an automated toy with a dead battery, Ibrahim suddenly stopped his frantic pacing.

"Tell me something, Sayid," he said calmly. "What did Caliph Umar do when he captured the city of Alexandria?"

History had never been Sayid's strength.

"He ordered to have the famed Library of Alexandria burnt to the ground, along with its vast collection of pagan scrolls!" Ibrahim said without waiting for the answer. "And as he gave his order, he said: 'Everything in accordance with the Quran is mentioned in the Quran, and everything that contradicts the Quran is unneeded.' The Quran does not tell us what components lightning is made out of or why rivers flow into oceans and not out of them. The Quran's purpose is not to explain the detailed schematics of chemistry or physics, but you will find no contradiction. Now ask yourself this question. If these Jinn Arts were meant for mortals, why are they not mentioned in the holy texts? Why didn't Allah's angels teach them to the Prophet and his men? And since the magi of Ancient Persia had knowledge of this powerful craft, where were they when the warriors of Islam were crushing the armies of the fire-worshipping Persian shahs on the battlefields?"

Sayid was not sure what to say; he hoped Hamza would join the discussion, back him up with counter-arguments. But he stayed silent.

***

Sayid turned to the side as he lay in bed in the dark of the following night. He wanted to get some sleep, yet he was denied even the shortest nap. He would close his eyes, but no dream would come, and familiar voices would fill his head over and over again. He would hear Nishwari and then Awal. And if that was not enough, the voice of Ibrahim Falai would join the fray like a musician that arrived late for the performance. Sayid would hear their allegorical, moral-filled monologues about right and wrong, about having faith and the consequences of making grave mistakes. And he no longer knew what to think about any of this. He had prayed, but had heard no answer to his question.

He roughly pulled his blanket aside and staggered to the moonlit window. He damned the day these Jinn Arts pushed their way into his world, turning everything upside down like a vicious hurricane. It was much simpler before: there was the goal and there was the zeal, and little else mattered. Both were still there—just, one more method was available as well. But this new method was so strange and so otherworldly that it could cast even the most seasoned fighter and ruthless killer into a state of dread.

He grabbed his jacket from the back of a chair; the night could be rather chilly. Intending to get some fresh air in the courtyard, he rushed out without turning the lights on in the corridor.

The aging stairway creaked underneath his heavy steps. He did not take safety into consideration, so when he slipped, there was nothing he could do. Pain hit different parts of his body as he tumbled down the stairs.

***

Sayid could only come to one conclusion: he had died. The scenery before him was nothing like anything he had beheld before.

He was standing on a stony platform, like the top of some cliff. Behind him was a screen of grey fog, so thick that even a distorted silhouette could not be seen through it. In contrast, morning light was breaking in front of him. And there, far in the distance but unnaturally accessible to the naked eye, was another platform of stone. It served as a foundation to an enormous gateway made out of pure light, which, in the absence of the sun, appeared to illuminate the surroundings. A figure in long, lustrous white robes stood beside it. It was not human; the bird-like wings sprouting from its back attested to this fact. A small cloud hung in front of it, concealing its face from Sayid's gaze. A hanging bridge, not grand but wide enough for one person to cross, stretched across the void, connecting the two platforms.

Sayid remembered a story his grandfather told him many years ago, a folktale that described the way into the Hereafter. In his adult years, he'd laughed many times upon remembering this superstitious account. It now appeared there was truth to it, much more than a grain.

Shock and surprise kept Sayid standing on the platform, unsure of his next move. He watched the angel—and the distant figure could be nothing but an angel—raise its hand and beckon him forward.

Anxiety tingling through him, Sayid walked onto the bridge. He'd made just one step when a horrendous sound assaulted his ears, making every particle of his being tremble. It sounded like an anguished cry...no, not a single cry, but a cacophony of countless wails.

Shaken, he looked down. He could not see the bottom of the void beneath the bridge, so deep it was. It glowed with hues of orange and crimson. Pillars of flames kept springing out of it all around. They appeared to have no equal in height; the tallest skyscrapers of Dubai would have seemed toy models in comparison.

And the pained wailing...it just would not stop. Down below him lay Hell, as bottomless and nightmarish as Ibrahim had described it.

Sayid looked up and started walking forward again, quickening his pace. Though he could see the angel and the gateway, he still had a long way to go.

Then he noticed that the celestial bridge was getting narrower as he crossed. Panic began to poke him in the back. What would happen if the bridge faded away completely? He preferred not to think about it. He sped his pace up, but the bridge kept contracting. Soon enough, he understood that if he continued in the same manner, he would fall off the edge of the ever-narrowing bridge.

With his options diminishing, he proceeded with caution. Soon enough, he neared the edge of the other platform. By that point, the bridge had become just slightly wider than the blade of a sword. He had to make use of all the agility he could harvest as he crossed the thin bridge like an acrobat walking a tightrope.

Only a few steps remained until the edge of the platform. The angel would soon be in reachable distance. But the wails from below never ceased. Sayid threw another look at the chasm and its fiery radiance.

He looked back up; he was almost there, a mere step away from the platform. But the angel was no longer there. Instead, an old hag stood in its place. Her dress was no white robe, but a black rag, torn and dirty. She was undoubtedly the most hideous creature he had ever had the misfortune of seeing. The skin of her face and hands was covered with disgusting pustules, like she was ridden with the most horrible type of plague. Her dark, messy hair clung to her head like seaweed, her eyes were dead, and the few teeth remaining in her mouth were disfigured with rot. The sight made Sayid tremble.

All of a sudden, the hag shrieked as she pounced at Sayid, making him cry out in sheer terror. Having lost balance, he fell backwards and plunged into the blazing abyss...

CHAPTER TWENTY-FOUR

Lauren stood beneath one of the trees that grew in the courtyard of the old inn, having retreated into the little world inside her head. Whenever the events of that horrendous night emerged, her mental defences kicked in, pushing the painful memories back into the shadows.

The evening was peaceful, free even from the blowing of the land's dry winds that would have otherwise made the leaves whisper in their floral tongue. The evenings at the inn were dull, even more monotonous than the days, mostly spent in her small room devoid of any form of entertainment. Without other options, strolling in the courtyard was the only way to free herself from complete boredom for at least some time.

The sound of footsteps echoing in the dusk drew her attention to the stone stairway that led to the inn's upper floor where the guest rooms were located. She saw Elliott coming down the steps slowly, quiet as a phantom. He failed to notice her as he concentrated on his own thoughts. With his back turned to her, he headed towards the ever-open gates of the inn.

"Elliott!" she called out to him, breaking the courtyard's tranquil silence.

He stopped and turned around. She started towards him at a fast pace.

"What a surprise," Elliott said whilst she was approaching. "I thought you'd be resting."

"Trust me, I've had enough rest for today," she responded. "What are you doing?"

"Going out," he said casually.

Lauren's eyebrow shot up as though an electric charge ran through her body. "What do you mean, you're going out?"

"I mean out, doing some exploring outside of this place." He gestured at their surroundings. "I, both of us, have been cooped up here for days."

"Are you sure that's a good idea?" she asked.

"As far as I'm aware, we're not under house arrest. And I want to see what it's like outside this enclosure. For all we know, maybe the world ended last night and the only thing left is this inn floating in the middle of nothing. You're welcome to join me if you'd like," he added before she had a chance to say anything.

She pondered for a few moments, not sure about the wisdom behind this idea. She had caught a glimpse of the town whilst they were riding to the ransacked campsite and back. But that was all it was: a momentary peek. And it was tempting to do something else for a change. But still, the facts urged her to maintain caution; after all, they were in the middle of an uncharted oasis in a remote area of an unfamiliar country.

"Ok, you can stay here if you're not up to it," Elliott said. "But I'm going anyway."

Lauren could sense light disappointment in his voice, and it felt awkward. The two of them had never really hung out together. There had been different reasons for that, none positive, and yet it appeared her cousin was regretting the fact that she would not be tagging along on this occasion.

"You know what," Lauren said, "I'll go as well. But you do realise that I still have reservations regarding this."

"I would have been more surprised if you didn't," Elliott joked.

She already knew that the inn stood by the road on the outskirts of the settlement. One could see the nearby houses, very traditional-looking ones, by just walking out on the road. The road, too, was rather old-fashioned. Paved with neither stone nor asphalt, it had likely never seen a car driving its surface, being meant for those travelling by foot, horse, or carriage.

Between the inn and the nearest house, the road forked, branching out towards the right. From there, it led to what was likely the biggest if not the only landmark of the settlement. The bulbous dome of a mosque rose from behind the walls of an enclosure. The tops of other buildings peeked out as well, an obvious clue that the walls hid an entire complex within their margins.

Naturally, Elliott's curiosity drove the pair towards the compound. The gateway leading into the complex lacked a proper gate, instead two chains sprawled from the top of each side, crossing in the middle. They had to crouch and bow their heads to get through. Lauren wondered what the purpose of this was as she slid underneath the chains.

The complex enclosed within the walls was a jewel of planning and architecture. Darkness could not devalue its antiquated beauty, only adding to its tranquillity. Elliott and Lauren walked the pavement cobbled with stones, old and smooth. The buildings stood looking back at them with their arch-supported façades. Some of the structures were rather large, big enough to contain several rooms; some would have fitted nothing more than a small shrine. Most stood around the edges, next to the walls; a few were scattered randomly.

"Wow, this place is surreal," Elliott said as he caught sight of the calligraphic engraving above the mosque's entrance.

"It is, isn't it?" Lauren agreed.

The only noise other than their voices was the sound of running water. A small fountain stood in front of the mosque, its basin inlaid with turquoise tiles.

"You know, I bet this could make a great film set," Ellliott said as he leaned over the side of the fountain and looked into its pool.

"Yeah, like something about Lawrence of Arabia," Lauren agreed, looking at the soothing sight of water erupting out of the fountain. "Or Sinbad."

The place was quiet and lifeless. Every building stood vacant, at least for the time being, darkness concealing the interiors on the other side of the windows. And so, when they saw a feeble glow of light escaping through the window of a building they stumbled upon after turning around the corner the mosque, it caught their attention instantly.

"I guess we really aren't the only ones here," Elliott said.

With a wave of his hand, he gestured for Lauren to follow him. Like a couple of infiltrators, the two sneaked closer. The window, in reality, was a pair of windows, separated by a mullion. Rectangular in shape and crossed with geometric latticework, the windows were set low in the wall. Elliott had to crawl under them to avoid possible detection. He rose up, leaned against the wall and carefully peeked into one window. Lauren did the same.

The interior consisted of one single large space, more of an atrium than a room. Oil lamps hanging around it illuminated the place quite well, though the latticework created obstacles when it came to a more detailed observation. Across the room, opposite the window, a man knelt on a mat, clad in attire Lauren had become used to seeing: a blue cloak and brown conical hat. She saw about ten more people, dressed the same way. Kneeling as well, they formed a row facing the lone figure. Lauren was certain that the man on the mat across from her was none other than Sheikh Ismail. The architectural acoustics of the building allowed the echoes of chanting to be heard outside.

The chanting soon stopped, only to be replaced with a set of different sounds that could only have been made by musical instruments. There appeared to be three of them, springing one after the other and quickly uniting into an elegant and thoughtful rhythm. Her place by the window did not allow her an opportunity to see the musicians, but Lauren made an attempt to recognise the instruments. The one that was mellow and whistling belonged to a flute; the hard beating was that of a drum. She was not sure about the third sound, the sharp one, but she assumed it came from some stringed instrument akin to a sitar.

Ismail stood up and the others followed his lead. Step by step, the sheikh began walking slowly, anticlockwise around the room. The other men set forth on the same path, one by one. Ismail turned around gracefully and gave a bow to the man following him, who bowed to him in return. The man then turned around to bow to the man behind him. And this continued until every man in the chain had been paid his respects. By the end they were all back at their original places.

Ismail raised his hand in prayer and chanted a sentence. The music that had ceased to allow him to speak resumed, more lively than before. As if on cue, all of the brethren, sans their leader and one more man, threw off their cloaks, revealing a set of robes hidden underneath. Being of a pleasant, clean white colour, their outfits consisted of three pieces: a shirt with long sleeves, a skirt-like cloth that fell to their ankles, and trousers, the edges of which stuck out from under the skirts.

The white-robed men began moving in the same direction yet again. But this time there was no slow walking and there was no bowing. The first man shot forward whilst rotating like a spinning top. The next one in line followed suit, then the third, and the fourth one, and so on. Soon the men were spinning around their axes like a set of whirligigs launched into motion by a playful child.

It was not only the unusual whirling motions that caught Lauren's attention; the positioning of their hands did as well. At first, a participant would hold them at the level of his waist, but as his enchanted dance went on, he would raise them higher and higher. Eventually, he would hold his palms above his head, pointing at the ceiling with the tips of his fingers.

Ismail and the other man who remained cloaked—and it already became clear that was Yussuf—did not follow the others into this mystical swirl. Instead, they split up and walked around the hall in the midst of spinners like pilgrims, bowing their heads before each of the men. The surreal atmosphere, the enthralling music, the detached feel of the dance—everything gave the impression that the men were charmed.

Because of this, she did not pay attention as Elliott crawled back underneath the window. She almost screamed in surprise as his side collided with her leg by accident.

"Elliott!" she hissed in anger.

"Oh, sorry." He whispered an apology before getting up straight. "I think we've seen enough for today. What do you say? Perhaps we better go back to the inn. Just in case," he added.

The idea of leaving did not really appeal to Lauren at that moment; the mystifying performance intrigued her, and she was curious to find out how its ending was supposed to play out. But even Elliott had the capability of making logical suggestions every now and then. And then, the rule-abiding part of her reminded her that perhaps their hosts did not like being spied on by outsiders.

"You're right," she admitted. "Let's go."

Calmly and quietly, they made their way out of the complex, crouching underneath the hanging chains at the gateway.

"Ah, why did they even hang them here?" Lauren mumbled to herself whilst straightening up, unable to resist the urge to complain.

"That was something I haven't seen before," Elliott commented as they walked into the evening.

"Yes, something very different."

"What type of celebration do you think it was?"

"I don't think they were celebrating," Lauren said, looking at the path before them. "They appeared to have fallen into a trance of some sort as they danced. If anything, I would say it's some form of meditation."

She now had something to think about for the remainder of the evening.

CHAPTER TWENTY-FIVE

The grimmest thoughts entered Neil's mind the moment the view of the gallery disappeared behind the heavy slab. He could not shake off the premonition that he was bound to remain in this room until his final breath.

His fist pounded against the wall like a hammer trying to sink a nail in.

"Nouri!" he shouted as shock, fear, and panic mixed together into an anxious cocktail. "Nouri!"

"Neil!" He heard the familiar voice reach out from the other side of the slab. "Can you hear me, Neil?!"

These words bore no potential for salvation, and yet they brought some form of relief.

"I hear you!" Neil said into the barely noticeable gap that existed between the door and the wall.

"Great. Neil, do not worry. I'll find a way to get you out of here—any way I can. Just bear with me."

"Ok," Neil said and took a few steps back.

His head, after the initial shock had worn off, began to clear up. He turned around and studied the chamber again. It was foolish to assume that there was a way to open the door in here; booby traps were meant to keep intruders in. There was nothing he could do about this situation by himself. All hope lay on Nouri.

He found himself drawn again to the highlight of the chamber—the piles of ancient artefacts. Returning to the same heap, he picked up the miniature incantation bowl. He studied the calligraphy as if trying to make out what the silent script was trying to convey to him. Yet the symbols did not give away their mystery, and perhaps that was their allure.

He tucked the bowl under his shirt; luckily, its small size promised it would not become an impediment in any situation in which he had to run. He could not deny the possibility, taking the surreal events of the day into account, that he might make use of the bowl in some paranormal capacity. The ancient token might have failed its original owner centuries ago, but perhaps it could still prove useful in warding off some evil spirit.

Neil heard the door rumble back again. He turned around and saw the slab move upwards, revealing the corridor beyond bit by bit. Seeing Nouri in the doorway again made him almost as jubilant as a child during a birthday party.

"Get out quickly!" Nouri called, gesturing as he did. "Or it might be too late! I don't know how this mechanism works!"

Neil dashed towards him, faster than he'd ever run, even when under fire during his stints on the frontlines.

"How did you reopen it?" he asked when he got outside the chamber.

"Trap doors often have secret triggers that allow you to open them from the outside. I had to put pressure on a number of stones before I got the right one," Nouri explained, pointing the sword's blade at a block in the wall that was visually no different from its neighbours to its left and right, above and below. "Now, let's go," he said, and led the way.

The next gallery seemed different from the rest; only one chamber led off its northern wall.

"Wait," Nouri said as he froze in his steps. Neil stopped immediately. "Look over there." The guard raised his sword, pointing at the wall to their right. "You see the section of wall I'm pointing at? Notice that it's thinner."

And indeed, Neil could see the spot where the wall appeared to lose a few inches in thickness.

"I see it," he said.

"That's exactly how the chamber you were trapped in looked like from outside when the door was down."

"You mean it's another trap door?"

"Yes."

Even if Nouri had not approached it, Neil would have done so on his own.

"Jake? Jake!" he carefully called through the needle-thin gap between door and wall.

"Is somebody there?" a voice responded, though it was not Jake's. Perhaps it was due to the acoustics of the complex, but the voice sounded quite feminine.

"Are you the aid worker from the refugee camp?" Nouri asked.

"I recognise that voice!" somebody else said from behind the wall. "Neil! Are you there?"

"I'm here, Jake! I'm here!" Neil answered, barely resisting a chuckle as relief rushed through his body like an adrenaline shot.

"Everybody, stay quiet. We'll get you out," Nouri instructed them. "Neil, start pressing the stones of the wall. One has to be a trigger."

Neil began searching for the hidden mechanism. Yet not a single stone moved under his touch. A rumbling sound to his side let him know that Nouri had found it. The door rose upwards and, as soon as it had completely withdrawn into the lintel, two figures bolted out of the chamber. One was undoubtedly Jake; the other was a blonde woman he had seen at the refugee camp, though he could not recall her name.

"Thank you," the woman whispered.

"Neil, I've never been so happy to see you," the cameraman said. He seemed so relieved and excited that Neil got an impression Jake could barely contain the urge to hug his colleague.

"Yes, this is quite a jam," Neil muttered.

"How did you guys manage to get here?" Jake asked.

"There will be a time to share stories," Nouri said impatiently. "But not now and not here." He turned to the freed captives. "For now, there's only one thing we need to know. Do you two know of a way out of this complex?"

"I can't remember how we ended up in that chamber," the woman said.

"It's unbelievable—we were brought here through some sort of magic," Jake said. "I'm serious."

"I'm sure of it," Neil said without the smallest tint of sarcasm.

"Then let's not waste any time," Nouri told them as he skilfully swirled the sword in his hand. "Follow me, be as quiet as possible, and watch your every step." Upon saying this, he made his way towards the northern wall.

The chamber they entered was somewhat bigger than the artefact storage area. Unlike every other room they had explored, this one had an identical entrance in the opposite wall. A big terracotta pot stood in the middle of the room. It was made of the simplest and crudest clay, though it was as wide as a cauldron. The rim rose to the level of Neil's chest.

And again, the mysterious source of lighting made Neil uncomfortable. They had to be deep in the complex. There were no torches on the walls, no lanterns on the floor, and no chandelier hung from the ceiling, yet the chamber was even brighter than all the galleries they had crossed.

Neil and the others followed Nouri up to the vessel. Inside, it was filled with sand, almost up to its rim.

"This room..." Neil said, looking around. "It reminds me the sanctum of the temple we saw last night."

"That's because it's intended to be a dark imitation of a fire altar. But instead of fire, which is the holy element according to the Zoroastrian tradition, burning inside this pot, you see it is filled with sand, the element of the daevas," Nouri said coldly. "Now I know the purpose of this structure: the daevas use it as a temple."

"A temple?" Neil raised an eyebrow. "But who do they pray to?" He would have readily paid money to find out the answer to this question.

"Gods," Nouri answered bluntly.

"What?" Neil said, dumbfounded. "But they're demons."

"Trust me, demons too can worship gods. Some gods, that is."

Neil decided not to ask any additional questions on this topic for the time being. The things he had seen and heard in this one day had already completely annihilated a worldview he had held for many years. He would have time to study this subject if he got out of this place.

"I've got a hunch about the way we can take," Nouri said and led them through the opposite entranceway.

Not surprisingly, they entered another gallery. From there, he led them on and on in the same direction through more and more galleries. The temple was enormous; even Angkor Wat, the largest temple ever built on the surface of the Earth, would not have occupied even a tenth of this unholy shrine.

But it turned out that Nouri was indeed on the right track. He led them into another vestibule with its own ceremonial entrance. Outside, a long cavern stretched out from the gate.

Neil had no clue where it promised to lead them to, but at least it was possible to walk it.

"We're lucky," Nouri said, peering down the tunnel. "This has to be the physical way in and out of the temple."

It stood to reason that the other entrance point was not particularly physical. But there was no point in thinking too deeply about that right now.

Eventually, the passageway guided them back towards the surface. Neil could see a light at the end, but unlike whatever glow had suffused the underground chambers, this radiance felt very familiar. Few things in the world were more natural than daylight.

The group emerged out of a desert cave that sat within the lower part of a large dune. Nouri urged them to follow him further, and only when the dune and the entrance into the underground domain were left far behind did he let them take a well-deserved break behind the cover of another dune.

"Are you sure we're safe here in the open?" Neil asked, dreading the thought of coming across another desert fiend.

"Positive. The daevas are not all-seeing and they are not omnipresent. And there's no reason to assume that there are demons lingering around every part of the desert."

"So how did you manage to figure out where the exit out of that temple was?" Neil asked.

"It's easy when you locate the sanctum of a temple. I told you it seemed to be inspired by the fire temples of old. A fire altar stands in the very heart of a temple and there tends to be at least one direct path towards it. As for there being a way out... Well, remember that the folklore of the Middle East is full of tales about magic caves leading to miraculous underground domains. Do you really think these stories came from nowhere?"

Neil could not even bother to comment on this.

Their break was also a time to share stories. Neil had thought that the things he had gone though were extraordinary. And indeed, Jake's eyes were wide with surprise as he found out that their guard was a skilled practitioner of magic, not to mention that he had tracked him via his graphic novel.

But the tale told by Jake and the blonde—Alice, as he was reminded—turned out to be even more bizarre. So many things were crammed into it. He learnt of the dark cult responsible for human sacrifices, the traces of which he had seen; an apparently high-ranking figure whose face was concealed behind a metallic mask; a strange artefact called the Tear of Set.

"Of course, Was Peraa," Nouri said, revealing this was not the first time he had heard this name. "They are an ancient society of mystics which, according to one account, was founded by the God King Set himself during his rule over Egypt thousands of years ago to serve as his enforcers. Though initially Egyptian, with time, they expanded to include people from other nations: Babylonians, Assyrians, Persians, Canaanites, Phrygians, Greeks.

"Back two and a half thousand years ago, after spending centuries in the shadows, they forged an alliance with the sorcerer Gaumata, who usurped the throne of the Persian Empire posing as Prince Bardiya, the late son of Cyrus the Great. They were the ones who had the Persian King Cambyses assassinated during his campaign in Egypt.

"However, Gaumata's reign was short-lived. His deception was revealed. One night, a group of seven conspirators broke into the royal palace and murdered him in his chambers. The leader of the coup, Darius, became the new king. I assume this event destroyed the society's attempt to spread their influence across the Persian Empire and become the dominant power behind the throne of the Achaemenid dynasty.

"After coming to power, Darius responded with a crackdown on the society. Some perished but some survived and fled Egypt. But it appears that the story of Was Peraa did not end there."

"But why did they need seven people specifically?" Neil asked. "Why not three, or five, or seventeen?"

"That's because seven has been a sacred number across different traditions of the Near East throughout the centuries," Nouri explained as he leaned on his sword. "Take Zoroastrianism, for example. There are seven divinities, the Amesha Spentas, which emanate from the god Ahura Mazda. There are seven holy feasts in the in the Zoroastrian calendar. So again, what we are seeing is a dark inversion of the symbol: there were seven sacrifices and, as I noticed, seven blows with a knife."

"These...Dae..." Jake said when Nouri questioned him for more information. "Daeva?" He had issues remembering this word. "All negotiation from their side was carried out by their leader...

very creepy type, but still more human-like than the others. His name starts with 'A', but I can't remember the rest."

"I think it was Aposa or something like that," Alice added.

For a brief moment, Nouri pursed his lips. "Apaosha?"

"Yes, I think that's how he pronounced it," Alice said.

"You've heard it before?" Neil asked Nouri.

"Yes. An ancient Persian myth talks about a powerful demon with the same name who once unleashed a terrible drought upon the known world. The rain god Tishtrya went on to battle the demon to relieve the curse. They fought for three days and three nights, and on the fourth day, Tishtrya was able to vanquish his foe. The myth does not reveal what became of Apaosha after that battle, but it appears that while weakened, he survived and retreated to these remote parts, where he succeeded in building his own fief."

"Unbelievable." Alice shook her head. "So, what you're saying is that an ancient myth is actually an account of an event that took place during the Stone Age?"

"Not necessarily the Stone Age. It could have happened during a later period like the Bronze Age. It could have even taken place during the early Iron Age, maybe even in the time of Zoroaster."

The way Neil saw it, it required real talent to explain something so shocking so casually.

Around them, the day was coming to an end. The desert sky needed only moments to cover itself with its dark shroud.

"So, what now?" Neil asked. "Will we be able to find our way back to the jeep?"

"We will. Don't worry about it," Nouri assured him. "But there is something that cannot be ignored: the Tear of Set. Personally, I have never heard of this artefact before." His gaze wandered from Jake to Alice. "But I can conclude from your story that it is powerful. Whatever purpose the cult and the daevas have for it is bound to be vile. It must not remain in their possession. Do either of you remember the way from the cult's camp to the site of the sacrifice?"

"Yes." Alice nodded.

"Wait, you want us to steal that artefact?" Jake asked, looking at the guard like he was some raving madman.

"No, I don't expect you to take an active part. I'll snatch it away from them myself. However, I will need as much information about their encampment as possible."

***

The night air felt cold but dry as Neil took a deep breath, bracing himself for the upcoming stunt. His looked at the holstered gun on his belt. Though he had wasted a chunk of ammo on the daeva, there were still some bullets left. It had not taken Nouri much effort to convince Neil to aid him in this operation by providing cover. After all, he owed the magician for the instrumental role he had played in locating Jake.

With Nouri and magic on his mind, Neil turned to the side. Nouri was kneeling some distance away. Though his back was turned to Neil and the group, it was obvious that he was in the middle of enacting some sort of spellwork. His hands were gliding over the sand, drawing symbols. Neil was certain he was quietly chanting incantations.

Neil glanced back at Jake and Alice, who silently stood nearby, before looking ahead, trying to imagine the hostile encampment hidden behind those distant dunes. He still found it funny to think that they had required no map or navigator to locate it. Nouri had used his psychic talents to lead them back to the vicinity of the sacrificial site, drawn to his own dagger, the one he lost whilst battling the daeva. From then on, it was all about following Alice's directions.

The sands began to rise, swirling in the air around them. The sight immediately brought thoughts of the daeva, and though Neil knew his weapon was useless against the demons, he still reached for the gun by sheer instinct.

The sand danced in the air around but not between them; the wind did not howl, hinting that some other power was involved on this occasion. Neil turned to Nouri again as the magician calmly stood up.

"The spell is complete, but it will only be active for a limited amount of time," Nouri said as he rejoined the trio. "Neil, let's go, we mustn't waste a single minute." He drew his sword. "As for you two..." He turned to Jake and Alice. "Stay here and remember what I told you about prayer."

Nouri began to climb the dunes with Neil right behind him. Neil shielded his face in an effort to avoid the unpleasantness of getting sand in his eyes. But this time, he did not step into the sandy tempest—the sandstorm was moving in front of them like a herald.

"Don't worry about your eyes," Nouri told him. "The spellwork in place is unlike the powers of the daevas. There is no sandstorm; the spell I cast is that of illusion."

Neil lowered his hands. They kept walking for some time before the edges of the camp came into view.

"Do you remember what your part is?" Nouri asked.

"Of course," Neil said as he withdrew the pistol from the holster.

"Perfect."

They were getting closer and closer to the camp and its streets of crimson tents. Anxiety grew inside Neil at the thought that they were practically walking into the enemy's base through the front door. Even through the whirling sands he could see a guard standing at the boundary of the camp. Clad in a breastplate and holding a sword, the man looked like an image from a textbook on ancient history. He kept staring at the strange sandstorm, making Neil fear that he had managed to see though the magical charade.

"Now." Nouri gave the order.

Immediately, Neil bolted towards the nearest tent and took his position behind it.

Nouri remained where he was for a few moments. Then, lifting his sword, he charged at the guard. He jumped out of the sand tempest as though he were a desert demon himself. The illusion faded away instantly. The armoured guard did not get a chance to even raise his weapon before he got cut down.

Several camels grunted from the depths of the camp, having felt the presence of an outsider. Then came the long boom of a horn as another guard sounded the alarm. One by one, more sword-wielding fighters emerged from the tents; some wore the same breastplates as the first, and others wore dark shrouds over their armour. Upon seeing new foes, Nouri charged to face his opponents, his blade sparkling in the moonlight. Neil moved out from behind the tent, holding the gun in front of him. He did not know how skilled these swordsmen were, but against Nouri they seemed like new recruits fighting a seasoned veteran. Nouri cut and sliced through every single one of them; even the best of them could only exchange a few blows with the invader clad in the navy cloak before getting struck down and joining their fallen comrades on the sand.

Another fighter arrived at the scene, raising a javelin over his head. Neil bolted towards the battlefield. He took aim and pulled the trigger. A bang erupted, and a moment later the javelin-thrower collapsed, struck in the head.

Quickly, looking left and right in search of any potential surprises, Neil moved closer to Nouri. Walking up the corpse-clad path, he noticed the silhouette of a man peeking from behind one of the tents.

"Look! The tent to the right!" Neil shouted.

But it appeared Nouri had noticed the man too; the magician's stern gaze alone sent the dark-clad figure into flight. Nouri gave chase. He whipped a throwing knife from his belt and threw it at the runaway. The man gasped as the blade sunk into his back, and he fell face down.

Nouri and Neil stood back-to-back, waiting for a second wave of opponents, the former gripping the hilt of his sword, the latter holding the gun ever-ready in his extended hand. But only the camels grunted from their stables.

"There," Nouri said, briefly pointing at the large tent that stood in the centre of the camp beside a large banner adorned with some kind of hieroglyphic.

Nouri went towards it and Neil crept behind him, covering his back. The inside of the tent contained nothing aside from a plinth with a box on top of it. Various hieroglyphics inlaid in gold leaf on its wood surface almost looked like they were glowing in the dark. Neil turned around to watch for any signs of danger as Nouri opened the box and withdrew the relic. A semi-transparent object that could be held in one hand, the Tear of Set was neither diamond nor glass. And yet nothing felt particularly otherworldly about it. Nothing gave him the notion that he was looking at an artefact that heralded doom.

Nouri put the Tear into a small sack he carried.

"I need to check up on one of them," Nouri said once they exited the tent.

Moments later, they were beside the sprawled body of a man dressed in a hooded robe, the same one who had made his brief attempt to flee. Neil heard a weak moan as the man moved his head.

"He's alive." Nouri passed the sack to Neil before dragging the man towards the closest tent and sitting him up. Weakened, the man leaned against the tent's pole.

"You've wandered too far from the Nile Delta, priest," Nouri told the man in Arabic as he pointed the sword at him. "This is not Egypt; you're in Mesopotamia. Now tell me what business you and your ilk have here!"

But the man—the priest, if Nouri was right in his assumption—said nothing. The shadows underneath his hood concealed most of his expression, but his eyes gleamed as he glared daggers at his interrogator.

"I must warn you," Nouri told him firmly, "I don't have any problems with resorting to torture if I need to."

The priest growled something out in a language Neil did not understand.

"So you speak Classical Aramaic?" Nouri said with a smirk. "Well, I'm fluent in that language as well." He then addressed the cultist in the same language; most likely, repeating his earlier statements.

The hooded man chuckled upon hearing him. "Fool!" he said in Arabic as he grinned, exposing his teeth like a jackal.

With a psychotic roar, the priest threw himself forward, making use of the last remnants of energy left in him in an act that stunned both the guard and the reporter. Nouri's blade went through the man's head, as though the cultist had tried to swallow it.

Nouri's questions were left unanswered.

***

Daylight in the desert arrived just as suddenly as it had retreated. The morning air was already baking the surroundings as Nouri, Neil, Jake, and Alice made their way towards the jeep.

"It feels odd," Neil commented. "They were in possession of a powerful artefact and they kept it lightly guarded. There were, like, what—less than ten guards on the grounds of the camp? And armed only with cold weapons.”

As he walked, the sack containing the mystic crystal kept bouncing off his thigh.

“They probably didn’t expect any humans to stumble upon them. After all, we’re in quite remote parts,” Nouri responded. “However, they did take precautions. I sensed powerful spellwork meant to ward off harmful spirits placed around the camp. If anything, their main concern was possible treachery from the daevas.

“Moreover, something tells me the lot we dealt with was something akin to a ceremonial guard. More like standard-bearers than enforcers. I’m sure there is more to their forces than just Iron Age-type warriors.”

“And what about that Masked Man Jake and Alice talked about? Where was he?” Neil asked.

“He and his party had probably not yet returned from the domain of the daevas. And that’s a good thing. There is no doubt that he is a sorcerer. Having to deal with one is the last thing we needed.”

After the four had trekked a while longer, the landscape opened, revealing the hidden jeep.

“You can’t imagine how happy I am to see Big Boy here,” Jake said.

Neil rushed ahead and opened the door. He leaned inside to put the bag into the glovebox.

“And I just can’t wait to finally get out of this goddamn desert,” Jake added, withdrawing a bottle of water from his backpack. He feverishly consumed half of it in a single swig before putting it back. “Is anybody thirsty?” He turned to his companions. “I’ve brought enough bottles for everybody!”

A feeble gust of wind blew past Neil, and he shuddered as he heard an unfamiliar voice carried on the air currents.

“Nobody evades the daevas,” it whispered with venomous glee.

CHAPTER TWENTY-SIX

Dawn had long since broken by the time Elliott walked onto the terrace overlooking the courtyard. He was beginning to realise how addicted he had become to the comfort of modernity and how excruciating it could get at times without access to a laptop or a smartphone. Not that having possession of one would have been that helpful anyway, when there were no sockets or electricity around to recharge a battery.

He was ready to give Lauren's newfound habit of walking around the courtyard a shot. But unlike his cousin, he thought it was best done in the morning; at least, in daylight one minimised the risk of tripping over a loose stone and smashing one's face against the trunk of a tree. Perhaps he could have even done some meditating of his own...if the scraping of a broom against the cobbled surface had not been a distraction.

The figure of the attendant, the same young man who had looked after him whilst he had been unconscious after his ordeal in the drylands, appeared in view, sweeping the courtyard. The hat-wearing man walked to the nearest door to the inn's ground floor and headed in, most likely to continue with his chores inside.

Curiosity again got a hold of Elliott; he was eager to see what was behind this door. Hands behind his back, he strolled down the stairs and through the courtyard in a walk that would appear leisurely to anyone who noticed him, gazing at the tree branches above his head. But when he was passing that door, he threw a calculated glance into the room. Inside, a big glass case stood by the wall. The polished metallic surfaces of the items kept inside reflected the morning light entering through the doorway. They appeared to be weapons, ones from days gone by. Even a momentary glance gave him enough opportunity to recognise a shield. This brought back memories of the re-enactment event from months back, images of Norm and Hollie.

He wandered around the courtyard, giving an impression of a tourist visiting a new place for the first time. When the attendant finished sweeping the room, he exited, closing the door behind him, but not locking it. He went past Elliott, casually saying something in Arabic or Kurdish, which Elliott took for a greeting. He greeted him in return in English. The man went to a different door, entered, and emerged without the broom—it must have been the broom closet. He then headed for the gates.

Elliott spent the next ten minutes or so standing in the yard, occasionally bursting into sessions of humming and tapping his foot to pass the time. By then, he was certain that the attendant was not coming back anytime soon, so he made his way towards the room that had caught his attention. He opened the door and entered.

And indeed, the display case contained exhibits of weapons. There were a couple of shields of different sizes with calligraphic motifs engraved on their bright-yellow fronts. A set of five swords accompanied them, their blades curved. A spear hung beside them, along with a quiver full of arrows, and a bow. The collection might have been small, but its size did not reduce Elliott's interest as he continued to marvel at the display. He wished he could hold one of the weapons in his hand, grip the curved hilt of one of the swords.

"I see you've taken notice of our collection." A familiar voice came from behind Elliott's back, startling him.

He turned around and saw Yussuf, the Master of Service, standing by the door, which Elliott had kept open to let the light in; the room's miniature window, smaller than a brick, did not light the room well enough alone.

"Sorry." Elliott scrambled for an excuse. "I saw the display when the door was wide open, and, since it was unlocked, I thought about having a better look."

"That's alright," Yussuf said, joining Elliott in front of the exhibit. "As for the doors...we never bother to lock them. None of the doors of this inn have been locked for centuries. This community is a close-knit one; nobody here steals another's possessions."

His words made Elliott remember his hometown of Bristol. Back home, he would not dare to go out to buy a bottle of beer from the off-license without making sure the door was locked.

"Then it's a great community you have here," he said.

"Thank you. So, what do you think about our display?" Yussuf asked.

"Honestly, it's very interesting." Elliott looked at the display and back at the sheikh. "I have an interest in old weapons."

"Really?"

"Yes, back at home, I've taken part in re-enactment events that bring historic combat to life. I've been trained in sword fighting," he explained. "Using replicas, of course."

"I see," Yussuf said. "But these weapons before us are not replicas. And our ancestors cut down many enemies whilst wielding them."

Elliott looked at the shield. The proud weapon revived memories of the re-enactment event. Though it was authentic, it was plain in appearance, lacking any of the stylised ornaments his and Norm's shields had borne at the distant camp in East Anglia.

"How old do you think these weapons are?" Yussuf asked.

"I don't know." Elliott considered it as he rubbed his chin. "Four hundred years old? Five hundred?"

"Around eight hundred years old," Yussuf said.

"They really are old."

"And they played an important role in the history of this community. It happened in the time of the Mongol invasions. In the year 1258 of your Western calendar, the same year when Hulagu Khan ransacked Baghdad and killed the Abbasid caliph Mustasim, a troop of Mongols made their way to the drylands with the intent of laying waste to the villages located by this oasis. Back then, these settlements were surrounded by walls; the ruins of some sections can still be seen above the ground. Aided by a few outsiders, our people stood up to fight for their land and households, and the Mongols failed to breach their defences. The decisive battle took place in the drylands just outside the oasis. The invaders had their swift horses and their experience of overrunning hundreds upon hundreds of villages, but our ancestors had the resolve to triumph and the grace of Allah.

Most of the Mongols perished that day and still lie buried under the crust of the drylands; the rest retreated, never to return. In the aftermath of the battle, the elders decided that the weapons wielded by the most accomplished of the fallen warriors would be preserved and taken care of throughout the generations as a reminder of the victory that saved the communities of this oasis from doom."

Elliott listened keenly, taking note of the part mentioning several outsiders that fought alongside the locals. A gut feeling told him that there was an entire story there as well.

"Since none of the settlements here have a museum or a town hall, these weapons were moved to be stored in this inn at some point in time, though occasionally they do get taken out during celebrations," Yussuf concluded.

"So that's how it was," Elliott said.

"But speaking about stories," Yussuf said suddenly. "I was speaking to Sheikh Ismail this morning and he was wondering if you and your cousin would like to have a short tour that would introduce you to our way of life. What would you say to it?"

"Sounds interesting."

"Indeed, Ismail is a man of rare mind and remarkable mental capabilities. It always surprises me that he can be in a deep state of meditation and yet also be fully aware of his surroundings at the same time. For instance, yesterday, during one of our ceremonies, he noticed human shapes by the windows. I myself was not paying attention." He went silent for a few moments. "I assume it was you, right?"

"Yes..." Elliott drew out the word. A sense of light embarrassment tickled him, colouring his cheeks with a blush of shame.

"There is no need to feel discomfort," Yussuf said, as if he had just read Elliott's mind. "Our ceremonies are not secretive. We do not have issue with outsiders observing, as long as they show respect and do not interrupt."

That was a relief to hear.

"You are quite an adventurous type, aren't you?" Yussuf laughed. "Anyway, perhaps you could go upstairs and tell your cousin about our offer?"

***

Lauren had gone on tours before, both in Britain and during holidays abroad, but this excursion felt unique. For starters, this was the first time her guide also held the mysterious title of Master of Service.

The complex wall and the dome behind it grew bigger as she approached the enclosure. The sun was shining over the rooftops, yet even daylight could not make the ambience of mysticism emanating from this place fade away.

"Let me ask something before we enter," Yussuf said, stopping at the gateway. "What faith do you think we locals follow?"

"Islam?" Elliott answered like pupil at school.

"Correct." Yussuf nodded. "But there are different movements within Islam too."

Lauren rummaged through her brain for any relevant information she had acquired throughout the years.

"Sufism," Yussuf said.

She had heard of Sufi Islam before, yet she had never read about its tenets.

"And this complex before you is the base of our fraternity, which is almost as old as Tubsir," the guide explained. "We are called Dervishes. All of the members of our order come from either Tubsir or the other settlement that lies within this oasis. And though we are a monastic community, the sheikhs of the order have traditionally taken the roles of elders, imams, and judges in our settlements. Sheikh Ismail is the head, and I, as Master of Service, am third in the hierarchy. Now follow me."

With that, he crouched and slipped under the crossed chains. He had to duck even lower than they did, holding on to the ceremonial cap on his head to make sure it did not fall off. Elliott and Lauren slipped in behind him.

"I have a question," Lauren said. "What is the purpose of these chains?"

"A way to remind visitors that this is a holy place and make them pay their respects," Yussuf said. "If a man arrived at the gate atop his horse, he would have to dismount in order to enter. If a man enters on foot, he would bow his head before the holy site of our mosque."

The purpose of the chains was a mystery no more.

Yussuf led them towards the first landmark of the complex: a long, rectangular building that stood conjoined with a section of the wall. It had only one storey, yet many doors led into it, and every door was accompanied by a window.

"Are these the residential quarters?" Lauren asked,

"Correct," Yussuf said as he came up to one of the doors.

"Is this one yours?" Elliott asked. To Lauren's ears, it sounded like a stupid question to ask.

"No," the older man replied. "This one is vacant."

He opened the door and gestured for them to take a look inside. Lauren had thought that her room in the inn was small, but this monastic cell made her room seem if not spacious then at least adequate in comparison. A simple couch stood by the side wall, covered with a quilt. A carpet was sprawled on the floor. An arch-shaped storage space had been made in the opposite wall, likely intended to keep books in. It would have taken only two steps for the resident to get out of bed and leave through the door.

Yussuf continued the tour. He directed their attention to one of the smaller buildings. "This is the library, and this," he said as they passed the dome-crowned building, "as you have likely guessed by now, is the mosque."

He brought them to the building where the previous days' ceremony had taken place. It was circular in form, and it, too, was topped with a dome, albeit a smaller one.

"And this building is called a khanqah. This is where many of our gatherings and ceremonies take place," Yussuf said. "The ceremony you witnessed yesterday was a Sama-zan, Whirling. For us, music and dance have spiritual significance. Sama-zan is one of the ways that allow us to reach balance and get closer to God."

He led them to the next building. Its door was wide open, and the aroma of various spices speared Lauren's nostrils even from the outside.

"And this is the kitchen," Yussuf said. "And I should mention that this is where the meals you receive at the inn are prepared. Let's go inside."

Unlike the open-air areas of the complex, which appeared to be empty even during daytime, the kitchen was alive. Several

Dervishes were scurrying around the spacious room. Some were preparing dough at the table, one was checking the stock, another was attending the pots simmering over the hearth in the corner of the spacious room.

"They are hard-working," Elliott commented.

"They are indeed." Yussuf watched the place and those inside with a look of pride. "Moreover, this part of the complex is of personal significance to me. I am the one who oversees the work in the kitchen. It is my responsibility to make sure that all the brothers and all our guests are fed."

"You've mentioned that you are third in the hierarchy," Lauren said. "So I guess this means that the kitchen has a major place in the operations of the community of the...Darvishes." One mention was not enough for her to remember the correct pronunciation of this new, exotic word.

"It does," Yussuf replied. "Any new initiate into the fraternity starts by working in the kitchen. And he is expected to work here for the duration of a thousand and one days. Moreover, during this time he would not just be running errands; he would actually be living here, not in the quarters you saw earlier.

"Now look over there." The Master of Service extended his hand towards the doorway.

To the left of the entrance, by the wall, there was a low-rise stone platform that drew visual parallels with a bed bunk.

"That...bunk...would serve as the bed," Lauren theorised.

"Correct, but naturally he would be provided with a mattress."

She'd definitely learned a few new things during this excursion.

***

"Consider yourself lucky, brother," Hamza said, sitting down on a stool. "You could have snapped your neck and died."

He looked at Sayid, who lay on the couch under a thin cover. Sayid did feel lucky, having survived a fall down the stairs the other night. And though different parts of his body had been aching ever since, he'd sustained no broken bones or dislocated joints.

"So, how are you feeling?" Hamza asked.

"Terrible, if you want me to be honest."

"Do you want me to get a doctor to see you? If you think something might have been overlooked—"

"I'm not talking about bruises," Sayid said, raising his head from the soft and comfortable fabric of the pillow. "It's inside me."

He began to describe the dream he'd had whilst he lay senseless at the base of the stairway. He shared every part of it, describing every detail as best as he could remember: the flames, the narrowing bridge, the hag.

"Ever since the day I gave an oath to fight to the death in the name of the Almighty, my zeal has been akin to a pitcher with a missing bottom. It could not be filled. I was certain that the moment I perished, I would find myself in Heaven, wandering its gardens that bloom with eternal bliss," Sayid uttered weakly, an uncommon manner for him. "I am certain that I have seen Heaven in my dreams; it's just that I cannot remember it. But this one time, I dreamt of Hell, and I can still describe every detail of that dream. And now that I'm lying here, I keep thinking. If I had died that night, where would my soul have been bound to: Heaven or Hell?"

"Do not pollute your mind with the misguided thoughts that dream stirs," Hamza said.

"It's all Falai's fault!" Sayid spoke back, somewhat roughly. "The damned imam spent the whole sermon talking about Hell. And now I dread to think if he was right in some respect. Can the Jinn Arts really lead to our downfall? Let's say the Shura bans it—but the damage has already been made. What judgement will await our souls? And what if the Shura comes to an incorrect conclusion?"

"I don't know, my friend," Hamza said. "I am as confused as you are. But as long as we keep praying, Allah will reveal the right answer to us."

"Praise be to the Almighty," Sayid uttered.

CHAPTER TWENTY-SEVEN

If Neil had had a choice, he would have rather seen a ghost than heard a daeva. At the sound of the voice, his eyes shot wide as if he had taken steroids, quickly scanning his surroundings for the nightmarish fiends. He could read the startled expressions on the faces of his companions, who froze in place, having heard the same whisper.

And then the sands began to swirl again, but not in the air—on the ground. The sand did not hover like a tempest, but churned like a maelstrom under their feet. Neil watched in horror as the desert itself began to pull them under its scorched surface. The front of the jeep began to sink as though it had been driven into a swamp. Neil's reflexes kicked in; he immediately jumped back. Panicking, he rose to his tiptoes, looking down as if his surroundings were roiling with poisonous snakes. But the ground beneath him remained solid; he appeared to have evaded this unnatural quicksand. He remained safe for the moment, unlike his companions, who slowly continued to sink into the sand.

Nouri was better off than the others. Using his mystical powers, he shot in the air like a firework. He spun into a backflip before landing on safe ground some distance away. Jake and Alice were not so lucky. Each of them made sudden motions like they were trying to run or jump, but this only made them sink even quicker. Nouri threw both hands forward as if he was a mime performing an act. With his left palm opened towards the jeep and the right turned to Jake and Alice, who had already sunk to knee level, he gritted his teeth as though he had suddenly come under immense pressure.

"The spellcraft the daevas are casting is too powerful!" he shouted. "My magic is not strong enough to pull both them and the vehicle out of the sand!"

Treading carefully, Neil crept closer to the edge of the pool of whirling sand. Jake was close, close enough for Neil to see the desperation in every aspect of his being: expression, body language, even aura.

"We need the vehicle if we are ever to get out of this desert!" Nouri declared.

His statement had only one meaning.

"Jake! Grab my hand!" The cameraman was not far, and yet Neil shouted as if a canyon kept them apart.

He reached out and caught Jake's hand in his. And on the other side of the sandy maelstrom, Nouri lowered his right hand, turning his full attention to the vehicle, applying some form of telekinetic power.

"Jake! Try grabbing Alice's hand!" Neil instructed, his heart bleeding at the sound of the blonde's shriek. He had no idea if he was strong enough to pull both of them out, but he was willing to try.

Jake extended his free hand towards Alice, but though she kept reaching frantically, pushing and pushing forth, she was unable to get a grip. Mere inches separated his fingers from hers.

"I can't!" she shouted as she made one more push.

"Neither can I!" Jake said, turning to Neil.

Neil said nothing, just kept pulling, investing all his strength in order to at least get Jake out of the quicksand that had already consumed him up to his waist. He felt pain under his skin, as if his muscles were ripping.

He glanced at the jeep and saw the heavy form nudge forward and the upper part of the tyre emerge out of the sand. Jake, on the other hand, sunk deeper and deeper.

Neil felt like a dozen wounds had opened on his body. But pain only increased his fervour. He kept pulling back ferociously, but to no avail. Even worse, the suction power of the infernal quicksand was dragging him towards it.

"Don't bother, Neil! You'll just get stuck as well!" Jake told him, now submerged up to his chest.

"Don't say anything!" Neil ordered. "It just needs a bit more effort!"

He tried and tried...and if he hadn't been able to re-establish a proper foothold, the quicksand would have welcomed him as well. He could no longer hear Alice. He looked past Jake, only to catch the moment the sand covered her crown of golden tresses. The desert's maw had consumed the medic fully. Jake threw a quick glance beyond his shoulder before turning back.

"Leave it, Neil," he said, sighing deeply. "Perhaps I just wasn't fated to get out of this hellhole."

"It's not over yet!"

"It is! Let go of me and save yourself!"

"No!" Neil howled like a wounded animal.

"Neil! If you don't let go, I swear I'll bite your hand!" Jake shouted back at him. By the tone of his voice, he was dead serious.

"Jake..."

Neil sighed and let go. Meeting no resistance, the sand encased Jake's chest and shoulders.

"Thank you, Neil! Thanks for everything! You even came to this damned place for me!" Jake's voice was trembling, but he tried to present an image of calm in order to keep Neil's spirit up.

Neil felt a moist sensation on his cheek, a soothing contrast to the harsh air, as a tear slid down.

"Perhaps we won't be able to work together anymore, but maybe we'll get a chance to meet again...if not in this world, then in another." Jake smiled sadly.

Jake's fingers curled to give Neil a thumbs up before he dropped his hand beneath the sand. Moments later, the rest of him followed.

"Jake..."

A roar from Nouri made Neil's head turn to see the jeep getting completely pushed out by an invisible force.

"Get inside, ignite the engine, and reverse!" Nouri ordered. "I'll join you once you're done!"

Neil scrambled into the vehicle, taking a peek into the compartment in order to make sure the bag had not been snatched away during the commotion. Seeing it was still in its place gave him some relief.

The engine rumbled heavily as the jeep began to reverse. Through the windscreen, Neil saw Nouri rush towards him.

"I remember...the course we took...to get here," Nouri said once he jumped into the vehicle. "Just follow...my directions... whenever I tell you." Heavy breaths interrupted his speech.

Neil could not remember a time when he'd seen the guard so worn out: Nouri was sitting, leaning against the back of the seat as he gasped for air. Duress had definitely taken a toll on him.

"Now drive!" he ordered.

Neil slowly drove in reverse for a few more minutes before turning the vehicle around and driving off at a higher speed.

"We need to get as far as we can away from this place as quickly as possible," Nouri said. "We don't have much time before the daevas fully transcend into our plane. But be assured, they will give chase once they do."

"So, how do we escape them?" Neil asked. "I mean permanently?"

"The daevas are very territorial beings. They are most likely to leave us alone once we leave their tribal lands behind."

"And where are the boundaries of their tribal lands?"

"I have no idea; it might be the nearest highway, for all we know. Just keep driving. Hopefully, they'll lose our tracks."

***

Time lost any meaning to Neil as he drove through the desert, following Nouri's directions. His mind kept wandering back to the events of the last few days, filled with miracles, chaos, and horror. And all of this lingered in the company of a deep sense of loss as he thought about Jake.

"Damn it." Neil heard Nouri curse from the passenger seat. "They've picked up our tracks."

Having no need to keep his eyes on the road—for there was nothing in front except for many miles of barren terrain—Neil turned and found the guard looking back through the window. Neil lowered the window on his side and peered out.

The scene he beheld was one that he did not expect. Three thick whirlwinds raged by the horizon, coursing with sand. Tightropes that seemed to connect Heaven and earth, the sight instilled fear and hopelessness. They were a great distance behind the moving vehicle, but they, too, were advancing. It was only a matter of time before they caught up.

"Are those..."

"Yes, the daevas," Nouri said.

"Talk about dust devils," Neil remarked, but his sarcasm evaporated in the blink of an eye. "What do we do?! We're already driving in high gear! But they might still catch up to us."

"We might actually be in luck," Nouri said.

"What do you mean?"

"Do you remember the abandoned fire temple we stumbled across? We're on course towards it. We just need to make it to it."

"Holy ground?" It suddenly clicked in Neil's head.

"It was when it was still in use, but not anymore." Nouri's prognosis was not optimistic. "However, if the ground can be made holy again, at least temporarily, not only will it become a trap for our pursuers, but it'll also disorient any daeva in its vicinity."

"So how do we do that?"

"We have enough coal to make a fire, right? You said so back at the temple."

"Yes."

"Great," Nouri said. "Remember that giant pot? That was a fire altar, the centrepiece of any Zoroastrian temple. You will need to rekindle the fire that used to burn in it."

"Me?" Neil could not hold back his surprise.

"Yes. I will give you cover by fending off the daevas."

"I guess I get the easier part."

"But it is important that you keep your mouth covered with a veil or a cloth of some sorts as you light it. Human breath taints the holy fire."

"I'll keep that in mind."

"But there's more to it. You will need to say the right words."

"What words?" Neil asked. The task was getting more complex.

"When kindling the holy fire, ancient priests used to recite hymns from the Yasna, a collection of sacred Zoroastrian liturgical texts. According to tradition that goes back millennia, the hymns need to be chanted in their original language—which is Avestan, an ancient language related to Farsi."

"What?! How am I going to do that? I don't even know modern Farsi!" He withdrew his earlier claim: his part of the task was just as complex.

"Luckily, that's only the ideal scenario. Uttering a prayer simply based on the Yasna in any language ought to be enough in this instance. Now pay close attention to what I say. You will need to recite these same words at the altar whilst rekindling the fire."

"Got it."

"Holy Fire, great—"

"Wait!" Neil had to interrupt him. "There's no way I'll be able to memorise an entire incantation in one go. Give me a moment."

He pulled out his smartphone, relieved to see some power left in the device. He swiped at the screen a couple of times before selecting the voice recorder.

"You may start," Neil said.

"Holy Fire, great son of the God Ahura Mazda!" Nouri began. "I offer you praise. I praise good thoughts like I celebrate good deeds and honour good words. I denounce evil in all its forms: in thoughts, in words, and in deeds. Burn brightly by the side of those who stand facing the wickedness of the daevas!"

Nouri nodded with a confident expression that implied he had said everything. Neil clicked on the touchscreen, making the gadget repeat the magician's words. He replayed the recording over and over again, repeating the incantation, both in his mind and aloud.

In the meantime, the old fire temple appeared in view. Its domed roof and square shape made it easily distinguishable from any dune or rock. Behind the vehicle, the encroaching whirlwinds kept getting closer and closer.

Nouri explained a couple more details about the ritual whilst Neil pulled the jeep up beside one of the entrances to the temple.

"Make sure you take everything that's needed! I'll keep them distracted!" the guard said, opening the car door. "And take the Tear of Set with you!"

Neil nodded and shoved the bag containing the artefact into his backpack. He exited the vehicle, and the vicious winds slapped his face almost immediately. He joined Nouri, who was standing close to back of the jeep, looking at the incoming demonic dust storms. Neil opened the rear hatch and grabbed a sack of coal in one hand and a canister of fuel in the other.

"Let this end in success," Nouri said before pulling his sword out of its scabbard.

Neil scuttled towards the nearest entrance to the temple. His muscles ached under the weight of the load he carried, strained by earlier toils; his feet kept stomping heavily on the sand. He made it inside and dropped all of it—canister, sack, even backpack—on the floor behind the fire altar. The temple's shape allowed him to fully see what was going on outside. He saw Nouri walk to the side entrance, then turn to face the monstrous storm closing in on them, becoming a miniature yet strong obstacle in its way.

"Accursed spawn of the Malevolent Spirit!" a defiant Nouri yelled at the dust devils whirling just a few hundred feet away from him. "You want our lives and souls? Then come and claim them! I dare you!"

The open palm of his free hand suddenly illuminated, glowing with magical light. All three whirlwinds stopped upon hearing him speak. They raged for a few more moments before dying out like the flame of a match. Three grotesque figures now stood on the ground in their place, beings that Neil would never again mistake for any other creature. Maces materialised in their hands as they charged at Nouri, their eyes alight with bloodlust.

Watching this spectacle any longer meant wasting precious time. Neil roughly tore the sack of coal open and poured its contents into the bronze vessel. He then splashed it with petrol.

Still, he could not resist checking out the situation outside. To his amazement, Nouri was holding out against three adversaries. The magic-wielder manoeuvred among the demons, evading and exchanging blows. He delivered a kick to the chest of one daeva, making it stagger backwards. The light in his palm continued to glow; the sorcerer threw a couple of blasts of magic at his foes.

Neil ducked down and hurriedly rummaged through his backpack in search of the lighter. He found it in one of the small compartments and stood up. A tiny flame lit up when he pressed the sparkwheel, and he held the lighter before the vessel.

"Damn, almost forgot," he muttered.

He needed to cover his mouth lest he'd defile the fire with breath and ruin the whole endeavour. Neil turned the lighter off and placed it in his pocket. Again, he looked at the battle raging in front of the temple. And as he looked at the combatants, one of the daevas glanced at him. With Nouri distracted by its brethren, the demon bolted towards the temple. But before Neil could even react properly, a bolt of light broke out of the demon's chest like the tip of a harpoon. The roaring monster was then sent flying back. Neil caught sight of Nouri holding the other end of this magical weapon, the same way he had during the duel the previous day. The guard swung his beaming rope and hurled the daeva against the other two demons.

Neil withdrew a pocket knife out of the backpack. Careful to avoid injuring himself, he ran the knife through the soft material of his shirt just below the shoulder. He heard the sound of ripping fabric as the blade ran down the sleeve. It was a pity to ruin the shirt, but sacrifices had to be made. He grabbed the sleeve, now hanging loosely, with both hands and pulled as hard as he could, tearing it off. He then tied it over the lower part of his face, transforming it into an amateur veil.

"Holy Fire, great son of the God Ahura Mazda!" Neil began to chant. "I offer you praise. I praise good thoughts like I celebrate good deeds and honour good words!

"Miserable mortal!" An angry voice roared from the opposite entrance.

He looked round and saw a daeva, no doubt the same one that had tried to get to him just moments before, standing in the entryway, having somehow circumnavigated the temple.

Neil felt a familiar tickling of panic as he realised Nouri was too preoccupied with the other two demons to come to his aid. The small incantation bowl that he still kept hidden, the one pressing against his stomach, might have been his only defender that moment. He reached under his shirt, feeling the hard clay with the tips of his fingers.

"I denounce evil in all its forms!" he continued, looking at the daeva, waiting for its next move. He withdrew the bowl; it was small enough for him to conceal it from the demon with the back of his hand.

The demon rose above the ground. Almost immediately, it bolted forward, not running but flying towards the human.

"In thoughts, in words, in deeds!" Neil chanted, extending his hand, presenting the magic trinket towards the monster.

The demon fell to the ground like a wounded bird. It hissed in rage as it struggled to get up. Wasting no time, Neil pulled the lighter out of his pocket. The sparkwheel moved under the pressure of his finger, freeing the flame from the lighter's confines. He turned around and dipped his hand into the vessel before swiftly withdrawing it to leave the lighter inside. He barely avoided scalding his fingers on the tongues of fire that burst from inside the large bronze pot.

"Burn brightly by the side of those who stand facing the wickedness of the daevas!" Neil called out to the holy flame.

And suddenly the atmosphere inside the fire temple changed. It grew lighter, more serene. The daeva, that had just got back on its feet, hissed again, this time in agony, before exploding in a burst of sand that scattered across the sanctum. Neil looked the other way in time to witness the two demons outside meet the same fate.

"We did it, Mister Feaver," Nouri said, still holding the sword as he walked up to the fire temple with a triumphant smile on his face.

It was indeed a moment of triumph, and yet Neil could not shake the feeling of loss.

This one's for you, Jake.

CHAPTER TWENTY-EIGHT

Lauren woke up gasping for air. The night was sweltering. Sweat ran down her face like water dripping from a melting icicle, and breathing became a difficult task. For some time, she lay in her bed, having thrown the burdensome cover aside, trying to fall back to sleep. Yet it was to no avail; too much heat had accumulated in the room. A fan was beyond wishful thinking in this place, so the room needed to be ventilated the old-fashioned way.

She got out of bed and opened the door, letting the night air in—not particularly cool but an improvement. She turned to the window and pulled the shutters open. Nearby, the small, ornamented oil lamp she had forgotten to put out before going to bed burnt atop the wardrobe trunk. Its glow drove back the night's shadows, as did its siblings that hung outside on the terrace.

Lauren stayed by the window, aimlessly looking at the moonlit sky and the nearby grove enveloped in dark shadows. Nocturnal insects buzzed outside, comforting her with their little serenade.

Thoughts of Dr Mergham returned like they had time and time again over these past several days. Scouts had never found any evidence that he perished that horrendous night, so hope remained that he was still around somewhere in the drylands, perhaps even outside them, back in the big world.

Lauren heard slow steps outside in the courtyard. It had to be Elliott going about some night-time business of his. She went back to thinking and imagining. She could not wait to get back home, to scroll through her smartphone whilst lying on a sofa, to go out with her friends, to listen to the concerns of her parents and get softly rebuked for getting caught in a bizarre situation even if it had come to be through no fault of her own.

Lauren leaned down and lay her chin on her crossed hands resting on the windowsill. Detached from thoughts of the moment, she remained like that, inhaling the night air, until she heard a thud behind her. It came from the doorway, ruining the simple idyll her room had become.

"What is it, Elliott?" she asked before turning around to face her cousin.

Elliott was not there, yet she was not alone. And she was not in human company. The thing—for it was hard to describe it as anything else—stood in the doorway, its pointy muzzle turned to her.

She would forever be able to recognise a being of this type. To a level of hardly imaginable horror, it was standing there by the door on its hind legs. Its long front paws, tipped with claws, were hanging by its sides like hands. Elliott had claimed he had seen one of these hyena beasts walk like a human, and whilst she had not truly doubted his word, she had not known what to think of such claims, even after seeing the ferocity of these infernal creatures.

Not a single doubt remained. Lauren screamed. Instinct made her jump back, but all that she accomplished was bumping against the windowsill and feeling a sting of pain in her back.

The hyena-esque monstrosity, this "ghul" as Ismail called it, opened its pointy canine mouth, revealing a set of sharp teeth. It growled at her—a predator in the presence of its prey. In terror, Lauren's eyes scrambled around the room in search of anything that could help ward off the monster. The burning oil lamp was in arm's reach; she swiftly grabbed it by the handle.

The ghul took a step closer and entered the room. It growled again as it raised its clawed hands.

"Stay back!" Lauren screamed at it.

But her shriek held no authority. The spotted beast pressed on. The room was small, and every step the ghul made meant a significant decrease of the space between them.

Thinking quickly, Lauren tore the lid off the oil lamp and lunged forth, her blazing weapon in front of her. Hot oil burst out of the lamp and splashed into the monster's face. The beast released a soul-ripping howl as it convulsed in pain. It shivered feverishly as it tried to soothe itself and shake the burning substance off its face, no longer paying attention to its surroundings or its prey.

Lauren knew this was the best moment to make her escape. She rushed past the ghul. She jumped over her bed, and slipped round behind the beast's back. She dashed towards the exit, only to slam into something else the moment she got outside.

***

Elliott was not sure whether he had been sleeping or just lying in bed in a bleary state when a loud scream made him bolt up. It sounded feminine, and as far as he knew, there was only one woman on the premises. More than that, Lauren was the only other guest staying at the inn.

Elliott jumped out of bed and grabbed the silvery pitcher used to store water for washing up in the absence a proper water supply—it could prove useful in whatever he was about to get into. Without a second thought, he rushed out of his room. He could have sworn he heard a howl, though he was not certain if it was real or if his imagination was toying with him.

Further down the terrace, he saw the door to his cousin's room was open; his hold on the pitcher's thin handle tightened. He was about to turn into Lauren's room when something collided with him. For a second, a red-orange coloured wave flashed before his eyes. Then he felt hundreds of strands of hair tickling his face.

"Lauren!" he exclaimed upon realising he had bumped into his cousin. "What the—"

An uncomfortably familiar feral noise cut off his sentence mid-way. Elliott looked up and saw a bipedal hyena-beast in the middle of Lauren's room. His memory flashed back to the events of the gruesome night. He was there again, gripping the hookah like a club, having just witnessed Joe get dragged away by the monstrous predator like a turkey by an eagle.

The fiend was shaking as though it was having a seizure. Its back was turned to them—this was the best chance they'd get to try to take it out. Elliott threw himself at it.

"Elliott, no!" he heard Lauren yell.

Alerted by its animalistic senses, the ghul turned around as Elliott swung the pitcher. The blow collided with the side of the ghul's muzzle. It was immediately followed by another one.

"It has hot oil in its eyes!" Lauren shouted. "It can't see right!"

Elliott hit it once more. Visually impaired or not, the fiend still had reflexes. He had to duck to avoid a clawed swipe that could have easily ripped his face off. His experience of schoolyard fights was certainly paying off now. Elliott then kicked the thing in the stomach, making it stagger back.

But he had to accept the surreal reality of his predicament: he was a human trying to go hand-to-hand against something that was akin to a werewolf at best...and a demon at worst. He burst out of the room.

"C'mon!" Lauren urged him as he slammed the door shut, leaving the beast snarling in the room.

They scuttled back down the terrace like a pair of crabs, keeping their eyes on the door.

"Hopefully, this will keep it inside," Elliott whispered, throwing a quick glance back.

"What makes you think so?"

"In some movies, zombies are not clever enough to open doors by themselves."

"But that thing is not a zombie."

And then the door opened, forever solidifying Lauren's statement amidst the greatest philosophical quotes of all time... at least in Elliott's frenzied mind.

He glanced back; the stairway was just behind them. The hulking form emerged and looked across the corridor, seeming to have mostly regained its vision. It let out an ear-tormenting sound, a mix of a roar and a chuckle, the moment it saw them.

"Run!" Lauren shouted.

An oil lamp hung next to the stairway. Before following, Elliott grabbed it from the hanger. He gritted his teeth as his skin touched the searing surface.

Releasing another howl, more ghostly than feral, the ghul dashed at them, moving on its hind legs. Elliott momentarily thought about charging at it and trying to splash more of the burning oil in its eyes. But shock, fear, and uncertainty made him act differently. Instead, he threw the oil lamp at the fiend. But the hot projectile did not hit its intended target; it fell in front of it, and the blistering contents quickly spilled into a small puddle on the floor. Still, the monster slipped on the oil and fell backwards against the floor. At least he'd bought more time to flee.

Elliott followed Lauren down the stairway.

"We should...run...for the complex," Lauren whispered, out of breath and gasping for air. "It's on holy ground. That should keep it away."

"I'm not sure we'll be able to make it that far. They're quite swift in the open," Elliott argued. "Plus, who knows how many of them are lurking outside, waiting to ambush us. Remember, hyenas hunt in packs!"

Like a sudden omen, a gunshot shrieked in the night. It sounded like it came from a distance. Another shot followed, even further away. That was not a good sign.

Elliott looked upwards. Above them, on the terrace, their pursuer was getting back on its feet. It gazed down from its lookout point, catching sight of its prey.

"I know!" Elliott grabbed his cousin by the hand as the thing released another soul-curdling howl. "Follow me!" he exclaimed and pulled Lauren further into the courtyard.

An echo of Yussuf's words sounded in his head: "None of the doors of this inn have been locked for centuries." This was the key to changing everything.

His course was set for the door that had intrigued him earlier. Reaching it, he and Lauren glanced back. The beast, now on all-fours, hopped down the stairs; it took a moment to snarl viciously before continuing pursuit.

Elliott let Lauren into the room before following her inside. He slammed the door shut and kept a hold of the handle. He heard the ghul stop outside and hiss. Suddenly, he found himself bracing against the door as the beast tried to force it open. It kept pulling at the door, making the room quake. Elliott pressed his foot against the wall in order to get more support. It was becoming a tug-of-war.

"What do we do?!" Lauren asked as she, too, grabbed hold of the handle in order to aid him.

"Do you see that display case behind you?"

"So?"

"I have a plan, but you need to break that glass. Look around and find some stone lying around or something!" he practically shouted. "I can hold it!"

She did as he asked, falling back into the room.

Let's just hope this glass isn't bullet-proof, Elliott thought as the door kept rocking.

On this occasion, the sound of glass shattering behind his back sounded as pleasant as the flow of a stream in a secluded valley.

"I did it!" Lauren declared.

"Great!" he said. "Now I need you to cover me at the door for two minutes."

Lauren ran back to the door and took the handle.

"Take over," he said as he let go.

He got up to the broken display case and looked at the weapons. He removed a shield from its place and slid his left arm through the enarmes on its back. Then he pulled out one of the curved swords.

This was the first time he'd held a real, old Arabic sword in his hand. Yet the soreness in his palm from touching the hot lamp and fighting for the disputed door did not let him appreciate this moment properly. With the ancient armaments ready for battle for the first time in centuries, Elliott stepped forth.

"Let it go, Lauren, and move away!" He gave the order.

She let go of the handle and swirled aside like a ballerina. The door flung open with inhuman force. Elliott charged like an armoured vehicle. Holding the shield firmly against his body, he ran straight into the bipedal hyena fiend. The force of the collision threw the monster back, but it was not down. Elliott lifted the sword, intent on bringing it down on the beast's neck, but his opponent dodged it. He swung again, and again the beast avoided the blade. He made several more attempts, swinging the weapon as though he was cutting a path in the middle of the jungle. But the ghul's sight had returned, at least most of it, and the creature was proving to be quite agile as it hopped back on all four feet.

It swiped at him, but Elliott blocked with his shield. He was glad for all those sword fighting sessions he had taken at the re-enactment society.

He could hear Norm's voice in the back of his head. *Motivate yourself. If there are no stakes, pretend there are.*

And the stakes were high on this occasion. With another snarl, the ghul attacked again, only to retreat suddenly. It shifted as though aiming for Elliott's side, but Elliott kept his eyes on the opponent, shifting the same way.

He felt like a gladiator fighting a lion in the arena. And then it suddenly dawned upon him: he was underestimating his opponent. The ghul was not an animal; he had no idea what its true level of cunning and intelligence was.

Carefully, Elliott began to retreat, taking a step back. If he could make it to the doorway, his back would be covered. But the ghul began attacking from different sides, trying to wear him out and outflank him.

"Stay back, freak!" Lauren shouted angrily from behind Elliott's back.

A spear popped out from the right of him, making the ghul jump back to avoid getting stung. Elliott was grateful for the assistance, but he really hoped that Lauren knew what she was doing; combat was not horse riding.

The ghul moved swiftly and grabbed the new nuisance by the shaft near the spearhead. Growling, it pulled back as it tried to rip the weapon out of Lauren's hands. It was then that Elliott went for another strike. The beast succeeded in tearing the spear out of Lauren's grasp. It retreated before Elliott managed to have it decapitated, but this time, it failed to dodge the blade fully; the ancient steel left a mark across its side.

Just as the ghul resembled an animal in appearance, so too did it have an animal's instincts. It is sometimes said that a wounded predator is more dangerous than a healthy one. The injury left it enraged. It spat the spear out and immediately went for another attack. This time, it was more brazen.

It lunged at Elliott with its full weight, almost as if it was mirroring his earlier move, and tackled him onto his back. His every muscle screamed as he hit the hard ground. He heard Lauren call out his name as he fell. Luckily, he did not hit his head. The double weight of the shield and the monster were pressing against his chest as the nocturnal horror hung over him, saliva dripping out of its open maw. The fact that he was lying in such a way that the shield was concealing his neck was probably the only thing stopping the ghul from tearing his throat out.

Elliott felt a weight in his right palm, and realised he was still clinging to the sword. Then there was no thinking, no calculation, no manoeuvring. His sword-hand stabbed up as if it had a mind of its own, plunging the blade into the beast's neck.

The ghul shrieked into Elliott's face one more time, blood bursting out of its mouth. Elliott saw the medieval spear rise behind the beast; a glimpse of Lauren appeared as she thrust the weapon's sharp tip into the creature back. The ghul convulsed for a second before its body went slack and collapsed on top of the shield.

Chapter Twenty-Nine

The moment the doors opened, Neil burst out of the lift and walked down the corridor to his hotel room. He let Nouri in before entering himself, heavily slamming the door behind his back. Rubbing his forehead, Neil leaned back against the wall, listening to the air conditioner murmuring above him. Nouri walked further into the room, looking around like an inspector.

"So now what? Neil asked.

It had been a long journey. After re-emerging from the desert they had made their way back to Karbala to collect Furqan; from there, they returned to Baghdad.

"Here is what we are going to do," Nouri said. "Your hotel room has a safe. Put the Tear of Set inside it and keep it there at all times when you are in. If you go out—for example, to have breakfast—take the artefact with you. Keep it close to you at all times."

"Wait, I'll put it inside the safe now," Neil said.

He confined the item within the thick metallic vault.

"Good," Nouri said. "If possible, try not to go outside the hotel today."

Neil nodded tiredly.

"As for me, there are some...matters...that I need to attend to. I will come back tomorrow morning to let you know what we can do with the Tear in order to prevent it from falling back into the wrong hands."

There was always a swathe of secrecy that the guard held on to like a player who got a good combination of cards in a game. Neil did not bother finding out what his secret was at this time; as long as everything looked like it was going the right way, he was content with being kept in the dark about some things.

"Be safe, Mister Feaver." Nouri bowed before making his exit.

A deep melancholic feeling possessed Neil moments after the door shut. It was a strong, uncomfortable sensation that pressed against his chest like a stone slab. He walked to the bathroom and looked in the mirror, seeing his reflection stare back at him with a miserable expression.

And as the mirror reflected his image, he could not help but reflect on everything that had transpired since he landed in Iraq to film his documentary. The whole project had been a fiasco. Yes, he had hours of footage and material, but the project was still incomplete. And it would probably remain that way, especially since he no longer had a cameraman.

And that part was what made him feel so dismal. He no longer cared about this documentary; it was Jake's unfortunate fate that made him depressed. At that moment, if he was given the option, he would choose to drown in the sand in the cameraman's stead.

A quick shower did not make him feel better. He was not in the mood to eat, so there was no point in ordering room service. But his urge to chase the grim thoughts away turned into a basic need. He got everything in order, donned his backpack, and left his suite.

The bar's Art Deco atmosphere welcomed him again with the sounds of jazz music and ringing glasses. He sat down by the counter and ordered a glass of whiskey. He emptied it fast and asked for another, and then another. Alcohol drove the depressing thoughts to the back of his consciousness, but the troubles in his thoughts gave way to physical discomfort. His head began to revolve like a merry-go-round; his stomach began to roil.

And just to make things worse, a troubling thought slapped him across the back of his head. *Wait, did I bring the Tear with me?* He could not recall properly. The hotel might have been a respected joint, but even the best apple tree was bound to bear some rotten fruit. He remembered hearing stories about crooked staff stealing money and belongings from rooms even in the most posh hotels.

Neil jumped up, unzipped his backpack and reached inside. He felt relief the moment he grabbed hold of the bag and pulled it out.

The whiskey was still getting back at him. His stomach cramped; he found himself on the verge of throwing up. Crouching, he reflexively brought his hands to his mouth, unintentionally dropping the sack in the process.

He heard a familiar voice behind his back. "Are you alright, Neil?"

Whatever reaction Neil might have had to the alcohol descended back down into his stomach. He straightened up.

"Yes, fine," he muttered.

"You dropped something," Claude Faucon said as he leaned down. "Don't worry. I'll pick it up."

He grabbed the bag and lifted it up. However, Nouri had never bothered to tie the sack. The semi-transparent crystal slid out and fell back on the floor.

"No, that's alright!" Neil declared anxiously.

He picked the artefact up, clutching it possessively. He practically ripped the sack out of the hands of the surprised academic.

"That's an interesting example of glasswork," Claude said. "I don't remember seeing anything like this before."

"I bought it from a souvenir vendor in the south of the country," Neil lied as he put the Tear back in the sack. "I don't think it even serves any purpose."

He returned the bag to the backpack, and Claude sat down on a nearby barstool.

"So, how's the work on your documentary progressing? And where's Jake? I thought I would find him in your company at the bar."

"Terrible," Neil confessed, his head still in disarray. "As for Jake...he was abducted when a militia raided a refugee camp we were filming the documentary at."

"Oh, God..."

"Listen, Claude, please don't be upset, but I feel like shit at the moment. I'll tell you about it later. Please excuse me."

"Of course, I understand."

Giving the older man an apologetic look, Neil grabbed the backpack and darted out of the bar.

***

"I have done much thinking about what to do with the artefact," Nouri said after making sure the door of the hotel room was locked. "I hope you don't mind going on one more trip. This one should only take a few hours and be practically uneventful."

"The contract with the driver is still in force. But where do you want us to go?" Neil asked.

"Naturally, we cannot surrender the Tear of Set to the authorities. Nobody will believe our story and, if anything, we will just be labelled insane. So the only option we have is to safely dispose of the artefact in order to make sure that neither Was Peraa nor the daevas ever get their hands on it again."

"So, what do you have planned?"

"At first, I thought of just burying it somewhere in the countryside, but any plot of land could potentially go through some development project. I thought about throwing it into a marsh, but any marsh could later be drained to make way for arable land. I mean, Saddam did something like that in the south a few decades back," Nouri explained as he walked back and forth. "But what are the two eternal things in Iraq?"

Neil shrugged his shoulders.

"The great rivers: Tigris and Euphrates," Nouri said. "We will hide it at the bottom of Tigris, but we ought to do it outside Baghdad, away from the eyes of any witnesses, just in case. There is no better place to hide a magical artefact associated with deserts and droughts than at the bottom of a river." He sat down in a chair by the wall.

"Good idea. I'll call the driver. He'll get the vehicle here in no time," Neil said, taking his phone out his pocket.

"You can take the Tear out of the safe now," Nouri said as they waited.

Neil nodded and went over to the vault to type the combination in. A draught entered the room through the open window, hitting him with a cooling breeze.

"I don't think you'll get any fresh air by keeping the window open," Nouri commented. "After all, Baghdad has quite a high level of air pollution."

"I don't know why I opened it." Neil finished inputting the combination. "And frankly, I can't even remember opening the window. I'm still not thinking completely straight."

He opened the safe door and took the bag out.

"Here," he said as he turned around.

His gaze briefly fell on the floor lamp. Tall and lean, it stood in the corner, casting a shadow…two shadows.

"I think I'm seeing double." Neil lightly shook his head to get over whatever daze he was in.

Then, one of the thin shadows shot at him like a black arrow, a dark spear. Neil could not tell whether he was pushed, punched, or struck, but something knocked him to the floor, hard. Next thing he saw was a shadow, now with recognisable human characteristics, hovering over him like a phantom, clutching the bag in its ethereal night-dyed hand.

He heard Nouri's battle cry as the guard swooped to strike the thing with his dagger. But the shadow dodged the blow and flew out of the window within moments. Nouri hopped to the window and threw one of his knives after it. He missed.

"Damn it!" Nouri proclaimed in anger. "Damn them all!" His fist violently descended on the windowsill as though he was trying to punish it.

"What…the hell…was that?" Neil uttered, getting back on his feet.

"A jinn," Nouri said, still looking out of the window. "And if it's not affiliated with the daevas, then it's affiliated with Was Peraa."

"But how did it find us?"

"It's probably been trailing us since we came out of the desert."

"But why did it wait until now to strike?"

"A jinn can move through solid objects, but it cannot make a solid object pass through another solid object. And the safe could not be opened without a combination." Nouri turned away from the window. If he was not truly composed again, his acting was realistic. "This is why you couldn't remember opening the window. You didn't open it; the jinn did as it was preparing its escape."

"But there was a time yesterday when I took the Tear from the safe. Why didn't it attack then?"

"I don't know. Maybe it thought the artefact was still in the vehicle, so it followed the jeep when we got out and made its way back to the hotel after realising it was not with the driver." Nouri shook his head. "I don't know."

"And you didn't feel its presence in the room? I mean, you were able to sense the daeva back in the desert."

"I can sense the presence of very strong energies: good or evil. The daevas are unconditionally evil beings. But this is a different case. It's likely a tamed jinni: a slave involuntarily serving wicked masters."

Neil found the whole scenario truly disturbing; to realise that he had been all alone in the presence of a paranormal entity, fully at its mercy without even realising it.

"So, what do we do now?" he asked. He did not really know what to make of this situation. Concern mixed with a sense of farce.

"I don't know," Nouri said.

Still, one fact could not be disputed: their foes had outmanoeuvred them.

***

The meeting had been going on for some time. The commanders leading the forces taking part in the offensive had assembled around a table, looking down at the map spread on its surface. Marked on it were settlements, strategic heights, and notable infrastructure in the vicinity of Baghdad. One after another, the warlords spoke about the situation in each of their respective sections of the front. They shared details of attacks, raids, and reconnaissance missions.

Mullah Nishwari was standing at the helm of the table, listening to his subordinates' accounts. He had remained silent throughout the meeting, aside from its very beginning, when he'd declared that from this point onward the Jinn Arts practitioners would be taking part in the final push to Baghdad.

Sayid could barely believe it. Baghdad. God's grace had brought them to the gates of the Iraqi capital. Whilst the government and its foreign allies were bracing for the defence of the capital, the leaders of the Liwa were holding this meeting mere miles away from the outskirts of the great city.

The sound of footsteps resonated from the corridor leading into the group's secret operations room. Jalil al-Quwaiti stopped talking, and with a look of annoyance, the impulsive warlord turned to the entrance. Sayid, just like the others, looked the same way.

A moment later, an old man staggered into the room, limping so badly that it seemed moving his legs was a task for him. Initially, Sayid mistook him for Khaleed Awal. But then it dawned upon him that Awal, not being a military commander, was not expected to attend the meeting. The old sheikh was not even supposed to be in these parts. Plus, he had never seen Awal limp.

Sayid realised that he had never seen this man before. The man was not just old—he was ancient, no doubt pushing past his nineties. His attire gave him an archaic feel. He wore a long, red-gold kaftan over his tunic. The embroidery was elaborate. If anything, he seemed like he would have been more at home in the court of an ancient caliph than by the side of a militant group's leader.

But a more important question demanded an answer. How did he get past the security guards? Instinctively, Sayid pulled his gun out and pointed it at the old man. He was beaten to it by Jalil, who, too, aimed his weapon at the newcomer.

"Who are you and how did you get here?!" Jalil barked.

"And the angels Harut and Marut descended on Babylon. 'We came not to teach but to judge,' they said," the old man uttered as he looked at the group.

The sound of a gunshot boomed across the room; Sayid blinked, startled. Since Sayid had kept his finger off the trigger, it meant that Jalil had fired the shot. The next thing he knew, the old man was there no more. There was no sign of him at all, no lifeless body sprawled on the floor. He had disappeared like he was never there in the first place. Behind the spot where he had stood, a bullet hole adorned the wall.

"What was that?" said one of the commanders.

"And who was it?" asked another amazed witness.

Sayid heard sighs, chatter, and footsteps behind his back.

"Not even a bloodstain?" said Shamil as he knelt down to have a closer look at the concrete floor.

"The words he said—he was alluding to a verse from the Quran," said another commander, al-Pirani. "But what message was trying to convey?"

"Why did you shoot so quickly?" Sayid asked Jalil, raising his voice. "We needed answers!"

"He made his way past security and located a room he was supposed to have no knowledge of. I do not take risks!" Jalil stated, paying little care to Sayid's condemnation. "Nobody knows what other tricks we might have expected from him. And secondly, look!" He pointed the gun at the empty spot. "Does it even look like somebody died here?"

Sayid and Jalil turned to Nishwari.

Yet the mullah said nothing. He stood there, stroking his greying beard with a thoughtful expression on his face.

***

The last few days had been nothing but a conga line of bad luck. Jake was lost. The artefact Nouri and Neil had gone to great lengths to obtain had been snatched away right under their noses. And now the two appeared to be stuck in a besieged city.

"The week saw a sudden and rapid advance by Liwa al-Qadisiyyah forces as the terror group gained ground around the Iraqi capital." Neil scrolled down the screen of his smartphone, reading the article from the news website.

Nouri stood by the window, leaning against the sill. The thoughts he kept hidden hardened his facial expressions, which he wore heavily, like a clay mask.

"The Iraqi military was dealt another significant blow earlier today when the militants succeeded in capturing Baghdad International Airport, effectively cutting the capital's main link with the outside world," Neil continued to read. "Coalition air forces have retaliated by launching a series of air raids on the terror group's positions around the city."

Neil scrolled down to check the length of the article.

"Sources say that the Iraqi government has fled Baghdad. A number of foreign governments have urged their nationals to leave the country. Due to the loss of the airport, the US military will be carrying out evacuations of foreign nationals still trapped Baghdad to Basra via helicopters. They are set to begin tomorrow morning from several locations across the Green Zone, including Grand Festivities Square."

Nouri stayed silent. Neil refreshed the contents of the live feed on the webpage; a new entry popped up, coming attached to a video. The sensationalist title made him click on it. The footage had supposedly been shot during the fighting that took place in the vicinity of the airport.

"What the hell?!"

The video was definitely worth rewatching.

"What is it?" Nouri asked as he sprang out of his semi-meditative state.

"You certainly need to see this."

The guard came up to him and leaned in to look at the small screen. A scene of fighting on the street of some town or village played out in front of their eyes. The focus then shifted to one of the Islamist positions hidden behind the makeshift street barricades. An enormous ball of fire suddenly materialised above it. A militant appeared from behind the barricade, and with a gesture, sent the flame flying towards his enemies.

"Fire magic," Nouri commented when the video stopped playing. "And no doubt it was the decisive factor in their swift advance."

"So, what, the Liwa has its own wizards now?"

"After everything that you've already witnessed, are you still surprised?"

"I guess not." Neil let out a light chuckle.

"Well, your mystery might have been solved," Nouri stated. "Those ancient trinkets uncovered during the raid, the ones you have pictures of...they were not meant for the black market. They, or at least some of them, must have been intended for use as part of this practice."

"Where did they even learn it from?"

"I have no idea," Nouri said. "There were fire mages in the past, but they have been unheard of for centuries. Fire magic is especially hard to master because fire as an element is very hard to tame. And who knows how many of these new-generation fire mages the Liwa has managed to train and send out to the battlefield. They might be only semi-prepared, possessing less than half the skill of the masters of old, but they are a force to be reckoned with even in such a state. This is troubling."

They both stayed silent for a few moments.

"So, what now?" Neil asked uncomfortably.

"Foreign nationals have a chance to be airlifted out of Baghdad. Use this opportunity, Mister Feaver."

"And what about you?"

"I will get out of the city by other means. Do not worry about me, I've sneaked past the noses of different militants in the past." Nouri smiled lightly. "I guess we will be parting ways tomorrow."

Neil was left speechless. He had not known the enigmatic guard long, but the thought of never seeing him again brought him further sadness. He knew the extraordinary things they had gone through together would never fade from his memory.

In the meantime, Nouri went over to the window again.

"And you don't have to pay me anything for my services," he said, looking out at the city's skyline.

"What?" Neil said. Surprises kept following surprises.

"I was never in it for the money. I had a discovery of my own to make," Nouri said, back turned to his employer.

"Are you ever going to let me in on anything?" Neil asked, somewhat angered. Jake had lost his life, and yet for Nouri, it was all about some sort of *discovery*. It sounded like something a person suffering from a mid-life crisis would claim to embark on in order to bring more flavour into his life.

"Yes. After all that has happened, you deserve to know." Nouri turned around.

"I hail from a community that dwells in a very remote part of Iraq. This is all that I will say about my people," he explained. "You know of my psychic powers. I've had them since childhood. Yet, in the last few years, I've begun having visions of a horrible blight that is to fall upon this land."

Neil shivered to hear the guard speak in this gloomy voice.

"I saw different types of visions of people and places, literal events and allegories. But I could not make out a full picture. They followed no chronology. These visions are fragmentary and often ripped out of context. I left my community to investigate this matter. My journey took me to different parts of Iraq, but I still could not find the truth. Eventually, my visions brought me to the coffee shop, where I foresaw I would meet you. And it came to pass that we crossed paths.

"I had no idea whether you would have an important role to play in all of this or if you are just a background character in a large mosaic. I tagged along with you, and indeed now I have the answers to at least some of my questions.

"To be honest, I feel bad about it—for keeping you in the dark throughout all of these events. I hope you can forgive me for it, for all of it," Nouri said, lowering his head.

"Don't worry," Neil said. What else could he say at that moment?

***

It had taken Neil much effort that night to finally fall asleep. Yet sometime later, he found himself shaken awake by the shoulders.

"Wake up!" Nouri declared loudly, rocking Neil by shoulders like a madman. "Wake up!"

"What is it?" Neil said as he sat up, his sleepy eyes adjusting to the room's lights.

"Look." Nouri pointed towards the window.

The curtains had been drawn back, showing the skyline Neil had looked at many times before. But this time it was painted thickly yellow, and the winds were beating against his window.

"What's that?" he asked. "Smog?"

"No, the daevas." Nouri shook his head, slowly, worriedly. "They've come in their full might."

CHAPTER THIRTY

It had been a calm night. No exchange of artillery fire and no bombing raid disrupted its tranquillity. For the first time in a few days, Sayid was certain he would get some proper sleep.

Without the sound of hostilities to wake him up, one of his aides chose to take this task upon himself. Still spellbound with sleep, Sayid listened as the aide urged him to go outside. Whatever was going on, it sounded like it was worth checking out.

Putting effort into keeping his eyes open, Sayid emerged out of his shelter. He had been expecting to behold darkness and moonlight, but the street was glowing in a dim yellow light. He could have sworn that some nearby oil rig had caught fire, but then the aide directed his attention towards the skies.

There he saw no moon and no stars, only a blot of a dirty brown colour. Vast, thick, and shapeless, it had eclipsed all celestial bodies. It continued its journey towards the besieged capital, moving like a cloud.

"What's this?" Sayid asked—no, theorised. "A sandstorm?"

***

"The daevas?" Neil asked.

Outside, the city quarter now appeared through a sandy haze.

"Yes," Nouri said.

"We're not even close to the desert!"

"Remember what Jake described: the cult offered the daevas the chance to amplify their powers with the help of the Tear of Set. It appears that is what they've done. Only I do not think this empowerment is permanent. Even Was Peraa will not just give unchecked power to desert demons."

A powerful gust of wind struck the window. Sudden and ferocious, it made Neil jump up, mouth agape. It was followed by another, and then several more, as if an intruder was trying to break into the room. A crack formed in the glass; it expanded, running down the window like a drop of water. All the while, the invisible assailant continued to deliver his blows.

"Get away from the window!" Nouri ordered as he grabbed Neil by the shoulders and pushed him towards the wall.

Unable to resist any longer, the window shattered, and a long stream of sand burst into the room like water out of a burst pipe. It surged through the room before hitting the wall and spattering sand all around.

"We need to get out of here!" Nouri said as he ran for the door. Neil followed, grabbing hold of his backpack on the way.

The corridor greeted them with shouting and screaming and more sand. The windows here, too, were smashed and sand was slowly filling the place. The hotel guests had begun coming out of their rooms, most still in their nightwear. There was panic and commotion all around; after all, what else would people who had never encountered anything even vaguely miraculous done at that moment?

"Why are they attacking this hotel?" Neil asked, his voice drowning among the screams and shouts.

"Revenge for the troubles we caused them," Nouri said. "The jinn stole the artefact right from your room, so they know we are here. It appears the daevas can be quite petty as well. This hotel is turning into a death trap. We need to get out."

He turned along the corridor, and shouted, "Everybody! Listen to me!"

At least for a brief moment, the bewildered guests gave Nouri their attention.

"Do not remain in one place! Make your way towards the fire exit!"

And he led by example, ducking under a torrent of sand bursting out of a broken window as he did.

Whether in the case of fire, an earthquake, or even dark sorcery, emergency exits always appear to offer a route to salvation. As sand kept filling the corridors, the passage remained clear sans a few specks that had managed to get past the door.

Nouri guided the group on their way down. With every floor they passed, they were joined by more people who had thought of the same idea.

Another flight of stairs brought Nouri and Neil to a familiar figure, Claude Faucon, who had joined a group of escapees from his floor. There were no formal greetings; Neil immediately advised the academic to follow them.

Upon finally reaching ground floor, Nouri ripped the seal off the emergency door. The group was now outside, but though they had evaded the hammer, they remained standing on the anvil, for the unnatural sandstorm was raging around them.

Lingering in the vicinity of such an unnatural phenomenon could prove to be suicide, and at least some of the people realised that. The crowd scattered like a flock of lambs that had broken out of an enclosure, rushing for the nearest safe spaces. Nouri gestured for Neil and Claude to follow him down a nearby alley.

"Can anybody explain what is going on here?!" Claude asked, bewildered.

"I'll tell you this," Nouri said. "If you do not believe in the existence of demons, then you ought to, and be wary of them for your own sake."

Neil was not sure how to read the facial expression Claude made within the yellow-brownish mist: anger, surprise, or amusement.

"So, what do we do?" Neil asked Nouri.

"We need to get as far away from this place as possible. For all we know they might decide to check if we're dead. And if they don't find the bodies, they might decide to scour the surroundings." Nouri threw a quick glance back at the towering hotel and the clouds of sand coiling around it like a monstrous python. "We need to go to the nearest mosque or temple and find refuge there. The daevas cannot walk on holy ground," he said before leading his companions onward.

Clouds of sand danced in the air above their heads as they made their way through the city's streets. The winds blowing through the city had truly gone mad; it felt like they were coming from all sides, all at once. Every street and alley the trio sneaked through was completely empty. Not a single window had a light burning in it. The dim hues of the magical sandstorm were making the urban landscape particularly eerie.

The scene became truly apocalyptic when they came across a checkpoint. Lack of security had been a problem in the city for years. Due to this, checkpoints had become a common sight on the streets of the capital, though their effectiveness had long been a matter of debate. The checkpoint in front of them was completely ravaged. Four armoured vehicles had been turned upside down as if they were hit by a powerful cyclone or tsunami. The soldiers that had manned them lay scattered around on the pavement. Not a single one of them even twitched a muscle. Neil counted eight bodies.

"The work of the daevas," Nouri said, kneeling before one of the soldiers.

Neil looked at the lifeless body, and the enormous bloody tear on the man's chest. Even the bulletproof vest the soldier wore had not been enough to save him from whatever blow he had sustained, having been pierced like a plain tunic.

Neil's gaze slid to the soldier's sleeve, which bore the insignia of the Iraqi Army.

"What are their intentions?" he asked.

"Did you really think that the daevas have made it all this way just to bury us alive under a ton of sand at the hotel?" Nouri said, standing up. "No, revenge is not their main motivation. This is an attack on the city."

Neil found it a horrifying thought.

"Let's keep going," Nouri said.

Their path was leading them southwards. The walk was not a pleasant one; every now and then they'd stumble across bodies of soldiers, policemen, militiamen, and even civilians. They kept appearing at random, as if they had been dropped from the sky.

"It all makes sense now," Nouri said as they walked past another body.

"Can you explain?" Neil asked.

"The nature of this attack and its timing. The forces of Liwa al-Qadisiyyah are outside the city. No matter what success they might have had on the battlefield, capturing a city the size of Baghdad would be a hard if not impossible feat for the group, even if they used fire magic. The daevas are wearing out the army's defences inside the city. The military has enough manpower and weapons to resist an attempt to capture the city by militants.

However, most weapons are useless against the daevas if they have not been blessed. So, for the demons, slaughtering the city's defenders is just as easy as plucking a chicken out of a farmer's backyard is for a hawk." Nouri looked Neil straight in the eyes. "They want to give the city to the Liwa."

"What?" Claude mumbled.

Neil looked at the academic, feeling sorry for the guy who was probably still trying to find some rationality in all of this.

"So, what you're saying is that the daevas and the jihadists are..." Neil struggled to complete the sentence as he raised a baffled brow. "...allies?"

"Perhaps not allies, but at least co-belligerents."

Neil had to admit that Nouri's hypothesis made sense when no other theory could.

"They're all in this together, one way or the other: Was Peraa, the daevas, the Liwa?"

"Yes, a game with kings and pawns." Nouri nodded. "But the greatest mystery is this: what is their endgame? And whose plan is it really?

"Change in plans!" he declared suddenly. "You are supposed to leave Baghdad in the morning. We might as well start making our way to the Green Zone now. The closer we get by morning the better, because if the Liwa moves its forces in once the daevas have done their work, it might be too late, and if we waste time hiding on holy ground throughout the night, we'll find sneaking through the streets of an insurgent-controlled area during daytime more risky than what we are doing now."

Neil could not agree more. As terrifying this supernatural evil was, the cruelty of radical extremists could give it a run for its money.

They walked in silence for some time, and all the while the sensational theory nagged at Neil's mind.

Every minute brought them closer to the Green Zone. The Green Zone was not Baghdad's beating heart—it was the city's nerve system. A district of government buildings and foreign embassies, this small part of the riverbank metropolis was without question the safest part of Baghdad. Not a single militant group had the power to breach all the levels of security. Grand Festivities Square, where the airlift was supposed to commence in a few hours, lay within the boundaries of the area.

But this night was unlike any other night throughout the long war. Extremists were not the carrying out the current attack: demons were.

"Is there a way to stop the daeva attack on the city?" Neil asked.

"Not one that I know of," Nouri said. "This is not some old Arabian folktale where there is a miraculous solution to every problem. This battle cannot be won; our goal isn't to become victorious—our goal is to survive. Let's hope this power upgrade the Tear of Set has given them will wear out by morning. And let's hope at least part of the Green Zone will remain somewhat intact by the time evacuations begin," he added cynically.

"And what if the daevas leave nothing remaining?"

"Then we will we use other means of exiting Baghdad. Together."

A blaze of light suddenly erupted in front of them, catching the trio by surprise. Neil flinched at its brightness. It took him a couple of moments to realise it was coming from the projector mounted atop a nearby checkpoint.

"You three, stop!" a voice commanded in Arabic.

The strong beam of light had already made them stop, but the barrels of automatic rifles sticking out from behind the sandbags that served as the checkpoint's wall served as further incentives.

Another order came from behind the barricade. "Raise your hands!"

They obliged.

A soldier stepped from behind the checkpoint, rifle in hand.

"Where are you people going?" he asked them in a steely tone.

"Towards the Green Zone!" Nouri answered. "For the evacuations!"

The soldier took several cautious steps forward.

And at the same time, a long, yellow bolt lanced down on the checkpoint. It could have been mistaken for lightning had it not seemed to consist of a hard material. Crashing and ripping sounds mixed with short screams played a blood-curdling tune behind the barrier.

"What is that?!" the soldier exclaimed, turning his back on the trio.

Moments later, a tailed, barely human-looking monstrosity appeared, rising into the air above the checkpoint. It dragged another soldier up with it, clutching him by his vest. The man was still alive, twitching and screaming in fear; the bloodiest battle he had survived was nothing compared to the grasp of a demon.

"Almighty Allah, help us," the first soldier whispered a prayer, pointing his weapon at the monster.

The daeva spun around in the air and threw its whimpering captive into the distance like a pebble. The trooper on the ground immediately fired at the fiend. But bullets left no wounds on the desert demon. It darted down like a falcon that had spotted prey. A mace materialised in its hand, and it decapitated the serviceman with a single blow.

The demon's death-heralding flight continued as it set its sights on the trio. Nouri jumped forth, drawing his sword. Metal rang as he parried the incoming strike from the mace. The demon, no doubt irritated by the resistance, pulled back and leapt high into the sky.

Wind and sand began to revolve in a vortex around the daeva, hiding its hideous form.

"Oh no," Nouri whispered, worried. His sword screeched as it returned to the scabbard.

The unnatural vortex expanded rapidly, becoming a dust devil. Wind had been blowing violently all night, but suddenly it felt like its strength increased a hundredfold. Before Neil could even adjust to the change, the ferocious currents tore him off the asphalt. He yelped in shock as he was sucked into the demonic whirlwind like a flower petal.

Neil's senses were in flux, but he felt someone's hand clasp around his wrist and pull him down roughly. He slammed against the pavement, squawking in pain. However, he was better off than Claude, who got pulled high into the air by the cyclone and disappeared into the vortex in a matter of seconds.

Horrified, he looked over to see Nouri resisting the whirlwind. The guard stood his ground, his left knee bent, firmly holding on to Neil with his right hand. His left hand was pointed at the dust devil; the mysterious orb of light was burning in his palm again, just as it had in the desert.

But the whirlwind seemed intent on devouring Neil. The insane air currents kept trying to pull him in, making him feel like the rope in a tug of war.

"Try to stand up, get behind me, and grab hold of my shoulder!" Nouri commanded through gritted teeth. It was clear he was under great pressure.

Neil's senses might not have been all there, but somehow, he managed to get up and hide behind Nouri, grabbing his shoulder tight.

A few inches really did seem to make a difference. Sheltered behind Nouri, he found himself resisting the whirlwind's suction. Nouri's magic was working.

"I did it!" Neil said, holding on to the guard's shoulder as hard as he could.

"Good!" Nouri said, letting go of his hand.

Neil heard another metallic screech, and a second later Nouri held a dagger out towards him.

"Here, take this!" He did not look at his former employer, keeping his eyes on the dust devil. "This weapon has been blessed!" he continued, still speaking loudly in order to be heard through the wind. "This should give you some protection against the daevas! If one gets close to you, strike it!"

"Got it!" Neil said, grabbing the weapon.

"Perfect! We're not that far from the Green Zone and the square!" Nouri said, now pointing both his hands at the whirlwind. "Get as far as possible, find a place to hide, and when things are safer, you can cover the distance by yourself! Use GPS if you need or can!"

"But what about you?"

"My magic should keep this whirlwind contained for some time!" Nouri explained. "But thanks to the Tear's power, the daeva's sorcery is stronger than it was in the desert! I won't be able to resist it for long! However, I'll try to destroy this whirlwind from inside; that's where its weakest point should be! I'll do it once you are far enough away!"

"This is insane!" Neil tried to argue.

"Don't worry about me! I've survived through worse! I might even come to say goodbye to you during the evacuation in the morning!"

Neil could imagine a sad smile on the guard's face as he uttered these words.

"Now run!" Nouri declared. "And don't worry about me! Just keep moving!"

"I guess I will see you later, Nouri Samir!" Neil said.

"Likewise, Mister Feaver!"

Reluctantly, Neil let go of his shoulder and began to run. Every moment, he expected the demonic cyclone to pull him back, but Nouri's magic seemed to protect him from it.

Neil stopped for a short moment to look back. He saw Nouri still holding his ground, his position unchanged. The guard slowly turned around and saw him watching. Neither tried to shout anything; it was unlikely that they would have heard each other over the distance and the wind's howl.

Nouri calmly turned in the daeva's direction once more, lifting both hands up as if he was capitulating. The whirlwind immediately plucked him off the ground.

Neil ran.

CHAPTER THIRTY-ONE

The feral currents within the whirlwind kept throwing Nouri up and down in a spiral pattern. But even this crazed ride could not overpower his senses. His mind and willpower were strong, sharpened over years of training in both martial and mystical arts. He began chanting an incantation as he tapped into his powers.

The demonic cyclone around him raged at full strength, yet the moment he uttered the final word of the spell, Nouri no longer moved with it. He was now floating in the air, suspended in the middle of the chaos. Random objects the dust devil was picking up from the nearby streets flew past him: empty soda cans, plastic, even somebody's lost wallet. A panicked shriek reached his ears, and a moment later, the winds hurled a living human right in front of him before throwing the man upwards.

"Claude!" Nouri shouted.

Readjusting the power that was coursing through him like adrenaline, Nouri flew up like a rock spat out of an erupting volcano. Within a matter of moments, he caught up with the academic and grabbed him by the hand. His mystical aura embraced Claude as well. No longer was the man thrown around by the winds, but he remained suspended in the air by Nouri's side.

"What is all of this?" Claude shouted into his ear. "What the hell are you? How are you levitating—"

"Hush!" Nouri told him. He was not in the mood to explain anything to the man. Countering sorcery, especially demonic, was a draining task. Nouri could already feel the strain on both his body and spirit. "I'm trying to save us both! But you'll need to stay calm!"

It took Claude a moment to get himself together before he responded with a nod. Nouri raised his free hand, and pale-blue light danced in his palm. He immediately dropped his hand, pointing it down. The light turned into a beam that shot from his palm into the bowels of the whirlwind. He was not sure what it hit in that abyss of wind, sand, and darkness, but he heard a loud roar resonate around him. It appeared the daeva was in anguish.

Everything within the whirlwind remained in a state of constant motion. Still, he felt a shift, a series of constant pushes. Its meaning was obvious: the dust devil had begun to move. Nouri found himself getting dragged forward. He realised that the cyclone was moving north, the opposite direction to the way Neil had run, but it was not the time to celebrate.

He diverted more of his power into the magical beam ripping through the daeva's aether-made form. The demon's howl became louder. Nouri invested more and more of his strength into the magical assault. But whilst his magic was hurting the daeva, Nouri too was in pain, feeling as if his very soul was getting torn out of his body.

The magical light he unleashed kept pouring down into the whirlwind's depths. Suddenly, his surroundings rumbled, shaking like a building caught in an earthquake. The dust devil exploded as if a bomb had detonated inside it; its remnants scattered across the air. Nouri could see the paved ground beneath him— and then he plunged down, along with Claude. Nouri heard the man yelp as he cast one more spell. They both fell on the hard surface, miraculously landing on their feet, but the fall was still a hard one. Their feet gave out beneath them, and they both collapsed on the asphalt.

It took Nouri a minute or so to get back up. His navy cloak was flapping in the wind behind him as he made a note of his surroundings. The twin minarets of a nearby mosque immediately caught his attention. Just a few feet to his left, another dead body lay sprawled in the middle of the road. The armband on the dead man's sleeve, dyed in a mixture of yellow and green, indicated that he belonged to one of the sectarian Shia militias that had come to aid the defence of Baghdad.

Destroying the cyclone had been a hard endeavour, but it had ended in success. Nouri was somewhat surprised he'd managed to survive.

Perfect, Urumshamim, the magician thought, congratulating himself.

Urumshamim was his real name. He had used the alias of Nouri Samir for years. And though he had come up with it himself, he had never truly learnt to like it.

"Damn! There's another one!" He heard Claude's voice behind him.

Urumshamim turned around. And indeed, another daeva was hovering in the air not that far away from their spot, eyeing the two of them with its ice-cold gaze. And yet, this demon looked different from the ones the magician had fought. It lacked a tail; its head and face were human, lacking the animalistic features of the other daevas. Practically all of its body, sans its head and clawed hands, was encased in armour made out of countless iron plates, and though it was ancient, it resembled no armour worn by any ancient army the magician knew of. Assyrian warriors were not clad in similar gear when they swarmed the Near East on top of their chariots, and the Persian King Cyrus wore nothing like it when he victoriously marched through the gates of Babylon.

The creature appeared to be kin to the vermin-like fiends, yet Urumshamim could sense a regal tint infused within its wicked aura. It had to be a daeva of a higher caste, most likely one of their lords. For all he knew, it could have been Apaosha himself...

The previous battle had left Urumshamim drained, like a fruit that had had all the juice extracted out of it. At that moment, he had no energy left to fight another daeva, especially one of greater power. And if Apaosha was truly in front of him, then he definitely did not stand a chance. A demon that was able to go against a rain deity during his prime would easily obliterate any mortal that had the folly to challenge him, especially one in a weakened state.

Claude scrambled for the handgun that lay next to the fallen militiaman. He picked it up and pointed it at the hovering demon. "Stay back!" he shouted.

"Don't bother! It's immune to bullets!" Urumshamim shot the man a quick look. "Run for the mosque—they cannot set foot on holy ground!"

He did not need to repeat his words in order for Claude to take flight towards the landmark. Urumshamim ran too, briefly throwing a look back. The daeva did not pursue, continuing to hover above the ground in silence.

They made it into the courtyard of the complex, where the walls that enclosed it hid them from the demon's view. The atmosphere was completely different; not a single gust of the infernal winds was able to reach this space. Still, the duo kept on moving until they reached the prayer room of the mosque.

Lanterns bathed the large, colonnaded room in their dim glow, not bright enough to allow a visitor to marvel at the calligraphic inscriptions adorning its walls.

Urumshamim had never been to this place before, yet a sense of strange familiarity overwhelmed him soon after they stepped inside. He gently rubbed his forehead.

"Are we safe here?" Claude asked.

And then a scene manifested in front of Urumshamim. He had seen it before amidst the other chaotic visions that had ultimately led him on this quest. The event had not yet happened, but it was replaying before his eyes. He heard a voice coming from both past and future...

"What mosque is this?" Urumshamim suddenly turned to Claude, looking at him like an interrogator.

"The Baratha Mosque," Claude replied.

"They will be here," Urumshamim uttered, looking aside.

"Who?"

"Liwa al-Qadisiyyah, or their leadership, to be more precise."

Looking around like a tourist, he took a few steps towards the nearest columns. "I saw them pray here in a vision I had."

Claude looked at him like at a madman. Urumshamim could not blame him.

"But this is a Shia mosque, and the Liwa are Wahhabis, Sunni radicals," Claude said. "But come to think of it, they can still pray here," he added after a short pause.

The next silence lasted longer.

"So, what do we do now?" Claude asked eventually.

"I don't know about you," Urumshamim said. "I'm not sure what to suggest. But I can tell that the city will fall to the jihadists today. It's not safe outside with the daevas roaming the city, so perhaps your best option is to linger in the mosque for some time. The local imam might help you out and get you to safety when—if—he comes here in the morning."

"And what about you?" Claude asked.

"I thought this battle was lost." Urumshamim's gaze wandered towards a ring of lanterns hanging nearby. "However, now I see an opportunity to achieve a significant victory through other means."

He reached under his cloak and felt the reassuring touch of the sword's hilt under his palm.

"I will kill the jihadist serpent by cutting its head off," he stated.

***

The crimson disk of the early morning sun was slowly rising over Baghdad's Victory Arch. The landmark looked even more imposing during dawn. One almost got the impression that the pair of titanic hands rising out of the ground were flesh, not casts from stone and concrete. Each hand held on to an enormous sword with a firm grip. The two curved blades crossed each other far above the tops of nearby trees and lampposts, but no matter how monumental the sculpture was, the sun ascended to heights far beyond the reach of its swords.

Neil had seen the monument before and, tired and worn out, he had no desire to have one last close look at the landmark. He could already hear the buzz of propellers coming from afar. He looked upward to see the forms of several transport helicopters making their way through the colourful morning sky. He heard several exalted cries coming from around him. Many evacuees had made their way to Grand Festivities Square, and the sight of these flying machines, bulky but not devoid of their own type of elegance, presented a notion of hope.

The weather was calm—a sweeping contrast to the dreadful atmosphere during the night. The only winds frolicking across the square were conjured up by the rotation of heavy propellers as the craft slowly landed.

Members of the American armed forces were already making all the arrangements related to embarkation. Neil found some familiar faces among them; he was certain he'd seen them among the servicemen stationed at the military base where he and Jake filmed a segment of the documentary weeks before.

It feels like it happened a lifetime ago, Neil thought as a sad smile appeared on his face.

It was a perfect time for some recollections, but the events of the previous night were the first thing that came to his mind. He had been surprised to find the Green Zone at least partially intact. True, the district had not been spared of the daevas' destructive spree, but most military positions remained manned. However, dread and confusion had reached the servicemen guarding them. Having never encountered a supernatural situation such as this one and having no idea of what was going on across the city, they'd grown paranoid. Had a breakdown in communication occurred when a group of coalition soldiers spotted Neil's approaching figure from their hiding spot, the reporter was certain he, too, would be lying dead on the asphalt.

Neil could not help but wonder what had stopped the daevas' ravaging assault and prevented them from turning Baghdad into a completely unmanned outpost. But it appeared that this riddle was not up to him to crack.

"Sir, please make your way towards the helicopter." The voice of a marine snapped Neil out of his thoughts. The serviceman motioned him towards the nearest aircraft, the ramp leading into its cabin already lowered.

"Yes, of course," Neil said, giving a nod.

He set on his path towards the helicopter, one step at a time. Every moment, he turned his head left and right in hopes of spotting one familiar face in the crowd, but he saw not even a glimpse of him. The guard had not come to say goodbye.

"Stay safe, Nouri," Neil whispered under his breath.

***

There has to be some catch to all of this, Sayid could not help but think as his pick-up truck carefully navigated through the city's lifeless streets.

This was not the situation he had anticipated. He was riding through Baghdad, the capital of the country and home to millions. He had expected to step into an utter bloodbath, the Mother of All Battles that would devour thousands of men once it opened its maw. The city was supposed to be defended by many different forces: the Iraqi Army, coalition troops, Shia paramilitaries.

And yet he felt like he was on a fieldtrip. More effort had been required to capture Hisad al-Shaeir, and that town fell easily. But here, deep within the limits of Baghdad, he was meeting no resistance whatsoever. Not a single sniper even tried to shoot at him. Communications revealed that the other commanders were faring the same.

Two decades before, the Americans, at a culminating point in their invasion of the country, had been able to capture Baghdad with relative ease, but even then, it took the infidels days to secure the city. At this rate, the Liwa was set to have the city under their control by evening.

Sayid wanted to think that it was God who had enlightened the minds of the city's defenders, making them desert their positions and scatter. But all the checkpoints Sayid personally came across had not been abandoned—they had been destroyed. And it looked like neither shells nor bombs had ravaged the entrenchments of the enemy, but some unknown weapon he had never seen in use.

"I've seen fiercer battles over a farmstead," Sayid grumbled to his bodyguard prior to jumping out of the truck to look at another devastated checkpoint.

It might have been a bright spring afternoon in the city, and yet Sayid had an urge to shiver, as if the temperature had suddenly fallen below zero.

The soldiers who used to man the checkpoint lay dead, scattered all around. Sayid went from one to the next, inspecting the bodies. Their equipment and insignias revealed that they were Americans.

He tried to formulate a reasonable explanation for all of this. Perhaps there was a guerrilla group operating in the city: a fifth column, a cell of Wahhabi sympathisers. Perhaps they had struck unexpectedly, catching their adversaries off guard and overwhelming them. But this theory was weak; after all, Sayid, as an important commander, would have been aware of any inside job. The fact that the streets were not being patrolled by their local allies buried the theory completely.

"Not a single one of them sustained a bullet wound," he commented, having had a look at the corpses.

At least one had been struck with a blunt object; the blood-crusted dent on the side of his head made that clear. Others had long tears running down their chests and throats. In one case, the gashes were so severe that it seemed the body had intentionally been mutilated.

"Commander!" Sayid turned around upon hearing one of his subordinates.

He saw two fighters practically dragging an American soldier by the hands from whatever gutter they had extracted him from.

"We found him cowering in a nearby alley," one of the men said.

The soldier was not resisting, but his whole body was seized by a strong fit of shivering that made him incapable of moving on his own. If it had not been for the fighters holding him up, he would have collapsed on the pavement.

"American dog!" Sayid raised his voice, speaking in English, as he stormed towards the captive. "What happened at this checkpoint?" He grabbed the man by the collar.

His face mere inches away from the soldier's, Sayid looked into his eyes, reading dread in them. The man before him was like a child separated from his mother: scared, lost, and alone.

"Tell me what happened, and I personally guarantee you life and safety," Sayid said, trying the carrot tactic but keeping his voice solid.

The soldier moved his lips, but whatever he whispered, he uttered in such a quiet tone that Sayid was unable to hear. Impatient, Sayid whipped out a handgun, pointing the barrel right in the soldier's face.

"I said...TELL ME WHAT HAPPENED HERE!"

"Sand and fury," the soldier mumbled.

"What do you mean? Sayid asked.

"Sand and fury," the soldier repeated.

"Yes, I heard that. Now say something else!"

"Sand and fury."

"Do you know who I am?! I don't play games!" Sayid warned him, shoving the gun closer to the man's face, making sure that the barrel was a mere inch away from his eye. "Start speaking with sense!"

"Sand and fury."

And it was then that Sayid realised that the man in front of him was not talking to his interrogator; he was talking to himself. The pitiful soul was a madman, so disconnected from his surroundings that he was probably unaware who the figures in front of him even were. Sayid barely resisted the urge to plant a bullet into his brain; the creature before him was not worth wasting a single piece of ammunition.

"Get this filth out of my sight!" Sayid spat out, lowering his gun.

***

A couple of hours later, Sayid entered the courtyard of the Baratha Mosque, the place Nishwari had chosen as their assembly point. Most of the commanders had already arrived; a couple of others turned up within the next few minutes.

"I have excellent news, Mullah Nishwari," Jalil al-Quwaiti declared triumphantly. "The city centre is under our control. The banners of the Liwa are flying over the Presidential Complex, the Parliament, and the Constitutional Court."

"But do any of you find it strange that Baghdad was taken so easily?" said Shamil. "It's as if lethal wounds simply opened on the bodies of our enemies, making them fall dead on the ground."

"Certainly not all of them," Jalil said. "Helicopters were spotted departing from the centre just before my forces entered Baghdad. Some of them seem to have escaped the city."

"I've had my men question some witnesses." Nayaub got involved in the discussion. "The stories they tell sound fantastical. Some claim they've seen angels descend from above. And others say they saw jinn walking the streets of the city."

This made the commanders and their aides start chattering among each other. Sayid remained silent. He, too, had had a chance to ask some of the locals questions once his men had dragged some of them from their basements, but he would have been more content if he'd got useful information from captured enemy combatants.

"Angels, jinn, poison, or disease—what difference does it make?" Jalil spoke out to everybody. "Baghdad is ours now, and we took it without a fight."

Sayid found it disturbing how the other commander managed to shrug the whole thing off so easily.

"Allah grants victory whichever way he wills," Nishwari commented, finally speaking out. "Now let us stand here no more and go inside the mosque. It's almost time for the Asr prayer."

An invitation to prayer was enough to cast aside all debates about superstitions.

"So, Mullah, why did you want us to assemble at this particular mosque?" Shamil asked their leader as the group made their way inside.

"You probably do not know this, but this mosque is one of the oldest monuments of Islam's presence in Iraq, founded long before Baghdad itself," Abdulaziz explained. "But since then, the miserable Shias defiled this holy site with their practices, even erecting a shrine on its territory. Back when I was residing in Baghdad, many years ago, I would often pass this site, looking at it with regret as I hoped to see the day when justice was restored. And today is that day. From now, all prayers here will be held in accordance with our tradition, the only true way..."

***

The prayer room of the mosque was large. Sayid had no idea how many people it could have fitted nor how many attended prayer on a usual day. But on this day, the group were the only ones inside, gathered together in one section of the room.

The mullah led the service from the top of the minbar. Not surprisingly, victory was the topic of the sermon he was giving.

"And indeed, Allah commands the forces of both Earth and Heaven," Nishwari said, referencing the Quran. "And it is to his faithful followers that he grants unlimited victories."

A loud thud came from behind their backs. To Sayid's ears, it sounded like the large door that led into the building had closed by itself. Nishwari stopped preaching immediately and looked towards the sound. Sayid looked around whilst still kneeling on the carpet.

It appeared that another man intended to join the group for prayer. But it was a man he had never met before. Medium height with a short beard, he would not have stood out from among the millions of Baghdad's denizens if it had not been for the navy cloak he wore. Sayid had no idea what tribe or group this stranger belonged to.

"I have to interrupt your sermon, Mullah!" the stranger said loudly, addressing the Liwa's leader.

Chapter Thirty-Two

The stranger seemed relaxed and unconcerned as he walked up to stand in the midst of the group's leaders and their aides. Noticing that the man had not even bothered to take his boots off before entering this holy site made Sayid grit his teeth in outright fury; it was starting to seem like this daring newcomer was intentionally trying to mock them.

"Who are you?!" Nishwari addressed the newcomer from the minbar.

"My name is Urumshamim," the mysterious man responded calmly but loud enough that even a person sitting in a distant corner would have heard him. "And this Son of Ea sends his regards to the Sons of Marduk!"

This cryptic greeting left Sayid confused. But before he could discern its meaning, the stranger made his first move, swift and precise. Like a serpent leaping in pursuit of its prey, his hand dashed under his navy cloak. Sayid heard the screech of metal, and a moment later, a sword appeared in the man's hand. The light coming through the mosque's glazed windows embraced it like an aura.

The stranger struck so quickly that nobody had the time to react. He swung his sword, decapitating the commander located closest to him, Shamil, with one strike. Blood stained the old carpet, forever leaving its mark on the rug as Shamil's kneeling body collapsed on the floor.

Before anybody even realised what was happening, the stranger ran the blade through the chest of one of Sayid's own bodyguards, then continued his lethal acrobatic display. Having danced towards one of Nishwari's aides, he raised his blade, dripping with blood, over his head and brought it down immediately, cleaving the man in two.

By that time, all the jihadists were back on their feet, but most of them were in disarray. Some were frantically searching the hall with their eyes, looking for the best way out.

"There is no way out!" the stranger hissed, having taken a battle stance with the bare blade raised in front of him. "I have sealed all the exits! And I assure you, I did it in such a way that none of you could open the doors without breaking them down!"

A sinister grin appeared on the stranger's face, exposing his teeth. Sayid was not the type to get disturbed easily, but in this moment he swore that the image of this smirk would haunt him until the final moment of his life.

He instinctively reached for his gun, but his fingers only grasped at empty air. In all of this chaos, he had forgotten that he was unarmed—all of them were. A mosque was a sacred place; they had left their weapons with the fighters outside the complex.

"You imbeciles! Why are you standing like this?!" Jalil yelled. "Tackle him! There is one of him and two dozen of us! A blade won't help him if he's overwhelmed!"

The stranger lunged at his next target. But this time, he was met with resistance as the jihadists practically tried to dogpile him. But the stranger had the agility of a jinn as he gracefully manoeuvred among his foes, avoiding getting locked down. He put everything he could into use against his enemies—his sword, his fist, his foot. Every single man surrounding the intruder was an experienced cutthroat or at least had the potential to be one. Yet the stranger was slaughtering them all with ease, like a boy stomping on a nest of ants.

Nayaub, Mahdavi, Wahid, al-Pirani—the Liwa's top leaders were falling by his blade, one after another.

The weapon's sharp tip passed mere inches away from Sayid's face. Blood splashed on his face, and Sayid stepped back, blinking constantly, trying to get it out of his eyes. His hands scrambled as he examined his face, neck, and chest with his fingers in search of any wounds. But no part of his body was stinging and his fingers touched no bleeding gashes: the blood was not his.

By that time, only a few of the jihadists remained. Sayid saw Jalil try another strategy. Having no concern for the survival of any of his comrades, the imposing warlord slammed his palms into his bodyguard's back, pushing him onto the stranger's sword with all the strength he could. The aide, not expecting this, released a short yelp before getting impaled. But the strategy seemed to work. He fell on the blade with his full weight, slamming into the stranger and knocking him off his feet.

Jalil instantly dashed towards them. Sayid could recognise a perfect moment for him to act too...

The stranger had to let go of the sword, but got back on his feet in no time. It was unclear what technique Jalil was intending to use against him, for he did not get a chance to show it off. The stranger countered by delivering an impressive kick to Jalil's chin, knocking him down.

But, at least for a couple moments, the stranger was vulnerable from the back. Sayid lunged, and locked him in a rear naked choke, encircling his neck with his arm from behind and pressing hard. He applied more pressure into the chokehold as he frantically sought to suffocate his opponent.

The stranger began to gasp; his body trembled. His fingers dug into Sayid's arm, trying to claw through the fabric of his sleeve.

"Got you, you son of a bitch," Sayid hissed with absolute hatred.

The stranger's arms fell to his side, his hands convulsing...

And then pain erupted in Sayid's gut, making him let go of the stranger in an instant. Staggering back, Sayid looked down to see the hilt of a dagger sticking out of his stomach. The area around it was getting moist, and blood darkened the fabric of his fatigues. Now he felt like he himself was in a chokehold, as he looked back and forth between the wound and the stranger.

He heard movement coming from the side and turned to see Jalil drawing the sword out of the body of his dead bodyguard. Letting out a battle cry, he lunged at his enemy with the blood-soaked blade in his hand, but the stranger put his skills to full use, dodging and ducking away from every blow. Neither opponent realised how much their confrontation resembled a ceremonial dance on an eerie stage as they manoeuvred around the lifeless corpses littering the blood-soaked carpets.

Jumping away from the blood-craving blade once again, the stranger ripped his cloak off in one rough movement and threw it at Jalil like a snare. The warlord snarled in rage as it entangled his upper body, blinding him behind its navy screen. The stranger immediately threw himself forward and kicked his enemy straight in the chest. The weapon fell out of Jalil's hand as he teetered backwards, but he tore that shroud off with feral vigour, as if it was a chemical-drenched cloth that was searing his face.

The stranger was in no rush to pick his weapon up. He rushed forth and punched Jalil in the face. Almost immediately, Jalil received another punch. The stranger was very charitable when it came to delivering blows. He kept punching Jalil's face as if his opponent was a practice dummy. Jalil could no longer respond to any blow, only stepping back with every hit he received. And when the right moment came, the stranger's palm enveloped Jalil's face and slammed his head against a nearby column.

It was unbelievable: the stranger had killed or neutralised every man in the group that had tried to tackle him.

And he was not even bleeding.

Blood continued to cascade out of Sayid's wound as he slid down against a nearby column, his strength draining out through the wound along with his blood.

As for Mullah Nishwari, all this time he had been on top of the minbar, watching the brawl unfold.

The stranger extended his hand towards his sword, and in one of the most extraordinary scenes Sayid had ever beheld, the weapon shot through the air like a projectile and found its way into his grasp.

This had to be a hallucination caused by blood loss...

"You can finish your prayer, Nishwari!" the stranger declared, pointing the blade at the group's leader from afar. "I will give you this privilege before I send your soul to devour dust in the underworld!"

"You have martyred my best men!" Nishwari told him as he slowly descended from the minbar. "But their deaths will be avenged!"

Fire enveloped the mullah's palms and fingers, but Nishwari did not appear to burn. He raised his hands up in a boastful demonstration of his miraculous abilities.

It was clear that the group's leader too had mastered the mysterious Jinn Arts. The dying Sayid was not sure if he was meant to be surprised by this revelation. He had never thought to ask. As far as Sayid knew, nobody had...for some unexplained reason.

"It appears you have learnt fire magic!" the stranger said, somewhat jokingly. "But tell me this, Mullah: what does the Quran say about it?!"

"This is not magic. Magic is an illusion," Nishwari responded coldly. "These are the Jinn Arts!"

"Magic is magic no matter what you wish to call it!" the stranger declared. "And it's very un-Islamic of you to practice these...Jinn Arts."

"No institution gave you the authority to issue fatwas on this matter!" Nishwari snarled at him.

The stranger reached for his belt and pulled out a knife. The weapon shot through the air, but a precise strike from Nishwari's blazing fist ended its flight before the blade could sink into his throat. The part-melted, disfigured blade fell to the floor.

"Die!" Nishwari cried out.

He pushed his hands forward and a thick stream of fire burst from his palms. Even the stranger appeared to be startled by this deadly display of Nishwari's unnatural might. Grabbing the hilt of his sword with both hands, the stranger brought the blade in front of himself. The mystical fire collided with the blade, but was unable to pass beyond it, as if the sword was sucking the magic into its thin metallic form.

When the attack ceased, the stranger hurriedly cast the sword aside, as though it was a log he had picked out of a burning fireplace. Energy began to form around the stranger's palm. Its hues mixing blue and white, it seemed more akin to light than fire. The stranger cast the magical bolt at his rival, but the surprisingly agile Nishwari dodged away. The bolt dissolved in the air upon hitting the wall.

Nishwari responded by conjuring up a fireball, which he threw at the stranger. But their mysterious enemy sent one of his own bolts to meet it. The two projectiles neutralised each other with a bright flash.

The stranger jumped to the side as he began to draw some invisible signs in the air. A corona of the same mystical energy formed over him before splitting into seven bolts that immediately shot at Nishwari.

His hands still blazing, the mullah swirled around his axis and an enormous wall of pure flame encircled him. The stranger's magical projectiles were unable to penetrate it; they disappeared in the unnatural conflagration. A pyre of such magnitude would have burned the whole building to the ground in a matter of minutes if the unnatural force that fuelled it had not decided to keep its devouring flames restrained.

Nishwari's laughter crackled with the fires, reverberating through the colonnaded hall. It reached Sayid's ears, but he could barely recognise it, though he had heard the leader's laugh before. This sounded many times louder and deeper, acquiring a menacing tone capable of making the bravest man shiver.

The flaming wall concealed Nishwari from view. The stranger took a couple of careful steps forward, the magic circulating around him ever-ready. Two long tendrils of fire emerged from the burning wall. They moved and coiled like a pair of tentacles belonging to an enormous squid-like monstrosity that had emerged from the most macabre part of Hell. It might not have been possible to see Nishwari, but the mullah definitely saw his opponent, for the fiery tendrils descended on the stranger. The man braced against the pressure as a shield made of the mystic blue energy formed around him, becoming a bulwark against fiery sorcery. The monstrous tendrils hit against it repeatedly, but were unable to break through the barrier.

But a minute later, both the wall of fire and the shell of energy suddenly extinguished, and a barely conscious Sayid came to conclude that he would never find out why.

Nishwari and the stranger now stood facing each other. Nishwari brought his hands forward, unleashing another stream of fire. The stranger practically mirrored his act, shooting a blue-white beam forth. The two torrents collided; fire and energy danced in the air in a spectacle that could put the most extravagant fireworks to shame.

For some time, it appeared that the two were evenly matched. And then Nishwari put more force into his effort. Bit by bit, the fiery beam began consuming its rival, moving closer towards the opposing magic-wielder.

The stranger let out a loud groan. Then the tide changed. Most of the fire beam suddenly turned blue-white.

"No!" Sayid heard Nishwari yell.

Both combatants were putting everything they had into the latest phase of their duel.

Then the two contrasting beams exploded like a bomb. The stranger fell to his knees. Nishwari fared noticeably worse. Thrown back by the shockwave, he was propelled through the air and slammed against the minbar.

It looked like the mind-boggling duel had come to an end. The stranger coughed out blood, the first sign he'd given of any vulnerability. He slowly rose up, his body shaking as if coming down from a high.

"Bastard," Sayid whispered under his breath.

The stranger turned as though he had heard him. For several seconds, his dark eyes lingered on him before he casually turned away, no longer viewing him as a threat. And he was not wrong—having lost much blood, Sayid could barely move a finger.

The sword floated back into the stranger's hand as if some invisible chain kept the weapon attached to its wielder. Limping, the stranger staggered towards the minbar, the blade clutched in his hand.

It was obvious that Nishwari was the loser in the mystical duel. He lay at the foot of the dais, drained of all energy, so when the stranger grabbed him by the collar of his robe and pulled him up like a ragdoll, the mullah showed no resistance.

"Whatever you envisioned dies with you," the stranger said, slowly but harshly, as he raised the sword to deliver the final blow.

A sound echoed across the large colonnaded room, the last thing Sayid expected to hear on this occasion—the boom of a discharged gun.

The stranger fell to the floor, dead, completely silent in his final moments as blood burst out of the back of his head and sprinkled his surroundings like drizzle. Nishwari fell with him, but found the strength to raise his upper body off the floor with his arms.

Sayid's gaze wandered towards the entrance. Though his vision had blurred, he distinguished a Western-looking man slowly walking towards Nishwari, holding a gun in his lowered hand. Sayid had no idea who he was, how he had entered the building, or how he could have remained unnoticed for so long.

"Are you alright, Mullah Nishwari?" This new arrival, whether friend or foe, sounded genuinely concerned.

"Who are you?" Nishwari asked.

"Claude Faucon. And I am the man the Samnite notified you about."

Sayid would not hear the remainder of the newcomer's introduction. The whole world suddenly ceased to be...in his eyes and in his mind.

EPILOGUE

Yussuf had passed through these gates many times before, but on no other occasion had he experienced such anxiety as now enveloped him in its troubling hug. The two men standing just one step in front of him remained tense, their hunting rifles pointed at the entrance to the inn's courtyard. However, their potential game was unlike any creature usually spotted in these parts. Only the grace of God would offer the best defence against the beasts they were up against.

Sheikh Ismail stood by Yussuf's side, as stoic as always; two more men were guarding their backs. Their guards slowly moved towards the entrance, their fingers on the triggers of their weapons, ready to discharge their deadly projectiles at the mere sight of a hideous canine muzzle.

The shadows of the night offered many potential shelters for beings that roamed in the hours of darkness, but the blazing lanterns that hung around the courtyard had somewhat reduced their options.

"Look over there," one of the armed men whispered, drawing their attention to the distant part of the courtyard.

And indeed, the Master of Service saw a big lump lying on the ground near the old armoury. The hunting party carefully moved closer to the motionless form. A dark-grey hide served as its shaggy exterior. A puddle of blood had formed around it, and Yussuf recognised the antique sabre and spear sticking out of the body. But what disturbed him the most was the trail of blood and footprints that seemed to have originated in the crimson pool and led a path upstairs.

"Allah, Master of Creation!" he heard one of the men whisper in awe.

Ismail stepped from behind the guards and moved closer to the vanquished ghul.

"I do not think this is a good idea, Sheikh. Just because something seems dead does not mean it is," Yussuf told him. After all, some predators play dead to mislead their foes and victims before striking unexpectedly.

"Allah will keep me safe," Ismail said calmly.

The men who'd come with them were whispering to each other, unable to keep their eyes off the creature.

"I have never seen a creature like this before," Ismail uttered. "This cannot be a hyena."

"Indeed," Yussuf agreed. "If it got up on its hind legs, it would be as tall as a man."

And as he thought about it, he had to admit that the creature's paws did not look as if they belonged to a canine. There was something particularly human-like in them...

This was the first time he, or any of them, had seen a ghul. The fiends had crept into the settlement and attacked several houses and barns, wiping away the lines that were meant to exist between folklore and reality. The locals had managed to drive them away, but to Yussuf's knowledge, this was the only one slain.

"What about the guests?" Ismail asked.

And indeed, checking up on them was the main reason for their presence.

"Elliott! Lauren!" Yussuf called out their names over and over again.

"Sheikh Yussuf!" He heard a female voice coming from above. "Thank God!"

The Dervishes looked up to see the young woman standing on the terrace, her red hair reflecting the radiance of the flames burning in the nearby lantern. She ran down to them.

"Please...the ghul attacked...Elliott...is injured," Lauren said, tripping over the words in her distress.

Yussuf could now see the large swathes of blood on her shirt. Yet she looked unharmed; the blood was someone else's.

"Calm down, my girl," Yussuf said. "Where is he?"

"I helped him get upstairs to his room. He's still there."

"How severe are his injuries?" Ismail asked.

"He suffered quite a bad fall when the monster pinned him to the ground. The ghul also fell on top of him when he killed it."

"Are there any bites or claw wounds?" Yussuf asked.

"I didn't see any."

"Do not worry," Ismail said. "Sheikh Yussuf will have a look at him. He has no equal in this town when it comes to skills in medicine. Now please, go attend to your cousin. Sheikh Yussuf will be upstairs in a matter of minutes."

Lauren curtsied before she turned around and went upstairs.

"When morning comes, take the body and bury it in the drylands." Ismail turned to one of his men. "I do not want this carcass to foul the soil of our oasis."

The man responded with a nod and assurances.

"We will know the true amount of damage the ghuls wrought on the town as the day progresses," Ismail told Yussuf. "Go check up on the boy. I need to do some pondering." He finished his statement with a deep, saddened sigh, then turned and began to walk towards the gate.

"Sheikh Ismail?" Yussuf addressed him.

Ismail stopped immediately and looked back at him.

"I thought a prayer would be enough to pacify the ghuls," Ismail said. "But I was wrong. If anything, it only infuriated these jinn even more. Before, they raided our cemeteries; now they target our homes. I need to think about how we can ward off this threat."

Ismail went on his way. Yussuf ascended the stairs that led onto the terrace. There was a lantern hanging from every arch. He looked at one for a few moments. The fire burning within was driving the gloom away from the vessel. *Even the darkest shadow can be vanquished,* he thought.

***

Sand covered the floor of the hallway like a second carpet, crunching under the soles of Claude Faucon's shoes as he made his way to his hotel room. The hotel stood lifeless and silent. He saw no guest or member of staff in sight. Not surprising, really. Not only would the events of the previous night frighten anybody unprepared for them, but the city's fall to Liwa al-Qadisiyyah meant that the order of things was bound to change.

The lock clicked as he turned the key. Claude entered the room and looked around. The place remained the way he had left it. Unlike many other windows in the hotel, the window in his room had coincidentally remained intact, having avoided the wrath of the daevas.

"What a relief. The last thing I need is to stay in a sand-covered room," he said to himself, a habit that often activated when he was all alone.

He sat down on a chair.

He had to admit that the Fates could bring plans to fruition in some peculiar ways. Some plots were destined to succeed thanks to meticulous planning, perfect organisation, and rapid action. And some... These achieved success through a series of coincidences, sometimes incredibly farcical in nature.

Was Peraa had planned everything carefully. Like a master blacksmith, they had tried to make sure that every link in the chain they forged was solid and immune to damage. Yet they had almost been thwarted, and it was due not to treachery or the efforts of an enemy. A pair of reporters and their bodyguard had stolen the key component for their plan from right under the noses of their ancient mystics. And that was when the ironic coincidences played their fated role. By chance, he and the reporters had stayed at the same hotel, and by chance had he met Feaver at that lounge.

Coincidences are born from the chaos of the moment but can have far-reaching repercussions. History is filled with countless examples of coincidences bringing down the mightiest leaders and deciding the rise and fall of entire empires.

Luckily, he was able to overwrite the failure of Was Peraa. Neither Feaver nor his guard could have figured out that it was he, Claude Faucon, their acquaintance, who sent the jinn to retrieve the artefact for the ancient society. They had no idea that during the night of the daeva attack, he had tagged along with them to make sure they would create no more problems. He had never intended to leave Baghdad; on the contrary, his mission was only beginning.

But then things had turned for the worse. His gambit came with high risks. The daevas had no knowledge of him, so there were several times during the night when he'd had a chance to have a meeting with death. Ironically, it was Nouri Samir who saved him. Again, it was chance that brought him and the guard to the mosque where Nishwari was meant to preach his fated sermon...

Claude had never considered Feaver a threat—the reporter never had the potential. His mysterious bodyguard, on the other hand, was a completely different story. Nouri might have been dead, but the secrets he took with him into the afterlife only fuelled the intrigue surrounding him. Who was he really and where did he come from? It was not just Claude's own curiosity that sought an answer to this question; this information would prove valuable to Was Peraa.

"I will kill the jihadist serpent by cutting its head off," Nouri's words echoed in Claude's ears.

Claude could only shake his head at the memory. He had no idea what the guard really hoped to achieve by assassinating the leadership of the terror group. A foolish and misplaced attempt to set things right; after all, others would just come in the place of the slain and continue from where their predecessors left off.

"You're wrong, Samir," Claude said, as if the man was standing right in front of him. "There is no jihadist serpent. Liwa al-Qadisiyyah, just like the groups that came before it, is not a serpent. It's a hydra. For every head that gets cut off, two new ones grow in its place. You can prevent the heads from regenerating by burning the neck stumps, yet still you will not destroy it; one head always turns out to be invincible, instinctively hissing and biting even when detached from the body. And even if you are able to seal that head away, that will still not be the end, for the venom oozing out of its rotting corpse would pollute the surroundings for years, if not decades, to come."

And outside, the sun was shining over a new Baghdad.

***

Drawing his sword, the Norman knight stepped forth, proudly displaying the green-yellow sigil of his duchy on the shield he held before him. Elliott, once again in the guise of a Saxon warrior, gripped the hilt of his sword, feeling its leather dressing under his fingers. The medieval world around them played its own tune, the cheers of spectators mixing with the melodies of flute and psaltery.

Elliott smirked as he thought about the upcoming duel. He had gained more experience in swordsmanship, having fended off a real monster with a bare blade. This time Norm was most certainly bound to lose.

It was great to be back where he truly belonged, at another historical re-enactment event with all of its décor and sounds and atmosphere. No drylands, no digging in the dust, no wandering under the scorching sun, no hyena-monsters.

He raised his blade and lunged at his opponent...

Then found himself lying flat on his back, staring at the ceiling. He felt the pain in his joints as he realised that he was still at the inn at the oasis in the middle of nowhere, in a distant corner of the world.

"Damn." He could not hide his disappointment.

"Elliott, you're awake."

He turned his head and saw Lauren sitting on a stool beside the closed door in the bright light that was pouring into the room through the archaic window.

"Yes, I am," Elliott said, regretfully. "Is that thing dead?"

"Yes," Lauren said.

For the next few moments there was only silence.

"You know." Elliott spoke again, his tone as weary as his mind. "I had a dream where everything was back to normal, where all of this craziness was over."

"Trust me, it's far from over," Lauren responded, her voice devoid of emotion.

And there was absolutely no way that Elliott could disagree with her this time.

END

GLOSSARY

The novel contains terms, names, and allusions that many readers might find unfamiliar. This glossary was compiled in order to provide context and explanations. The terms are listed in order of appearance in the novel.

Historical Characters/Dynasties/Events

Euclid (III-II centuries BC): An Ancient Greek mathematician. Euclid's treatises and theorems have played a major role in the history of geometry.

Harun al-Rashid (r. 786–809): A medieval Arabic ruler. His reign corresponds with the zenith of the Arabic Caliphate, when the empire stretched from the Maghreb to north India. He was known as a benefactor of arts and sciences and also for the lavishness of his court. Though not much of his biography is known, many legends and anecdotes surround him.

Salah ad-Din (r. 1174–1193): Commonly known as **Saladin** in Western sources. Salah ad-Din is one of the most famous characters from medieval Middle Eastern history. He started out as a general under Egypt's Fatimid dynasty. However, he carried out a coup that overthrew the Fatimids in 1171 to become the Sultan of Egypt. His military campaign resulted in the conquest of Syria, Palestine, and parts of Iraq. In 1187, Saladin besieged and captured Jerusalem, which triggered the Third Crusade. He fought against the Crusader forces led by the English King

Richard the Lionheart and French King Phillip Augustus. The Third Crusade ended in draw with neither side achieving their tactical objectives. Despite being an adversary of the Crusaders, Saladin received a great deal of respect from medieval European authors, who praised him as a noble opponent and a wise ruler.

Abbasid Caliphate (750–1517): The second dynasty to rule over the Caliphate, following the overthrow of the Ummayyads in 750 AD. The first centuries of the dynasty can be considered a golden age of Middle Eastern history with political stability as well as thriving commerce, culture, and science. Nevertheless, the dynasty also oversaw the empire's decline and fragmentation into feudal kingdoms. What followed was a dark age during which the region lived through numerous feudal wars, as well as the Crusades and Mongol invasions.

Caliph Umar (r. 634–644): One of the aides of Prophet Muhammad and the second Caliph. Under Umar's command, the Arabs conquered Egypt, the Levant, Mesopotamia, and Iran.

Ibn Rushd (1126–1198): Also known as **Averroes**, a famous medieval Arabic philosopher and theologian.

Ibn Sina (980–1037): Known as **Avicenna** in the West, a Persian philosopher, scientist, and medic who wrote treatises on a variety of subjects. He has frequently been recognised as one of the most influential thinkers of all time.

Xerxes (r. 486–465 BC): An ancient Persian King. Xerxes is most famous for his failed invasion of Greece in 480 BC. His troops fought the numerically smaller Greek force led by the Spartan King Leonidas at Thermopylae in an event that gave rise to the famous tale of the 300 Spartans. Though he managed to capture Athens, his forces were later defeated at Salamis and Platea.

Seljuks (11–12th centuries): A Turkic dynasty that came to rule a large part of the Middle East, creating an empire stretching from Central Asia to Anatolia.

Hammurabi (XVIII century BC): An ancient Babylonian king. He is especially known for the Code of Hammurabi, a legal text containing laws regulating different aspects of Babylonian life. Very often, the punishment delivered to the offender mirrored the crime he committed. In the most famous example, it states that a man who blinds another man gets blinded himself as punishment.

Sargon of Akkad (XXIV–XXIII centuries BC): The ruler of Akkad, one of the kingdoms of ancient Mesopotamia. He conquered the neighbouring Sumerian city-states and founded the first known empire of Mesopotamia.

Gilgamesh of Uruk: The mythological king of the Sumerian city state of Uruk. The ancient Mesopotamian epic poem the *Epic of Gilgamesh* tells the story of Gilgamesh's adventures, including his friendship with the beastman Enkidu and their battles against different monsters, as well as Gilgamesh's failed quest to achieve immortality.

"What did Caliph Umar do when he captured the city of Alexandria?": The Great Library of Alexandria was one of the largest libraries and major research centres of the ancient world. The library was destroyed during one of the sieges of Alexandria in Antiquity or the Early Middle Ages, though the exact year and event are still a matter of debate. According to some accounts, it was burnt down under the order of Caliph Umar after the capture of Alexandria by the Arabs in 642 AD, though there is no substantial evidence to prove that this is anything more than a legend.

Cyrus the Great (r. 559–530 BC): The founder of Persia's Achaemenid empire and one of the most famous conquerors of ancient history. He overthrew Medes' rule over Persia and went on to conquer Babylon and Asia Minor.

Achaemenids (r. 559–330 BC): An ancient Persian dynasty that established the first Persian empire. At the height of their reign, the Achaemenid dynasty ruled over vast territories stretching from Egypt to Afghanistan. Ironically, the empire itself became a victim of expansionism and was overthrown by Alexander the Great during his conquest of the Middle East in 335–330 BC.

"...when Hulagu Khan ransacked Baghdad...": In 1258, in a culmination of the Mongol conquests of Iraq, Mongol forces led by Hulagu, Genghis Khan's grandson, laid siege to Baghdad for 13 days. After Baghdad's fall, the city was plundered and reduced to ruins with most of its population massacred, according to historical sources. The level of destruction and atrocities shocked contemporary authors and made the Sack of Baghdad one of the darkest moments of medieval Islamic history.

Society/Culture/Religion

Souq: A traditional Arabic market.

Amir/Ameer/Emir: An Arabic title. Though the title is most commonly associated with royalty and aristocracy, it is also used to refer to high-ranking military commanders and other figures of authority.

Haram: The Islamic concept of sin.

"Thousands of jinn built palaces and dug wells...": According to Quranic tradition, God gave King Solomon (Suleiman) rule over a large group of jinn as reward for his piety.

Fatwa: In Islam, a decree or ruling issued by a figure of religious authority (such as a Mufti or an Ayatollah) on issues in situations when an act's compatibility with Islamic law is under question. Contrary to common misconceptions, fatwas are not necessarily binding.

Shura: A council consisting of figures of authority summoned to give advice and debate matters. Depending on its nature, a shura can be either secular (made out of administrators and officials discussing affairs of the state) or religious (consisting of Islamic theologians and clerics debating on matters related to faith).

The Night Journey: The 17th chapter of the Quran. Also known as Al-Isra.

Sunah Al-Jinn: The 72nd chapter of the Quran.

Asr: The third out of five Islamic daily prayers. This prayer is held in the late afternoon.

Author Profile

A self-described amateur scholar, Dennis Tsarson has been interested in the world's mythology and folklore traditions since reading Greek myths as a boy. That interest grew into an undergraduate degree in history and archaeological training, which he incorporates into his fantasy retellings while travelling the globe. When he's not writing or exploring new countries and their cultural histories, you can find him settled in the United Kingdom, studying the comparative tendencies in folktales around the world.

What Did You Think of Here Be Jinn?

A big thank you for purchasing this book. It means a lot that you chose this book specifically from such a wide range on offer. I do hope you enjoyed it.

Book reviews are incredibly important for an author. All feedback helps them improve their writing for future projects and for developing this edition. If you are able to spare a few minutes to post a review, that would be much appreciated.